By the same author:

The Art of Friendship
The Promise of Happiness
Second Time Around

ERIN KAYE

Always You

AVON

AVON
A division of HarperCollins*Publishers*
77–85 Fulham Palace Road,
London W6 8JB

www.harpercollins.co.uk

A Paperback Original 2013

1

Copyright © Erin Kaye 2013

Patricia Gibb asserts the moral right to
be identified as the author of this work

A catalogue record for this book is
available from the British Library

ISBN-13: 978-1-84756-203-6

Set in Minion by Group FMG

Printed and bound in Great Britain by
Clays Ltd, St Ives plc

FSC™
the resp
FSC lab
fr

To my big brother, Jim

Chapter 1   1992

'So, have you told your father about us yet?' Cahal lay on his back, head propped up by two pillows, staring at a patch of green mould on the ceiling. A chipped saucer, full of ash, balanced precariously on his athletic chest.

'Have you told yours?' said Sarah, tracing her finger around the whorl of thick, black hair that surrounded his left nipple. The room smelt of cigarette smoke, stale beer and sex – the smell of sin. Golden February sunshine filtered through the thin floral curtains and 'Goodnight Girl' by Wet Wet Wet played quietly on the radio. The laughter of high school kids on their lunch break floated up from the street below.

'Yep.' He brought the stub of a roll-up to his lips, pinched between nicotine-yellow finger and thumb. His chest rose as he inhaled, stilled, then deflated slowly as a plume of grey smoke escaped from the corner of his mouth.

Sarah propped herself up on her elbow, and pulled the

slightly musty duvet around her naked, shivering shoulders. She tucked a lock of long, blonde hair behind her ear. 'What did they say?'

He stubbed the cigarette out on the saucer with a faint fizzing sound and carefully placed the saucer atop the bedside table. 'Not much.'

'Oh,' she said, disappointed, and sank back down on the bed again.

He rolled onto his side and the well-defined muscles beneath his pale skin flexed. 'Don't take it personally. They aren't that interested in anything I do.' But though he smiled, his eyes, the same blue-green colour of the sea in Portstewart bay outside, were sad.

Sarah frowned. 'Not like my Dad. He rang the flat the other day, you know, asking me what mark I got in that psychology paper. He's always ringing me. Or if not him, Aunt Vi. I wish we didn't have that phone. You manage perfectly well here without one. He insists that I come home every weekend. You'd think I was twelve, not a grown adult.'

He cocked his head in reply and was quiet for a few moments. Sarah waited, used to the way he always thought before he spoke, a trait that lent everything he said an air of authority. 'I wouldn't knock it. At least he cares about you.'

'He cares too much,' grumbled Sarah. 'He didn't want me to leave Ballyfergus. He wanted me to go to Queen's in Belfast and live at home.'

A pause. 'So why didn't you?'

'I had to get away. Living in that house was suffocating. I had to attend church twice on a Sunday and my father always

2

had to know exactly where I was, and who I was with. My aunt was even worse. And if I was ever late, oh, what a carry-on. You'd have thought Jack the Ripper was on the loose.'

He grinned lopsidedly, a dimple appearing in his left cheek, and revealed the crooked tooth in his lower left jaw that would've been an imperfection in anyone else. He placed a hand, rough and hot, on her hip. 'So you escaped?'

'Something like that.'

The smile faded from his face. 'I did too.'

'What were you escaping from?'

He stared at the wall for a few moments and said at last, 'My family have lived in Ballyfergus and worked on the docks for three generations. I'm not knocking the town, or them, but I wanted something more out of life. It wouldn't have been possible before for people like me to go to university but the grant system's changed all that. So long as I work every holiday and keep my job in The Anchor bar, I should be all right.' He smiled and looked at Sarah. 'You should've seen my Ma and Da's faces when I told them I was going to university.'

'They must've been pleased.'

'They were astonished. No one in my family has ever got past O levels, Sarah, never mind gone on to uni.'

Sarah stared at him thoughtfully. 'There's far more to you than meets the eye, Cahal Mulvenna.'

'You think so?' he laughed, his dark eyes twinkling.

She knitted her eyebrows together. 'You give the impression of being one of the lads. You act like all you want to do is get pissed and have a good time.'

3

He grinned. 'Well I do want to have a good time. You're only young once. And sure there's nothing wrong with that.'

'But you're not the pisshead you pretend to be. Beneath that exterior, you're actually quite determined and focused, aren't you?'

'This is my chance to make something of my life. I'm not going to screw it up.' He paused and twirled a lock of her hair around his index finger. 'You know I've never met a girl like you before.'

'But there have been other girls?' she teased, looking at him from under her eyelashes. Beneath the covers she found his leg and rubbed his hairy calf with her foot.

'A few,' he acknowledged, letting go of her hair and slipping his hand under the covers.

'Tell me about them.'

'Ach, now, you don't want to know that.' His hand made contact with her ribcage, then moved swiftly down her smooth, boyish hip. 'You must've had your fair share of boyfriends,' he said, looking up at her questioningly from under long lashes. 'I bet I'm just one of many.'

She stopped rubbing his leg and stared at him. Didn't he realise what he meant to her? She'd dated a few boys, but she'd never loved any of them. 'I've had boyfriends,' she said, looking at his chest, and feeling her face colour. Her voice dropped. 'But I never slept with any of them.'

His hand stilled and his voice softened. 'What?'

She raised her eyes to meet his. 'I never loved any of them, Cahal. Not the way I love you.'

'Oh, sweetheart,' he said. 'You never told me.'

'You never asked.'

He gathered her to him in his hard arms, and pressed his lips to her temple. Coarse dark stubble rasped against her face with painful, exquisite discomfort. 'Sarah, Sarah, Sarah,' he intoned like a prayer, his voice breaking up like static on the radio. 'I love you too.'

Sarah's heart swelled with happiness and with the sense of power and protection that his love instilled in her. Every breath was in time with his as if they were one, and in that moment her world contracted. Everything she'd ever wanted, everything she would ever want, was in that small square room, with the tired wallpaper, the wardrobe with one door missing, the creeping mould on the ceiling.

'If you'd loved someone before me,' he said into her hair after a long silence, 'I'd be jealous, you know.'

She laughed. 'How can you be jealous of someone who happened in the past?'

In reply he kissed the top of her head and held her closer. The still afternoon wore on and they lay for a long time, listening to the sound of traffic and conversation drifting up from the promenade below. And yet she was not at peace. She pressed her face into his chest and closed her eyes but all she saw was her father's face, sporting the reproachful, wounded expression she knew so well. A police detective, he saw the world in terms of black and white, and was crystal clear about who was on the side of good – and who wasn't. And the Mulvennas, low-class and of dubious background, would, she suspected (though she had never asked), fall on the wrong side of her father's carefully calibrated moral fence. Cahal's father had even served time in prison.

His voice broke through her thoughts. 'What're you thinking?'

She blushed, glad that her face was pressed against his chest, so he could not see. 'Isn't it weird that we grew up in the same town and never so much as spoke to each other before?'

He pulled away and looked into her face, smiling. 'I suppose so. But that's Ulster for you. Two different cultures, not so much rubbing along as steadfastly ignoring each other.'

'Except when they're trying to murder each other.'

'Yeah,' he said and gave a little laugh. 'I saw you once, you know. In your grammar school uniform in the library. Last year, when I was home for my gran's funeral.'

'I used to go there for peace and quiet to revise for my A levels.'

'I thought you were beautiful even then. I watched you for ages, pretending to choose a book off the shelf. I never thought a girl like you would look at a guy like me.'

'Why not?'

'Because you're an uptown girl,' he said, referring not just to the fact that she lived in a house on what locals called 'The Hill'.

'Well, maybe I like a downtown guy,' she said playfully.

Cahal sat half upright, his elbow digging into the pillow, and looked down at her. His face was serious. 'You haven't answered my question.'

'What question?' she said, knowing full well what he meant.

'Have you told your family about us yet?'

'I told my little sister that I was seeing someone.' She raised her eyebrows in the faint hope that this might satisfy him.

'And the rest of the family?'

She twisted a lock of hair around her forefinger and examined the split ends in the shaft of sunlight that sliced through the ill-fitting curtains. 'Not yet.'

'You said you would.'

'The right moment hasn't … presented itself.' He opened his mouth to speak but she silenced him with a smile. 'But I will. I promise. But back to your parents. They must have said something about me?' His left shoulder twitched. She sat upright and stared at him. 'What? What did they say?'

He stared at her for some long moments as if weighing something up in his mind. 'My Da asked me if you were David Walker's daughter.'

'And?'

'He said I had no business walking out with the daughter of an RUC man.' RUC stood for Royal Ulster Constabulary.

'Oh,' said Sarah, feeling slighted, and her head sank back into the pillow. Having a father in the police had always been a point of pride, of honour. Never before had anyone attempted to make her feel as if it was something to be ashamed of.

'It's not personal,' said Cahal, seeing her unease. 'You have to understand that my father has a certain, how shall I say it, *disregard* for the law and those who enforce it.'

'Hmm,' said Sarah, only partly mollified. 'And what did you tell him?'

'You really want to know?'

She nodded.

7

'I told him to mind his own effing business.'

She blinked, suddenly so proud of him for standing up for her against his father that her throat swelled up and she found it hard to speak. 'You did?' she squeaked.

'Pah,' he said, brushing off his father's objections like dandruff. 'I'm not having a layabout like him telling me what to do.' He smiled then and placed his palm on her cheek, his big hand curled around her face like one half of a shell. 'I know what I want, Sarah. I want you. And I'm not going to let anything, or anyone in this world, come between us.'

'Me neither, Cahal.'

'Do you mean that, Sarah? Do you really, really mean it?'

Her heart pounded in her chest. 'With all my heart and soul. I have never loved a man as I love you and I never will again.'

'Stay there,' he said, as a wide, triumphant grin spread across his face. He jumped out of bed and crossed the room in two strides, the gluteal muscles in his tight, stark white buttocks flexing as he walked. Above his backside, a narrow waist widened into a deep, strong back and broad triangular shoulders. She propped herself up on both elbows and butter-flies born of lust, not nerves, made her stomach churn.

He crouched down and rummaged in the bottom of the wardrobe, his muscled body vulnerable in a crouched position, like Atlas preparing to take the weight of the world upon his shoulders.

He stood up, faced her front on. 'Found it,' he grinned, holding out his closed right fist. His knuckles bore dark red crusty scars from hurling, a game she'd never seen until yesterday, when she'd stood on the sidelines astounded by its pace and warrior-like qualities, the sticks brandished like swords.

He came over and knelt on the bed, seemingly oblivious to the chill in the room, which the early spring sunshine did nothing to dissipate. If she breathed out hard enough, her breath misted. She sat up, leaned against the pillows and pulled the covers up to her chin.

'I want you to have this,' he said and he held out a small gold ring in the palm of his calloused hand.

She hesitated.

'Go on. Take it.'

She picked it up and examined it. It was a curious design featuring two hands entwined around a heart with a crown on top, all wrought from pale yellow gold. The edges of the ring were worn with age, like the weathered sandstone gargoyles on Ballyfergus town hall that had fascinated her as a child.

'It belonged to my grandmother on my father's side, Sarah. It was her wedding ring.'

Sarah breathed in sharply and her heart began to pound.

'She left it to me when she died,' he went on. 'By tradition Claddagh rings get passed down the female line but she never had a daughter of her own, and she never got on with my sister. So I got it.'

'It's … it's beautiful.'

He smiled, his eyes all glassy and bright. 'I want you to wear it, Sarah.'

'I … I can't. It's a family heirloom.'

'Exactly.' He stared at her intensely, and the quietest of silences settled between them. And then he said, 'That's why I want you to have it. You are my family now.'

Her whole body flooded with happiness. 'Oh, Cahal.'

He plucked the ring from her open palm. 'Will you wear this ring as a token of my love?'

She gasped and, letting go of the covers to reveal her naked torso, clapped both hands over her mouth at once. Under her fingers, her face burned, and she felt foolishly giddy. She stared into his eyes, steady and calm and the giddiness evaporated. Her hands dropped onto the bed cover and she said solemnly, 'I will.'

He took her right hand and slid the ring onto her third finger. 'There,' he said and grinned. 'You see the way the heart faces inwards towards your heart?'

Her hand trembled. 'Yes.'

'That means your heart is taken.'

She smiled. 'Oh Cahal, that's so sweet.'

'And it is taken, isn't it?' His right eyelid twitched.

'Completely and absolutely. Forever.'

He squeezed her fingers tightly in his and kissed the back of her hand. 'You understand what this means, me giving you this ring?'

She looked at him blankly.

'Claddagh rings are passed down from generation to generation. And one day I hope it will seal our marriage.'

She looked at her hand but she could not see the ring, only the blur of tears in her eyes.

He slid in beside her then and pulled her fiercely against

his hard cold body. They wriggled down under the covers and both held their arms aloft, forming a tent-like space under-neath the duvet where it was warm and dim like a cave.

'This is our world, Cahal, under this duvet. Under here it's just you and me, and the rest of the world doesn't matter.' She tried to forget about what would happen when Cahal graduated in the summer. 'Just each other. In our wee world.' In the dimness, his pupils were large and black. The space was filled with the smell of him and already his body was radiating heat like a furnace.

He inched forward but she placed a hand on his chest. 'Promise me you'll never leave me, Cahal.'

He smiled easily and, moving closer, teased, 'Of course I'll never leave you, you eijet.'

She pressed her palm against his flesh. 'You have to say it. You have to say the words.'

'Sarah Anne Walker. I'll never leave you. Not so long as I have breath in my body.'

The next day, Sarah strolled down the corridor, clutching a folder to her chest and thinking of Cahal. Rain battered the glass walls of the building and the wind howled around it like a demented ghost. She felt guilty about the three lectures and tutorial she had missed yesterday, even more about spending an entire day in bed. But it had been the most wonderful day of her life. Cahal wanted to marry her.

'What are you smiling about?' said a male voice and she started.

It was Ian Aitken, one of her oldest friends from Ballyfergus.

She clutched the folder even tighter across her breasts – tender from Cahal's passionate, rough love-making – as if it might hide the guilty secrets of her heart.

'Nothing.'

'I missed you at the Physics Society talk last night,' he said, staring down at her with pale blue eyes, his gaze as resolute as his character. His ginger hair was carefully combed in a side parting and his terribly unfashionable dark blue jeans had a crease ironed down the front of each leg. 'I only went because I thought you'd be there.'

She chewed her lip and looked away. 'Sorry. Had some work to catch up on.' She glanced up into his face and gave him a quick smile. That bit at least was true. She'd left Cahal's flat in the late afternoon and gone home and started an assignment.

After a moment's hesitation his face relaxed into a forgiving smile. She felt as if he could see right through her and she blushed. She could not see him approving of a full day spent in bed. Ian was conventional, old-fashioned even, in his outlook.

'Have you got time for a coffee, Sarah? I haven't spoken to you properly in ages.'

'Sure,' she said brightly.

'Come on then,' he said and fell in beside her as she walked, his clean, white trainers squeaking on the floor. 'You haven't been avoiding me, have you?' He sounded a little wounded.

'Don't be silly. Why would I do such a thing?'

They got coffees and sat facing each other, the rain pattering relentlessly against the window. She arranged her bag and folder on the floor, then crossed her hands primly on her lap, feeling like she was about to be interviewed. Conscious of Cahal's ring on her finger, where she had never worn one before, she hid her right hand under her left.

They chatted about inconsequential things and then Ian leaned back in the low chair and folded his arms across his chest. 'Is it true that you're still seeing Cahal Mulvenna?'

She frowned crossly. It was impossible to keep anything private in the small uni community. 'Yes. What about it?'

He looked at the floor and his features twisted into a grimace. 'How long have we known each other, Sarah?'

'All our lives?'

'Almost. You were seven when we moved to Ballyfergus. I remember the first time I saw you.' He unfolded his arms and leaned forward, his big hands dangling awkwardly between his long legs. 'At first, I thought you were an angel.'

'I'm no angel.' She shifted uncomfortably in the chair, recalling Ian as a child – a bookish redhead with brown freckles splattered across the bridge of his nose. He'd annoyed her so much with his intense wide-eyed stare, that she'd stuck her tongue out at him.

He smiled. 'I found that out later, didn't I? The first time I saw you, you wore a pink dress and white ankle socks. I'd never met a girl with such blonde hair. Or such a stubborn character.'

'Me? Stubborn?'

'Oh yes. Don't you remember how you refused to partici-pate when Mrs Banks took Sunday school because you'd taken a dislike to her? You spent months sitting in the corner, staring at the wall.'

'She was horrible. She told me I was vain and that vanity was a sin. She told me that, if I didn't mend my ways, I'd burn in hell.' Sarah pouted crossly. 'I've never forgiven her for that.'

He laughed indulgently. 'See what I mean?'

Sarah laughed too. In spite of getting off to a bad start, she and Ian had eventually become friends, more through circumstance than a natural affinity in character. Their fathers knew each other through their jobs in the police – as young men they'd served together in Ballymena – and the families often socialised together. She wondered what Cahal would've been like as a little boy. If they'd met, she was certain that they would've recognised kindred spirits in each other and become instant, inseparable friends, she thought with a smile.

When Ian's laughter faded, she said carefully, 'You know, Ian, that was a long time ago. I've grown up a lot since then.'

'We've both grown up. But some things never change, Sarah.' His eyes were bright and shining. 'And some people never change.'

'I have.' It was a challenge and they both knew it. Their eyes locked.

He stared, unblinking. 'I don't know about that. I think that underneath you're the same Sarah you always were. I know I'm the same.'

'Yes,' she said and it was simply an observation, meant as neither criticism nor praise. Ian had always seemed so certain of himself, even as a child. And now that he was an adult, he reminded her more and more of her father. Conservative. Steadfast. Staid.

He looked away. 'About Cahal,' he said, picking his words carefully. 'Are you sure that he's right for you?'

'Really, Ian,' she snapped, her patience worn thin, 'I don't mean to be unkind, but it's none of your business.'

His face fell, and she felt mean for hurting him.

'You know that I care for you, don't you, Sarah?'

She swallowed and looked away. 'Yes.' She'd dated him the previous summer and it had been a mistake. She'd never seen a guy so happy, nor so heartbroken when, three months later, she'd finished the relationship. She'd given him hope and even now, when she was with someone else, he had not relinquished it.

'Well, it's just that since you started seeing him, you've become quite distant. I'm worried about you.' He wasn't worried; he was pissed because she was dating Cahal and not him.

She gave him a tolerant smile that belied the irritation she felt inside. 'Well, you don't need to be. I ...' She sought for the words that might accurately describe how being with Cahal made her feel – whole, complete, sated – and settled for, 'I've never been happier in my entire life. I'm sorry that I haven't had much time for our friendship lately.'

'I feel like I'm losing you, Sarah,' he said glumly.

She reached for the coffee cup and tried not to show her exasperation. He talked as if she was his to lose. She suspected that he'd followed her to uni. He'd got straight A's. He could've gone anywhere, yet he turned down places at St Andrews and Durham to come to The University of Ulster at Coleraine, which filled a fair whack of its places through clearing. Sarah's reasons for being here, on the other hand, had nothing to do with grades. She needed to be far enough away from home to achieve the independence she craved, yet close enough to keep an eye on her little sister, Becky.

'I'll always be your friend, Ian. You will always be able to count on me. But going to uni is all about growing and changing, not holding on to the familiar,' she said, rather pointedly. Ian had surrounded himself with people who were almost carbon copies of his geeky friends at home.

His eyes flashed. 'Well, I think it's important to keep old friends and stay true to who you are.'

'And I think it's important to expand your horizons, to question who you are and what you've been brought up to believe.' She took a sip of milky, lukewarm coffee. 'We should be opening our minds to new experiences. Being a student isn't just about getting grades, Ian. It's about learning in the broadest sense.'

He looked at her as if she'd just spouted forth ancient Greek, then focused on her hands cradling the cup. His brows knitted together – he cocked his head to one side and squinted. And making no attempt to hide his dismay said, 'Did *he* give you that ring?'

She set the cup down and twisted the ring between the finger and thumb of her left hand. A sudden burst of rain hit the glass wall of the building like peppercorns.

'It's just a ring, Ian,' she said, trying to make light of it. Why did she say that? The ring meant everything to her. Cahal meant everything to her.

'You really are going over to the dark side, aren't you?' he

16

said, though there was no humour in his voice.

Sarah inched forward in her seat and lowered her voice. 'Don't be like that, Ian. You should be more open-minded. We only fear those who are different from us because we fear what we don't understand.'

But she had never feared Cahal. She'd been inexorably drawn to him. She thought back to the first time she'd seen him all those months ago, playing the bodhran drum in The Anchor bar.

The sound came from a small room at the front of the bar. She fought her way through the crowd blocking the doorway and stood there, transfixed by the scene in the smoke-filled room. Musicians sat on the wooden benches on either side of the fire dancing in the grate, the air filled with such music – the moving cadence of the fiddle, the high, sweet tones of the flute and the fierce, primeval beat of a drum. And it was Cahal, the drummer, who caught her eye. His head was down, his entire body vibrated in time to the wild pulse of the small round drum balanced vertically on his left thigh. With an expert flick of his right wrist, a stubby, double-ended stick skimmed the skin of the drum while his foot pounded out the beat on the floor.

Dark curls, damp with sweat, fell over his forehead and muscular thighs filled the legs of his faded, ripped jeans. Her breath caught in her throat – and her heart turned over. The spirited rhythm made her heart stretch and contract like a bellow. He'd looked up and smiled at her through the fog of smoke, a cigarette in the corner of his mouth, ash falling unheeded to the floor. And she'd stared back into those black, glittering eyes, knowing that her life was changed forever...

Ian coughed and ran the flat of his hands down the long, slim thighs of his jeans, as if brushing something off them. 'I understand the likes of Cahal Mulvenna perfectly well, Sarah,' he said coldly. 'But clearly you don't. I'm really surprised that you've been taken in by him.'

She opened her mouth to defend him but someone beat her to it. 'Hi, Sarah.'

At the sound of Cahal's voice, Sarah jumped up and spun around to find him standing there with damp patches on the thighs of his pale blue jeans and across the broad shoulders of the battered brown leather jacket he always wore. His hair, wet from the rain, was plastered to his chiselled features. Just the sight of him was enough to set her heart pounding.

'You're soaked through!' she cried and put a hand on the sleeve of his jacket.

He acknowledged her touch with a look and Ian with a nod of the head. Then he grinned at Sarah and ran a hand through his hair. A black curl fell in front of his face. It took all of Sarah's self-restraint to resist the urge to reach out and brush it from his brow. She wished she was in bed with him right now, away from prying eyes and interfering busybodies like Ian.

'Aye, it's wild out there all right.' He tossed his head and the curl flopped to one side. 'Listen, have you got a minute, Sarah? There's something I need to talk to you about.' Cahal stared pointedly at Ian and Sarah looked at the floor.

Ian stood up, taller than Sarah by several inches, but the exact same height as Cahal – the only thing, as far as Sarah could see, that the two had in common. 'I was just leaving.' He turned to go, then paused and gave Sarah the faintest of smiles. 'See you around, Sarah.'

'Yeah, see you, Ian.'

As soon as he was gone, Cahal said, with a twinkle in his eye, 'S'pose he was giving you a wee lecture about the evils of associating with a guy like me?'

She put a hand over her mouth and giggled. Then she bit her lip to stop herself from laughing. 'Don't. Ian's all right, really.'

Cahal made a sound like a neighing horse. 'He's a boring sod.'

'There's worse crimes.'

He shrugged, grabbed her hand and pulled her down onto a seat by both hands. 'I didn't come to talk about him.'

'What then?' she said, slightly alarmed by the firmness of his grip.

He spoke quickly, the words tumbling out, one of top of the other, totally unlike his usual measured way of talking. 'I've been thinking. You know the way I graduate this summer?'

She stared at the rain running in rivulets down the glass. It was all she thought about these days. Although they kept separate lodgings, they practically lived together, rarely spending a night apart. And even though it was months away, the thought of it made her palms sweat with panic. 'I don't think I could bear for us to be separated,' she said, and bit her bottom lip to stop it quivering. Tears were not far away.

'I don't think I could live without you.'

He grabbed her shoulders and squeezed. 'You don't have to, Sarah.' He grinned into her face. 'What if I got a job right here in the university?'

'What job?'

He pressed his palms together as if praying and touched his bottom lip with his fingertips. 'Lab technician. I've just been talking to my tutor and he says they're looking for a replacement for Phil Lynch – he's taking up a post in Edinburgh. They need someone to start after the summer and he thinks I would be ideal. He's more or less offered me the job, Sarah. What do you think?'

'Oh, Cahal,' she said, clasping her hands together and crying with relief. 'That's wonderful.'

'I'd get a decent starting salary. Enough for the two of us to live on. We could move in together.'

'Oh.' What would her father say to living in sin? And Aunt Vi?

'Or,' he added hastily, seeing her reaction, 'we could get married. Whatever you want.'

'Married?' she said, her head filling immediately with images of her in a white dress and Cahal by her side in a penguin suit, both of them smiling, delirious with happiness.

'Yes. And then we'd never have to be apart ever again.'

She threw her arms around him and pressed her face into his warm, damp neck. He smelled of cigarettes and last night's curry. Her stomach churned with desire. 'Oh let's, Cahal. And then no one, and nothing, can ever come between us.'

Chapter 2 2012

Carnlough beach, at the foot of Glencloy and just twelve miles north of Ballyfergus, was bleak on this bright but bitter February day. Carved out of the landscape by a massive ice age glacier, the glen, framed on either side by gently rising hills, swept gracefully down to meet the beach like a vast, winter-faded green velvet skirt. On its northern hem, the buildings of Carnlough village, mostly hewn from local limestone, clustered like pearls. An icy wind blew down the valley from the west, chilling the four people walking on the shingle beach.

Sarah's nose was red with the cold and spits of cruel rain speared her left cheek like painful darts. Sarah's sister, Becky chatted away beside her and, up ahead, Sarah's children – eleven-year-old Molly and nine-year-old Lewis – stumbled gracelessly along the coarse sand, hindered by ill-fitting wellies. Molly, blonde-haired and grey-eyed, was very like Sarah. Lewis, with short red hair standing up in spikes and brown freckles sprinkled liberally across his face like hundreds and thousands, was the spitting image of his Dad.

Not for the first time, she wondered idly what Lewis might have looked like had she married Cahal instead of Ian. He might've had dark curly hair instead of red, and blue-green eyes instead of pale, almost translucent, blue ones. And then, just as quickly as the thought came to mind, she pushed it crossly away, annoyed that she had allowed Cahal to occupy her thoughts even for a second. He had done the thing he promised never to do – he had left her. She would never forgive him. In the same way her father used to dampen down the coal fire every night with a layer of slack, she buried her curiosity under a layer of determination not to think of him again.

'So,' Becky was saying, 'after watching me for ages at the bar, this guy comes over and starts chatting. He was a postgrad. Nice looking. A few years younger than me I'd say, but that didn't seem to put him off.'

A sudden gust unwound Sarah's navy and grey cashmere scarf and whipped it in her face. She secured it round her neck again. 'What were you wearing?'

'Oh, my grey dress.'

Sarah knew the one – slinky jersey with a v-neck as deep as the Grand Canyon and a skirt that stopped mid-thigh. Becky liked to wear it with black fishnets and killer heels. She had even been known to wear it to work, though with flat boots, thank God, not heels.

'Anyway,' Becky went on, 'we had a few drinks. Well, more

than a few drinks.'

Sarah glanced at Becky, taking in the bags under her eyes and her rather carelessly applied make-up. Was that last night's make-up with a fresh layer slapped on top?

Becky grinned and dug her hands deeper into the pockets of her padded red duvet coat, which made her look big and plump compared to Sarah. But the figure underneath the coat was more curvaceous than fat and, while she was well-upholstered, it was in all the right places. 'And he was so hot. You should've seen his pecs.' She pursed both lips together and pulled a crude, lustful face in the manner of Dawn French.

'It wasn't his personality you were interested in then?' said Sarah with a raised eyebrow.

Becky chuckled. 'Well, let's just say the rest of him wasn't a disappointment.'

Sarah opened her mouth, but Becky didn't wait for her to ask the question that was on the tip of her tongue. 'He had a flat up near the university. We went there and I drove home this morning.'

Sarah stopped dead in her tracks. 'Becky! You said you'd stop picking up strangers in bars and sleeping with them! He could've been an axe murderer for all you know.'

Becky wrinkled her nose and the crystal stud in her left nostril glinted like a dewdrop. 'He wasn't a stranger. Well, not really. I'd seen him in the uni café a few times and we spent all evening talking. I wouldn't have gone home with him if I didn't think he was sound.'

Sarah tutted and shook her head. She understood Becky's desire to rebel against their strict upbringing – hadn't she done it herself? – but this behaviour was positively reckless. Lowering her voice, Sarah said, 'What if he had an STD or HIV?'

'I'm not completely stupid, Sarah. We used a condom. Condoms, I should say,' she added, and gave Sarah a saucy smile.

'They're not always safe,' said Sarah sniffily, not that she knew much about the subject. Since the divorce from Ian eight years ago, she'd not had much need for contraception. She squinted into the wind. Eight years of celibacy. What a depressing thought.

'Have you met anyone nice lately?' said Becky, as if she could read Sarah's thoughts.

Sarah gave her a weary look. 'You know I haven't.'

'You're never going to meet someone if you don't get out on the dating scene,' said Becky gently. 'I'll go out with you. We'll hit Belfast together!'

Sarah bit her lip and kicked sand with the toe of her boot. 'I know,' she said quietly.

'So what's stopping you?'

Sarah shrugged and looked ahead. Lewis, oblivious to the cold and the sharp needles of rain, twirled his navy hat in his hand, his red head exposed to the elements. 'The kids. Work. Running the home. Lack of time.'

Becky glanced at her sharply. 'And the real reason is?'

Sarah took a deep breath and smiled wryly. Becky would not let her away so easily. But how could she possibly explain that the love she had known with Cahal had been so perfect, so all-encompassing that she knew she would never experience the like of it again? And even if it were possible to love another man like she had once loved him, she would not take the risk. His betrayal had hurt too much. 'I've been so disappointed in love. I guess I'm scared to give it another chance.'

'Oh, Sarah,' said Becky. 'It makes me so sad to hear you talk like that. But you and Ian have been divorced for a long time now. You must put all that behind you.'

Sarah looked away guiltily and failed to correct Becky's assumption about Ian. 'I'm really happy with my life. Honestly. A man isn't the be-all and end-all. You mustn't worry about me.' She linked arms with Becky and said brightly, 'So tell me, are you seeing this guy again?'

'I doubt it. We didn't swap numbers or anything.'

'Didn't you like him?'

'I did like him but he … well, it was just a one-night stand.' She ducked her head. 'I don't expect him to appear on my doorstep bearing a dozen red roses.'

How could he, when he didn't even know where she lived? Sarah sighed, exasperated. She slipped her arm out of Becky's and turned her back to the wind, so that she could see her sister's face more clearly. She chose her next words carefully. 'You jumped into bed with him too quickly.'

Becky guffawed. 'Oh, Sarah, that is so old-fashioned. People sleep with each other on first dates all the time.'

'Do they?'

'Yes and anyway, I like sex. A lot of the time, that's all I want. I don't want them to marry me.'

'But you would like to be in a long-term relationship. You told me you'd like to settle down one day and have a family. And if that's what you want, you're going about it the wrong way.'

Becky came to a halt, turned her back to the wind and whipped a packet of cigarettes and a lighter out of her pocket. She put a cigarette in her mouth and, after several attempts at lighting it, the white tip burned like a cinder.

'I wish you wouldn't,' sighed Sarah. 'Do you want to end up like Mum?'

'Oh, come on, give me a break.' Her hazel eyes, the same as Mum's, flashed under thin, arched eyebrows. 'Mum didn't die from smoking. A blood vessel in her brain burst. And she never smoked a cigarette in her life. You have to stop worrying so much.'

'I can't help it.'

'Come here,' said Becky and she put one arm around Sarah's shoulders and gave her a big, rough hug. 'Better?' she said, holding the cigarette at arm's length, her breath sour with the smell.

Sarah smiled, feeling for a rare moment as if the heavy mantle of responsibility that she felt towards Becky had been lifted – as if she was the little sister and not the other way round. 'Yeah.'

They started walking again. The edges of Sarah's coat flapped like black wings, and the feeling of lightness evaporated, as if blown away on the breeze. She took a deep breath. 'To get back to the subject in hand, the problem with sleeping with someone on the first date is that you completely destroy any sense of mystery. Men like a bit of intrigue. If you just give it all out on the first date, you spoil the romance, or rather, the prospect of romance.'

Though she had slept with Cahal on their first date, she

did not feel any sense of hypocrisy in dishing out this advice to Becky. Her relationship with Cahal had been different from the start.

'Did you enjoy the seisiún?'

She'd returned to her friends and had not seen him come up. He leaned against the bar and crossed his ankles. Her friends all stared while she blushed and groped for words.

'I could see it in your eyes,' he went on, staring at her as if she were the only person in the room. 'The way you connected with the music. The way it connected with you.'

The music had touched her. 'I thought it was beautiful.'

'I'm Cahal by the way.'

'Ca-hal,' she said, trying out the unfamiliar name. 'Sarah. How did you learn to play like that?'

He shrugged as if his talent was nothing. 'I've tickets for a Chieftains concert next week. Will you come with me?'

She did not hesitate. 'Yes.'

'So says Miss Celibate.' Becky grinned to take the sting out of her comment.

'That's not fair. I did have a sex life once,' said Sarah.

'And you will do again,' said Becky confidently.

Sarah smiled doubtfully. 'Seriously, you should think about what I said.' She spied Lewis' hat on the ground, picked it up and shook the sand off it. 'What happened with that promotion at work? Weren't you to hear this week?'

Becky sighed. 'I didn't get it.'

Sarah's heart sank. It was the third promotion Becky had

been knocked back for. She worked as an admin assistant at Queen's University Belfast, a job she'd taken straight after leaving school with three good A levels. Sarah had tried to encourage her to go to uni but Becky, under the influence of a no-good boyfriend at the time, had refused.

'They recruited externally,' Becky went on. 'You know, I'm really cross about it. I wouldn't have minded, but you should see the nerd who got the job. He can barely switch on the computer. Has to ask me every little thing.'

'I'm sorry,' said Sarah and glanced furtively at Becky. The nose piercing was a recent one and it still looked raw and sore. 'Did you get any feedback on why you didn't get it?'

Becky shook her head. 'Just vague feedback about not being right for the job. My boss said I should've got it, but it was up to the interview panel, not her. And I didn't know any of them.'

They walked on, arms linked. Up ahead, Molly veered left, onto the seaweed-strewn pebbles at the top of the beach, and Lewis trailed in her wake. 'Have you thought that how you present yourself might have something to do with not getting the job?'

Becky sighed crossly. 'I'm an admin assistant, not a model. Surely what I do is more important than what I look like?'

'It ought to be. But the thing is,' said Sarah tentatively, 'first impressions are ever so important. Everyone who knows you thinks you're lovely but to someone meeting you for the first time, well, they might not think so.'

'Why not?' snapped Becky, shaking off Sarah's arm.

'The piercings and the tattoos and the dyed hair. They give

out a message, Becky. Quite an aggressive one. Why don't you let your hair go back to being brown? It's the most gorgeous chestnut colour.'

Becky lifted her chin and her eyes narrowed. 'I'm not going to change the way I look just to fit into other people's idea of what's acceptable. And I wish you would stop trying to change me into a clone of you. Just because you have it all – the house, the kids, the high-flying career. And the figure and looks.'

Sarah gasped in surprise. 'How can you possibly say that? I'm a single mother struggling to run a home and hold down a full-time job. I'd hardly call that having it all.'

Becky blushed. 'Well, you did have it all until you got divorced.' There was an awkward pause and she sighed. 'I just wish you would stop telling me how I should dress and what I should do.'

Sarah looked away, chastened. 'I don't mean to boss you around. I just want things to work out for you. In and out of work.'

Becky sighed and patted Sarah's arm. 'I'm okay, Sarah, really. I'm happy the way I am. You don't have to be so protective. You've been mothering me ever since Mum died.'

Sarah swallowed, the mere mention of their mother bringing a lump to her throat.

The rain had stopped. A shard of sunlight broke through a chink in the pale grey, skitting cloud – and just as quickly vanished again. In the blank canvas of the sky, Sarah saw the stark grey-whiteness of the hospital ward where her mother had died.

She perched on the edge of her mother's bed, the metal bedframe digging into her thigh. Crisp white sheets crunched between her fingers. The low hum of equipment, like a beating heart, filled her ears. The room was hot and smelt of floor polish and the fragrant sweetpeas that Dad had picked from the garden two days ago and which now sat, wilting, on the bedside table. Fear, terrible fear, ballooned in her chest.

'Sarah.'

She leaned over her mother's body, already still, like a corpse. She held her ear close to her mother's lips, her heart tight and cold in her breast, and waited.

'Take care of Becky.' Her mother's breath was a caress, like a summer's breeze. 'You're sister and mother to her now.'

The last words her mother had said to her.

Becky's quiet voice cracked through the memories. 'It wasn't right of Mum to ask you to take care of me,' she said, harbinger of a message that Sarah stubbornly refused to own. 'You were little more than a child yourself.' Becky paused. 'You must know that.'

Sarah looked away, her heart heavy with old, well-worn guilt. There was logic and truth in what Becky said. But her mother had asked. And she had promised. She'd spent the rest of her life trying to fulfil that promise. Such a contract, so solemnly made, could not be broken, despite Becky's plausible arguments to the contrary. She blinked to clear her vision. 'But if I don't look out for you, who will?'

'I'm thirty years old, Sarah,' smiled Becky, 'I think I can look after myself.'

Sarah returned the smile but knew in her heart that this wasn't true. Becky was always borrowing money off her, though to be fair she did pay it back – eventually. She'd been thrown out of accommodation twice in her early twenties for not paying her rent and she was still living in a rented flat with no prospect of buying somewhere of her own.

Becky bent down, picked up a couple of glassy, grey, sharp-edged stones and stood up again, holding them in her mittened palm for Sarah to see. 'Do you know they found evidence of Neolithic people living in this bay? They made tools from this flint. It's over two hundred million years old.' She turned the stone in her hand and gazed dreamily along the beach. 'It's amazing to think that we're walking in the footsteps of Stone Age humans who lived over six thousand years ago. They reckon they lived in caves up there on the hill.' She pointed at the green plateau that rose high above sea level. 'And came down to the seashore to forage for shellfish.'

'How do you know that?'

Becky slipped the flintstones into her pocket. 'I quite often go to the library at lunchtime. I like the idea of learning about our ancestors by the evidence they left behind.'

'Well,' said Sarah, pulling the collar of her coat tighter. 'I wouldn't have fancied running about in nothing but animal furs, trying to kill your dinner with a bit of stone tied to the end of a stick. It must've been a bleak existence.'

Becky laughed. 'A short one too, by all accounts. They rarely made it past forty.'

The age at which their mother had died. And their father, whom Sarah had believed invincible, had fallen apart.

It was shortly after the funeral. She was filling a glass with water at the kitchen sink, her swollen eyes gritty and sore from crying. Dad was in the back garden bringing in the washing, an expression of grim determination on his face. When he came to Mum's favourite pink nightdress, he unpegged it tenderly and stood for some moments with it clutched against his breast.

Suddenly, he dropped to his knees on the damp grass, wooden pegs spilling out from the bag in his hand like kindling. Sarah rushed to the door but stalled at the sound of his sobbing, coming through the opened window. A kind of mewling, like a cat caught in a trap. It was unbearable, a private moment of grief never meant for sharing. Quickly, she turned and walked away.

Sarah's heart pounded in her chest. It astounded her how, all these years later, she could still be so unexpectedly ambushed by moments of grief. She pushed the image resolutely out of her mind and focused on the present.

The children were absorbed by something in the seaweed which Molly was poking with a big stick. 'Hey,' she called out. 'Time to go.' She peeled back the sleeve of her coat to consult her watch and said to Becky, 'We'd better make tracks. If we don't hurry up we'll be late meeting Dad and Aunt Vi for lunch.'

'And we'll never hear the end of it if we are,' said Becky, rolling her eyes.

Lewis came over and held up fingers, as red and stiff as a cooked lobster. 'My hands are cold, Mum.'

Sarah smiled indulgently. 'No wonder, sweetheart, when you refuse to wear gloves.' She put her arm around him and kissed his coarse hair.

'Last one back to the car's the loser,' cried Becky and she set off across the shingle followed by the children.

By the time they'd all made it back to the car and driven the short distance to the Londonderry Arms Hotel in the middle of Carnlough village – where good home cooking was the order of the day and attracted clientele from the length and breadth of County Antrim – they found Aunt Vi and Dad already seated at a table by the window.

'Thank goodness, you're here at last,' was the first thing Aunt Vi said from behind steel-rimmed glasses, her right hand splayed on her sternum like a starfish, her lined face full of anxiety. 'We were getting worried.'

'I'm sorry,' said Sarah, peeling off her scarf. 'Lewis, don't leave your coat lying there on the floor. Put it on the back of a chair. That's a good boy.'

'Come and sit by me,' Dad said to the boy, patting the seat beside him. 'Molly, pet, you sit on the other side.'

Sarah and Becky shed their outdoor things and filled the two remaining seats beside their aunt, who was still bristling with annoyance.

'Sorry Aunt Vi,' said Sarah again. 'We didn't mean to be late. We were on the beach. We lost track of time.'

'That's okay, love,' said Dad, staring wistfully out the window, with eyes the palest shade of sky blue. 'Your Mum used to love walking on the beach here.'

Sarah smiled at him warmly, taking in his white dentures

and thinning white-grey hair. His gnarled hands lay motion-less on the table – the skin across his knuckles was wrinkled and papery. An old man's hands.

Becky said softly, 'Yes, Dad, I remember. We used to take a run up the coast most Sundays in the summer. We'd get an ice cream and eat it over there, on the harbour wall.' She pointed through the window to the limestone harbour constructed in the 1850s. The white stone had weathered, tinged now with a golden yellow, reminding Sarah of another childhood treat.

'Do you remember Yellow Man?' she said, referring to the brittle honeycomb toffee that had been one of the highlights of 'a day up the coast'.

'Oh, yes,' said Becky. 'I loved that stuff when I was little.'

Aunt Vi jumped into the brief lull in the conversation. 'All I'm saying is that you should've phoned.' She glanced at the mobile phone poised squarely on the table in front of her, like a reproach. 'Or texted.' Despite the fact that she cut a decidedly old-fashioned figure with her steel grey hair scraped back in a bun and a stern black roll-neck, adorned only with a simple gold locket, she was surprisingly up to speed when it came to cutting-edge technology.

Becky said, 'Who's for a drink?' and caught the eye of a waiter.

Sarah lowered her voice and said patiently, 'We were only ten minutes late, Aunt Vi.'

The children chattered excitedly to Dad and Aunt Vi said, folding her arms across her chest, 'Ten minutes is a long time when you're waiting for someone. Anything could've happened for all we knew.'

Dad looked up sharply. 'That's enough, now, Vi,' he said gently.

Aunt Vi unfolded her arms and pushed up the bridge of her glasses and soon everyone was distracted by ordering drinks and food.

'Well, Molly, you'll be moving up to the high school after the summer,' said Becky, when the waiter had left.

'I hope she's not in the same class as those nasty girls,' said Aunt Vi under her breath. Sarah hoped so too. Lately, some girls in her class had been picking on Molly.

'I can't believe you're growing up so fast,' said Becky. 'Next thing we know you'll be a teenager!'

Molly sat up straighter in her chair and beamed. 'Mum says I can cycle to school and back every day.'

'Even in the winter?' quizzed Aunt Vi. 'When it's dark?'

Sarah bit her tongue, reminding herself that Aunt Vi couldn't help herself. She'd moved in shortly after their mother died – and with her came a new era of curfews and surveillance on a par with the secret service. Dad, stricken with depression, had pretty much let Vi take charge of the running of the house and the raising of his daughters. Sarah didn't blame him for it – he'd done the best he could.

And, on the whole, Aunt Vi had done a good job, certainly the best she knew how, considering she'd never married or had children. There was no doubting Vi's love for Sarah and Becky, nor her compassion – she had given up her job as matron in Coleraine hospital to help her brother raise his two motherless daughters.

'Lots of kids cycle to the high school, Aunt Vi,' she said cheerfully. 'She'll have good lights and a helmet and a fluorescent vest for when it's dark. And she's done her cycling proficiency.'

Molly nodded vigorously and a look of genuine fear crossed Aunt Vi's face as she gazed upon her great-niece. Sarah felt a wave of compassion for her. 'Honestly, Aunt Vi, we wouldn't let her do it if we didn't think it was safe.'

After they'd eaten, Dad gave the children two pounds each and they went off in search of Yellow Man. It wasn't long before they came running in, clutching bags of mustard-yellow toffee that shared a close resemblance in appearance, if not in texture, to natural sponge.

'We just saw Daddy!' cried Lewis.

'With Raquel,' said Molly, breathlessly.

'Where?' said Sarah, glancing at the door.

'In Daddy's car,' said Lewis.

'They waved but they didn't stop,' added Molly.

Inside, Sarah bristled. How could Ian drive past his own children without pulling over, if only for a few moments? That would be down to Raquel, of course. She had no time for Molly and Lewis.

'I can't stand that woman,' said Aunt Vi; Sarah shot her a warning look. She was no fan of Ian's new wife either but, for the children's sake, she tried to hide it.

Dad asked to see the hoard of Yellow Man and pinched a bit out of Molly's bag, which resulted in lots of loud laughter and good-humoured recriminations.

'She's so common,' mouthed Aunt Vi to Sarah over the

noise.

Sarah leaned across the table to Aunt Vi and said quietly, 'Like it or not, Raquel's their stepmother now. We all have to make the best of it.'

Her aunt snorted. 'Some stepmother. She's never there half the time they're at their Dad's. Honestly, Sarah, I don't know what Ian ever saw in that woman.'

Chapter 3

'I hope this ATS conference is a one-off,' said Jessica, referring to the Australian telecommunications giant that had just bought over Vision Telecommunications Services, or VTS, for whom she and Sarah both worked. 'I don't fancy organising this every year.' Jessica was a very pretty redhead with pale skin and green eyes – and Sarah's friend.

They were standing at the entrance to the banqueting hall in the glamorous Europa Hotel on Great Victoria Street, Belfast's 'Golden Mile'. Outside, the February cold had given way to a wet and windy March. Jessica peered into the room, ticked something off the list on her clipboard and tutted crossly to herself.

'If I don't get a drink inside you soon, you'll turn into a gremlin,' said Sarah. 'Come on.'

Jessica looked at her watch, hugged the clipboard to her chest and pulled a disappointed face. 'I can't, honey. I have to check the visual display equipment is working,' she said, pointing with the biro into the banqueting hall.

Sarah looked down at her rose red satin pencil dress, all folds and pleats, which clung to her figure like it was sprayed on. She screwed up her face doubtfully. 'Do you think this is okay? I bought it for a wedding last year and thought it would do for cocktail parties, but now I'm thinking it's a bit OTT.'

'Nonsense,' exclaimed Jessica with an approving nod of her head. 'It's gorgeous. Adds a bit of glamour to an otherwise rather dull occasion.'

Sarah smiled gratefully and Jessica added, 'You might even catch the eye of one of the Australian change management guys. They arrived an hour ago.' She raised her right eyebrow like a challenge and said huskily, 'A couple of them are rather tasty. Kind of makes me wish I was single.'

Sarah laughed off the suggestion and made her way to the drinks reception alone. As soon as she stepped into the wood-panelled room, the soft buzz of civilised conversation closed around her like a blanket. A beaming waitress held out a silver tray of champagne flutes, filled with fizzy, straw-yellow liquid. 'Prosecco, madam?'

She took a glass and, spying a group of familiar faces, threaded her way through the crowd, holding the glass aloft to avoid spills on her precious dress. 'And here's Sarah,' said her boss Andy, with affection in his deep Home Counties voice. 'Looking absolutely gorgeous.'

'You don't brush up too badly yourself,' teased Sarah, who regarded portly, grey-haired Andy as a kindly father figure.

'We were just talking about whether or not ATS might

centralise HR,' said a worried-looking, slightly breathless Trevor, his slightly too-big suit hanging off his shoulders.

'If they do, they'll put us all out of a job,' said Lizzy, one year out of uni and dressed in a royal blue bondage dress that suited her dark colouring but could've covered more of her well-built modesty.

Sarah considered the possibility of redundancy and took a gulp of bubbly. Then she glanced at Trevor and Lizzy's solemn faces and said, 'I don't think we've anything to worry about. I reckon they'll need us more than ever once these change management consultants have finished.'

She looked at Andy for support. 'Sarah's right. If there're going to be job cuts, you guys will be busier than ever.' Lizzy nodded in grim understanding and everyone looked glumly at the floor.

In an effort to lift the mood, Sarah said, 'Don't be so downhearted. Change can bring problems, but it also brings opportunities.'

Andy said, 'Here, here! Listen, kids, it's not often we get a free jaunt on the business, so let's stop imagining the worst. Here's to free bubbly and a good dinner!' He raised his glass, radiating bonhomie like heat from a fire.

The mood immediately lifted and Sarah took a big gulp, determined to banish the blues and have a great time.

Trevor said, 'God I'm starving. I could eat a horse,' and everyone laughed for, in spite of his slight frame he was always hungry.

'I wish I had your constitution,' said Andy patting his big, round stomach. 'If I so much as look at cream cake, it goes right on here.' He pulled a face, distorting his mobile features into a caricature, making everyone roar with laughter.

Sarah tossed back the rest of her drink, her way of indicating to Lizzy and Trevor that it was okay to relax and have fun tonight, maybe even get a little drunk. Andy took Sarah gently by the elbow and steered her away from the other two. 'There's someone you must meet over here,' he said, business-like all of a sudden.

'See you at the table, guys,' Sarah called out over her shoulder.

'Love your dress,' mouthed Lizzy, her eye running down Sarah's figure.

'Yours too.'

'Now,' said Andy peering through the throng, which was becoming more animated by the minute as inhibitions took flight along with the steady consumption of alcohol. 'This guy's in charge of the change management team, external consultants brought over from Oz to realign us with the VTS way of doing things. They'll be here for six months, maybe longer.'

Sarah sailed across the room in his wake, the crowd parting like a sea in the face of his enormous bulk. She'd drunk the wine too quickly on an empty stomach. It had gone to her head making her feel slightly giddy.

Andy called out a salutation and the circle of people in front of them parted to admit Andy and Sarah into their little group. Sarah smiled and stepped into a space.

She glanced at the tall figure opposite her – and emitted a strangled cry. All the blood drained from her head and her fingers went rigid, the glass in her hand nearly slipping to the floor.

'Sarah, are you all right?' said Andy.

She looked at him blankly.

It was impossible.

Blood pounded in her ears, filling her head with the noise of crashing waves and making it impossible to make out anything of the conversation around her. And then, in a lull in the noise inside her head, she heard it.

'Cahal,' Andy said in the midst of a mouthful of gibberish. And under that deep, dark tan, the man's face coloured.

Sarah took in a great gasp of air and looked away. It *was* him. *Oh my God, Oh my God*, said a voice inside her head and she looked right, then left, ready to bolt. She had never expected to see him again. And certainly not here, not in this too-hot room where people pressed up against her and there wasn't enough air. Her legs shook beneath her but somehow she held her ground.

'Sarah, I want you to meet Cahal Mulvenna,' said Andy, his voice sounding like it came from the end of a tunnel. More incomprehensible mumbling and then, 'Cahal, meet Sarah Aitken, HR manager here in Belfast.'

Cahal's eyes came to rest on her once more and he smiled grimly. 'Aitken,' he repeated, and she caught a glimpse of the little crooked tooth in his lower jaw, absolute confirmation of his identity. 'Sarah Aitken.'

Sarah formed her mouth round words but managed only to squeak, 'What …' before her throat closed over. She swallowed and found her voice at last. 'It *is* you.' She touched the pulse at the base of her throat – blood pumped through her veins so fast and hard she thought her heart might give out.

A sad, thoughtful look passed briefly across his face. 'Yes. It's been a long time, Sarah.'

She stared at him wordlessly. This was not the Cahal Mulvenna she remembered – the skinny student she'd loved with all her heart – but a mature, sophisticated man dressed in the finest apparel money could buy. He was in his mid-forties now; grey peppered his dark, curly hair. Irish gypsy hair, she'd teased him once, running her hand through his luscious locks, while he made love to her in the single bed in her student digs ...

'Do you two know each other?' said Andy, sounding a little put out.

'Yes.' Cahal extended his hand to Sarah, all smiles. 'G'day, Sarah, it's great to see you again.'

She stared at his hand and furrowed her brow. The voice was all wrong. The predominantly Australian accent had softened the hard vowels of the East Antrim one, like a pebble worn smooth by a river. But the underlying accent was still there, unmistakably Ulster in origin.

Hesitantly, she took Cahal's cool, dry hand in hers and a tiny static shock travelled up her bare arm, making the fine, downy hairs stand on end. On the cuff of his pristine white shirt, a gold cufflink winked in the light like a diamond. He smelt faintly of pine and spice. Quickly, she pulled her hand away.

She'd never seen Cahal in a shirt and tie, let alone a suit. Back when she'd known him, he'd been firmly anti-establishment.

How had he gone from a scruffy student in a black leather bomber jacket and jeans – who'd barely scraped a third class degree – to a high-flying management consultant?

Andy's voice broke the stretched silence. 'So how do you know each other?'

Cahal's face went from red to pale under his tan. 'I … er … we went to university together, didn't we, Sarah? At least that's where we met …' His voice trailed away and Sarah's gaze slid down to the glass she held in her hands like a chalice.

His words had pierced her heart like needles in a pincushion. Was she nothing more to him than an old university acquaintance? Her throat constricted with anger and she hated him.

Unable to look him in the eye, she mumbled, 'Yes, it *was* a long time ago.' A time when she believed that love could overcome everything …

Inside Morelli's coffee shop it was warm and steamy but outside the wind howled and, now and again, waves came crashing over the black railings onto Portstewart Promenade. Cahal reached across the table and stroked her damp hair, his eyes soft as chocolate velvet.

'We were made for each other, Sarah. We're such a perfect fit in every way.'

She grinned, thinking of the way they lay together at night like spoons, and lifted the cup of hot, sweet tea to her lips. They were inseparable during the day, meeting up between lectures and for lunch, eschewing the company of all others. She set the cup down carefully in the saucer. 'I never thought that I could love someone as much as I love you, Cahal. When

44

we got together, in those first few weeks, I worried it wouldn't last, you know. It seemed too perfect, too good to be true. I thought that you would tire of me.'

'I'll never tire of you, Sarah.'

She smiled. 'I thought that as I got to know you better, I would find out things about you that I didn't like.'

His face fell. 'And have you?'

She grinned. 'The more I find out about you, the more I like you.'

A dimple appeared in his left cheek. 'Even when I bite my nails?' It was a habit of his when he was worried.

'Especially when you bite your nails.'

Their hands met, his cold fingers laced with hers. She'd never seen him wear gloves.

'Do you have to go home tonight?' he said, squeezing her hands tight, and sending a little shiver deep down inside her. 'I miss you so much at the weekends.'

'I miss you too.'

His Adam's apple moved in his throat. 'You do know that one day you'll be mine, Sarah?'

'I am yours already,' she breathed into the humid air. 'I was from the first moment I saw you.'

'I mean properly mine.' His hands tightened round hers like a vice. Slow, steady, exquisite pressure. 'And then we'll never have to spend a night apart ever again.'

Andy's voice broke through her thoughts. 'Well, isn't that a wonderful coincidence? Just shows you that the world is a lot smaller than we think.'

And yet not big enough, apparently, for her and Cahal. He shouldn't be here, encroaching on her patch. She had trusted him, blindly, stupidly. And then he'd left her, never to be heard of again. Had he tired of her after all? The bitterness in her mouth was sour and tangy, like blood.

Suddenly, the tall young woman beside Cahal, all sun-bleached hair with teeth like a horse, thrust her hand forward and, positioning her body in front of Cahal's, said, 'Hi, I'm Jody.'

'Pleased to meet you,' said Sarah, offering a limp handshake. The woman grinned into Cahal's face and Sarah swallowed the lump in her throat. She had to get away. She tapped the empty glass with a red-painted fingernail and said, 'If you'll excuse me a moment, I'll just go and get another drink.' And then she turned and fled.

She pushed her way impatiently through the crowd towards the loos, her heart going ka-thump ka-thump against the shiny red fabric of her dress. The sight and smell of Cahal filled all her senses; her eyes pricked inexplicably with tears. She fought them back with ferocious determination.

In the cool, quiet privacy of a cubicle, Sarah sat down on the closed toilet seat and tried to calm herself. Cahal had been in her thoughts since the day he'd boarded the plane to Australia two decades ago, the job as a lab technician long forgotten and their dreams of a life together in tatters. His face was as pale as a ghost, his lips pressed tightly together, thin and colourless. She remembered standing motionless, blinking in dry, wide-eyed disbelief as the metal tube containing the love of her life taxied down the runway and took off.

She'd never seen or heard from him again. She'd been proven right in the end – their love had been too good to be true. Too perfect to last. Too insubstantial to survive in the real world. She'd tried to forget him but, in the years that followed, she'd never stopped wondering about him. And then one day, standing behind his mother in the post office queue, she overheard her tell the postmistress that she was going out to Australia for her son Cahal's wedding. Sarah went home and cried, and that day a little bit of her died. Two weeks later she accepted Ian's proposal of marriage.

And now Cahal had been air-dropped into her life, turning everything upside down. She placed a hand over her heart and wondered why it felt like it was cracking open. She hated him for being here, for standing there so cool and collected and dismissing her as a nobody. But most of all she hated him for breaking her heart, a wound which had never healed, never mended, despite everyone's assurances that it would. Time had merely sealed over the hurt with a thin scab, making life bearable. But now that the scab was picked off, the hurt was just as raw and painful as the day he'd left.

She ran cold water over her blue-veined wrists in the sink and stared at the sad-faced woman in the mirror. She was a good-looking woman for her age, pretty even, but the bloom of youth was gone and every year that passed etched another fine line on her face. She'd spent her best years trapped in a loveless marriage, and she found it hard to forgive herself, or Cahal, for that. But looking back was pointless, and regret is the most damaging of emotions. She would not let herself wallow in it. Sarah dried her hands, smiled grimly at her reflection in the mirror, and walked out.

Back in the drinks reception, she lifted a glass off the silver tray and made her way back to where she'd left Lizzy and Trevor – she had no intention of rejoining Andy whose voice she could hear rising above the bright hum of conversation like a foghorn. But when she got to the middle of the room, her colleagues were gone. She took a sip of Prosecco, hoping dinner would be announced soon, when suddenly Cahal appeared beside her, smelling like a spice market.

'Sarah,' he said, shoving both hands into his trouser pockets. 'I … I never expected to meet you – here of all places.' He glanced around the room, and then his gaze, intense and steady, came to rest on her. He inclined his head a little and lowered his voice. 'I can't tell you what a surprise it is to see you again.'

A tingle travelled down Sarah's spine and her heart leapt foolishly. But then she frowned and reminded herself that his word was not to be trusted. 'Well, you know what a small place Northern Ireland is.'

He glanced appraisingly at her figure. 'You haven't changed a bit.'

'You must be needing glasses, Cahal.' He laughed at this, and she added, 'You've changed.'

He ran a hand through his short hair and his smile faltered. 'For better or worse?'

She blushed at this allusion to the marriage vows she had once believed they would exchange. 'Neither,' she answered shortly. 'Just different.'

'That's a relief.' He allowed himself a small smile, revealing the crooked tooth she had once loved so much.

'So, you're HR manager for VTS,' he went on. 'You've done well, Sarah.'

She felt herself grow an inch, at the same time hating that she cared what he thought. 'I am proud of what I've achieved,' she said, referring to her successful transformation from stay-at-home mum to businesswoman. Seven years ago she'd updated her qualifications, brushed up her image and gone back out to work. She'd been promoted three times since then and hadn't looked back.

He took a hand out of his pocket and rubbed his chin, dark with stubble even though the night was yet young.

'You know, I was going to look you up when I got here,' he said.

'Really?' she said sourly, disbelieving him. And then she recalled the earlier conversation with Andy. 'Why did you tell Andy we were just university acquaintances?'

He held out his hands in supplication and smiled disarmingly. 'What did you expect me to say? That we were lovers once?'

She looked away, embarrassed. Not only had they been lovers, they had been in love, and the best sex she'd ever experienced had been with him …

She opened her mouth to ask why he had wanted to look her up, when a voice shrieked, 'Cahal!' They both looked in the direction it was coming from. Jody teetered towards them. She was tall anyway and in heels she towered, like a caramel-coloured gazelle, over all the women and most of the men in

49

the room. She hooked her arm around Cahal's and, turning a cold, glassy eye on Sarah, she said, 'Ah, here you are.' Then she turned her laser-like attention on Cahal. 'I wondered where you'd gotten to.' She pouted girlishly into his face, lowered her gaze and pressed a forefinger into his chest. 'Everyone's looking for you.'

Sarah looked away, annoyed by the interruption and faintly embarrassed by Jody's physical intimacy with Cahal. Were they an item? She disapproved, she told herself, because Jody was young enough, almost, to be his daughter.

Regarding Jody from under slightly hooded eyes, he said playfully, 'You make me sound like a wanted man.'

Heat rose to Sarah's cheeks. He *was* flirting with Jody!

Quick as a flash, Jody said, 'Oh, you are.' There was a long silence while she let all the possible meanings of this sink in, and Sarah's emotions see-sawed between admiration at her boldness – and outrage. Once she'd recovered her equilibrium, she said, 'Excuse me, I have to go,' and she marched purposefully into the crowd.

Eventually she stumbled across her work colleagues. Lizzy teetered towards her on three-inch heels, red-faced and clearly the worse for wear. Trevor wasn't far behind, smiling goofily, his tie loosened. 'Come on,' said Lizzy. 'They've called us through for dinner. I'm starving.' She placed one hand on her stomach and grabbed Sarah's arm with the other to prevent herself from toppling over. Sarah smiled indulgently – and tried to put the image of Jody pawing over Cahal out of her mind.

Chapter 4

On the way home from work, Ian took the short detour to Lough View, the nursing home on Greenbank Road where his mother had lived for the past two years. He found the place depressing and the fact that he'd been unable to secure more salubrious surroundings for his mother's final home filled him with guilt. It wasn't for want of trying – or for lack of money. His father, who'd risen to the rank of chief superintendent in the police, had left Evelyn very comfortable. When Ian had set out on the quest to find a suitable nursing home, after the second stroke had left his mother partially paralysed on her right side, this was the best of an unimpressive bunch. As soon as the door opened he steeled himself for the smell that wafted out on stale, overheated air – overcooked vegetables and the unpleasant odour of cheap disinfectant, a game attempt to disguise the faint, sour smell of urine. Though lately confined to bed by yet another persistent chest infection, his mother was not incontinent – not yet – and for that he thanked God. He prayed she would be spared that indignity. 'How is she today, Jolanta?'

The care assistant thought for a moment and then shook her head. 'Not good today, Mr Aitken. Not good.'

This news did not disturb Ian unduly. In fact he smiled to himself for this was what Jolanta had said every day he'd visited for the last two years.

Ian nodded, and walked through the door with his hands shoved in his trouser pockets. He avoided touching anything in this place – it felt unclean and shame engulfed him once more. His mother ought to be living with him, her only son, not here in this awful place. If he had married a different sort of woman to Raquel, perhaps it might have been possible. If he'd still been married to Sarah, so kind and compassionate, he was almost certain it would be so …

He found her in bed, her head propped up, staring at the ceiling and clutching a white tissue in her sinewy, liver-spotted hand. She tilted her head to look at him standing in the doorway and gave him a lopsided smile, which made her eyes almost disappear in her crinkly face. Ian had been a late and only baby – a miracle his mother used to say in wonderment, gazing upon him as a small red-haired boy. She was now eighty-one years old.

'Hello, Ian,' she said a little slowly. Her speech had been affected by the stroke and, though it sometimes took a little longer to find the words, she was still perfectly intelligible. It was just she sounded different, like an old woman, not the pretty, bright mother with the sing-song voice that he

52

remembered from his youth.

'Hello, Mum,' he said and sat on the chair placed on the left side of her bed. 'I can't stay too long. Raquel'll be home soon.'

'Mmm, Raquel, yes. Tell me, is she still working as a shop assistant?'

Poor Raquel, with her platinum blonde hair and lack of tertiary education, she had never quite lived up to his mother's exacting standards. 'No, mother,' said Ian patiently. He suppressed the more robust retort that sprang to his lips, choosing to ignore her snobbishness and the intended provocation because he was pleased, in spite of both, that she still had all her wits about her. The day these left her, the fight would leave her too. 'You know perfectly well that she's been promoted to manageress. Of a very upmarket boutique.'

'Oh, yes, I'd forgotten.' A whisper of a smile played about one corner of her mouth followed by a long pause during which the smile evaporated. 'Is everything all right between you two? You don't talk about her very much. And I can't remember when I last saw her.'

Ian rubbed his hands together and looked at the floor. Part of him wanted to tell her that his four-year-old marriage to Raquel was on the rocks. He couldn't remember when they'd last slept together, though sex had once been the most important aspect of their relationship. He'd lusted after her, but his old-fashioned, outdated scruples would not allow him to take her outside of marriage. And so they'd wed. What had he been thinking?

He looked at his mother and forced a smile. She'd warned him not to marry Raquel and she'd said some rather unkind things about her. Sadly, they had mostly proved to be true, though at the time, he'd been too seduced by her sexuality to listen. It was difficult now to admit that he'd been wrong, that he'd been blinded by lust (so much more humiliating than being blinded by love). He could not bear to hear his mother say she'd told him so. 'Everything's fine, Mum. Raquel's just very busy at work. She works six days most weeks. She's so tired come Sunday, she just wants some me time.'

'Me time,' she said with a faint raspy snort. 'We didn't have that in my day.'

'Well,' he said in Raquel's defence, trying to sound like a loyal husband, 'times have changed.'

Thankfully, she lost interest then. He heard someone come into the room and his mother's eyes crinkled up with pleasure when she saw who was there. 'Oh, look, it's Sarah!' she cried out in a small voice. 'Do come in.'

Ian looked round to find Sarah standing by the door with a battered biscuit tin in her hands. He drew in his breath, for a moment not recognising this glamorous apparition for his rather frumpy former wife. The black dress and matching Jackie Kennedy-style jacket skimmed her curves in all the right places. Glossy tights sheathed her well-shaped legs and black patent heels added several inches to her height. She'd put on a lot of weight after having the kids and she'd struggled with it over the years. But he was aware suddenly, even though he'd seen her only a few days ago, that the excess weight was all gone. She looked once more like the Sarah he had married. Her natural blonde hair was tucked behind one ear; the rest fell like a curtain of gold about her face. And while he was pleased to see her smile, full and warm, directed at Evelyn, he wished she would smile at him like that.

'Hello, sweetheart,' she said, approaching the bed. When she bent down to kiss his mother on both cheeks, a waft of perfume drifted across the bed; it filled Ian with longing. Evelyn let go of the tissue in her good hand and clasped Sarah's hand instead. Ian blinked and looked away, the moment of intimacy between the two women making him both uncomfortable and glad. He and Sarah had had their differences, but he would forever be indebted to her for her affection towards his mother.

'Hello, Ian,' she smiled when Evelyn had released her, and then looked from Ian to his mother with a little frown between her arched brows. 'I got home from work early and thought I'd just pop in and see how you were. But,' she said, her intonation at the end of the sentence turning it into a question, 'I can come another time?'

'No,' said Ian and his mother simultaneously. Ian stood up, smiled, and gestured towards the chair he'd just vacated. 'Please, come and sit down, Sarah.' He liked her being here; she'd always made the relationship between him and his mother easier, like oil between two slightly out-of-sync cogs.

She placed a hand on his shoulder and gently pushed him back into the chair. 'You stay right where you are, by your Mum,' she whispered. She patted his shoulder, then withdrew her hand. This gesture of solidarity conveyed so much – recognition of the perilous state of his mother's health and the grim, inevitable outcome that lay ahead. And he was grateful. 'I'll pull up another chair.'

She sat on the opposite side of the bed and Evelyn said, 'Well, isn't this nice?' She paused to cough. 'My two favourite people – not counting Molly and Lewis of course – come to see me at the same time.'

Sarah grinned. 'Like buses. We all come at once.'

'You should have brought the children,' said Evelyn, out of one side of her mouth, a little dribble of saliva running down her chin. If she was aware of it, she showed no sign.

While he was wondering if he ought to wipe his mother's face, Sarah got up and discreetly dabbed the corner of her mouth with a tissue from the box on the bedside table. Her smile never wavered as she carried out the task, but she gave Ian a quick, knowing glance.

'Maybe next time. When you're feeling a little better,' she said.

Evelyn closed her eyes and Ian said, 'Isn't your chest any better?'

'Never mind that now. Tell me about the children, Ian,' she said holding out her hand.

He took it, cold and frail, in his own. 'The kids are fine, Mum. What did the doctor say?'

Her voice had dropped to a whisper. 'Didn't Lewis have a swim gala this week? You know how much I love to hear all about –' A coughing fit took hold and the sentence was left unfinished.

'Mum!' cried Ian, gripped by sudden fear. The infection wasn't shifting. If anything it sounded worse! She'd had that cough for over a month now.

The coughing subsided. 'Shush,' she commanded, her tone

firm in spite of her affliction. 'What's in the tin, Sarah?'

'Have a look.' She prised the lid off the tin and tipped it so that Evelyn could see the contents.

'Homemade wheaten bread!' she exclaimed breathlessly, trying to lift her head off the pillow. 'My favourite.'

Sarah picked out a piece and held the moist, buttered bread to Evelyn's lips so that she could take a bite. Her head sank back into the pillow, her gums working slowly, and Sarah said, 'I know.'

Sarah held out the tin to Ian. 'Want some?' He shook his head.

Evelyn chewed and swallowed. 'That was delicious. The wheatgerm'll play havoc with my dentures. But what the heck. You only live once.'

Ian smiled, slightly envious of the easiness between Sarah and his mother. Sarah got up, lifted the glass of water from the bedside table and held it to Evelyn's lips. They'd always been like this together, easy in each other's company. Even when Sarah was a girl she'd gotten on well with his mum, and their relationship had always operated independently of his marriage.

'Want some more?'

'No thanks, love.'

'You gave me the recipe. Took me ages to get it right.' Sarah stared doubtfully into the tin. 'It's still not as good as yours.'

'The secret's in the flour. Got to be Morton's. And a light touch.'

The first day he'd brought her home as his girlfriend, Sarah and Evelyn had ended up in the kitchen together, where Evelyn revealed the secret of her famous wheaten bread. He'd known then how much his mother approved. He'd always known that he wanted her to be his wife, but that day simply confirmed it. When she'd said yes, he was thrilled, though if truth be told, he'd not expected her to accept.

He cleared his throat and looked about the room. 'Raquel said she sent you some flowers a few days ago.'

His mother broke eye contact and, picking up the tissue on the bedspread, squeezed it between her fingers. For one awful moment, he thought Raquel might have lied to him.

'Oh, yes,' said Evelyn, making eye contact again. 'Though you'd have thought someone was getting married. There were enough flowers to fill a church.'

Ian laughed nervously. She was not pleased. Why on earth not?

She dropped the tissue, captured it again and Ian said, 'So where are they?'

His mother looked at him blankly.

'The flowers, Mum. Where are they?'

She looked away again and said, with studied airiness, 'Oh, I told the girls to put them in vases in the day room. Let everyone enjoy them.'

'But those flowers were meant for you, Mum. They cost Raquel a fortune.'

His mother brought her gaze to bear on him and her features hardened. 'They were lilies, Ian. There must've been two dozen of them.'

Ian blushed and looked at his feet. 'She must've forgotten,' he mumbled. How could Raquel be so thoughtless? She'd been at his father's funeral five years ago when the church was festooned with the pure white flowers, their musky scent as overpowering as the grief. How many times had Mum said in conversation since then that she'd come to hate lilies? How she could not look upon them, nor catch the faintest whiff of their perfume, without thinking of that day.

'I'm sure she meant well,' said Sarah.

'Hmm.' Evelyn pressed the hankie to the tip of her nose. 'Flowers are all very well, but why doesn't she come to see me?'

'She's er ... busy,' said Ian. He glanced at Sarah who lowered her eyes to her lap. The last time Raquel had visited was four weeks ago. She'd been sitting beside an old man in the day room, waiting for the staff to finish attending to Evelyn, when the man soiled himself. She'd been horrified, though not as much as the poor old bugger who, though he'd lost control of his bodily functions, was still compos mentis. Raquel hadn't been back since.

Sarah stood up and said, 'Well, I'd better be getting along. I don't want to be late picking up the children.'

'Be sure to give them a kiss from me,' said Evelyn. 'Tell them I love them very much.'

'I will,' said Sarah, her eyes bright and glassy. 'And we'll bring them to see you very soon, won't we, Ian?' He nodded and swallowed, unable to shift the hard lump in the centre of his chest. She bent over, gave Evelyn a hug and ran the flat of her hand down the side of his mother's wrinkled face.

'See you,' she said. She reached over, touched him lightly on the arm and then was gone, leaving him feeling oddly bereft.

'If you'll excuse me, Ian, I must go to the loo.' Evelyn peeled back the bedcovers and slowly swung her legs over the other side of the bed. Her bare feet made contact with the floor.

'Do you need some help, Mum?' he said, standing up.

'No, I'm fine.'

But she wasn't fine. As soon as she stood up, her legs buckled beneath her and she crumpled onto the floor.

Ian cursed, slammed the emergency call button on the wall with the flat of his hand and rushed to her aid. She was lying on her side, her knees bent up. 'Here, let me help you. Are you hurt?'

She wheezed and shook her head, a hand pressed to her chest.

Jolanta came running in and, as soon as she saw what had happened, helped Ian lift his mother back into bed, though he hardly needed her assistance, his mother was so slight.

'Are you hurt, Mum?' he said, blinking back tears.

'No. I don't know what happened, Ian,' she said in bewilderment. 'My legs just gave way.'

'It's okay, Mum. Everything's okay.'

'She was trying to go to the toilet, Jolanta,' he said. 'She's never fallen like that before, has she?'

Jolanta shook her head and touched his arm. 'It's okay, Mr Aitken. You leave this to me. You go outside and wait.'

It was dark by the time he left the nursing home. He stood in the car park, ill at ease and worried. Light drizzle settled on his head and shoulders in glistening, translucent pearls. He needed to talk to someone about his mother, someone he could trust, someone who would understand the fear in his heart and the feeling of impotence that consumed him. He glanced at his watch, pulled out his mobile and called home. There was no answer. He remembered then that Raquel had gone late night shopping followed by a drink with her girl-friends. He left a message saying he would be home late. Then he got in the car and drove to someone who would understand his pain.

Her car was parked outside the house on the leafy street. He turned the engine off and glanced at the clock in the car. They would be in the kitchen at the back of the house having tea around the pine kitchen table, the windows steamed up and the scent of good home cooking in the air. The closest Raquel came to home cooking was opening a packet from Marks and Spencer.

Sarah, Molly and Lewis. The three people he loved most in the entire world. Why had he not been able to hold on to them? He leaned his head on the headrest and closed his eyes. He should not have come. But he could not go home alone to that empty house with its pale carpets and ridiculous white ostrich feathers in a vase on the hall table.

Waiting nervously on the doorstep, Ian stared at his reflec-tion in the glass panelled door. His reddish-blond hair was receding, making him look more like his father every day. He had not expected to keep his hair, of course – his father had been bald by the time he was fifty – but now that the time had come for him, he found it hard to accept. It made the gulf between him and Raquel, ten years his junior and devoted to physical perfection, seem even greater. He'd even toyed with the idea of a hair transplant – until common sense kicked in.

Inside a light came on, his reflection disappeared and the door opened.

Sarah was wearing sweatpants and a hoodie, her hair tied up in a spiky ponytail, her feet bare. 'Ian,' she said, looking past him into the darkness as if looking for an accomplice. 'What're you doing here?'

He shuffled awkwardly on the doorstep, his hands shoved deep in his pockets, regretting the decision to come.

'Is everything all right?' she said and her eyes widened in alarm. 'Is it Evelyn?'

He rubbed the end of his nose. 'No. Yes … she had a fall on the way to the toilet but she's okay.'

'Is she hurt?' gasped Sarah.

'No, she's fine, really. Jolanta says they'll make sure she's accompanied on trips to the loo in future. I … I was just wondering if you could spare some time for a quick chat. About her care.'

Immediately she stood aside and ushered him in. 'Of course.'

'I haven't come at a bad time?' he said, nearly falling over the pile of schoolbags, shoes and coats in the hall. Bisto, the brown-and-white cat Sarah had rescued from the cat home, came and circled his legs warily. He bent down to stroke his back, but he immediately scarpered up the stairs.

'No, not at all,' said Sarah, brushing crumbs off the front of her hoodie. 'We've just finished eating. The kids will be thrilled to see you.'

Molly and Lewis, drawn by the sound of voices, appeared

at the end of the hall. As soon as Molly saw him, her face lit up in a smile and she bounded along the hall like a long-limbed gazelle and latched on to his arm. Lewis barrelled up the hall at full pelt, colliding with his father and wrapping his arms around his waist. In spite of his worries, Ian laughed. Lewis lifted his head to look his father in the face, grinning cheekily. Ian leaned down and planted a kiss on his tomato-sauce-stained cheek. 'Let me guess? You had spaghetti bolognese for tea.'

'How did you know?' said Lewis suspiciously, while Ian kissed the top of Molly's head, her hair the same colour and texture as Sarah's. He hadn't done much right in life, but his children made his heart swell with unfettered pride.

'That'd be telling,' he said.

'How's Gran?' said Molly.

'She's fine,' said Ian without missing a beat. 'Lewis, will you take your swim medal in to show Gran on Sunday? She'd love to see it.'

'Come on kids,' said Sarah. 'Dad and I need to have a little chat. Why don't you switch the TV on in the lounge?' She glanced at the clock. '*The Simpsons* are just coming on. I'll bring you through some ice cream.'

'Ice cream on a Wednesday?' said Molly with an exaggerated look of surprise on her face. 'What's got into you, Mum?' Sarah, who was a big fan of healthy eating, gave Molly a withering look. Ian was a bit shamed to admit that the children were spoiled when they came to him. Raquel seemed to think that plying them with sweets and sugary treats was the secret to winning their affection. It hadn't worked.

'Seeing as your Dad's here,' said Sarah with a conspiratorial wink at Ian. 'Now scram before I change my mind.' That was enough to send them scarpering into the lounge, slamming the door shut behind them.

In the kitchen, strewn with pots and pans, Ian smiled. Sarah had always been a messy cook, never tidying up as she went along. 'Take the weight off,' she said. 'I'll be right with you.'

He sat down at the table, pushed a plate out of the way and dabbed ineffectually at the spills on the table with a used napkin. He missed the mess of family life.

'I don't know about you but I could use a drink,' said Sarah, as she came back into the kitchen, taking a half-empty bottle of white wine out of the fridge. 'Want some?'

He shook his head. 'No thanks. I'm driving. Some orange juice would be nice.' He watched her drain the juice from a carton, toss the carton at the bin – and miss. She shrugged and he smiled, feeling himself relax for the first time that day. The homeliness of Sarah's chaotic kitchen reminded him of happier times.

She handed him a tumbler of juice and half-filled a stubby-stemmed glass with wine for herself. Oblivious to the state of the place, which would've had Raquel hyperventilating, she sat down opposite him, the bottle of wine close at hand as if her glass might need replenishment soon. 'What's up?'

'It's just that ... well. I wanted to ask your advice.'

She stared at him with grey eyes, steady and clear. 'About Evelyn?'

'Yes. I spoke with the staff on the way out. They assured me that she'd finished the antibiotics two days ago but that fall just made me realise how weak she is. That's the second dose in the last four weeks. She just doesn't seem able to shift that infection.'

'Did you speak with Linda?' Linda was the manager and a trained nurse.

'No, she wasn't there.'

'Hmm,' said Sarah, took a drink of wine and added, 'And what have the staff done about it?'

'Nothing, as far as I can see. They said she was tired and needed a chance to rest.'

There was a long pause. Sarah looked into her glass, held between both hands. 'I think you should get Dr Glover back to see her tomorrow. If the chest infection's not cleared, she might need stronger antibiotics. Left untreated, it could turn into pneumonia.'

He nodded glumly and took a swig of juice. She'd not told him anything he had not thought himself, but it was reassuring to hear that she agreed, that his instinct had been right. He swallowed, and emotion – something akin to, but not quite the same as anger – welled up inside him. 'You know,' he said, his eyes stinging the way they did when he took the kids to the chlorinated pool, 'I don't think the staff in that place know what they're doing.'

He set the glass down on the table with more force than he intended and some juice slopped out, to mingle with the blob of bolognese sauce he'd smeared across the vinyl table-cloth. 'How come they didn't volunteer the information about her antibiotics? How come they haven't called in a doctor already? They just leave her lying in that bed, hour after hour, all alone.'

Sarah sighed. 'I'm sorry, Ian. I know how much it hurts you to see her like that. Me too.'

He put his hands over his face and his shoulders shook. 'I hate to see her in that place.'

'Don't beat yourself up over that again, Ian. You had no choice. She needs professional care. And she's in the best place possible.'

He removed his hands and looked into Sarah's sympathetic eyes. 'But they stole her Bible.'

'I know.' Sarah paused and added gently, 'But we don't know if that was the staff, another resident or a visitor. And from what I can see, they're kind to her. And professional.'

He blew air out his nose noisily. 'Professional, huh! That's a joke. Half of the staff look like they've just left school and the other half can hardly speak a word of English.'

Sarah blinked and said carefully, 'I know you're upset, Ian, but that's really not fair. They're doing their best.'

His shoulders slumped and he suddenly felt desperately tired. He rubbed his forehead with the heel of his hand. 'I feel as though I've let her down.'

'You haven't,' she said softly. 'It wasn't really practical to have her come and live with you, was it? Not with you and Raquel out at work all day.'

He attempted a smile of gratitude for the kind words, though they did little to assuage his guilt. He ran his hand across the top of his head and thought for a few long moments.

'Right, we need a plan.' If he could inject some order into what was happening, maybe he could control things, maybe he could get his mother well again. 'I think someone should go in and see her at least once a day now until this crisis is over,' he said, the words that had been swimming around in his head all afternoon tumbling out too fast, one on top of the other. 'Keep on top of the staff. I can do most days, except Tuesdays. Probably best not to take the kids too often – we don't want to freak them out, seeing her unwell.' He focused on the swirly pattern on the oilcloth in an attempt to slow down his thoughts. 'Maybe we could both take them at the weekend and you could take them away after a few minutes. I think it'd do her good to see them, don't you? And we could take turns to visit on the days when the other one's got the kids. And –'

'Ian,' said Sarah gently and when he looked up her cheeks were red. 'You know how much I love Evelyn and I'd do anything for her.' She paused, stared at the table, and then went on, twisting the stem of the glass between her finger and thumb. 'I'll do whatever's required. But don't you think you should be having this conversation with Raquel?'

She was right, of course. A cold chill settled in his stomach. He had no right to be here, no right to ask this of her. And yet, who else could he ask? He had no siblings to call on. And Raquel, well, she would visit if he asked her, but it would be done out of a sense of duty, not of love. And there would be little compassion.

He cleared his throat and said disloyally, his cheeks flushing, 'But there's no bond, no connection, between Raquel and my mother. No … affection. They've never clicked. Whereas you two, well, you're like mother and daughter. At least that's how it's always appeared to me.' He would've married Sarah without his mother's approval – but it had always pleased him that both his parents liked her so much.

Sarah lifted her eyes, held his gaze and said solemnly, 'You're right, that's how it is. I love your mother as if she were my own. That's why I'll do whatever it takes to make what's left of her life as happy and comfortable as possible.'

'I knew that I could rely on you, Sarah,' he said, relief and gratitude flooding through him. 'Thank you.' Instinctively, he reached his hand out towards hers, lying on the table, then snatched it back when he saw the look of puzzlement on her face.

'I'm doing this for Evelyn, Ian,' she said quietly as her hand slid off the table onto her lap.

'Yes, of course. And I'll never forget that, Sarah. I'll never forget that you make time to visit her, no matter how busy you are.'

Sarah shook her head. 'After all she's done for me … for them, it's nothing. And the divorce didn't change anything between us. She treated me just the same. Do you know she paid for the kids' childcare so that I could go back to work?'

He shook his head. 'I didn't know. But it doesn't surprise me.'

Suddenly, Sarah put her hand over her mouth and her eyes filled with tears. 'She's always been so good to me,' she choked. 'To all of us.'

He let the comment settle between them like a feather drifting slowly to the floor. The silence between them was comfortable, a blanket round their shared grief. And it seemed like the right moment all of a sudden to say what had been on his mind lately. He took a deep breath. 'I know I've said it before, Sarah, but I am sorry for walking out on you and the kids. I'm sorry that I hurt you.'

Her hand fell from her mouth but she said nothing for a few moments. She took a sip of wine, high colour in her cheeks, and said, 'I appreciate you saying that, Ian, really I do.'

'I just want you to know, that's all. Sometimes I feel like a real heel. I just wish … well.' He looked at the palms of his hands, white and smooth, and left the sentence unfinished. He wondered if he'd stayed, would the marriage have survived?

'I don't blame you,' she said and his head snapped up. She cocked her head to one side the way she did when she had something difficult to say.

He'd walked out before Lewis could even walk and Molly was still in nappies. He'd hated himself for it. But he couldn't stay. The Sarah he'd loved had simply disappeared, consumed entirely by motherhood. At least that was what he thought had happened. It wasn't until after Lewis' birth that he'd realised Sarah did not love him the way he loved her. If she loved him at all.

Her love for him had always been an elusive thing, rarely voiced. She'd maintained that words were cheap and that she preferred to show love rather than constantly declare it. As a new bride she'd been kind and attentive but her interest had waned over the years and towards the end of their marriage, he'd felt nothing but loathing emanating from her like heat from a fire.

'If you'd been happy you never would've left,' she went on.

'And I was largely responsible for that unhappiness.'

For some reason he shook his head, though what she said was true.

'No, I wasn't a good wife. I pushed you away. I built barriers between us and then I couldn't seem to pull them down.'

'Why?'

'I don't know.' She looked away and he felt, as he had often done in their marriage, that she wasn't being entirely straight with him.

'Once Molly was born, I felt that you lost interest in me, Sarah. And it only got worse when Lewis came along. I couldn't see a future for us. I couldn't see how we would ever be happy again. I gave you so much and got so little back in return.'

'Maybe we shouldn't talk about the past, Ian,' she said, rubbing the back of her neck. 'We both made mistakes and it doesn't change where we are now.'

'Yes, let's look to the future.' He smiled at her then, resisting the urge to reach out and touch a strand of hair that had escaped her ponytail. 'And let's not be too hard on ourselves. I mean, there aren't many divorced couples who can sit down and talk to each other like this.'

She smiled weakly. 'I guess that's true. I'm glad we've remained friends. In spite of everything.'

He stared into her silvery eyes, the pupils wide and black as night. From somewhere deep inside, courage and hope rose in his breast like twin flames, and he blurted out, 'I loved you the first moment I set eyes on you. All those years ago in Sunday school.'

She looked at him with wide eyes and her mouth opened

slightly. Her face paled.

He blushed and smiled. Now that he'd broached the subject of his feelings for her, there was no going back. Nor did he want to. 'I deeply regret our divorce, Sarah. I wish I'd fought harder to save our marriage.'

She shook her head slowly, a look of bafflement on her face. 'It wasn't just down to you –'

'It's bound to have affected the children, hasn't it?'

'Well, naturally, but the children are fine, really. They've grown up with you not living at home. It's all they've ever known, in Lewis' case anyway. In that respect they're much luckier than other kids of divorced parents.'

'Still,' he said, steering her gently back to the topic that had lately come to preoccupy his thoughts. 'Wouldn't it be so much better for them if their parents were together?'

She lifted her shoulders and looked away. 'Well, yes, in theory that's what everyone wants for their children.' Her shoulders dropped and the corners of her mouth turned down. 'But life doesn't always deliver dreams.'

'Why did you never marry again?'

Colour rose to her cheeks once more and his heart leapt in his chest. He'd thought long and hard about it and he'd come to the conclusion that she must still have feelings for him. 'You do care for me, Sarah, don't you?'

She frowned, her expression deeply troubled. 'I'm fond of you, Ian, of course. But you're married to Raquel.'

He broke eye contact then and looked at the floor. Raquel. The thorn in his side. And then, as if on cue, the phone rang and Sarah jumped to her feet. 'I'd better get it, in case it's the nursing home.'

Ian stood up and pulled his mobile out of his pocket. The battery was dead. Damn! What if the staff had been trying to contact him? His mother was asleep when he'd left, but what if she'd taken a turn for the worse?

Sarah snatched up the phone, listened for a moment and frowned. 'Yes, he's here,' she said rather coolly, then thrust the receiver into his hand.

He took the phone from her hand, as cold dread settled in his stomach.

'What are you doing over there?' said a sharp, ill-tempered woman's voice and, while the dread evaporated instantly, his heart sank. Why did Raquel have to ring now when he and Sarah were having the most important conversation of the last eight years?

'Raquel,' he said, and sat down abruptly on the nearest chair. 'Thank God it's you. I thought it was the nursing home.'

'I've been home for over half an hour. I tried calling you on your mobile.'

'You got my message?' he said, watching Sarah wipe splashes of tomato sauce off the cream tiles behind the cooker. Tiles he'd spent an entire weekend putting up. He'd done a good job and Sarah had been so thrilled.

'Yes, but you didn't say where you were going. What are you doing over at Sarah's?'

'I'll explain when I get home.'

'It had better be good,' she said meanly and hung up.

Ian sighed. 'Sorry 'bout that,' he said apologetically. He put the phone in its cradle and Sarah yawned.

'Tired?'

She nodded. 'Late night last night. Work thing.'

'Well,' he said, fumbling in his jacket pocket for the car keys. 'I guess I'd better go. I'll just pop into the lounge and say goodbye to the kids. Give me five minutes.'

He sat between them on the sofa, an arm round each of them, marvelling at how big they'd grown, how two unpromising scraps of life had turned into the most beautiful children he'd ever seen. Molly placed her head on his shoulder and Lewis cuddled up in the crook of his arm. Oh, what he would give to be back here, on this sofa every night, with his children in his arms.

His hand was on the front door latch when Sarah called his name. He turned and she padded noiselessly up the hall, the now empty wine glass pressed to her chest, her hair fallen from the ponytail. 'Between us, we'll take care of her, Ian. And everything's going to be all right. Try not to worry.'

Her blonde hair, back-lit by the lamp on the hall table, was like a halo. Goodness shone from her, pure and bright. Why hadn't he fought harder to save his marriage?

Chapter 5

When the children were in bed and the house was finally quiet for the night, Sarah threw together a stiff gin with out-of-date tonic she'd found lurking in the bottom of the fridge. Standing over the kitchen sink she swallowed the bitter drink in one, grimaced, and waited for the alcohol to slow her racing pulse and unscramble the thoughts inside her head. Bisto rubbed his back against her leg and meowed.

'Oh, I'm sorry, Bisto. I've forgotten to feed you, haven't I?' He meowed again as if he understood. She spooned half a tin of cat food into his bowl and he gobbled it down appreciatively.

She'd got home late last night from the Europa Hotel and then lain in bed for hours, tossing and turning, unable to sleep, replaying over and over her meeting with Cahal.

She remembered every little detail of his changed appearance; the smattering of grey hairs in his dark sideburns; the deep zig-zag crease across his brow; the slight slackness of the skin on the back of his tanned hands. She'd noticed too the things that hadn't changed like the barely visible, half-moon-shaped scar on his cheekbone, a war wound from a long-ago hurling match. Lying in the darkness staring at the digital clock display, as the minutes and hours ticked by, sorrow and anger welled up like twin demons. She tortured herself with scenarios of what might have been. The life they might have had. All the old regrets came rushing back and with them came anger. She had been a fool to believe in him. For all his talk of love, his promises had been empty. He should not have come back. He should not be here, invading her space and making her question the life she had so painstakingly constructed.

After a restless night, she'd been exhausted all day at work, on edge the entire time, expecting him to walk through the door at any minute. Yawning, she rinsed out the glass and decided on an early night.

Upstairs, in the bedroom where she'd slept alone these past eight years, she changed into her pyjamas and opened the heavy bottom drawer of a mahogany chest – one of many items that Ian, in his haste to shed his old life like a skin, had left behind. Under a pile of lycra gym wear she'd bought after the divorce and never worn, she found the old shoebox that was home to her special things. She sat down on the bed with her legs crossed and took off the lid.

Under the black-and-white photographs she found the small, hand-carved green-and-blue lacquered box that she'd owned for so long she could no longer remember how she'd come to possess it.

She opened the hinged lid that didn't quite fit properly. Inside was a magpie assortment of tarnished trinkets collected in her youth, which she could not bring herself to throw away. Pieces of insubstantial jewellery from old boyfriends; a thin silver bracelet she'd bought with her first pay packet from her Saturday job in the hairdressers; a silver alloy and marcasite bracelet with a broken clasp that had belonged to her maternal grandmother.

Finally she found what she was looking for. Her fingers closed around a twist of tissue paper, yellowed and crisp with age. She set the box on the bed, unravelled the paper and a delicate necklace and a ring, both dirty with neglect, fell onto the dove grey satin bedspread. She picked the necklace up and stared at the tiny pendant that hung from the chain, browned with tarnish like coffee stains.

Cahal had given it to her on her nineteenth birthday, a silvery disc suspended within a half-moon-shaped arc. Back then, the silver had gleamed bright and shiny like her hopes. The pendant had peculiar markings on it, resembling hiero-glyphics, that didn't at first seem to make any sense.

'Let me show you,' he said. He flicked the little disc with his nail, sending it spinning, and conjuring out of thin air the words 'I Love You'. She gasped silently and watched the words floating in the space between them. But, as soon as she touched the pendant, they were gone.

She placed the necklace in the palm of her left hand, closed her fingers around it and sighed. For six months, she'd worn that necklace nestled between her breasts, never taking it off even to shower or bathe.

'Mammy,' said a voice and Sarah, looking up, blinked back tears and smiled at her thin and willowy daughter, dressed in fleecy tiger print pyjamas to ward off the chill of the cold March night.

'What're …' she croaked, cleared her throat and found her voice. 'What're you doing out of bed, Molly?'

'I couldn't sleep. When I lie down my throat gets all tickly and then I cough and cough.' She coughed as if to prove her point and her whole body shook. Her face was as white as the stubborn pockets of snow that still clung to the north-facing pavement outside. She sat down beside her mother and looked at the things on the bed.

'If it's not any better in the morning, you might have to go to the doctor's.'

Molly shook her long hair, thin like Sarah's but a lighter shade of blonde, and picked up one of the photographs that were spread across the bed. 'Who's this?' she said, holding up a picture of two women, in fifties-style skirts and buttoned-up cardigans, leaning against a railing with a shoreline as backdrop.

Sarah craned her neck to see more clearly and smiled. 'Oh, that's your nan and Aunt Vi.'

Molly frowned. 'It doesn't look like Aunt Vi.'

'That's because it was taken a long time ago.' She took the picture from Molly and peered at it. The women's full skirts flared in the wind and they fought to hold the skirts down in an effort to protect their modesty. Maybe that was why they were laughing so hard. She smiled, warm memories of her mother flooding back. 'Look how young they both are. I think it was taken when your Gran and Grandad were going out together, before they were married. I guess Grandad must've taken the picture.'

'Aunt Vi was really pretty,' said Molly, sifting through some more photos.

'Yes, yes, she was,' said Sarah, wondering how the carefree girl in the picture with the tiny waist and shapely legs had turned into such a worrier. And why too, she had never married.

Losing interest in the photographs, Molly plucked the ring off the bedspread. She held it between her finger and thumb and observed, 'This is really dirty.'

'Yes,' said Sarah, dropping the photograph. 'It's been in the box a long time. It'd come up fine with a bit of gold polish though.'

'What is it?'

Sarah swallowed. She had not shown the ring to anyone in over twenty years. She told herself that talking about it now was harmless. It was a relic from her personal history; that was all. But still, her voice caught in her throat when she said, 'It's a Claddagh ring.'

'What's a Cla-da ring?' said Molly, stumbling over the unfamiliar syllables.

'It's a friendship ring. Sometimes people use them as wedding rings. It's named after a little village in Galway. Here, let me show you.' She held out her hand and Molly dropped the ring, cold as clay, into the palm of her hand.

'The heart in the middle stands for love,' she said, holding the ring up to the light, its history told in the rounded corners of the soft metal and the many little scratches that covered its surface. 'The two hands holding the heart mean friendship, and the crown here, on top of the heart, it means loyalty.' She paused. 'At least that's what people say,' she added.

'Loyalty?' frowned Molly, staring at the ring.

'You know, being true. Always standing up for someone. Like the way you and Nicola are with each other.'

The mention of her best friend's name ironed out the frown on Molly's brow. 'Did Dad give it to you?'

'No, love. A friend.' She dropped it into Molly's outstretched palm.

'If Dad didn't give it to you, why don't you wear it?'

Sarah flinched. She had thought that the child would not notice that she no longer wore her wedding or engagement ring, nor any other piece of jewellery Ian had given her. But of course she had noticed, because children miss nothing. 'Because it was a long time ago. And I'm not really friends with them, not anymore.' She plucked the ring from her daughter's palm and stared at it, remembering the thrill when Cahal had slipped the ring on her finger. And the horror on her father's face, and her aunt's, when they'd first seen it, one evening after tea …

'Where did you get that?' Dad said, with a quick, sharp glance at Aunt Vi on the opposite side of the kitchen table.

Sarah nervously twirled the ring around the ring finger on her right hand, her pulse quickening. 'Oh, from someone I'm dating,' she said as casually as she could muster.

'Who?'

Sarah thought of the promises she had made to Cahal and told herself determinedly that she was nineteen now and an adult and free to make her own decisions and choices. So why did she feel like a kid again, caught doing something wrong? She'd always known her father and her aunt wouldn't approve of Cahal, but she had to face up to them sooner or later. She and Cahal would be engaged soon and married before the summer was out. Steeling herself with this knowledge, she took a deep breath and said, 'Cahal Mulvenna.'

'Mulvenna?' said Aunt Vi and stared at Dad, her eyes wide open. 'Where from?'

'Ballyfergus. His family live in the Drumalis estate, though I've never met them.'

There was a long and heavy silence.

She didn't of course expect them to be cock-a-hoop at the news that she was dating a boy from the Drumalis council estate. And her father knew without being told – because he knew everyone in Ballyfergus – that Cahal was a Catholic. Which wouldn't exactly help matters. But their reaction was a whole lot worse than she'd expected. Aunt Vi's face went pure white and Dad said, as grim-faced as she'd ever seen him, 'I don't want you seeing him again.'

'What?' said Sarah in disbelief.

'You heard what I said.' He tapped the handle of a teaspoon on the table and Aunt Vi stared wordlessly at the table, her mouth, which was never usually at rest, hanging slightly open.

'That's ridiculous.' Indignation inflamed Sarah's cheeks.

'You heard what your father said,' said Aunt Vi.

'Because he's not good enough?' demanded Sarah, glancing

at her aunt, then focusing on her father again.

'Yes,' he said.

'Or because he's a Catholic?'

'That too,' he said and, though he would not look at Sarah, he gave Aunt Vi a hard, knowing stare.

Becky, who was only eleven at the time, bless her, said quietly, 'But isn't it up to Sarah?'

'No, it's not,' snapped Aunt Vi, her voice all high and shrill, like the way she sang in church. 'His father's been in prison, Sarah, for heaven's sake.' She clutched the neck of her blouse tight between shaking fingers.

'So what?' said Sarah, indignation giving way to anger. 'That's not Cahal's fault! I knew you two were prejudiced, but I didn't expect you to be out-and-out bigots.'

'We're not bigots,' said her father calmly, setting the spoon on the table. 'We respect other people's views and beliefs.'

Sarah blushed because she knew this to be true. Her father played golf with Dr Flynn and he was a Catholic. And her aunt was never done sending meals and home baking over to old Mrs Riley who lived alone next door and insisted on flicking 'holy' water over Sarah every time she stepped through the front door with a plate of food.

Anger made her brave. 'So what is it then? Because he's working class?' she said nastily.

Dad's face hardened even more, the muscles in his jaw twitching. 'I'm sure this Ca-, or whatever his name is –'

'Ca-hal,' interrupted Sarah, emphasising the two syllables slowly, taking offence at her father's inability to pronounce the name.

Dad's gaze flicked over her. 'I'm sure he's a decent boy but I didn't raise you to mix with people like that.'

'People like what?'

'Stick to your own kind, Sarah,' shouted Aunt Vi, who had never before raised her voice in Sarah's presence. 'That's what your father's saying. People who've been brought up the same way as you and believe in the same things. People with the same standards.'

'You're both just snobs, pure and simple,' cried Sarah, slapping the table with both palms. And she jumped up and ran out of the room.

'Can I have it?' Molly's dove grey eyes, the same colour as the bedspread, were wide, her expression expectant.

'What?'

Molly pointed at the ring in Sarah's hand.

'Oh, no, love. I don't think so,' said Sarah gently, letting her hand fall onto her lap, her fingers closing around the ring.

'Just to borrow?'

Sarah shook her head and her fingers tightened.

'Please?'

'It's too big for you.'

'I could wear it on a chain,' she said, touching the pale delicate skin at the base of her throat.

How on earth would she explain its appearance round Molly's neck to her father and Auntie Vi? They would recognise it immediately. Sarah put a hand on Molly's arm. 'Not this time, darling. You can have that silver bracelet though. I bought it for myself when I got my first job.'

Ignoring this comment, the child persisted. 'But what's the point of having it if you don't wear it?'

Sarah's hand slipped from Molly's arm. 'Because it's a … a memory, Molly. Sometimes people like to keep things to remind them of happy times.'

'But it's not making you happy. It's making you sad.'

Sarah forced a limp smile. 'Sometimes happy memories make you a little sad.'

Molly screwed up her nose, folded her arms across her narrow chest and shook her head stubbornly. 'I don't get it.'

Sarah sighed. 'It's a little hard to explain,' she began and floundered. How could she explain the bitter-sweetness of her memories? Or how the desire to remember, suppressed for so long, had been cracked open last night by the mere sight of Cahal Mulvenna. How could she admit to herself, never mind Molly, that seeing him again had brought with it not only pain but a stupid, fevered hope?

'I think I might give it back to the person who gave it to me,' she announced, realising as she said it that it was the right thing to do. The ring had never been hers, it had only ever been borrowed. It belonged to Cahal.

'Who's that?'

'Come on, time for bed,' she said sharply, dropping the ring and necklace into the box, and snapping the lid shut before shoving it back in the drawer, slamming it firmly shut.

'And let's see if we can find you some cough medicine, young lady,' she smiled and taking a reluctant, wide-awake daughter by the hand, led her into the bathroom.

Chapter 6

Cahal typed 'Ballyfergus' on the keyboard, hit the return button, and stared at the computer screen, unable to get Sarah in that red dress and high heels out of his mind. So she had married Ian Aitken. How could she? She'd had little to no time for Ian at university, even though the poor bugger was clearly in love with her. So what had changed? Or had she married him just to please her family? The thought repelled him.

She'd hurt him so deeply the pain had never really gone away and seeing her had only re-opened the old wound. She'd refused to go to Australia with him and she'd not responded to a single one of the dozens of letters he'd sent her from there, nor the phone call either. She'd effectively ended the relationship without the courtesy of an explanation, though he guessed what had happened after he'd left. Ian would've been waiting in the wings, all too ready to offer tea and sympathy.

But maybe she wasn't what she'd pretended to be. What if he'd never known the real Sarah? Maybe his going to Australia was the opportunity she'd been waiting for? An opportunity to end a relationship she was too cowardly to finish face-to-face.

He brought his closed fist down quietly on the table. She was here, somewhere, in this very building, Laganside Tower, going about her business along with the twelve hundred other staff. And these questions were driving him mad.

He had not known she worked for VTS, and when he saw her at the Europa Hotel two days ago, shimmering like a star amongst the drab suits and dreary conversation, he'd not, at first, believed his eyes.

He had not imagined that her appearance would be so largely unchanged from when he'd last seen her, twenty years ago. There were fine wrinkles on her skin, yes, but she had the same pretty face framed by that blonde hair, cut into a shorter, neater style than the one she'd worn at uni. The same big, grey doe eyes and slim, boyish figure that had entranced him from the first moment he'd set eyes on her folding her knickers with intense focus in the uni laundry … he swallowed and shook his head to dispel that particular image.

He was a little ashamed of the way he'd flirted with Jody in front of Sarah – but he'd been angry when he heard the name Aitken and he took a mean sort of satisfaction in her response. She'd gone red and stomped off in a huff almost as if she cared. And the idea that his tiny act of revenge might have made her jealous, might have hurt her, pleased him. She'd taught him that it wasn't what people said that mattered, but what they did. She'd talked of nothing but how much she loved him, but in the end, her actions spoke more loudly than any words she'd ever uttered. Her lack of courage had disappointed him almost as much as his heart hurt. He'd always thought her better than that.

Even now, thinking of it all these years later, he was angry. He'd come here to Northern Ireland for work, that was true, but he'd also come for answers. He put a closed fist to his lips and stared out the twelfth-floor window across a cityscape recognisable to him only by the mammoth yellow cranes of the shipyard and the Belfast Hills – Cavehill, Divis, Black Mountain and the rest – that surrounded the city on three sides, behind which the late afternoon sun was setting. Closer up, he barely recognised this vibrant, optimistic place as the grey, barricaded Belfast he'd known as a young man. Brand new buildings had sprouted up all over the place like saplings reaching for the sun, and everywhere he went he met bright young people full of energy.

A lock of blonde hair fell into his line of vision and he started.

'Hey, what're you up to, sunshine?' said Jody in his right ear, her cloying perfume filling his nostrils. Then she perched on the edge of his desk, crossed her long tanned legs, encased in nylons, and glanced at the computer screen. 'Oh, you're looking at rentals. In …' She peered closer. 'Bally-what?'

'Ballyfergus,' he said, wishing she would go away. It wasn't personal – he'd worked with Jody, fifteen years his junior, for two years and they'd always got on well. But right now he'd rather be alone with his thoughts. 'It's a little town, a port actually, twenty-five miles north of Belfast.' She looked a little puzzled and he added, remembering that she'd been raised in metric Australia, 'That's about forty kilometres.'

Leaning over, she stared more closely at the picture of a rather drab terrace house on the computer screen and frowned. 'Why would you want to rent a place there? I thought we'd all stay in Belfast for the six months.'

He shrugged. 'It's where I grew up.'

'Oh, I see, so you can be near your family. I'd love to meet them sometime,' she said, putting special emphasis on 'love' and leaning in even closer to peer at the screen.

He cleared his throat. Hell would freeze over before he'd introduce anyone on the team to his family. He never talked about his background at work. He clicked a button and the terrace house disappeared from the screen.

'I've been offered a room in a flat owned by one of the girls in admin,' she went on in the face of his silence.

'Take it. It'll be much nicer than living out of a suitcase in a hotel. You'll get to know the place better that way. Might even pick yourself up a Belfast man.' He winked at her and she pouted, then pulled her suit jacket tight round her slim frame and said, 'Hmm. Well, I don't know how anyone can live here. How they can stand the cold. Isn't this supposed to be spring?'

He smiled. 'Wait till it rains for days on end. Then you'll have something to complain about.'

She laughed more than the joke merited, then said, in that

peculiarly animated way of hers, her blue eyes wide like saucers, 'Some of the locals have invited us out for drinks and dinner after work at a place called Cayenne. It's owned by some celebrity chef and the food's supposed to be fantastic. Fancy it?'

He shook his head. 'I've got other plans for tonight.'

'Oh?' She picked up a pencil and twirled it between her fingers like a miniature cheerleader's baton.

'I'm going to Ballyfergus.'

'To see family?'

He shrugged non-committally. Something about the gleam in her eye and the way the baton stilled in her hand, made him even more cautious than normal.

'You wouldn't be going out on a date, would you, and not telling me?' The corners of her mouth twitched, though the big toothy smile remained in place.

He laughed falsely. 'No. What makes you ask that?'

She threw her head back and laughed, the sinews on her neck standing out, her long blonde hair like a mane. A man, walking by on his way to the photocopier, was so busy watching her he nearly walked into a filing cabinet and swerved to avoid it just in time. She was, he supposed, a fine-looking woman and it was surprising that she was still single. She brought her gaze to bear on him once more. 'Oh, it's just a feeling I have.'

'What feeling?' he said idly, hitting keys on the keyboard.

'About you and Sarah Aitken. I sensed there was a kind of …' She raised her eyebrows questioningly, '… tension between you two.'

He felt himself go hot under the collar. Heat rose up his

neck. 'She's an old friend.'

'That all?'

He cleared his throat. 'We used to go out together. But that ended a long time ago. It's history.'

The pencil stilled and Jody's eyes narrowed with sly understanding. 'Well, if you hadn't told me that, I would've said there was some unfinished business there. You could have cut the atmosphere between you with a knife.' She gave him a tight smile that didn't reach her eyes and set the pencil down carefully beside her on the table. 'But what do I know? Have a nice time tonight.'

Cahal parked self-consciously outside the grim block of flats, wishing that he'd chosen a much less ostentatious rental car than the shiny new Vauxhall Insignia. Here on the Drumalis estate where he'd grown up, where car ownership still appeared to be the exception rather than the rule, it stuck out like a sore thumb.

He stepped out of the car, pulled the edges of his coat together and shivered in the cold March wind blowing in off the Irish Sea. In his smart suit, open-necked shirt and overcoat he looked as out of place here as the car. Bright street lighting did little to dispel the despair that hung in the air like a fog. The mesh fence that surrounded the building was all rusted and the area of green space behind it, meant to be a garden of sorts, was a tangle of weeds. He wondered where Sarah lived – it could only be a few miles away – Ballyfergus was not a big town – but it would be nothing like this place, of that he was certain.

To his left, a group of hooded teenagers loitered on the street corner under a lamp post. The biggest, a muscular lad of about sixteen or seventeen, two diamond studs in his right ear and a familiar look about his large hooked nose and weak chin, stared hard at Cahal. He stared back, emotionless, until the boy broke eye contact, spat contemptuously on the pavement and looked away. Cahal would not be so easily intimidated. Once a Drumalis boy, always a Drumalis boy.

He walked heavily up the short flight of steps to the front door of the building. Movement on his left caught his eye. The boys, led by the big one, ambled slowly along the cracked pavement, hands stuffed in pockets, the hoods on their sweatshirts their only protection from the elements. Kids here learnt to do without from an early age. But their eyes weren't on him, they were on the car. Cahal turned, retraced his steps and approached the group on the pavement. The big one took his red-knuckled hands out of his pockets and curled them into fists. The rest of the lads watched their boss with hardened eyes, like wolves.

'How about ye?' said Cahal which elicited no response, nor did he expect one. He put his left hand in his back pocket and the boy tensed. Cahal froze, raised his right hand in the air and said, 'Easy.' Then he pulled out his wallet, opened it and extracted a crisp new tenner. He slipped the wallet back in his pocket and proceeded to fold the note up, slowly and methodically.

'How about you keep an eye on my wheels?' he said in his strongest Ballyfergus accent, his eyes fixed on his busy hands. 'When I come out, it'd be grand if the car was just the way I left it.'

The boy snorted derisively. 'How 'bout you hand over yer wallet?' he spat out, finishing the sentence with a choice selection of swear words.

Cahal looked up and then down the deserted street. In a second-floor window, curtains twitched, emitting a shaft of light, then stilled. No one would come to his aid here.

'You don't want to do that,' he said calmly and taking a gamble, he looked the boy straight in the eye and added, 'Yer da wouldn't be too pleased to hear you'd done over his best mate from school.'

The boy's face twitched and his thick brows furrowed slightly. Seeing his opportunity, Cahal slipped the note, now folded into eight, into the front pocket of the boy's hoodie. 'Tell yer da that Cahal Mulvenna was asking after him.' And with that he turned and walked inside.

The communal hallway was badly lit and the smell of stale cigarette smoke was the pleasanter of odours. On the top floor, he paused outside the red door of his childhood home and the feeling of dread that had been building on the drive here peaked. The doorbell hung off the door frame, severed wires exposed. Drumalis was a million miles from the middle-class, leafy suburb of Melbourne that was now his home. Taking a deep breath, he rapped the door three times with his knuckles.

'Oh there you are, son. Come on in out of the cold,' said his mother Bridget, dressed in brown polyester trousers with a crease like a knife down the front of each leg, and a beige nylon jumper. She shuffled backwards on black-velvet-slippered feet and he stepped into the cramped hallway which ran down the middle of the flat, each of the five small rooms opening off it. 'I've got the tea on already. There's some dinner if you want it. I made a bit of stew.'

'A cup of tea will be fine, Ma.'

Inside, it was overly warm and a fug of cigarette smoke hung in the air. The hall and the kitchen, which he could glimpse over her shoulder, hadn't been decorated in twenty years. The sound of the TV blared out of the open door to the lounge. He closed the front door, took off his coat and hung it on a peg behind the door.

Bridget cupped her cold hands on his cheeks and blinked up into his face, tears pooling in her rheumy eyes. 'You're looking good, son, so you are.' She let go of his face and tugged the sleeve of his fine merino wool jacket and took a step back to admire his figure. 'Look at you. Imagine a son of mine a business executive.'

He smiled, a little embarrassed, noticing that her hair was white now, all the grey gone, and her face looked more sunken. At fifty she'd looked like an old woman. Now seventy, she looked more like eighty plus.

'How are you, ma?' he said, swallowing hard.

'Oh, you know what he's like. Nothing changes round here. Your Da's in the lounge. Grainne too.' His heart sank at this news. She turned her head and shouted, 'Malachy, he's here.' Then to Cahal, 'I'll get the tea. Still milk, no sugar, son?'

'That's right, Ma,' he smiled kindly. She'd done her best to be a good mother, considering the circumstances.

She disappeared into the kitchen and Cahal went into the lounge where his father was lying on a big red leather reclining seat with a lit cigarette in one hand and a pen in the other.

As soon as he saw him, Cahal's stomach muscles tightened. A paper, open at the crossword, lay on his father's lap and a grey metal walking stick rested against the side of the chair.

Grainne got up off the sofa and smiled, revealing yellow teeth. She looked desperately thin in faded blue jeans and white trainers. Her greasy hair was streaked with grey and tied back in a fierce ponytail and her sallow face was bare of make-up. Though only a few years older than him, she looked ancient.

'How 'bout you, Cahal?' she said. He gave her a hug in response. She smelt of stale sweat and cigarette smoke. She stiffened in his embrace, and he stepped away.

'How are the boys?' She had one grown-up son and two younger ones, now fifteen and thirteen. All were by different men, none of whom had stayed around long enough to see their sons start school.

She looked at the floor. 'Pain in the arse. You know what boys are like.' She shoved her hands in the back pockets of her jeans and bit the inside of her mouth, a little habit from childhood that meant she was stressed or worried. He looked away, barely able to reconcile this haggard creature with the blonde-haired sister he'd loved. Why had she become trapped here? Why hadn't she the wherewithal to break free, to escape? He realised with horror that now he pitied her more than he loved her.

'Look, I gotta go.'

'But I've only just got here,' he said.

'I know. Sorry. I'll see you another time, eh?' She glanced at their parents and said, quietly, 'Let's talk in the hall.'

He followed her out into the narrow hall and watched her take a black jacket with shiny patches on the elbows off a coat peg by the door and put it on. Her hands were shaking so much she could barely do up the zip. But it wasn't nerves. He'd seen her like this before. The muscles in his stomach contracted. She looked like a tramp. A down and out. 'Does Ma give you the money I send every month?'

'Yeah. But ...' She glanced at him then looked away. 'But things are so expensive. Two growing boys. I've tried really hard but ...'

'But what?'

'I've got myself into a bit of trouble, Cahal.' She looked at him directly now, her eyes full of pleading and something else. Fear. 'I owe some money, like. Listen, you couldn't spare me five hundred, could you? This guy I owe money to ...' Her voice trailed off and she shook her head.

'Five hundred pounds?' How had she managed to borrow so much? She and her boyfriend lived on benefits. He swallowed the lump in his throat and the wad of money in his pocket burned like a hot coal. It would be so easy to give her the money. But would she pay off her debt like she said? Or squander it on drink and drugs?

He shook his head and she said, quick as a flash, 'A hundred, then.'

He folded his lips together.

'Fifty,' she said and placed a thin and bony hand on his arm. 'Give me fifty.'

'Okay.' His eyes stung. Blinking, he took the money out of his pocket, peeled off the notes and handed them to her. She stared at them greedily.

'Thanks Bro,' she said absentmindedly, as if her thoughts were already elsewhere. Then she opened the door and disappeared.

Back in the lounge, Malachy made no effort to get up so Cahal went over and offered his hand. His father's face was red and heavily lined from too much drinking and smoking. His looked at Cahal's hand before shaking it, then said, 'So you came to see us.' Then he looked back at the TV. His hair, receding from the brow, was thin and white and the front half of his ruddy head was almost bald. What hair clung to the rest of his head was carefully combed down with greasy hair cream and he'd put on a few pounds since the last time Cahal had seen him. Malachy had always thought of himself as a bit of a looker and even now, in old age, he was vain.

'Aye,' Cahal said over the sound of the adverts and sat down on the sofa opposite his father.

Mechanically, Malachy put the cigarette in his mouth and inhaled. His eyes narrowed to slits as he blew smoke out in a thin line. 'It's been six years.'

Cahal tensed, the anger in him, which was always at the ready in the presence of his father, coming to a simmer. 'Haven't I offered for you to come out to Australia year after year? The only time you came was for my wedding.'

Bridget came through the door with three mugs of tea on a small melamine tray and a plate of custard creams. As soon as she sensed the atmosphere in the room, the tight smile on her face disappeared. She handed tea to Malachy first, then Cahal.

'Ach, now, you're only in the door and you two are arguing,' she said, with faux breeziness, holding the plate of biscuits out to Malachy like a peace offering. During the handing out of the tea and biscuits, his father exchanged neither glance nor word with his wife. She sat down on the edge of the sofa beside Cahal with a chipped brown mug in her hand. 'Will you turn that TV off, Malachy?'

He grunted and partly complied by turning down the sound.

'I was just saying to Da that you never come out to Australia, Ma,' said Cahal taking a sip of the too-strong tea, the smoke stinging his eyes. He'd given up smoking as soon as he got to Australia, on insistence from a non-smoking hippy housemate. 'If it's a question of money, you know I'd take care of that. Haven't I offered loads of times before?'

But instead of answering him, Bridget looked at Malachy, and clutched the silver crucifix hanging around her neck. He said, knocking ash into a glass ashtray that had been nicked from a pub, 'We don't need your money.'

Bridget looked at her lap and Malachy took another drag on the cigarette. 'What do we want to be going out to Australia for anyway? It's too frigging hot.'

Cahal's blood boiled but, for his mother's sake, who sat mute and tense beside him, he held it in check. 'To see your grandsons? Anyway last time you came in summer – you should come in winter. The weather's not so different from Ireland then.'

'I can't come with this leg.' Malachy gave Cahal a stony stare and blew a cloud of blue smoke into the air between them. Cahal's stomach muscles tightened even more and he tasted metal on his tongue. He'd forgotten how much he hated his father.

He looked at his father's supposedly dodgy leg and shook his head. A lorry on the docks had backed into him thirty years ago, fracturing a bone, and it had prevented him from working ever since. He'd always been remarkably mobile, however, when it came to collecting benefits – now it was a state pension – and getting himself down to the betting shop and the pub at every opportunity.

Cahal turned to his mother and tried to engage her in eye contact but her eyes darted about like minnows. 'So why don't you come on your own, Ma? You could travel there with me in May for Jed's birthday. I'm only going for a fortnight's holiday and we could travel back together too. My treat.'

Her eyes lit up with hope but she looked at Malachy, not Cahal.

'Your mother's not going anywhere.'

'Why not?'

'Someone has to stay here and run the house.'

Cahal turned to his mother but she was already shaking her head, her eyes full of the desperate pleading that he had seen there hundreds of times before. She put her hand on Cahal's thigh, ever the peacemaker, and he bit back the retort that had sprung to his lips, the instinct to protect his mother just as acute as when he'd lived at home.

'Anyway,' said she with a weak smile, removing her hand. 'How are the weeuns?' She put the mug to her lips, and sipped.

'Not so wee now.' Cahal pulled out his wallet. He handed

a photograph to his mother and she set her mug of tea on the floor. 'That was taken just before I came away.'

'Look at the size of 'em,' said Bridget, holding the photo with both hands at arm's distance. 'Especially Jed.' She sighed and handed the photo back. 'Do you see them much?'

'They come to me one night a week and every other weekend. These next few months are going to be hard ... not seeing them. You keep the photo, Ma.' She pressed it to her chest with a grateful smile and he felt guilty that such a small gesture meant so much.

'Here, have a look, Malachy,' she said, but before she could rise from her seat he replied, without taking his eyes off the TV, 'I'll see it later.'

'And this guy of Adele's ... what's his name?' said Bridget brightly, looking at the photo again.

'Brady,' supplied Cahal.

'So they married, did they?'

'That's right.' Cahal stared at a patch on the carpet, worn thin with use, and tried not to resent the interloper in the home he still paid for. It was one of the reasons he was here. When Brady had moved in, he'd felt redundant, his manhood diminished somehow. He told himself that such Neanderthal emotions had no place in a modern world, that it was better for the boys that their mother was happy. But, still, it stuck in his gullet like undercooked pastry. It had nothing to do with his feelings for Adele – he no longer loved her – but he could not deal with the fact that another man was now effectively father to his kids.

'He's moved into your old house?' said Malachy, hitting

Cahal's raw nerve. He paused and looked quizzically at Cahal, as if he hadn't understood the conversation that had just taken place. 'With *your* weeuns?'

'Sure, I told you that the other day,' snapped Bridget.

Ignoring her, he took another drag on the cigarette that was now little more than a stump and shook his head. 'I would never have let that happen.'

'Of course you wouldn't,' snapped Cahal. 'Because you'd be completely incapable of putting the needs of your children first.'

His father smiled, the first since Cahal had come in. And it chilled him to the bone.

'So you're working for a phone company over here then?' said Bridget, staring at Cahal, her thin eyebrows high on her brow.

Malachy coughed and stubbed the cigarette out in the ashtray. He banged his chest with his fist. 'I told you not to buy those cheap cigarettes, woman. You know only Benson and Hedges agree with me.'

Bridget said, 'I'll get them next time, Malachy.'

Cahal took a deep breath and told himself to stay out of it. Hadn't he tried for years to get her to leave him? 'Telecommunications. I'm leading a change management programme for an Australian company, ATS. They've taken over VTS.'

Bridget's face brightened. 'I've heard of VTS.'

Malachy picked something off the tip of his tongue and looked at it. He would have no idea what change management was but it'd be nice if, just once in his life, he could acknowledge his son's success. 'And you think they'll listen to you?'

In that instant Cahal was a boy again, on the day he'd come home from school, burst into the lounge where his father was nursing his recently injured leg on a footstool, and told him that he'd won the third-year English prize. His father had laughed without humour. 'Made a mistake, did they? Don't be getting above yourself, Cahal. You'll leave school at sixteen and get a job just like your brother Sean did.' He tapped his leg with his walking stick. 'About time you started earning your keep.' Then he'd picked up the paper and opened it, obscuring his hateful face entirely.

But he'd proved them all wrong, Cahal thought angrily, looking around the childhood home that held so many, awful, memories. Cahal Mulvenna, whom no one, least of all his father, had ever expected to amount to anything, had made something of himself.

'Oh, will you look at the time,' said Bridget, with a glance at the sunburst clock on the wall. 'We're supposed to be down the club.' She leapt off the sofa and scooped up the empty mug that Malachy had discarded on the floor.

Cahal frowned. 'You never said anything about going down the club on the phone. I'd have come earlier.'

'But we always go on a Friday,' she said, looking at the carpet.

'Well you can miss it this once, can't you?' said Cahal, slightly incredulous. He'd only been in the house twenty minutes.

'Your mother doesn't like to miss her bingo,' said Malachy. 'And they do pensioner's rates at the bar.'

Cheap drink was the real reason they were going then because, to Cahal's knowledge, his father had never put

Bridget's wishes before his own.

'You could come too and have a pint with yer Da,' said Bridget tentatively.

Cahal looked at his father. 'No, I don't think so. I'm driving.'

'You could stay the night,' said Bridget, and she went on, warming to the idea as it grew in her mind, 'The back bedroom's full of junk. But you can sleep on the sofa. I have some blankets somewhere. Maybe up in the attic. They might need a bit of an airing mind. It can get a bit damp up there …' She looked hopefully at Malachy – and he looked at the TV.

The idea of sleeping in this smoke-filled room under damp, musty blankets filled Cahal with horror. Already he felt sick with the fumes and he hadn't been here half an hour.

'Thanks Ma,' he said without looking at her as he couldn't bear to witness the disappointment on her face. 'But I've got to get up for work in the morning. I'll need clean clothes.'

'Oh, well, another time,' she said with the brisk resignation of a woman used to handling defeat. She hovered over him, looking into the mug he held between both hands. 'Are you going to drink that tea?'

Cahal shook his head, stood up and handed her the mug. The cigarette smoke made him light-headed – or was it the tangle of emotions in his stomach?

'You'll come and see us again?' said Bridget, standing in the middle of the lounge looking so small and worn down that his heart went out to her, in spite of the anger he felt towards both of them.

'Of course I will, Ma.'

At the front door, he shrugged on his coat and pressed a thick wad of twenty pound notes into her palm. She shook her head half-heartedly, one eye on the cash, the other on the door to the lounge where Malachy still lay sprawled in front of the TV.

'Take it,' he whispered, touching her cold fingers. 'There's five hundred there.'

Her eyes opened wide in astonishment and he said, 'Grainne says she owes someone five hundred pounds.'

His mother scowled. 'It'll be Beaky,' she said. 'He runs everything round here.'

'I want you to give three hundred to him. To him mind, not Grainne. Tell him he'll get the rest next week. The rest of the money's for you and the boys. You get them what they need. Don't give any money to Grainne, now. And see that you treat yourself too,' he said, though he knew that she would not. Some of the money would go on cigarettes and whiskey to keep his father happy, the rest on things for his nephews.

'You're a good brother. And you're good to yer old ma,' she said, closing her gnarled, arthritic fingers around the cash.

His throat was so tight it hurt. He looked around the shabby hallway and whispered, 'If you'd left him I would've looked after you. You know that, don't you, Ma?'

She placed a hand on his arm and blinked into his face. 'Knowing that you are well and happy in the world is enough, Cahal. Try to understand that.'

He didn't understand, and he never would, but he smiled anyway to please her and placed a kiss on her wrinkled forehead.

Down on the street the big teenager was waiting, leaning against the car with his arms folded, looking pleased with himself. Cahal nodded.

'She's fine,' said the lad and patted the paintwork with the flat of his hand. 'I've not let any of them touch it,' he said.

Cahal nodded his appreciation and got the keys out of his pocket. The boy, who showed no sign of moving, cocked his head to one side and said, 'Me Da says you're some kind of big shot in Australia. Is that right?'

Cahal shrugged. 'I wouldn't believe everything you hear.' And with that he got in the car and drove off.

Chapter 7

When he saw Sarah sitting alone with a cup of coffee the very next day in the canteen at work, he froze. Her head was bent over her BlackBerry screen, a button of pale, vulnerable skin exposed at the crown of her head. Suddenly her nose wrinkled up the way it used to when she was annoyed with him – and something inside him melted.

She was the only person he had ever confided in about his family. Adele had seen for herself, but he'd never shared with her how he felt deep inside. How he'd spent his life wishing he was someone else.

Something made her look up at that precise moment and their eyes locked. Her lips formed into a nervous, fleeting acknowledgement that was almost a smile. She looked away and lifted the cup to her lips. Without thinking about it, he went over. 'Mind if I sit down?'

She glanced at the empty seats around the table and

shrugged.

He sat down opposite her, set his mug of tea on the table and rested his hands on his thighs. 'I never expected to see you again.'

'Nor I you,' she said and looked away. In the silence that followed, he studied the pale pink nail polish on the ends of her slender fingers.

'So, you married Ian?' he said, trying to keep the bitterness out of his voice.

'He's a good man,' she said coldly.

He frowned. Why was she being so hostile? If anyone had a right to be angry it was him, not her.

She set the BlackBerry on the table in front of her. 'You never liked him.'

It was so like her to go straight for the jugular. Small talk had never been her forte. But then again, they knew each other too well for meaningless chit-chat. 'No. And he never liked me much either,' he said evenly. 'I would go so far as to say he hated me.'

'He didn't hate you,' she said quietly. 'He hated what he thought you were. What you stood for. Just as you hated what he stood for.'

He shook his head, refuting this. 'He hated me because of you, Sarah. It was obvious to everyone that he loved you, even when you were going out with me.' She blinked, colour rising to her cheeks and he went on, 'But I like to think that under other circumstances, in another place and time perhaps, we might have been friends.'

She looked at him sceptically.

'I was prejudiced back then. Narrow-minded,' he explained, 'I hope I'm not now.'

She frowned and took another sip of coffee. Then she put the cup down and blurted out, 'Well, the marriage didn't last. Though it was a good divorce. If you can have such a thing.'

This news left him dumbstruck, his eye drawn to her bare ring finger. She was not another man's after all. She did not lie with Ian every night as he had imagined. A shutter creaked open in his heart.

'What I mean is,' she went on, 'we're not at each other's throats all the time, like some people. We always put the kids first.'

'Kids?'

'Yes, Molly's eleven-year-old and Lewis is nine-year-old,' she said, proudly, lifting her chin.

Children, he thought regretfully, that might have been his. It came as no surprise, really, that she had a family. But the knowledge lodged itself uncomfortably in his consciousness all the same. 'I have three boys.'

A smile warmed her face, softening her features. 'You must miss them.'

'It's like someone's taken a big chunk out of me, right here.' He placed a hand on his side. 'And it hurts like hell. I've only been gone a week and I've spoken to them on the phone every day. But it's not the same as being there.'

She shook her head. 'I could never leave my children.'

'I had to because of this job,' he snapped defensively, and then softened. 'And now I'm sorry I did.'

In the awkward silence that followed, Sarah looked away.

'Your father and your aunt,' he said, 'are they still both well?'

She looked at him, surprised. 'Both, yes, thank you.' She frowned, turning the mug between her fingers. 'The last time you spoke to me of them, you said you hated them.'

'I had reason to, hadn't I?' It had slipped out, more bitter and resentful than he'd intended. But honest too. He stared at her and she stared back.

And then her BlackBerry, on the table between them, buzzed like a wasp trapped in a jar. She picked it up and, without looking at the screen, said, 'I have to go. I've got a meeting in five minutes.' She stood up and swung a black leather handbag over her left shoulder. He got to his feet and they faced each other across the small table.

'Sarah?'

She paused, one hand on the back of the chair, her face a deliberate mask. 'What?'

'I think we need to talk.'

She looked away.

He took a step around the table till they were an arm's length apart. He still hadn't got the answers that he wanted. And even now, when he was angry with her, when he blamed her for so much, he was drawn to her, like a moth to a flame. 'Have dinner with me.'

A pained expression briefly marred her pretty features and she looked at the floor. 'I don't know if that's a good –'

'Please,' he cut across her, more of a demand than a request, and touched her lightly on the hand. Her skin tingled under his touch.

She looked at his hand, then into his face. Her eyelids flickered. 'Okay.'

'Quieten down you two,' hollered Becky, standing at the bottom of Sarah's stairs, her hand on the newel post, one foot on the bottom stair. 'Or I'll come up and ... eh ... sort you out.'

Upstairs, the whooping and squealing intensified and Becky rolled her eyes. 'They don't listen to a word I say.'

Sarah pulled on her smart black wool coat. 'That's because they know you're a soft touch. Not that that's a bad thing,' she added hastily. 'They love you just the way you are.'

A smile flickered across Becky's face and then she was serious. 'Listen, are you sure you really want to meet Cahal Mulvenna? Personally, I think he's got a cheek coming back after all this time, expecting you to be at his beck and call.'

Sarah did up the buttons on her coat. 'I'm not at his beck and call. We're just having dinner.' But now she was having second thoughts about it. For one thing, her stomach was so tied up in knots she didn't think she'd be able to eat a single mouthful.

A deep line appeared between Becky's brows. 'And he didn't say why he wanted to meet you?'

Sarah put her gloves back in the drawer. She would not need them. Her palms were sweating. 'He just said we needed to talk, that was all.'

'He wants you to forgive him. You do know that, don't you? So he can go back to Australia and feel good about himself.'

She slung her bag over her shoulder. 'Maybe.' It wouldn't change anything, but an apology would be something at least.

A kind of cold comfort.

'Is that why you said yes?'

Sarah smoothed down the front of her wool coat with sticky hands. She didn't know why she had agreed. Only that she couldn't say no. 'I guess I'm curious.'

'You know what they say: curiosity killed the cat.'

Sarah smiled weakly and Becky reached out and touched her on the arm. 'Just be careful, Sarah. I don't want to see you hurt.' She paused and added, 'Like the last time.'

'I won't be.' Sarah took a deep breath and threw back her shoulders. 'How do I look?'

Becky's arm fell to her side. 'Fabulous. He'll be sorry he ever let you go when he sees you.'

'Thank you.' Sarah bit her lip. 'Wish me luck.'

Becky smiled, though Sarah could tell she was faking it, and gave her a big warm hug. Then she held her at arms' length. 'You'll be grand. You can tell me all about it when you get in. I'll wait up.'

'You don't have to.'

'I want to. Anyway, I've got this great documentary to watch about Ephesus once the kids are in bed.'

'Who's Ephesus?'

'Duh?' said Becky and she knocked Sarah's forehead lightly with her knuckle. 'Only the best preserved classical city in the whole of the Eastern Mediterranean. It's in Turkey.'

'You cheeky cow,' said Sarah taking an ineffectual swipe at Becky's hand. But Becky had already jumped nimbly onto the stairs, well out of reach. She grinned and glanced at her watch. 'Hadn't you better go?'

*

Cahal sat alone at a table for two in Carnegie's, Ballyfergus's only fine-dining restaurant, waiting. Outside, new owners had done a good job of tarting up what used to be a grotty biker's hang-out, Peggy's Kitchen.

Across the road stood the old Carnegie library, where he'd spent many silent hours as a boy sitting cross-legged on the dusty wooden floor. With a book resting on his bare knees, and the warm sun streaming through the tall windows, he'd been transported to a world that could not have been more different from his own – an exotic land populated by ex-convicts, coal-black Aborigines and kangaroos. Inside, the restaurant was extravagantly done out in plush carpet, rich brocades and velvets in burgundy and gold with ornate mirrors on the wall and candles everywhere. The room smelt of candle smoke and good food. It was certainly atmospheric, but now that he was here – and it was too late to change – he worried that it was too romantic.

It was not a date, he reminded himself, even though his stomach flipped every time the door opened. The purpose of the meeting was to get answers to his questions. What had happened after he went to Australia? Why had she not replied to his letters and phone call? Had she ever really loved him? Or had he been a complete and utter fool to believe in her?

He finished his drink, set the empty glass on the linen tablecloth and immediately a young waiter, all in black like a shadow, was at his side. 'Would you like another beer, sir?'

He shook his head.

'Something else?'

He cleared his throat. 'No thank you.'

The waiter moved away and, nervously, Cahal pulled his mobile out of his pocket. Sarah was fifteen minutes late and there was no text to say why. He set the phone on the table and peered out the small window on his left which overlooked the almost empty car park. So she was a few minutes late? Big deal. She might have had trouble getting the kids to bed or maybe the babysitter was late. He let out a long, audible sigh and told himself to stop worrying. Then he closed his eyes, rolled his shoulders – still tense from the visit earlier in the week to his parents' – and tried to relax. His stomach felt like a wet sheet after the spin cycle – all snarled up in itself, a feeling he associated only with his family. It was, he supposed, what love, hate and guilt felt like all tangled up together.

He looked at his watch. It was twenty minutes past eight. He tapped the face of the watch but the time stayed the same.

His heart fluttered in his chest as the possibility that she might not show began to elbow its way into his consciousness. Perhaps her mobile had no signal. His spirits lifted then fell again when he realised that, if she wanted to get a message to him, all she had to do was phone the restaurant. He bit his lip and dialled into his voicemail – but there was nothing from Sarah. Finally, he sent her a text. *Where are you? C*

He placed the phone carefully on the table beside the gleaming knife again and took a deep breath. Give it five more minutes he said to himself, while his hands in his lap, hidden underneath the fine linen tablecloth, clenched into fists. And the rage that he had felt all those years ago at her betrayal began to surface once more.

The minutes and seconds ticked by and the collar of his new white shirt, bought specially for tonight in Belfast's upmarket Victoria Square, began to itch. The couple at the next table glanced at him and quickly looked away. The waiter, hovering near the door to the kitchen, checked his watch and consulted discreetly with a colleague. One of the elderly ladies, cutlery in hand, nudged her neighbour and nodded sympathetically at him. He caught her eye but she did not look away. Embarrassed, he did.

He would give her until half past eight.

Two minutes later the waiter came over, carrying an order pad and pen. 'Just to let you know, sir,' he said, looking almost as embarrassed as Cahal felt, 'the kitchen closes for orders at nine.'

Cahal gave him a grim smile and picked up the mobile. Eight twenty-nine.

She wasn't coming.

'I don't think I'll be dining tonight after all,' he said, slipping the phone into his inside pocket. 'I'm sorry.'

'That's quite all right, sir.'

Cahal pulled a twenty out of his wallet and pressed it into the waiter's palm. 'For the beer,' he said quietly. 'And your trouble.'

'Thank you very much, sir,' said the waiter, pocketing the note in one smooth movement without looking at it.

Cahal stood up slowly and took his time fastening the middle button on his jacket with fingers suddenly fat and clumsy. Then he strode casually out the door resisting the urge to run. He knew, if he glanced back, everyone would be looking at him.

Outside in the car park it was raining, the perfect end to a miserable day. He walked quickly to the car, head down, his fists curled into balls. Anger rose in him like sap. He hated to be humiliated. He oughtn't to be surprised. After all, it wasn't the first time she had broken her word. It wasn't the first time she had let him down. What on earth had made him think that he could trust her, that she had changed?

The rain merged into a blur and he swallowed hard as the anger turned to sadness. He'd wanted answers tonight but he'd wanted something else too. He wanted to know if she felt anything for him – anything at all. Her reaction to his flirting with Jody had given him hope. But now he knew.

He blinked, the muscles in his jaw twitching. Then he thrust the car into first gear and screeched onto the road like a teenager in his first car.

Hidden in the shadows outside Carnegie's, Sarah stared through the window at the warm and cosy scene inside. Half the tables in the restaurant were filled with old people and couples – and Cahal, sitting alone at a table for two facing the door, his face bathed in golden candlelight.

He was smartly, but casually, dressed in a navy sports jacket and crisp white shirt, opened at the neck just enough to reveal a triangle of brown flesh and black chest hair. The dark shadow on his chin made him look both slightly unkempt, and undeniably attractive. Her stomach flipped with desire and she placed a hand on her belly.

113

She had dressed with great care for tonight, rejecting outfit after outfit until her bed was piled high with clothes, and she finally settled on a red crepe dress and high-heeled black boots. Not too smart, not too casual. But now the shiny patent boots felt too sexy and the dress too tight. What the hell was she doing here? Cahal was a married man with a family. What did he want with her after all these years? Her stomach tightened and she pulled her wool coat tighter around her body.

Movement inside the restaurant caught her eye. A waiter went over and exchanged a few words with Cahal, then wandered off with an empty glass in his hand. Cahal pulled a mobile out of his pocket, frowned at it, then glanced at the window. And even though she knew he would see nothing but a reflection of himself in the glass, she jumped back all the same, her heart thumping against her ribs. She was already ten minutes late and it would be incredibly rude to keep him waiting any longer. She ought to go inside now. But her feet were rooted to the spot.

She leaned against the wall and looked up at the inky sky. A cool breeze fanned her flushed cheeks. He'd said they needed to talk. But what was there to talk about except the past and what had gone wrong between them? She hated to recall the painful memories, and the good ones were even worse. They only served as cruel reminders of the love and happiness she had known and lost. And a little, cruel part of her wanted to give him a taste of his own medicine – she wanted him to know what it was like to wait for someone. She was wiser now, more cautious, and she would never let anyone break her heart again.

*

Cahal stood as still and unyielding as a rock in the airport foyer, ignoring the people streaming around him. Flight information flickered on the screens above his head. Sarah stood before him, her eyes itchy from crying, legs swaying beneath her. She felt like she was swimming against the tide, against a current that she feared would prove too strong.

'Please, Cahal,' she said for the hundredth time that morning. 'Don't go.'

She clutched the arm of his battered leather jacket and stared into his red-rimmed eyes. But there was no softness there, only hard, glassy stubbornness. 'Please.'

'I have to.' He looked down and gently peeled her hand from his arm. It hung by her side like a dead weight. 'We've been through this a thousand times, Sarah. You know what I want.'

She stifled a sob. If she started crying again, she knew she would not stop. 'I can't. You know I can't. You know what it would mean.'

The corner of his mouth twitched and he gave her a withering look. 'That's what you keep saying.'

'Just give me two months. That's all I ask.'

'No.'

'When will I hear from you again?'

'I'll write to you,' he said, grim-faced. 'I promise.' And he turned and walked away.

She stood with her fist stuffed into her mouth, watching the back of his head and his broad, square shoulders disappear in the crowd, believing that he would turn round any minute, any second, and come running back to her. He would not leave her. She could not survive without him.

But his head remained resolutely fixed straight ahead and suddenly he was at the security gate. He handed over his passport and ticket. She started to move towards him, mouthing silent words, her eyes wide in disbelief. He would not do this, he would not leave her. But then, just like that, he was gone.

Sarah brushed a tear from her eye and felt a spit of rain, like a hot spark, on her cheek. Despite his promise, he'd never written. Not once. In desperation she'd tried to contact him. She'd no address for him in Australia, so she'd sent a letter care of his parents. She'd gone round to their flat one day and slipped the envelope through their letterbox before running away. But she'd never received a reply.

She closed her eyes. Becky was right. All Cahal wanted was the chance to say sorry, the opportunity to salve his guilty conscience. Her throat tightened. She clenched her teeth so tightly, her jaw ached. He wanted her to absolve him. He wanted her to say she forgave him for breaking her heart.

She opened her eyes. Through the restaurant window she watched Cahal pick the phone up, peer at the screen – and set it down again. What she'd said to Becky about being curious was true, but the real reason she'd agreed to meet him was more foolish. She wanted to feel once more the love they had shared, to relive the happiest days of her life. She still ached for the Cahal she had adored.

But that Cahal was long gone. The urbane, sophisticated man on the other side of the glass had a wife and family. She had an ex-husband and two children. It was too late to turn back the clock.

A car pulled into the car park. Briefly she was caught in the headlights. She covered her face with her arm and realised how ridiculous she must look, hiding in the foliage. The car parked and the couple inside got out, put up an umbrella and walked down the road without looking at her. She was really late now. But still she could not move.

Cahal could not be trusted.

If he'd only listened to her. If he'd only given her more time. But he would not do either. It was his way, or no way.

She could pinpoint the exact moment when it had all started to go sour.

It was Sunday night and she was returning from the long Easter break spent with her family in Ballyfergus. Cahal had stayed in Portstewart over the Easter holidays – just as he did every holiday. On the platform in Coleraine station, she saw him before he saw her, his hands shoved in the pockets of his brown leather jacket, which he wore in spite of the warm summery weather. He looked a little worried, his brow furrowed in concentration as he scanned the crowd of chattering students returning for the summer term. Her heart fluttered in her breast; she quickened her step, picking her way through the crowd. When he saw her, a smile that obliterated everything else lit up his face. She ran to him, her enormous bag banging against her legs, and threw her arms around his neck. He kissed her on the lips fierce and hard. She closed her eyes and drank him in.

'Jesus, I've missed you,' he said, holding her head in his

hands. His thumbs and fingertips pressed into her skull, at once soothing and stoking her desire. His gaze travelled up her face, searching, as if he was mapping out her features in his mind. He kissed her on both eyelids, then let go of her head.

She pressed her cheek against his rough, late afternoon stubble. He smelt of cigarettes and sweat. 'I missed you too, love,' she said, pulling away a little and running her hand through his thick, black curls. Every nerve in her body tingled.

His pupils dilated. 'Your place or mine?'

'Mine,' she said huskily. 'The flat's empty. No one's back till tomorrow.'

He grabbed her bag then and swung it over his shoulder as if it weighed nothing at all. Then he led her by the hand out of the station.

Outside, dusk was falling on a fair and still day. They stood apart from the other people waiting for the bus. She noticed that the skin under his eyes was grey. 'Have you been working a lot?'

He let out a long sigh. 'Yeah. I've been pretty much full time at the pub. The hot weather's been good for business.'

For the last three years he'd worked term time and the Easter and summer holidays at The Anchor bar in Portstewart, a favourite student haunt. But his exams were only weeks away. It wasn't fair that he had to work so hard. 'Did you manage to get any studying done?'

He shrugged. 'Not as much as I would've liked. But I'm not complaining. I need the money, Sarah.'

She bit her lip and thought about the cheque her father had just given her, burning a hole in her pocket. 'I could help you. Then you wouldn't have to work so much.'

His right eyelid flickered. 'Don't say that again. I won't take money from you. I can look after myself.'

The bus came, cutting the conversation short, and when they'd boarded and were seated together he said, 'Well, how did it go?'

Her stomach muscles clenched but not with desire. 'Fine,' she said breezily, taking a big breath to hold down the feeling of nausea. 'I got a lot of revision done but I wish I could've been up here with you.'

His grip on her hand slackened. 'That's not what I meant.'

She looked out the window at the red-pink sky and felt her face go the same colour, while her heartbeat fluttered. She had made him a promise and she had broken it.

He released her hand, discarding it like something unwanted, and she withdrew it onto her own lap.

'You didn't tell them, did you?'

She blinked at the setting sun, a ball of orange on the horizon, then looked at the Claddagh ring on the wedding finger of her left hand. The ring had spent the last fortnight in the zipped breast pocket of her jacket – she'd only slipped it on her finger when the train had left Ballyfergus station that afternoon.

'I tried to,' she said honestly. Every morning she had risen with fresh resolve but every day her courage failed. 'You don't understand what they're like, Cahal.'

Silence.

'I don't care so much what my aunt thinks. But my father.' She fought back tears. 'Him and Becky are all I've got. But I really think that if he got to know you –'

'Got to know me?' growled Cahal, his nostrils flaring. 'How can he get to know me if he won't even meet me? My family weren't exactly thrilled when I told them I was going out with you but at least they're not so bigoted that they refused to meet you.'

Sarah blushed with shame, reluctant to admit that, while religion undoubtedly played a part in her father's objections, Cahal's low-class background and his father's criminal convictions counted for far more.

She'd felt out of place as soon as she set foot on the Drumalis estate, which she had never before visited. The small flat stank of cigarette smoke and his mother made her uncomfortable, flapping about as if she were royalty and apologising for everything from the chipped mugs to the broken biscuits. His father sat mute in the corner, staring at her through a cloud of pale blue smoke.

She rubbed the Claddagh ring between finger and thumb as if it might produce a genie with an answer to the dilemma.

'And how come they didn't notice the ring then?'

Sarah lifted her right shoulder a little and lied to him for the first time. 'I guess they weren't paying attention.'

He stared at it coldly. 'Until you tell them, Sarah, we can't tell anyone else. And until that happens we're not engaged.'

'But we are,' she protested feebly, his words pricking holes in her happiness.

'No we're not. An engagement is a public declaration of an intention to marry.' His bottom lip quivered and she hated herself for inflicting pain on him. The same way she hated the look of quiet misery that crossed her father's face when Cahal's name was mentioned.

'I thought you loved me, Sarah.'

'I do.'

'Then show it.'

The phone in her pocket vibrated, bringing Sarah back to the present. Cahal was still sitting at the table in the restaurant. She pulled the phone out of her bag, her hands shaking. It was Cahal. When she touched her cheek, she was surprised to find cold tears clinging to her face.

Cahal had been wrong. She had loved him with all her heart but she had loved her family too. He could never understand her devotion to them. He made it sound so simple, but it wasn't. And what had he done to save the relationship? Nothing. When things got tough, he'd run away to the other side of the world.

On the other side of the glass, Cahal was talking to the waiter again, but this time there was no trace of good humour in his expression. She wished he had never come back. His presence reminded her of a past she would rather forget and forced her to examine the present – and find it wanting. She should not have come.

A trickle of rain ran into the collar of Sarah's coat, shockingly cold against her hot skin. Cahal handed something to the waiter and stood up. Her heart pounded so loudly it filled her ears with noise. Grimly she pulled the collar of her coat tight, turned her back on the brightly lit window, and fled into the night.

Chapter 8

'What's wrong?' said Becky, as soon as Sarah stepped inside, dripping water onto the doormat. 'Why are you back so early?'

Sarah dropped her bag on the floor and chucked the car keys on the hall table. A noise came from upstairs.

Becky put a finger to her lips and pulled Sarah into the lounge, shutting the door behind her. She picked up the TV remote and pressed a button. The image of a crumbling edifice bathed in hot Mediterranean sun disappeared from the screen. 'The kids aren't long in bed,' said Becky. 'Lewis is probably asleep, but Molly's reading. Do you want to go up and see her?'

Sarah shook her head miserably and ran her hands down her face.

'That bad, uh?' said Becky. 'Give me your coat. And I'll get a towel.'

Becky disappeared with the coat and came back with a

towel which she handed to Sarah and watched while she rubbed her hair. 'How come you got so wet?'

Sarah handed the towel to Becky, looked into her concerned eyes and her bottom lip wobbled. 'Oh, Becky,' she said, and promptly burst into tears.

Becky put her arms around her and held her until the tears had stopped. Then she manoeuvred her gently into the big armchair by the gas fire. 'Come and sit down, and you can tell me all about it.'

Once settled in front of the fire with a fleece blanket around her shoulders and a very large hot whiskey in her hand, Sarah started to feel better. Becky came in carrying a tumbler of steaming amber liquid with a slice of lemon floating in it.

Sarah took a swig of the whiskey and winced. It was strong and burned on the way down, setting her gullet on fire. She smiled weakly at Becky, warmth spreading through her. 'I chickened out.'

'What do you mean you chickened out? Hold on a minute, I need a cigarette. Do you mind?'

Sarah shook her head, too distressed to object to Becky smoking indoors.

Once she'd lit the cigarette and taken a couple of deep puffs, Becky said, 'Okay.'

Sarah looked into her drink. 'I stood outside in the rain watching him through the window – and then … then I just came home.'

Becky raised her eyebrows. 'But why?'

Sarah shrugged. 'It's complicated.'

Becky took another puff on the cigarette and her face

hardened. 'Well, maybe it's just as well you did, Sarah. And maybe you should give him a wide berth in the future. Don't you remember what a mess you were in that summer he went to Australia?'

Cahal had left in June, not long after his finals. By mid-July she'd given up hope of ever hearing from him again and had taken to her bed. 'How could I forget?'

Becky leaned over, tapped ash into a mug on the floor beside her chair and said, 'You waited months for a letter from him but none came. We were all so worried for you. We thought you were having a breakdown.'

'I think I probably did have one.'

As this comment settled between them Sarah said, 'I knew Dad was worried when he brought me that bunch of chrysanthemums to try and cheer me up. He'd never brought me flowers before – and he hasn't since.' As a rule, their Presbyterian father didn't believe in ostentation and undue expense, and cut flowers for the home definitely fell into that category, unless they came from the garden. 'He sat on the edge of the bed and he looked so miserable. He said, I'll do anything to make you better, Sarah. To make you happy again. Just tell me. Anything. I told him all I wanted was Cahal and … well,' she said, unable to go on, 'you know the rest.'

'He was beside himself,' confirmed Becky. 'Aunt Vi too.'

'The flowers did the trick,' Sarah said, swallowing the sadness like a pill, and attempting a laugh. 'Thinking about Dad's worry was the first time I'd thought about anyone but myself for weeks.' She stared into the distance for a few moments. 'You know, the hardest thing was accepting that

Dad and Aunt Vi had been right about Cahal all along. I believed in him but he let me down like they said he would. Anyway,' she said with a sniff, 'I got over him in the end.'

'Have you though?' Becky threw back the rest of her drink and Sarah felt her cheeks colour.

Becky set the glass on the floor and stared at the tip of her cigarette. 'Going by the state of you, I'd say you've some way to go.'

Sarah blushed.

'Why did you stand him up?' Said Becky.

Sarah sighed. 'I'm still angry with him, even after all these years. And I think what you said about him wanting me to forgive him was probably true. I didn't want to give him the satisfaction. Or, to be truthful, listen to him banging on about his wife and kids. Not when my personal life's been such a disaster.'

'Don't say that!' cried Becky. Ash fell from the end of the cigarette onto her lap. 'Okay, your marriage didn't work out but you had happy years with Ian before it went wrong. And you have the children.'

Sarah smiled. 'The children are the best thing that ever happened to me. But the years with Ian, Becky.' She swallowed and looked up sheepishly. 'They weren't happy. Not really.'

Becky stared, like a kid who'd just been told there was no Santa.

The truth stuck in Sarah's throat like a fish bone. She coughed. 'I … I never loved Ian.'

Becky blinked. She had always liked Ian – he'd been like a big brother to her – and she still had a soft spot for him.

'That's not true. You told me you did.'

Sarah looked her sister straight in the eye. 'I thought I did. I *wanted* to love him so much that I convinced myself that I did. I thought that everything that was good and kind and honest about him would be enough to make me. But it wasn't. I never should have married him. I respected him but I didn't love him, not the way I ought to have. Not the way ...' her voice trailed off.

'... You loved Cahal Mulvenna?' said Becky. She took another puff on the cigarette, the soft 'pah' of her lips round the filter the only sound in the room. Sarah had never admitted to anyone that she had not loved Ian. Winkling the truth out, she said at last, 'Yes.'

The corners of Becky's mouth turned down. 'I'm shocked. Why did you never tell me this before?'

'I was ashamed you'd think badly of me.' She paused, waited without breathing. 'Do you?'

'No ... I ... I'm sorry, that's all.' Sarah breathed out a sigh of relief and Becky went on, 'Poor Ian. Your marriage never really stood a chance, did it?'

'I guess not.'

There was a long silence and Becky said, 'So what happens now? Between you and Cahal Mulvenna?'

'I dunno.' Sarah pulled the blanket tighter around her shoulders. 'I shouldn't have run off like that, should I?'

Becky tapped the cigarette on the edge of the mug. 'I think you ran away from your feelings as much as from him.'

'I know,' said Sarah staring at the rug.

'Will you see him again?'

'I doubt he'll want to see me again after tonight.'

Becky let out a loud sigh and dropped the stub of the cigarette into the mug. 'Just be … careful, Sarah. That's all I ask.'

'I will.' Sarah smiled bravely and glanced at the clock on the mantelpiece. 'I think I'll have an early night, if you don't mind. I'm exhausted. You watch the rest of your programme. Just lock up when you go to bed.'

Becky yawned and stretched her arms above her head. 'I might as well go home to my own bed.'

'Sorry for mucking you about.'

'You haven't. Honestly.'

Sarah set the empty glass on the coffee table.

'I've got some news too,' said Becky, unfolding her legs.

'Really?' said Sarah. She draped the blanket over the back of the sofa and sat down again.

'Remember that guy I told you about that started coming into the office?'

'Oh, yes,' said Sarah, picking up the glass. 'You went out for a drink with him a few times. He's older than you by quite a bit though, isn't he?'

'Tony's forty-two.'

The same age as Cahal. Sarah sucked air in through her teeth. 'A bit of a sugar daddy then?'

Becky giggled. 'No, he's not. He doesn't look old at all. More like suave and gentlemanly.'

Sarah laughed and blurted out, though it was a little mean, 'That'll be a change from your usual toy boys then!'

'Stop it!' cried Becky, though she was smiling.

'Okay,' said Sarah, pausing to catch her breath as she was laughing so hard. 'But last time you mentioned him to me you weren't so keen.'

'Well,' said Becky, rubbing the carpet with her toe. 'I've gotten to know him a bit better, haven't I?'

'Have you been keeping secrets from me?' she teased.

Becky blushed. 'I didn't mean to. It all happened so fast. Usually when we've gone for a drink we've been joined by other people but last night it was just us.' She stared meaningfully at Sarah.

'Oh God, don't tell me you slept with him?'

Becky grinned. 'Of course I did.'

Sarah tutted, and shook her head in despair. 'Do you listen to a word I say, Becky?' How could she protect her sister, like she'd promised her mother, if Becky wouldn't listen to her? Then, seeing the dismay on Becky's face, she smiled and said lightly, 'Honestly, I don't know what to do with you.'

Becky grinned and wiggled her eyebrows. 'Well he did. He was amazing in –'

Sarah held up her hand. 'Enough! I don't want all the gory details.' And then softening, she added, 'But you like him, yeah?'

The crude expression on Becky's face was replaced with an earnest one that plucked at Sarah's heartstrings. 'I do. We just get on so well. It's as if we've known each other all our lives. He … he totally *gets* me, Sarah. I think he might be perfect!'

Sarah smiled to hide her concern and offered up a silent prayer that this man would treat Becky right. Trying not to sound too protective, she said cautiously, 'No one's perfect,

Becky. But I'd love to meet him sometime.'

'He wants to meet my family too,' said Becky, and a little of Sarah's pessimism lifted. Maybe he was serious after all.

'I really, really hope it works out,' she said. She set the glass down and went over and embraced Becky. 'And thanks for listening to me, sweetie.'

Becky gave her a fierce hug in return. 'That's what sisters are for, silly.'

It was nine o'clock on Monday morning and Cahal was in the office, on the phone to Jed. Outside, the sky immediately over the city was clear, but a great charcoal cloud loomed over the Belfast Hills, threatening more rain. He'd been in Northern Ireland for ten days now and his prophecy to Jody had been proven right – it had rained every day, bar one. 'Look son, it's a bit difficult to talk just now,' he said, nodding at Jody who'd just come in with a paper cup in her hand. 'I'm in work.'

'You say that every time I call.'

'I'm sorry, son,' he said, deflated. 'I've just been a bit distracted lately, that's all.' Jed shouldn't suffer just because he was pissed with Sarah. It was bad enough that he wasn't there for his son physically. At the very least he should be there for him emotionally. He turned his back on Jody, who'd sat down at a table nearby and opened her laptop.

'When are you coming home, Dad? I miss you.'

The knife twisted in his stomach. He felt a sudden, desperate need to see Jed, with his too-big nose waiting for the rest of his face to catch up and feathery down on his upper lip. He would need to start shaving soon. It was the most crucial time in Jed's life, the transition from boy to man. A time when a boy needs a father most. He swallowed. 'I'll be home for your birthday at the end of May. For a couple of weeks. We'll go up to the lake.' He cleared his throat. 'Now what was it you wanted to tell me?'

Jed took a deep breath and blurted out, 'Rory's having a sleepover on Saturday night and Mum says I can't go.'

Cahal frowned. 'That's not like your Mum. You've been to sleepovers at Rory's loads of times.'

'I know,' said Jed, sounding indignant. 'So can I go and tell her that you said it was all right?'

'You're not grounded are you?' said Cahal suspiciously.

Jed sighed down the phone. 'No. I'd tell you if I was, wouldn't I? Now, can I just go and tell her?'

Cahal rubbed his chin thoughtfully. Of the two of them, Adele had always been the free and easy parent, Cahal the disciplinarian. So what had changed? Brady, that's what. Blood rushed to his head and his heartbeat quickened. He took a deep breath and tried to remain calm. 'Where's your Mum now, son?'

'Er … in the kitchen tidying, I think.'

'Can you put her on the phone?'

'Um, she's a bit busy, Dad.'

'Put her on *now*,' he said firmly.

'All right. Keep your shirt on, Dad.' Muffled sounds followed, there was a clattering of metal, and Adele came on the line.

'Hey Cahal, how's it going?' she said, her voice relaxed and happy. He remembered something Sarah had said about her divorce being a good one. Though his had been desperately sad – the second great disappointment in his life, after losing Sarah – it had been amicable too. And Adele was happy – at least one of them was.

'Fine. It's bloody cold though,' he said grumpily, feeling a sudden affection for the sunny Melbourne he had left behind.

Adele's derisive laugh came down the phone. 'And you wonder why I only visited the place once. It's all blue skies and sunshine here.'

He imagined Brady tending the sunny garden that had once been his, and taking a break to lounge on the patio, sipping a freezing cold tinny of Vic Bitter. The muscles in his upper arms tensed. 'Look, since when has Jed sleeping over at Rory's been a problem?'

'What did he …' began Adele.

'Has Brady put you up to this?' demanded Cahal, the red heat of anger flaring up, the words slipping out against his better judgement. 'He might be living under the same roof as the boys but he's not their father.'

'Now just a minute, Cahal,' she said, her voice hardening. 'Three things. Number one, this has got nothing to do with Brady. Number two, you chose to swan off to the other side of the world. And now you think you can come on the phone and give me grief about my parenting? I don't think so, mate.'

'I didn't have any choice,' he said.

'There's *always* a choice,' she snapped back.

'Yeah, and lose my job?' he said, exaggerating a little. He wouldn't have been sacked, but it would have harmed his career prospects. Refusing to come would've been interpreted as a lack of drive. And now he was so sorry he had. He missed his boys and the vague notion that he might, somehow, rekindle his relationship with Sarah had fallen flat on its face. He'd not heard a thing from her since she'd stood him up on Friday night, and he was still angry.

'And number three,' went on Adele. 'You should make sure you have all the facts before jumping down my throat.'

'What do you mean?'

'Did he tell you that Rory's parents are away for the night?'

A flush crept across Cahal's face. The crucial fact changed everything. 'No, he didn't.'

'Well, then. What have you got to say now?'

He swallowed. 'I'm sorry, Adele.'

'I should think so too. And, for your information, Brady's doing a good job with the boys. He gets on really well with them but he respects the fact that me – and you – are their parents, not him.'

He ran a hand through his hair, jealousy nibbling at his stomach like acid. Was that supposed to make him feel better? Did the boys like big, easy-going Brady more than him, especially as he was exonerated from the onerous duties of discipline and boundary-setting? He sighed. 'I'm sorry,' he said again.

'You're an arse sometimes, do you know that?' said Adele, but her tone was soft and affectionate.

'Yeah, I know,' he said, running his hand down his face. 'Sorry. I guess you'd better put Jed on again.'

When he finally came off the phone, Jody looked up from her computer screen and said, 'Everything all right?'

'Fine,' he said stonily, 'if managing to alienate your son and

132

piss off your ex-wife before half past nine in the morning can be qualified a success.'

Jody laughed as if he'd cracked a joke. 'I'm sure whatever it is, it'll blow over.'

How he wished it would. But Brady wasn't going anywhere. Since she'd married him, Adele had never seemed happier. He'd no reason to dislike Brady, yet he couldn't warm to the sports teacher, a huge beer-swilling, ex-professional Aussie-rules footballer. They had absolutely nothing in common. He stood up and jangled the coins in his trouser pocket. 'Catch you later. I'm going to get a coffee.'

He took the stairs down eight flights, thoroughly dejected both by the phone call and by being stood up on Friday night.

Walking into the canteen, he caught sight of Sarah and stopped dead in his tracks.

Bent slightly at the waist, with eyebrows knitted together in concentration, she held a plastic cup underneath the spout of the water cooler. Her pert bum was silhouetted by a tight, black skirt and she wore a crisp white fitted shirt that high-lighted her small waist and cupped her rounded breasts. Desire stirred in him – along with simmering anger.

He started to perspire, beads of sweat on his upper lip. And, as the growing anger slowly displaced the desire, his resolve strengthened. She'd a bloody cheek standing him up. He gritted his teeth and walked towards her. 'I wondered when I'd bump into you.'

She made a little startled sound and straightened up with a full cup of water in each hand. Her eyes met his and her face went bright red. 'I … er … I was going to come and find you today.' She glanced at the door, as if searching for a means of escape, then held up the cups. 'The water cooler on our floor ran out.'

Her nails were painted apricot, as pale and delicate as the inside of a shell. He pulled his gaze away from her nails and fixed her with a fierce gaze. 'I'm not interested in the bloody water cooler,' he said in a hoarse whisper. 'I want to know why you stood me up the other night.'

'I ... I didn't mean to,' she said feebly. 'I was there, outside Carnegie's. I saw you through the window but ...' Her voice trailed off and her hands shook. Water slopped out of the overfilled cups onto the floor between them. She was no longer blushing. Her face was pale as death.

'But what?' he said gently, her obvious distress immediately diluting his anger.

'I couldn't go in.'

'What do you mean, "You couldn't go in?"'

She shook her head slowly, her lips slightly parted, as if confounded by the question. At last she said, 'I did want to meet you ... I planned to.'

'So what stopped you?'

She looked at the floor and an overwhelming sadness enveloped him.

'Do you hate me?' he said.

'No,' she said emphatically, looked away and added abruptly, 'I have to go. I'm late for a meeting.' And with that she brushed past him and disappeared out the door.

He spent the rest of the morning cooped up in a meeting room with the senior management team, and was glad when they finally broke for lunch at one o'clock.

'Fancy going down to the canteen?' said Jody, as they walked into the office together.

He threw a pile of papers on the desk and glanced out the window. The dark cloud he'd spotted earlier had miraculously passed overhead without disgorging its contents on the city. Now the sun peeked out from behind a scattering of pale grey clouds stretched out across the sky.

'I think I need a bit of fresh air.'

Jody peered out the window. 'What a good idea. I think I might join you.'

'No,' he said and she looked at him sharply, though the smile was back on her face almost instantaneously.

'No offence but I could do with a bit of space to clear my head.'

'No offence taken,' she said breezily. 'I'll see you later.'

Outside the late March sun had surprising warmth in it and the breeze was gentle on his face. He headed for the Lagan River, the source of the city's historical maritime wealth and commerce, and now the heart of the city's tourist industry. Clutching a sandwich in one hand and a bottle of water in the other, he marched purposefully north along the riverbank pathway, his heart pounding in his chest. On his left, traffic rumbled by on Donegall Quay; on his right lay the deep blue waters of the Lagan, its still surface patterned by little whorls and eddies. He was angry with Jed for attempting to manipulate him and more angry with himself for not being there. As for Sarah, his feelings towards her were utterly confused.

He was frustrated with her, no doubt about that. But her

135

reaction in the canteen also gave him hope, even though her words made no sense. She'd been there, right outside Carnegie's, watching him. She'd planned to join him. He needed to know what had stopped her.

By the time he reached Lagan Weir, the anger had given way to despondency and his goose march had slowed to an amble. The adrenaline-fuelled energy that had propelled him the half mile or so from Laganside Tower, had all but dissipated. His shoulders sagged, the muscles across the centre of his back ached, and his legs felt incredibly tired.

Just beyond the weir, on a slightly elevated platform, he came across a startling sight – an enormous sculpture of a blue fish, taller than a man and at least ten metres in length. Bewildered, he sat down heavily on one of the black benches and stared out across the river.

'I see you have the same idea as me,' said a woman's voice. He looked up and the eyes that met his were still and grey, like the Lagan at the turn of the tide on a dull Belfast day.

He stood up. 'Sarah,' he said, his voice little more than a whisper and further words failed him. Against her black funereal coat, which buttoned up to the neck, her face was as white and flawless as porcelain.

'Mind if I join you?' Her face coloured and he saw at once how much it had cost her to make this approach.

'Sure,' he said casually and sat down, his heart beating so loud he could hear it.

She sat down beside him and placed a paper bag on her lap. 'Must be near low tide.'

'Huh?'

She pointed and moistened her lips. 'Look at the difference in height between the river on this side of the weir and the other side.' They both stared at the water bubbling at the base of the weir and then she went on, 'It was built to stop the mudflats further upstream being exposed at low tide. Apparently they used to stink to high heaven, especially in the summer. It's the key to the whole Laganside regeneration.' She paused. 'It's kind of beautiful in a way.'

'Sarah.' He sighed and shook his head and stared downstream. The yellow cranes of Harland and Wolfe loomed over the docks that had built the most famous ship in the world, RMS *Titanic*.

'I'm sorry for standing you up,' she said. His head snapped round and she stared him straight in the eye, her face both beautiful and sad. Then her gaze slid down to her lap. 'I shouldn't have done that.'

He waited. A lone seagull circled overhead, screeching and cawing, then flew off across the river towards Queen's Quay.

'I shouldn't have agreed to meet you in the first place.'

'Why not? We were once as close as two people can be,' he said carefully. 'Surely that counts for something?'

She squinted, as if focusing on some particular thing on the opposite side of the river. 'That's true. That's what makes what happened to us so unbearable. Even now.'

His mouth went dry. He licked his lips. 'I'm sorry if I made you feel uncomfortable in some way. I didn't mean to pressurise you into anything.'

She scratched the side of her nose. 'You didn't.'

'Then I don't understand.'

She looked at him then, her eyes wide open, her eyebrows raised. 'I do … I did want to see you. But I'm not sure if remembering … if going over the past is a good idea.'

'We can't just pretend we never happened, Sarah. Being with you was the happiest time of my life.'

She looked away.

His chest tightened. Even though he had so much just cause, he tried not to be angry with her. Why was she so distant with him? 'Do you dislike me, Sarah?'

'Of course not.'

She looked out over the water once more and they sat in silence. The sun warmed his thighs and the busy sound of traffic filled his ears. Beside him, Sarah shifted on the bench, crossed and uncrossed her ankles, the paper bag on her lap rustling. 'Well then,' he said at last, 'let's not talk about the past. Let's pretend we're two people meeting for the first time.'

She looked at him guardedly.

'I could use a friend round here,' he said.

A cautious smile played on her lips. 'Why do you say that?'

The tightness in his chest eased and he returned her smile. 'Everyone seems to see us as the enemy. The management team are less than enthusiastic about the change programme.'

'It's not personal, Cahal. It's just that they're worried that your team is going to come up with recommendations that might hurt them. Like redundancies.'

'Doesn't make it any easier.'

'I suppose not,' she said glumly, looking out across the water.

Desperate to restore her good humour, he indicated the

138

sculpture behind them with a nod of his head. 'So what's with Moby Dick back there?'

She threw her head back and laughed, the same deep and throaty sound he remembered, then twisted round on the bench to look at the enormous sculpture of the fish. 'It's not a whale, you eijet! It's a fish. An Atlantic salmon, actually. It's titled Salmon of Knowledge but everybody calls it The Big Fish.'

'What's it doing here?' he said, raising one eyebrow in mock derision. He loved to make her animated and happy. 'Got stranded on its way upstream, did it?'

She tutted, though there was a twinkle in her eye, and proceeded to explain, 'It's part of the regeneration. There are three art trails with sculptures that go all the way from the Stranmillis Embankment at Governor's Bridge, right down to this weir.'

'So why a fish?' he said, raising an eyebrow.

'Since the river's been cleaned up, fish have started to return. It's symbolic in loads of other ways too.'

He raised his right eyebrow even further.

'Come on, I'll show you.' And she jumped up with the paper bag in her hand and led the way up the steps to the sculpture.

'Look,' she said, walking around the head of the fish, with its downturned mouth and copper-coloured eye, as big and shiny as a wheel hub. 'The scales are made from ceramic tiles printed with images of Belfast, or something to do with Belfast, dating right back to Tudor times.'

He tucked the water bottle under his arm and touched the cold, glazed surface of a tile. Under his hand, an advert for defunct Cowan's Celebrated Whiskies feted the city's long-lost distillery. 'Interesting,' he said, studying the images – an extract from some old piece of legislation headed up The Summary Jurisdiction Act; a young girl staring out of a grainy photograph, a child's drawing of the *Titanic*; another of a soldier; a photograph of The Dub tea room. 'It's like a visual potted history of Belfast.'

She came up beside him, so close he could smell her perfume, and said, 'That's exactly what it is.' Then she looked out across the Lagan and squinted into the sun. 'Years ago, tourists wouldn't have come anywhere near Belfast, or the Lagan, but that's all changed.'

He laughed. 'Yeah, I read about a new *Titanic* centre that's opening somewhere round here.'

She pointed downstream, across the river. 'It's over there in Queen's Quay.'

'That's Irish isn't it?'

'What is?'

'Celebrating what is arguably the greatest maritime disaster in peacetime with a visitor centre.' Sarah laughed, tiny crinkles appearing at the corners of her grey eyes. Encouraged, he went on, 'I mean, if you'd built the *Titanic* would you want to crow about it?'

She giggled. 'Now, to be fair, the flaw wasn't in the construction, it was in the design. And there were a whole lot of other factors at play too in the sinking. But I bet people will flock to see it.'

They were silent then for a few moments while he contemplated his next move. He'd made her laugh. He wanted to hold this fragile moment, and the sound of her laughter, forever. 'Are you going to carry that sandwich round with you all lunchtime or are you going to eat it?'

She smiled. 'Let's find somewhere a bit quieter to eat.'

'So you'll break bread with me then?'

She paused for a second. 'Yes.'

They crossed the river and walked the short distance to the Odyssey Complex where they sat on a bench seat built into the concrete embankment and ate sandwiches, overlooking the Lagan. A massive white Stenaline passenger ferry inched slowly into dock on the opposite shore.

'So tell me about your wife,' she said, and took a bite of her sandwich.

Her arm pressed lightly against his, the faint smell of her perfume carried on the gentle breeze.

'Adele. We got divorced two years ago.'

She fixed her eyes on the ferry and chewed slowly. It was impossible to tell what she was thinking.

'I live alone in a flat overlooking the Yarra River,' he offered.

She swallowed, kept her eyes fixed on the ferry. 'And there I was thinking you'd found your happily ever after, and it was only me that'd made a mess of things.' She turned her eyes on him, soft and sad. 'But turns out we both did, didn't we?'

Chapter 9

Ian pulled up outside Ballyfergus Golf Club and sat in the car for a few moments, collecting his thoughts. The hot April sun beat down on the green, and on the brown faces and arms of the four golfers teeing off from the first hole. In the far distance, the deep blue sea met the Antrim coastline in a froth of inviting white surf. But Ian had much more important things on his mind than golf or frolicking in the waves. He got out of the car, slipped the car keys in the pocket of his suit jacket and went inside.

'Ian,' cooed Isabelle, wafting across the function room in a floaty blue dress, her matronly chest leading the way. When she reached Ian, she cupped her cool papery hands around his cheeks and squeezed, as if he was a boy of seven. 'I'm so glad you could come.'

'I wouldn't have missed your seventieth for all the world,' he laughed affectionately, realising that the reason he liked

Isabelle so much was not because he'd known her all his life but because she reminded him of his mother.

'It's also a fundraiser for the mission in Natal,' she said, removing her hands from his face and becoming serious. 'I hope you've got your cheque book with you.'

'Er, yes of course,' he said and her face cracked into a smile, perfect white dentures on display. 'Only joking, kid.' She found his hands and squeezed them between her own firm grasp. Her blue eyes filled up with tears. 'I'm just sorry that Evelyn can't be here.'

He swallowed, Isabelle's compassion making his throat feel tight and his eyes itch. 'She's sorry too. She sends all her love.'

'How is she?'

'Much the same.'

'I'll take a piece of birthday cake in to her tomorrow.' She patted the back of his hand and let it go. Then she fixed a dazzling smile on her face and blinked her tear-glazed eyes. 'But this is a party! Let's not be sad. Evelyn wouldn't want that.' She pointed to a table groaning with food. 'There's loads to eat and we're going to have some party games for the children later. Eric's going to show a video of the mission. Molly and Lewis are here somewhere.' Immediately he started scanning the room for Sarah.

But it was the children he saw first. Molly, looking so grown up in black leggings and a sparkling pink tunic; he felt an ache in his chest, a longing for her childhood that was, little-by-little, ebbing away. Soon her head would be full of boys and fashion and pop music. And there was Lewis, in a long-sleeved shirt, playing hide and seek with another little boy under the vast tablecloth that covered the buffet table. He crawled out on his hands and knees, and stood up.

'Dad,' he shrieked and ran across the room.

Ian braced himself for the impact and, when Lewis ran into him, he scooped him up in his arms, gave him a big hug and a kiss on the side of his head, before setting him back on his feet. Molly, who was much more subdued, came over and gave him a brief hug. 'Hey, Dad, will you come to the school fair on Friday?'

He squeezed her shoulders. 'Course I will, darling. It's already in the diary. Where's your Mum?'

'Over there,' said Molly pointing, 'talking to Aunt Vi and Grandpa.'

She was watching them with a hesitant smile on her face. She looked so radiant, fragile even, in a yellow, fifties-style dress with a full skirt and fitted bodice and a little teal cardigan, the same colour as the flowers on the dress. He smiled back, and his palms started to sweat. Sarah blinked and looked away. Vi, standing beside Sarah with her hair scraped back into a tight bun and her usual dark attire, looked like the black widow.

He got himself a Coke from the bar, and stood and chatted with Isabelle's husband, Eric. Since that day at Sarah's house, when he'd admitted that he still had feelings for her, he'd thought of nothing but getting back with her. And the more he thought about it, the more he was convinced that it was what she wanted too, even if she wasn't as sure of it yet as he was. They got on better now than they did when they were married. Didn't the fact that she had never remarried speak for itself? He was certain they could rekindle the magic that had once sparked between them. Excusing himself, he strolled towards Sarah, where she stood by the buffet table chatting with her aunt. Close by, her father grazed at the food, bypassing the plate in his hand and popping morsels directly into his mouth. Ian approached, feigning interest in a platter of pink, curling ham – and waited for Vi to catch his eye.

It wasn't long before she called out, 'Oh, there you are, Ian,' giving him the opportunity he'd been waiting for to join the little group. She kissed his cheek and called out, 'Look who's here, David.' David finished cramming a sausage roll into his mouth, came over and shook Ian's hand vigorously, pastry crumbs falling from his lips to the floor.

'Hi Ian,' said Sarah and he tried to make eye contact with her but, frustratingly, she looked at the silver sandals on her pretty feet instead.

'The Golf Club has put on a good spread,' observed Vi, drawing his attention away from Sarah.

'And all for a good cause,' added David and patted his stomach. 'You should have some of those sausage rolls before they get cold, Ian. Delicious.'

'So how are you, Ian love?' said Vi. 'I feel like I haven't seen you properly in ages. How's Evelyn?'

At the mention of his mother's name, Sarah's head snapped up and she looked at him at last. They talked about Evelyn's failing health for a while and then Ian turned to Sarah.

'So, Sarah, are you going to the school fair on Friday? Molly tells me she's on the nail-painting stall.' He pulled a humorous face to show that he thought this a decidedly risky venture.

Raquel had never quite forgiven Molly for the fuchsia pink nail polish stain in the middle of the landing carpet.

'Eh … I plan to,' she said and looked at her watch, before craning her neck to see past him. 'I wonder where Becky is?'

'She's bringing someone, you know,' said Vi, leaning towards Ian slightly, as if letting him in on some great secret.

'Is she?' he said pleasantly, wishing he and Sarah could be alone.

'He a lecturer in biology at Queen's,' announced Vi, sounding impressed.

David made a sort of humming sound in the back of his throat and said grumpily, 'Let's just hope he's a decent fellow and not some sort of long-haired weirdo who doesn't know how to dress properly.'

Sarah laughed. 'Oh, Dad, you don't mean that, surely? Just because someone's not in a suit and tie, it doesn't make them a bad person.'

'Well, you have to admit, Sarah, some of her former boyfriends left a bit to be desired,' said Ian, perfectly at home talking about Becky whom he regarded as a lovely, but slightly wayward, younger sister.

'Ian's right. There's a certain way to behave and those chaps didn't know how to,' said Dad firmly, balancing the plate on the edge of the buffet table.

'Harry always dressed so well,' chipped in Vi, referring to Ian's father. 'I don't think I ever saw him without a jacket. Did you David?'

He nodded, the grumpiness replaced with a faraway look in his blue eyes. 'In the police we used to call him Slick because

Ian smiled, glad to have the chance to talk about a father he had loved. He listened to David regale them with familiar tales of his and Harry's days in the police, the basis of a friendship that had lasted until his father's death. And then the conversation moved on to more recent times.

'He was over the moon when Molly was born,' smiled Vi. 'He'd always wanted a grandchild.'

Ian looked at Sarah. 'Do you remember the little wooden stool he made for her first birthday?'

'Oh yes, she used to sit on it and watch TV,' she said warmly, making eye contact with him again. He drank her gaze in, hanging on every word. 'It's in the loft still. I'm going to keep it for her till she's grown.'

'Do you remember how she burned her hand on the birthday candle at the party, the wee pet? She didn't realise it was hot,' laughed David and Ian was forced to tear his gaze away from Sarah.

'Poor wee mite,' said Aunt Vi. 'I did warn you to be careful.'

Everyone let this comment pass unremarked and then Vi gave out a sigh of satisfaction and looked round the room happily. Lewis flew past in hot pursuit of another boy while, nearby, Molly bounced a pink-cheeked toddler in a white party dress on her hip. 'Well, isn't this just like old times, the four of us and the children all together?'

Sarah looked at her feet again and Ian's heart soared. Vi was right. It *was* like old times when he and Sarah were still man and wife. He hoped that today would remind her of what they'd both lost in the divorce.

She looked at her watch again. 'Becky said she'd be here by half two and it's just gone three.'

'You know what she's like,' said Ian, trying hard to keep the irritation out of his voice. 'She's late for everything.' If only she would look at him, instead of craning to see Becky ...

And then Molly appeared suddenly beside him, minus the toddler. 'Where's Raquel?' she said, bringing him back to earth with a bump.

Everyone stared at him and his heart sank into his shoes. He ran his tongue over his lips. How could he tell them what Raquel had said to him before he'd left the house: 'Nobody has a party in the middle of the day, not a half decent one anyway, and you know I can't stand those churchy people. They're so boring.'

She meant people like him. He scowled. It hadn't always been like that. At first, she'd been happy to accompany him to Sunday church where she'd hung on to his arm possessively, her figure emphasised by a tight skirt, a cocky little veiled pillbox hat perched on her head. And his chest had swelled with pride when he saw how the men, with their frumpy wives by their side, had stared at her.

But she no longer accompanied him to church, and she'd started drinking again and he'd long ago given up on the idea of converting her to Christianity. He now wondered if, in stating her objection to sexual intimacy before marriage, she had simply been mirroring his beliefs. She was certainly no virgin. Raquel was all about sexuality and titillation but these pleasures, he'd discovered, were passing ones. As his sexual fervour waned, the stark reality of their incompatibility became ever more painfully clear. The idea of spending the rest of his days with her was inconceivable.

'Is she working today?' said Vi, breaking into his thoughts.

'Er, yes,' he said, though he'd left her at home painting her nails fluorescent pink and watching reruns of *Coronation Street*.

'Oh, that's a shame,' said Sarah and he looked at her oddly, wondering for whose benefit she was saying this. Sarah had always seemed indifferent to Raquel, slightly hostile even.

'That's not what she told me,' said Molly. Ian felt his face flush red though, thankfully, everyone stared at Molly. 'She told me she didn't like Isabelle.'

Vi gazed at Molly for a few seconds, raised her eyebrows and said, 'David, be a dear and hand round the plates, will you?'

'You must've misheard her, Molly,' said Ian, more loudly than was necessary.

'No I didn't. She …'

'Leave it now,' whispered Vi, grabbing Molly's arm, and then, in her normal voice, 'Come and see the cake, Molly. It's in the shape of India.'

'Why India?'

'Because that's where Natal is, dear,' replied Vi as she propelled Molly by the elbow into the crowd.

David wandered off in search of more food.

At last he was alone with Sarah.

Sandwiched between Ian and the buffet table, Sarah held a plate, loaded with sandwiches, a mini-quiche and a dollop of potato salad, in front of her chest like a barricade. In the other hand she gripped a fork like a spear. For the last few months Ian had been behaving decidedly oddly and today he seemed determined to engage her in conversation when she had no desire to speak to him. Her last proper conversation with him, that night in her house, had left her feeling distinctly uncomfortable.

'So, do you think I should let her paint my nails?' mumbled Ian, affording Sarah a clear view of mangled egg sandwich on his tongue.

'Huh?' said Sarah, looking away. His habit of speaking with his mouth full had always annoyed her.

He washed the sandwich down with a swig of Coke. 'Molly. Do you think I should let her paint my nails?'

'If you like,' she said indifferently, standing on tiptoes to look over his shoulder for Becky. She had so much to tell her about Cahal. How she'd followed him out of the office that day and barely managed to keep up with him until he'd reached The Big Fish and finally come to rest on a bench. She didn't know where she'd found the courage to approach him but she was glad that she had.

The knowledge that his marriage had failed too made her feel less of a failure. And she'd been secretly pleased.

They'd parted on amicable terms and she no longer spent every moment in work on edge, fearful that she'd bump into him. She'd proved to herself that she could be civil to him, that she could mask the unsettling effect he had on her, at least to the outside world. Now all she had to do was get through the next six months.

'Sarah? Did you hear a word I said?' said Ian's voice.

'Sorry, what was that?' She nibbled at a salmon and cream cheese sandwich, and tried to look interested.

'I asked you how Molly got on at school this week. Has there been any more bullying?'

She chewed and swallowed. 'Not as far as I know. Since my meeting with the head teacher, things seem to have settled down.'

'I think it would carry more impact if I went with you to the school next time.'

She smiled gratefully. 'Thanks, Ian. But so far, so good. The school have spoken to the girl involved – and her parents. We'll know soon enough if there's any more trouble.'

'Good.'

She placed the cannibalised sandwich on the plate and scanned the faces in the room but all she could see was Cahal's eyes, the same colour as the flowers on her dress, and the dimple in his cheek.

'So I was thinking,' said Ian, as Sarah looked around the room, wishing that one of the kids would come and rescue her from Ian. Where were they when she needed them? Nervously, she took a bite out of the sandwich.

'We should make a point of going out for supper on a regular basis.'

Her eyes grew big and she chewed frantically, trying to get the sandwich down.

'It would give us a proper chance to talk about the kids,' he went on.

The sandwich had formed into a dry lump; the cream

cheese stuck to her teeth. She placed the fork on the plate and put a hand on her throat, willing it to go down.

He was more animated now than she'd seen him in a long time, waving the Coke about so that the coffee-coloured liquid came precariously close to flying out of the glass. 'And it would be good for the kids, you know, seeing us together more, getting along. What do you say?'

She swallowed at last with a faint audible gulp, and blurted out, 'But we're not together, Ian. It would just be a show of togetherness.'

His expression soured, his lips thinned and a deep frown appeared between his pale brows. But she pressed on hastily, determined to nip this fantasy of them playing happy families in the bud. 'And we manage just fine the way things are, discussing whatever needs to be discussed when we drop the kids off from each other.'

The sour look was replaced with one of bitter disappoint-ment and he downed the rest of the fizzy drink. Sarah's voice softened. 'You know you're always welcome to stay and chat when you drop the kids off, if there's something troubling you.' She offered an olive branch in the form of a smile. 'And there's always the phone.'

His eyes brightened and a look of dogged determination, that she knew so well and slightly dreaded, passed across his face. He smiled pleasantly and leaning past her, placed the empty glass on the table behind her. She held the plate under her chin.

'If things are fine just the way they are,' he said, his voice low and even, 'then why were we just discussing Molly's problems at school? At a party?' he said, making a sweeping gesture with his hand that encompassed the room and everyone in it.

Momentarily stumped, she said nothing.

'You have to agree,' he said, sliding his hand into his trouser pocket, 'it's hardly appropriate.'

'You chose to raise the subject,' she said a little nastily. 'We didn't have to talk about it here.'

'Come on now, Sarah,' he said all gentleness and smiles, 'let's not argue. Please?'

Suppressing her irritation with him, she nodded. 'Okay.'

'But you do take my point, don't you?'

She sighed and shook her head in exasperation. He never would take no for an answer. But he was right too – this wasn't the place to wash their family linen. She looked around, desperately trying to make eye contact with someone, anyone, in the crowd.

Ian inched closer and she noticed beads of sweat on his forehead. It was warm in the room, but not hot. 'Are you feeling okay?' she said.

'Yes, yes, I'm fine,' he said somewhat dismissively and she shuffled backwards until the edge of the table pressed into the back of her thighs.

'Tell you what, why don't we take the kids out for tea next week, just the four of us? They'd love that.'

'Er … I don't think that would be a good idea, Ian. I mean, what would Raquel say?'

He took a step backwards, his pale-eyed, steady gaze making Sarah feel as if he could see right into her soul. He ran his tongue over his lips and said very quietly, 'I haven't been entirely straight with you – or anyone for that matter – about Raquel. Possibly because it's hard for me to admit that I've made a mistake. A big mistake.'

Sarah stared at him, torn between embarrassment at being privy to this information, and curiosity. She'd always wondered what Ian had seen in Raquel, apart from the obvious – youth and sex appeal. Raquel wasn't a marriage breaker – she'd come on the scene after she and Ian had split up – but Sarah, like the children, had never warmed to the woman.

Ian looked at his feet and cleared his throat. 'Raquel and I … well, suffice to say we don't get on very well these days. In fact,' he said, his voice catching, 'to be brutally honest, we don't get on at all. I haven't been happy for a long time.'

Sarah felt her cheeks burn hot and said uneasily, 'Ian, I don't think you should be telling me this. You should be at home talking to Raquel, not me.'

He sighed loudly. 'I'm done talking. I'm thinking of asking her for a divorce.'

'Oh.' Sarah's immediate thought was for the children. The break-up of their father's marriage would be unsettling and would he have to sell the house? Was he likely to become depressed? She didn't think he was the sort of man who would be happy living for long on his own. 'I'm very sorry to hear that, Ian,' she said with genuine compassion.

His shoulders sagged and he said flatly, 'I never imagined that this marriage would end in divorce too.'

Sarah nodded grimly, knowing how much Ian believed in the sanctity of marriage and how deeply he would feel this

154

failure.

He brushed something off his cheek. 'We barely talk to each other, at least not in any meaningful way. Not the way you and I used to talk – in the early days, at least.' He paused briefly to smile sadly at her. 'The truth of the matter is that Raquel and I don't have anything in common. And it's not the differences that make a good marriage but the things you share, like values and beliefs. And children.' He paused to let this sink in, then went on, 'Don't get me wrong, I'm not blaming Raquel. She's … she's just what she is. I feel sorry for her because I don't believe that I can make her happy. I blame myself.'

'Oh, Ian, you mustn't,' said Sarah. 'Marriages break up all the time and sometimes it's no one's fault.'

'No,' he said firmly. 'The mistake I made was in not getting to really know her properly beforehand. Not like us. We've known each other since we were kids.'

'Familiarity is no guarantee of a successful marriage,' said Sarah quickly, 'as you and I clearly demonstrate.'

'That's true. But we had lots of good times.'

'We did,' acknowledged Sarah, who had long ago stopped beating herself up about the failure of her marriage and tried to focus on its high points instead.

'Do you remember the time we took the kids to Florida?' It had been their last holiday together as a family.

'Yes, Molly was just three and Lewis was still a baby.' Looking back they'd been crazy to take the kids so young. Molly barely remembered Disney World, and Lewis not at all. But she saw now that it had been a last ditch attempt on Ian's part to save the marriage – and his family. 'Do you remember the ice creams we bought on the first day? They were enormous. Even you couldn't finish yours.'

He laughed and she relaxed, pleased that she'd successfully steered the conversation onto the comfortable territory of the children. 'After that, we bought one of everything and split it between the kids.'

Sarah tried to remember other highlights of the trip – and tried to forget the huge distance between her and Ian that had only been made more painfully obvious.

'I sometimes think we gave up too easily,' he said, and she stared at him in astonishment. If anything, in trying to keep the family together, she'd stuck it out longer than she ought to have. She opened her mouth to protest.

But just then her attention was caught by the man who sauntered confidently into the room. It took her a few milliseconds to recognise him but, when she did, her heart froze and the retort died on her lips. It was Anthony McLoughlin, a close friend of Cahal's at uni – and someone she'd hoped never to see again in her entire life.

She stared at the easy engaging smile, the Roman nose and the mop of fair curly hair that was largely unchanged from the last time she'd seen him. What on earth was he doing here? Surely he wasn't a relative of Isabelle?

Ian said something but she did not hear. Her heart had started again, pumping violently against her ribcage. She shrank back against the table and glanced at the emergency exit. With luck on her side she could avoid him, make her excuses and leave early. She took a step closer to Ian, hiding behind his broad frame, and cautiously peeped over his shoulder.

'Do you agree?' said Ian.

'Huh …?' she said, absentmindedly. And then Becky came through the door, dressed in a modest knee-length black jersey dress, and Sarah's shoulders sagged with relief. If only she could attract Becky's attention and get her to cover for her escape …

'Sarah?' said Ian.

But what was this? Anthony turned and took her sister's hand in his and they smiled at each other. The secret, eyes-locked-together smile of lovers.

She shivered, goosebumps prickling her arms like a plucked chicken. Anthony and Becky? How could that be?

And then she remembered. Anthony had told her once, on that fateful night she'd rather forget, that he intended to stay on and do a PhD in biology. Becky's Tony was a lecturer in biology. How could she not have made the connection? She'd been too preoccupied with Cahal to pay attention to Becky's new man. Her stomach went cold, like she'd swallowed ice cubes.

'What is it?' said Ian. He followed her gaze to the happy couple. Tony cradled Becky's hand between his own while they chatted to Isabelle and Ron.

'Oh, so this is the mystery man,' said Ian and turned to Sarah with a puzzled look on his face. 'You look like you've seen a ghost.'

Sarah bit down on her lip till it hurt. And then, to her relief, she heard Aunt Vi's voice in her ear.

'At least he's wearing a jacket and tie. That'll please your father.'

From reserves somewhere deep inside her, Sarah managed to summon up a grim smile, and Ian said, 'He looks like a teacher.'

In crumpled chinos, a brown corduroy jacket with leather patches on the elbow and a thin burgundy silk-knit tie, Tony did look like the archetypal teacher. But it wasn't the way he was dressed that concerned her. It was the way he looked at Becky, and worse, the way she stared back at him, a look of adoration that she had never before seen on her sister's face lending her average features a luminous beauty.

'Well, he is a teacher of sorts, I suppose,' said Aunt Vi, the tone of her voice indicating cautious approval, in spite of the fact that Tony stuck out among this conservative group like a sore thumb.

'Well, Becky's clearly keen on him,' observed Ian. Sarah knew she had to escape. She tried to move but her legs refused to co-operate and her arms were leaden. She leaned one hand on the table to steady herself and the plate in her hand wobbled. As if in slow motion, she watched the fork slide off the plate. She tried to grab it, missed, and it landed on the floor with a loud clatter, attracting attention from everyone around.

'Oh, do be careful! You'll stain that beautiful dress,' cried Vi while Ian bent at the waist and picked the fork up off the floor. Sarah, previously hidden by Ian's body, ducked her head. But it was too late. Becky had seen her.

Ian straightened up, said, 'I'll get you a clean fork,' and

disappeared.

Becky's happy voice drifted above the soft buzz of conversation in the room. 'Oh, you must come and meet Sarah and Aunt Vi!'

With shaking hands, Sarah set the plate down carefully on the table among the platters of food and wiped her sweaty palms on the front of her dress, oblivious to Aunt Vi's protestations. 'Sarah,' said Becky's voice. Sarah lifted her head and stared her sister straight in the eye, dreading what would happen next.

Becky beamed. 'I'd like you to meet my sister, Sarah. Sarah, this is Tony.'

She could not speak, she could only stare at him wordlessly as her breath came quietly in little fits and starts. Tony's steady blue-eyed gaze met hers and the broad, friendly smile on his face did not waver. Only a flicker of his right eyelid and the contraction of his dark pupils gave any sign of recognition.

She must seize the initiative before it was too late. Finding her voice she thrust her hand forward and blurted out, with a manic grin on her face, 'Nice to meet you at last, Tony.'

And he replied, taking her hand, all ease and charm, 'Likewise. Becky's told me so much about you.' He pumped her hand briefly, then dropped it like a hot stone.

'And this is my Aunt Vi,' said Becky, and an exchange of small talk followed. The tension drained out of Sarah and she was filled instead with relief – and a new creeping fear.

The moment of danger was past. But for how long? Would he keep the secret forever or would he feel compelled to tell Becky everything? Suddenly Becky grabbed Sarah's arm and said in a confidential tone, 'Tony thinks I should apply to uni as a mature student.'

'I always said you were wasted in that office.'

Becky frowned. 'I thought you'd be a bit more enthusiastic.'

Sarah forced a smile. 'I think it's a great idea. Really.'

While Becky rattled off a choice of possible courses, the thought occurred to Sarah that perhaps she had misread the situation. Becky's track record with men was pretty dismal. Why should this boyfriend last any longer than the rest?

'Tony says he'll help me financially,' said Becky, cutting a swathe through Sarah's hopes.

'Really? He oughtn't to make promises like that unless he intends to be around in the long term.'

'He does,' said Becky happily and she smiled over at Tony. He winked at her and continued the conversation with Aunt Vi. Then she clasped Sarah's hand in hers and squeezed it tight. 'This time it's different, Sarah,' she whispered. 'He's like no one I've ever met before. And he loves me.'

'He loves you?' croaked Sarah.

'Yes,' said Becky firmly, her eyes misting up. 'And I love him. I never thought this would happen to me, Sarah. I never thought that I'd find true love.'

Sarah stared at her glumly and Becky's face fell. 'Aren't you pleased for me?'

'Why, yes ... of course I am. I'm thrilled.' Sarah forced a hollow laugh. 'After kissing all those frogs, you've finally found your prince!'

Becky roared with laughter and blew Tony a kiss and Sarah

felt as if her heart was breaking. Becky was utterly oblivious, of course, but Sarah knew that her relationship with her sister was irreversibly altered. Either the awful secret would come out or Sarah would be shackled to it for the rest of her life, always watchful, always wary lest she betray herself or Tony. She wasn't sure which was worse.

Tony said something to Becky and she joined in the conversation with their aunt while Sarah stood on the periphery wishing she could shut her eyes and disappear. Better still, go back in time and change the thing that had led her to this dreadful pass.

Ian came back and Sarah smiled, wide with relief, never before so happy to see him.

Becky introduced the two men. 'Tony went to Coleraine too, Ian, round about the same time as you.' They spent a few moments debating if they'd bumped into each other at uni, concluding finally that though they recognised each other they had never actually spoken.

'And Sarah too,' said Becky brightly. 'Didn't you bump into each other?'

'No,' said Sarah hastily, shaking her head to refute any connection, while Tony stood still as a statue.

Ian turned to Sarah and held up a sparkling clean fork. 'I see you've finished eating,' he said, staring at her empty hands.

She clutched her stomach. 'Sorry, I don't feel hungry anymore.'

His pale eyebrows came together. 'Are you okay?'

'I feel a little unwell, that's all. A little nauseous. I think I might need to lie down for a bit.'

'I thought you looked a little peaky,' said Aunt Vi. 'I hope it's not that terrible flu bug that's doing the rounds just now. Mrs Riley's been laid low for nearly a week. All she can keep down is my chicken soup. You'd better go home and we'll drop the kids off after the party.'

'Tony and me can run you home,' said Becky. 'And I can stay with you if you like.'

'No!' snapped Sarah and stretched her lips into a smile. 'Don't spoil your afternoon because of me. There's loads of people here dying to meet Tony.' In her desperation she turned to Ian. 'Would you mind awfully giving me a lift?'

He didn't need asking twice. Tossing the fork onto the table with a clatter, he yanked car keys out of his jacket pocket and grabbed her elbow. 'Come on then, let's get you out of here,' he said, giving her elbow a gentle squeeze.

And for the first time in over a decade she was actually glad to be leaving a party with him.

Chapter 10

Sarah was at the wheel of the car, with Aunt Vi beside her in the passenger seat and the kids engrossed with their consoles in the back.

Outside, the sky was blue and the April sunshine bright. But Sarah's head was too full of last Saturday's awful events to pay either much attention.

Life was complicated enough with trying to sort out how she felt about Cahal, while deflecting Ian's misguided attempts at a reconciliation. Tony popping up, threatening her relationship with Becky, was the last straw. All tied up in knots inside, she wondered if she was that different really from Aunt Vi, who lived in a perpetual state of worry.

She glanced at her aunt, who wasn't looking at the cloudless sky either, but staring grimly at the road ahead. Her left hand hovered uncertainly in front of the dashboard, poised to brace herself in the event of a sudden stop or worse.

In her last year living at home, Sarah had found Vi's presence suffocating, but over the years she had become more understanding. She'd read an article about people with the same phobia in a Sunday supplement once. It even had a name – Generalised Anxiety Disorder – and opened up sufferers to all sorts of worry, from the weather to being mugged on the walk home from church. Even though she knew it would make no difference, Sarah said kindly, 'It's okay, Aunt Vi. I'm a very careful driver. Try and relax.'

'It not you I'm worried about,' she said darkly. 'It's the other lunatics on the road.'

Sarah slowed down a little. 'Did you hear that Isabelle's party raised over three hundred pounds for the mission?'

'Really? That was a good idea, having a collection instead of presents. Let's face it, at our age we don't need anything.'

A car pulled out in front, Sarah applied the brakes and Aunt Vi made a sudden lunge for the grab handle on the door.

'I wish you wouldn't do that,' said Sarah.

Aunt Vi pursed her lips. 'I'm glad we got to meet Becky's man at last. And I have to say I was pleasantly surprised. Apart from the fact that he needed a good haircut, I thought Tony was really quite –' She broke off abruptly and cried out, 'You need to slow down here at these lights. They change very suddenly.'

Sarah pretended to focus on changing down the gears though she was really concentrating on changing the subject. She glanced in the rear view mirror. 'Kids, how many of those sweets have you had?'

'Five,' said Lewis.

'I wasn't counting,' said Molly.

'He's not what you would call handsome,' went on Aunt Vi. 'His nose is too big for one thing. But he is attractive in a way, I suppose.'

What her aunt was trying to say was that Anthony had sex appeal. Sarah blushed furiously and slipped the car into neutral. 'Five sweets is enough for now. You've only just had breakfast,' she snapped, gripping the steering wheel with both hands even though the car was barely moving. 'You'll end up losing your teeth. Save the rest for later.'

'Still, he's an intelligent man,' went on her aunt, picking a speck of fluff off her navy trousers. 'And he's a good catch for Becky. I mean, I don't know what lecturers are paid, but he has a very respectable job. He might even be a professor one day,' she added with a slow, approving nod of her head. 'Imagine that?'

Sarah came to a halt at the lights and took a deep breath, biting back the observation that Anthony was a Catholic. Her aunt would've divined this within minutes of meeting Tony, if not before through pointed questioning of Becky beforehand. And yet it had not been mentioned once, though it had been one of the main objections to Cahal. She resolved not to be bitter and reminded herself that Northern Ireland had changed a great deal since 1992. Even her aunt and father, it seemed, had moved with the times.

'Imagine having an academic in the family?' said Aunt Vi and Sarah cringed. She hadn't actually considered the possibility of a marriage between Becky and Tony. The thought made her come out in a cold sweat.

'Why do we have to pick up other people's rubbish?' demanded Molly from the back seat, and for once Sarah was grateful for her prickly intervention. 'None of my friends have to do it.'

Sarah turned onto the aptly-named Coast Road that hugged the East Antrim shoreline all the way north to the pretty glen village of Cushendall. She let Aunt Vi, who was chair of the Ballyfergus in Bloom committee, do the talking.

'Ballyfergus in Bloom is all about community involvement, getting everyone out supporting their local town and making it look the best it can. It's only once a month and sure you love it!'

'I used to,' said Molly disparagingly, 'when I was Lewis' age.'

'You're never too old to make a contribution, Molly,' said Aunt Vi briskly, choosing to ignore Molly's sarcasm. 'And it's a lovely morning. How can a blue sky like that not cheer you? And, oh, look at the sea.'

Sarah, who'd been too preoccupied with worrying about Tony to notice her surroundings, looked east. The Irish Sea, sunlight sparkling off the water like shards of blue glass, came into view. She smelt the sea as soon as she stepped out of the car – salt and fish and rotting seaweed on the shore – and smiled in spite of the knots in her stomach.

Molly got out of the car, grumbling, with the ear phones still in her ears, a metallic red iPod tucked into the pocket of her skinny pink jeans. Lewis stood with his arms outstretched, his hair blowing in the gentle sea breeze, and cried out, 'It smells like holiday!'

166

Everyone laughed, even Molly, then set about pulling litter pickers, black bin bags and gloves out of the boot. This was one of the rare occasions when Aunt Vi wore trousers. She looked like a spinning top – skinny top and bottom, round in the middle.

'You'd better put this on so you're clearly visible,' Aunt Vi said, handing Sarah a grubby fluorescent jacket. 'You do that side of the road and I'll stay over here on the pavement with the children, where I can keep an eye on them.'

Sarah took the jacket, held it gingerly at arms' length and pulled a face. 'Well, I don't suppose this can possibly make me look any worse,' she said, looking down at old jeans two sizes too big held up with a frayed belt and dirty grey trainers with mismatched laces.

Aunt Vi zipped up her jacket, handed Lewis a litter picker and eyed Sarah sternly. 'It's not a beauty contest.'

Molly rolled her eyes at Sarah and it was all she could do not to burst out laughing.

'Bet I can fill my bag first,' said Lewis, snapping the jaws of the litter picker in Molly's face.

'Will you stop that! It's disgusting. It could have poo on it for all you know. Mum, make Lewis stop.'

Sarah sighed. 'Lewis, put it down.'

'Right, you two. Come with me,' commanded Aunt Vi, grabbing Lewis' hand firmly in her own, even though he was past the age when such caution was strictly necessary. Sarah stood for a few moments watching them go, the sound of Molly's continued protestations carrying on the breeze. She was glad to be alone at the side of the road with only the rubbish and the passing cars for company.

Using the litter picker, she pulled a brown beer bottle out of the grass verge by the neck, and dropped it into the bin bag. Then she inched along netting drinks cans, cigarette packets, broken glass and sweet wrappers in the rubber teeth of the grabber. The work was methodical, rewarding even, and just the balm her troubled mind craved as she pondered the excruciating events of the day before. She was grateful to Ian for getting her out of the party, though she'd rather it had been someone else. He'd driven her straight home but insisted on coming into the house where he made tea for them both, parked himself at her kitchen table and kept going on about how happy they had once been. It had taken all her powers of persuasion to get him, eventually, to leave. After he'd gone, she'd collapsed on the bed upstairs and sobbed into her pillow until it was stained with mascara and she had no tears left.

With hindsight she had made a grave mistake. She should never have pretended that she didn't know Tony. It would've been much better to have acknowledged him as Cahal's friend at the outset. Because a lie that was close to the truth was a lot more sustainable than one that was complete and outright fiction. And now it was too late. There was no going back.

Sarah picked up a squashed orange juice carton, the white straw still sticking out the top of the carton, and added it to her increasingly heavy load. Then she stood stock still and stared at the blue ocean.

A sole yacht in full sail, its red spinnaker billowing from the prow like a silk balloon, cruised north. She wished she was out there too, sailing away from this intractable problem.

She could talk to Tony. She could ask him to swear that he would never tell. She thought him a decent guy – there was every chance that he would comply. But what then? Would he keep the promise? Even if he intended to, there was always the chance that the truth might slip out in some unguarded moment.

She could never be certain. It would forever tarnish her relationship with her sister and if they married, Tony's presence would be a constant reminder of a chapter in her life she'd rather forget. And if Becky ever found out, it would break her heart.

For when she looked at Tony, Sarah had seen in her sister's eyes, a reflection of herself as she had once been with Cahal. Back then she had believed that love was invincible, something that could stretch and bend like elastic in the face of opposition and yet not yield.

But she was wiser now and she knew that love was none of these things. It was as fragile as the fragment of bright blue thrush's eggshell, speckled with spots of black, she'd found on the drive that morning.

Sadness bubbled up inside her but she fought it back with the determination that had seen her through a divorce and eight long, lonely years of single-parenting. She took a deep breath, gritted her teeth and yanked a pink sweet wrapper out of a tangle of grass with the litter picker. But before she had time to drop it in the bin bag a car pulled up alongside, engine growling, and forced her onto the verge.

She frowned crossly, peered through the passenger seat

window and froze. Cahal was in the driving seat grinning at her, his brown arms bared, a red T-shirt tight across his biceps and chest. Folds of red fabric rippled across his flat stomach, and below that, mid-blue jeans hugged lean hips and thighs. She had not seen him in a pair of jeans in twenty years. He'd kept himself in good shape and dressed like this, he looked so much more like her Cahal. She swallowed and backed away from the car.

He pressed a button on the dashboard and the window rolled down with a quiet hum. Leaning across the passenger seat, he looked up at her face, his tanned brow all wrinkled, and grinned. 'It is you, Sarah!'

She smiled faintly as her heart sank into her grubby trainers. 'Hi there, Cahal.'

Why, of all the places and all the times she might have bumped into him in Ballyfergus, did it have to be here and now? A strand of greasy blonde hair blew across her face. She tried to ignore it.

He stared at the sweetie wrapper – still suspended in the teeth of the grabber. The corners of his mouth twitched and his eyes sparkled mischievously. Was he laughing at her? And what was so mesmerising about a bit of rubbish? She lifted her chin defiantly and followed his gaze. And when she saw what she had picked up, she gulped.

It wasn't a sweetie wrapper she had picked up by the corner. It was a pink foil condom wrapper, glinting bright in the sunlight, with the blue legend 'Durex' emblazoned across it.

'Is that what I think it is?' he said.

She blushed furiously, dropped the offending item into the

bin bag and stood to attention, with the grabber pointing at the ground like a sword. And then, unable to stop herself from sounding just like her aunt, she said, 'You'd be surprised what people chuck out of car windows.'

He placed a flat hand on his non-existent belly and chuckled heartily while she scowled at him. 'Sarah,' he said, when he could stop laughing, 'what in God's name are you doing?'

'What does it look like?' she said crossly. 'I'm litter-picking. We do it on the second Saturday of every month.' She glanced up. Her aunt and the children were fifty yards away plucking rubbish out of the fence, like raspberries off a cane. A car sped past into town on the other side of the road, immediately followed by another going in the opposite direction.

'But why?'

By the time she'd finished explaining Ballyfergus in Bloom the smirk had gone from his face and he was looking at her earnestly. 'Good for you,' he said, his face as straight as a poker.

She frowned doubtfully – she'd seen him keep a perfectly straight face before and still poke gentle fun at people, a talent that used to send her into hysterics. She had to look away and suppress the smile that sprang to her lips. She couldn't really blame him – she must look ridiculous. 'So, are you down visiting family today?'

'Nope. I've just taken a lease on a bungalow in Grace Avenue.'

'Oh.' She hesitated, on one hand surprised by the interest this news induced in her. On the other, a little wrong-footed that he was intruding on her patch. She looked at the double yellow lines under her feet. 'I thought you said the consultants are all staying in Belfast.'

'They are. But I'm not.' He stared at her and she felt her cheeks redden once more.

He had every right to stay where he wanted. It was nothing to her. And this was where his parents still lived after all. 'It'll be nice to spend some time with your family.'

He inclined his head to one side and lifted one shoulder slightly, a gesture of indifference. 'My relationship with my family hasn't changed, Sarah. And I haven't been good at staying in touch with my old friends, though most of them are still living on the Drumalis estate.' He stared straight ahead at the road, and his Adam's apple moved in his throat. 'Or else serving time.'

Sarah tried not to look shocked. She remembered things he had told her long ago about the lives of the people on the estate – generations of families who had never worked, rampant drugs and teenage pregnancies, domestic violence and a moral code based on clan loyalty and a universal hatred of the law. She'd found his accounts of this dangerous world faintly thrilling then. Now it just seemed desperately sad. How had he made something out of a life that had started with so little promise – and without the advantages she'd taken for granted? She admired him for it.

'I'm sorry to hear that,' she said, thinking of the girls she'd met at school. She was still in touch with most of them – they met once a year for a reunion. But they had all been middle-class girls like her – the daughters of respectable people, doctors, lawyers, high-ranking policemen, bank managers. She saw with sudden clarity that Cahal's alienation from his kins-

172

folk was the cruel price he'd paid for his success.

A car came up behind Cahal and tooted angrily several times before driving on past, making them both and Aunt Vi turn to look. She shaded her eyes from the sun with her hand and stared.

He said, 'I don't remember so much traffic on this road.'

She glanced up at the blue sky. 'When the sun comes out, everyone makes a dash up the coast.' As if to prove her point, another car overtook without slowing down. Across the road, Molly snapped at Lewis' heels with the litter picker, the sound of his shrieks carried on the breeze.

'Those your kids?' he said.

'Yeah.'

He nodded thoughtfully, watching them for a few short moments with a wistful smile on his lips. Aunt Vi was still watching, as if frozen to the spot.

'Well,' she said, snapping the tips of the litter picker together. 'I suppose I'd better get on.'

'Okay, I'll see you,' he said, slipping the car into gear. She watched the car round a bend in the road and disappear. Then, tilting her face to the sun she inhaled a deep lungful of the fresh sea air. But it did little to calm the giddy feeling in her stomach. The last time she'd felt like this she'd drunk too much champagne at a cousin's wedding.

Aunt Vi was walking towards her, litter picker and bin bag abandoned on the pavement where she'd dropped them. Sarah crossed the road and the women met on the pavement. Aunt Vi glanced in the direction Cahal's car had gone.

'Who was in that car?' she said, her expression rigid. And

when Sarah did not answer, she brought her gaze to bear on her and said, more urgently, 'Who were you talking to, Sarah?'

Sarah looked in the direction Cahal had gone, a lump forming in her throat like a lie. She hated the way her aunt made her feel. As if she was a girl again. As if she had done something wrong.

She pulled herself up to her full height and told herself sternly that she was an adult now. She could talk to whom she liked. She would not be intimidated. She looked her aunt levelly in the eye. 'Cahal Mulvenna.'

'Oh,' said her aunt, a single, desolate cry and she cupped both hands over her mouth and stared at the bend in the road as if Cahal's car might round it any moment and mow them both down. Sarah's hackles rose. She'd never thought of her aunt as a drama queen but wasn't this reaction a bit over the top? After a few long moments of silence, Aunt Vi looked back at Sarah, her face all crumpled up with confusion. 'I thought I was seeing things. But I ... I don't understand. What's he doing here? I thought he lived in Australia now.'

'He does. He's over here on business.'

'You don't seem surprised to see him.'

'That's because this isn't the first time we've met.' Sarah explained about the Australian consultants sent over to assist in the merger of the two telecommunications companies. 'Cahal's the senior consultant.'

'I see,' said Aunt Vi, bringing a hand up to her neck. 'And is he ... has he brought his family with him?'

'No. The job's only for six months.' Aunt Vi's face relaxed. 'They're with his ex-wife in Melbourne,' she added and Aunt

Vi blinked rapidly, like she'd something in her eye.

'And you never thought to mention this before?'

Sarah shrugged indifferently. 'I didn't think you'd be particularly interested. You were never interested in Cahal Mulvenna before.' She locked eyes with Vi. 'Except to break us up.'

Aunt Vi broke eye contact and looked out to sea. 'I only ever did what was for the best.'

Sarah swallowed. They had not spoken of this subject for two decades. She remembered how hard Aunt Vi and Dad had made it for her and Cahal. And how hard she'd fought back, only to be defeated in the end. 'Best for whom?' she said quietly but there was no answer.

'What're you talking about?' said Molly, appearing suddenly beside them and squinting into the sun.

'How much litter there is!' she said brightly. 'Come on, back to work. There's loads more to be done.'

Chapter 11

After the uncomfortable exchange with Aunt Vi which had left a slight coolness between them, Sarah left the kids at her father's house and slipped out to see Evelyn. Her spirits lifted when she entered Evelyn's room and found her sitting up in bed watching the too-loud TV. Cold April rain lashed the window, but inside the nursing home it was unbearably hot and stuffy.

Shrugging off her coat, Sarah walked over to the bed and smiled. 'Hello Evelyn. You're looking well. Haven't seen you watching TV in a while.' She draped the coat over the chair and patted Evelyn's hand. Her skin was dry and papery, her hand cold as ice, even though she was bundled up in yellow blankets.

'Sarah, darling, how good to see you. I am feeling a little better.' Evelyn looked at the TV and peeled off her wire glasses with a trembling hand. Her eyes were watery and red-rimmed.

'Turn that off, would you?'

Sarah flicked off the TV and the room fell silent, save for the distressing sound of someone shouting further down the corridor. It was probably Nancy Magill, a resident who was half-mad. She spent her days loudly accusing anyone who happened by – staff, residents, or visitors – of stealing her handbag, even when it was sitting squarely on her lap. Sarah shut the door, muffling the sound.

'Thank you, darling,' smiled Evelyn. 'Where are the children?'

'Up at Dad's.'

'You should've brought them.'

'Ian'll bring them on Sunday.' The children's visits to see their Gran were confined to weekends now, carefully orchestrated to take place in the late morning when she was at her best. Evelyn tired easily and the children were bored by the visits, and unsettled by the changes in their bedridden Gran who had once been so active.

Sarah noticed a photograph on the windowsill. It was an old black-and-white one of Evelyn in a silky evening dress smiling happily at her husband Harry, portly and bald in suit and tie. She picked it up. 'I haven't seen that photo before. It's lovely.'

Sarah placed the plain silver frame in Evelyn's frail hands and sat down on the chair beside the bed, sweating in the over-warm room. 'Ian brought it in,' said Evelyn, clutching the photo between both hands. 'He found it in a box of old photographs. It was taken at the police annual dinner. 1973, I think. Quite a swanky affair in those days. The dress was emerald green silk. And do you see that pendant around my neck?' She pointed. 'It was an oval emerald. Harry gave it to me on our first wedding anniversary. Doesn't he look handsome?'

Sarah's throat tightened. 'Yes.' How difficult it must be dealing with each day without him.

Evelyn touched the glass in the frame with the tips of her fingers, as if connecting with the picture might in some way enable her to connect with Harry once more. 'I loved him very much. We met when I was eighteen and were immediately inseparable. After we were married we never spent a night apart. He was the love of my life, you know. We were so very happy together.'

Sarah thought immediately of Cahal, her first and only true love, lost to her. The unfairness of it made her eyes prick with tears.

'I had a good and happy life,' Evelyn went on. 'More children would've been nice but that wasn't to be … but really I'm very thankful for the life I had. Don't be sad for me, Sarah.'

Sarah sniffed back the tears and shook her head. 'It's not that …'

'What then?'

'I guess I'm crying for myself,' she said, as a single tear slid down her left cheek. Hastily she wiped it away and fought to get her emotions under control. 'I'm sorry. I shouldn't bring my troubles here.'

Evelyn let the photograph rest on the bedspread and waited. Sarah, who had always been able to confide in Evelyn and valued her counsel even above Becky's, was unable to resist the urge to unburden herself. 'Do you remember … did Ian ever mention a Cahal Mulvenna to you?'

Evelyn frowned and folded her thin lips in on themselves.

'He's from Ballyfergus. His family lived on the Drumalis estate.'

Evelyn licked her lips. 'Mulvenna. I do recall that name.'

'He was the love of my life.' Sarah looked at her hot and sweaty hands clasped in her lap. 'We met at university, in my first year, but it … it didn't work out.'

'So, why are you thinking about him now, all these years later?'

Sarah looked up. 'Because he's back in Ballyfergus, Evelyn. He's taken a house on Grace Avenue.'

Evelyn nodded slowly but said nothing.

Sarah stared out the window. The rain had ceased, though the sky was still a solid block of grey. She told Evelyn the tale of her and Cahal, how her family had been so set against him and how he'd gone to Australia and she'd never heard from him again.

'And now he's back.' Said Evelyn.

'Yes. And the thing is … well, I find I still have the same feelings for him. I just don't know if it's wise to act on them.'

'I don't think wisdom has got much to do with it, Sarah. I think you have to follow your heart.'

'But I don't know if I can trust him. And then there's the problem of distance. His ex-wife and three boys live in Australia. And I live here.' Sarah inched forward onto the edge of the seat and laid her hand on the bed. 'You do know that

I'd never take the kids away from their father.'

'I know you'd never do anything intentionally to hurt Ian,' said Evelyn, patting the back of her hand. There was a short pause and she went on, 'You can't jump hurdles till you get to them.' She looked at the photograph once more. 'And the future has a funny way of taking care of itself. There's something I've never told you about me and Harold.' She leaned back on the pillows and stared out the window. 'My parents were strict Baptists and they expected me to marry a boy from the Church. When they found out about Harold, they banned me from seeing him. They told me that they would cut me off if I persisted. That I would be cast out by my family and the Church.'

Sarah, astonished, said, 'What did you do?'

'We eloped. We got married in Antrim registry office. I had just turned nineteen. His sister and brother stood as witnesses. There was no one else there.'

Sarah stared, trying to imagine Evelyn as a young girl packing a suitcase and slipping out into the night, placing all her trust and her future in the hands of a man only two years older than she. 'That was a very courageous thing to do.'

'I loved him, that was all,' smiled Evelyn. 'I would've done anything for him.'

Sarah blushed. Had she loved Cahal enough? Should she have run away with him like he asked her to? But she'd had more than just her father and aunt to consider. There was Becky too.

'It all worked out in the end. My family didn't speak to me for years but eventually we patched things up.' Evelyn smiled at the picture. 'I never regretted it for one second.'

Sarah swallowed, her admiration for Evelyn growing by the second. 'You were very brave.'

Evelyn smiled. 'I don't know about that. But it taught me that sometimes in life you have to take a chance. Or you risk losing the thing you love most.'

A thoughtful silence settled between them and then Evelyn said, 'How's Becky?'

'Oh, she's fine. She's met a guy. She seems really keen on him.'

'That's nice.'

Sarah sighed heavily and wished she could tell Evelyn the truth about Becky's new man. 'I worry about her. She doesn't have a very good track record when it comes to men. She seems to have fallen for him really quickly and I'm worried that he'll let her down.'

'You worry about her too much, Sarah.'

Sarah looked at her hands and said quietly, 'But I feel responsible.'

'I know you do,' said Evelyn kindly, 'but she's a grown woman now. She has to make her own choices – and you have to let her. All you can do is be there for her if it doesn't work out.'

'But I can't help but feel as if it's my job to ensure her happiness.'

'No one can make someone else happy. And I think that when your mother asked you to look after her, Sarah, she only meant for the time that Becky was a child.'

The muscles around Sarah's heart tightened. 'Do you think

so?'

'Yes, I do, Sarah.' Evelyn reached out and patted the back of Sarah's hand. 'It's time you let go, Sarah. It's time to let Becky live her own life.'

'But –'

Evelyn put her finger to her lips and smiled kindly. 'No buts. She's quite capable of looking after herself, you know.'

Back at her father's house, Molly and Lewis were curled up on the sofa with Becky in the lounge watching a Mr Bean DVD. Peals of laughter came from down the hall, temporarily relieving Sarah's anxiety, and bringing a smile to her face as she started to empty the dishwasher with her father.

'I shouldn't have stayed so long with Evelyn. I think I over-tired her.'

'I'm sure she was very glad to see you,' said Dad, lifting a cup out of the dishwasher.

Sarah picked out the cutlery. 'The doctors say it's her heart. It's just slowly packing up and there's nothing they can do. That's why she's always cold – her circulation's bad.'

'God bless her,' he said, pausing for a moment with the cup in one hand and a dishtowel in the other. He couldn't be persuaded from his habit of drying the dishwashed dishes, even though, bar the odd pool of water on the base of a mug or glass, they were dry already. 'But we all have to go sometime. Tough for Ian though. She's all he's got left.'

'Yes, I think he'll take it very hard,' said Sarah, taking a cloth to the greasy splashes behind the cooker that Dad and Becky had overlooked, but which Vi, when she returned, would not. 'But at least he has Raquel,' she added a little feebly. Based on recent conversations with Ian, she wasn't sure Raquel would be of much comfort to him when the time came.

Dad said nothing and they worked in companionable silence for a little while. When the dishes were all dried and put away, he closed the door to the hall softly and came and stood beside her, the damp tea towel still in his hands. 'I want to talk to you about something, Sarah,' he said, in the grave tone of voice she knew so well and which had always inspired anxiety in her. Her stomach tightened.

'Vi told me that Cahal Mulvenna's back in town.'

She busied herself rinsing the basin under the tap. 'That's right.'

He folded the tea towel carefully into four and laid it on the kitchen counter. 'And he works with you, is that right?' he said, smoothing the folded cloth with the palm of his hand.

She stared at her reflection in the black kitchen window – beyond, the garden was in pitch darkness. Standing here, in the house in which she'd grown up, with the man who'd been the most dominant influence in her life, she was a child again. 'We work in the same building.'

She wiped the basin carefully with the dishcloth and set it on the draining board.

'I see,' he said coolly.

She squeezed out the dishcloth and set it by the sink.

Dad sniffed. 'And you don't have … er … any feelings for him still, do you?'

Sarah blushed. 'Really, Dad, I don't think that's any of your business. I'm thirty-eight years old.'

'You're my daughter, Sarah,' he said evenly. 'Your happiness is my business, no matter how old you are. I don't want that man hurting you again.'

She touched his arm. 'Don't worry, Dad. I won't let him.'

He folded his arms and leaned against the counter. 'So you do still care for him?'

Sarah shrugged. She would not deny it outright.

The corners of his mouth twitched. 'You met his parents, didn't you?'

She could not pretend to her father, or herself, that she'd felt comfortable in that environment. 'It's not Cahal's fault that he was born into a family like that. And frankly, I think it's incredibly old-fashioned to judge someone by their background. We live in the twenty-first century, Dad, not the nineteenth.' She offered an olive branch in the form of a smile. 'Haven't you heard of upward mobility?'

'I believe he's done well for himself,' he said glumly. 'And I suppose he's to be congratulated on that. Given the background he came from.'

'Yes, he has done well. And I admire him for that.'

'Well,' said Dad and he lowered his head a little so that he was looking at her from under his eyebrows. 'You should know that Aunt Vi and I don't feel any differently about him now than we did twenty years ago.'

'Well, it's comforting to know that some things never change.'

Just then Becky burst through the door, chuckling, in grey joggers and battered slipper boots. Sarah smiled grimly, her face reddening. She couldn't look at her sister these days without an image of Tony springing to mind. By all accounts the romance was going swimmingly. They were even talking of moving in together. Sarah felt sick at the thought.

'It's not over yet,' announced Becky, clutching a red plastic bowl to her large chest. 'Mr Bean has just destroyed this priceless painting. It's hilarious.' She opened a cupboard door and peered inside. 'I've been sent in to forage for supplies. Any more Tayto cheese and onion, Dad?' She paused and looked from Sarah's red face to her father's grim one. 'What's up with you two? You look like someone's died.'

'Nothing's the matter,' said Sarah brightly, her instinct to protect Becky from anything unpleasant as honed as it had always been.

'I think there's some more crisps in that cupboard there,' said Dad, pointing. 'At least that's where Aunt Vi normally puts them.'

'Becky,' came Lewis' voice from up the hall, 'you said you'd only be a minute.'

'I'm coming,' she hollered back, pulled crisps out of the cupboard and said to both of them, 'You coming to watch the end of this movie or what?'

'Sure,' said Dad and he walked into the hall.

'I'll maybe give it a miss tonight,' said Sarah, pulling her smartphone out of her bag, and concentrating on the screen. 'I could do with catching up on a few emails.' And time alone to think.

Becky ripped open three crisp packets and tipped the contents into the bowl. 'Oh, come on. It's Friday night, Sarah. Take a break.'

Sarah shook her head and tapped the screen of the phone.

185

'No, you go ahead.'

Becky gave her a peculiar look. 'Sarah, what's wrong?'

'Nothing.'

'Are you sure? You've been acting weird for a while now, ever since Isabelle's party.'

Sarah's heartbeat quickened. 'I'm just busy at work, that's all,' she snapped. 'Can't you give me some peace?'

Becky picked up the bowl. 'Sorry I asked.' She left the room, kicking the door shut with a loud thud on her way out.

Ian picked up the note lying on the kitchen table and loosened his tie as he read Raquel's scrawl.

Working late. Will eat out. Don't wait up. Raquel.

He turned the paper over. *Special K, low fat yoghurt, Ryvita.* So this is what communication between them had come to? Messages hastily scribbled on the back of old shopping lists. He checked his phone – she hadn't even tried to call or text. He sighed, tossed the note in the bin and slipped the phone back in his pocket.

Upstairs he switched on the lights in the all-white bedroom, emptied his pockets onto a lacquered white tray Raquel had bought for the purpose and kicked off his shoes.

Then he sat down on the bed, laced his fingers together and listened to the oppressive, deathly silence. The room smelled of Raquel – expensive perfume, hairspray, fake tan and body lotion. He felt her presence all around and in a strange sort of way, he felt closer to her in her absence. For when she was here, they barely spoke. They hadn't slept together in months. The last time Raquel had come on to

186

him, he'd feigned a headache, full of guilt that he was being unfaithful, not to her, but to Sarah. Because it was Sarah that filled his waking thoughts, not Raquel.

He was to blame of course. He'd fallen in love with his ex-wife. No, that wasn't true. He had never stopped loving her. He sighed loudly, his heart heavy with remorse. He should never have married Raquel and wondered why she'd married him. He was glad that they'd never had kids together. He felt bad enough about the prospect of breaking up with her, without the added guilt of fathering yet another child from a broken home.

At least, from that perspective, it would be a clean break for both of them. And when he and Sarah were finally reconciled he would be making whole once again that which he had thought lost to him. His children would have their father where he ought to be – living at home – and he and Sarah would be together once more.

Cheered by this thought he changed into black jeans and a red polo shirt. He thought about the party and Sarah, so pretty in the yellow dress, and smiled to himself. The party had turned out better than he could have hoped. For when Sarah felt unwell, who did she turn to? He even wondered if she had feigned illness to get him alone. She'd been a little quiet, coy even, on the journey back to her house, but he'd taken that as a good sign. He understood how she felt. Being around her made the back of his neck prick with sweat and his palms go clammy with nervousness.

And it had felt like the most natural thing in the world when they returned to their home and he made her a cup of tea. He'd left on a high, certain that their relationship had reached a turning point. On the way out, he'd offered to fix the dripping tap in the kitchen and she'd agreed. He had his foot in the door now – and he wasn't for turning back.

The tinny chime of the doorbell interrupted his thoughts. He glanced at his watch and frowned. He wasn't expecting anyone. Checking his reflection in the mirror, he went downstairs.

Vi was standing in the rain on his doorstep, holding a potted plant in her hands, a profusion of gaudy crimson flowers peeking out of the cellophane wrapper. He opened the door wide and invited her in out of the rain, though she was already halfway across the threshold before he'd finished speaking.

'That's a terrible night out there,' she complained, bustling past him.

She'd only visited here a few times but her easy familiarity didn't bother him – quite the opposite. He liked the fact that Vi still treated him as a member of her family.

'The plant's not for you, son,' she said, setting it down on the glass hall table and dusting her hands together. 'It's for Evelyn. I'm not going to get up to see her tonight so I wondered if you would mind taking it in tomorrow?'

'Why, yes, of course,' he said, peering into the dark at Vi's small grey car parked in the drive, the nose almost touching the rear bumper of his car. It would've been just as easy to drive to the nursing home as here. He shut the door.

Vi pulled off a glove and a deep frown appeared between her brows. 'How is she?'

He recalled how he'd left his mother only an hour ago, pale as the white pillows propping her up. She'd been good the past fortnight but yesterday she'd taken a turn for the worse. It had taken an age to get her to eat half a meal tonight. He was glad he'd been there at teatime because he wasn't convinced the staff would've had the time or patience to persevere like he had. His hands were suddenly damp with sweat, his stomach tight with fear. 'Much the same. The doctor says the chest infection's gone but she's not herself. She's tired all the time.' He pushed the fear down, the way he compressed the rubbish in the kitchen bin.

Vi nodded gravely. 'I'll pop up and see her on Wednesday,' she said, then looked about and added a loaded, 'Well now.'

Clearly she expected an invitation to stay and the fact that she had turned up unannounced for no good reason made him think she had come here for some specific purpose. And it could well concern Sarah. 'Would you like a cup of tea?'

'I don't want to be a nuisance,' she said, although she'd already taken off the other glove and undone the top button on her dark green wool coat.

'You're not, Vi.'

She glanced at the half-open lounge door, then up the stairs. 'Raquel out again?' Her right eyebrow arched – and he reddened.

'Er, yes. She's not back from work yet.'

'She's working very late,' observed Vi. 'Though I suppose that's the way of it these days.'

Without answering he led the way up the hall. In the kitchen she draped her coat over the back of a chair, sat down and drummed the table with short, neatly trimmed bare nails.

189

They exchanged small talk over a plate of plain digestives. Eventually, having drained the cup of tea, Vi placed it carefully on the saucer, and cleared her throat. He forced a smile, the suspense making him impatient.

'I thought you and Sarah were getting on well together at Isabelle's party,' she said.

He shifted in the seat and smiled shyly, the apprehension that had been building inside him subsiding. 'We were. We had a good long chat when we got back, over a cup of tea. You know, reminiscing about old times.'

Vi nodded slowly, but her sour expression troubled him. The smile fell from his face.

'What is it?'

'Cahal Mulvenna's back in Ballyfergus.'

Ian froze. It couldn't be. Cahal Mulvenna had gone to Australia years ago – and hadn't been seen or heard of since, not by anybody Ian knew anyway. He stared at Vi, sitting there with a face like she'd sucked a lemon, and spluttered, 'But that … that can't be.'

'I'm afraid it is. I saw Sarah talking to him with my own eyes on Saturday morning.' She explained that Cahal had taken a house in Grace Avenue, was over here on business and worked for the same company as Sarah.

'By coincidence?'

'Who's to say?' said Vi, taking a sip of tea.

What did Cahal want with Sarah? He could think of only one thing and it filled him with jealous rage. Cahal had no right to come here and interfere between man and wife. Because in Ian's heart, he and Sarah were still married.

And what was Sarah thinking of? Why was she even giving the time of day to a man like Cahal Mulvenna? A man who, by Becky's account, had broken her heart? Ian had never underestimated Cahal Mulvenna and he did not do so now. Even he could admit that Sarah had loved Cahal more than she had ever loved him. 'Turns out he's divorced,' said Vi pointedly and Ian took the Lord's name under his breath. His stomach churned with anxiety and his heart beat so fast he was certain it must be visible under his shirt.

Ian swallowed the lump in his throat and tried to control his emotions. 'Sarah ... she's not seeing him, is she?'

Vi unfolded her arms and leaned across the table. 'Not as far as we know. But you have to understand he has a hold over her. I always said that.'

He felt his hopes slipping away. 'I thought ... I thought that Sarah and I might ... you know ... get back together. We've been getting on so well lately.'

'I know, Ian. It's what David and I have hoped for too,' she said, vocalising what he already knew.

In return for her confidence, he said, miserably, 'I was going to ask Raquel for a divorce.'

She regarded him for a few long moments, then her features hardened. 'Don't give up hope, Ian. Nothing's happened yet. Maybe nothing will. But I thought you'd want to know.' And with that, she got up, patted him lightly on the shoulder and pulled on her coat. 'I'll see myself out.'

After she'd gone, he sat for a long time at the kitchen table, clenched fists pressed to his eyes. He knew what Sarah saw in Cahal – or at least what she had seen in him all those years ago. Far too good-looking, in a battered leather jacket and tight jeans, he oozed disdain for authority and sex appeal in equal measure, like a raven-haired James Dean. Constantly surrounded by a fog of cigarette smoke and the smell of last night's beer, he was a walk on the wild side. He was, in short, everything Ian wasn't.

And now he was back, threatening to ruin everything that Ian had so carefully worked towards these last weeks and months. Step by slow, painful step he'd rebuilt the trust between him and Sarah until he'd been certain they would, ultimately, be reconciled. But now, with Cahal on the scene, all his plans were in jeopardy. How could he compete against him?

He was no fool. Even though his heart had soared with happiness on the day Sarah accepted his marriage proposal, he'd always known that she never would've done so had Cahal still been on the scene.

He stood up. A great surge of adrenaline coursed through him. Cahal had so nearly taken Sarah from him before. But Ian had bided his time and he had won her in the end. He would not let him win this time either. He would fight. For her and for his children.

Without any thought at all, his hands closed round a wrought-iron chair, the one in which Vi had so recently sat, picked it up and hurled it across the room. It clanged off the wall, one of the legs puncturing the plasterboard, and came to rest, with a screech of protest, on the limestone tiles. Shocked, Ian looked at his hands – and in the silence that followed he heard the slow, deliberate click of high heels on wooden floorboards.

He looked up. Raquel was standing in the hall doorway in a tight navy trouser suit and white silk shirt, opened just enough to offer a peek of honey-brown flesh and a pink lace bra. Her normally sleek blonde hair looked a little dishevelled, like she'd just run her hands through it, and her carefully applied eye make-up was slightly smudged under her eyes, making her look old and haggard.

He looked at the chair. How to explain what he'd just done, especially when he didn't understand it himself?

'I heard everything,' she said stonily and he looked up sharply. His heartbeat flickered with the fear of discovery. When had she come in? How much had she heard?

She cocked her head a little to one side. 'When exactly were you planning on telling me that you want a divorce?'

The air and anger went out of him all at once. He closed his eyes briefly and when he opened them he saw in her face, not the hurt he'd expected, but rage. 'I'm sorry, Raquel. This wasn't how I planned to tell you.'

She snorted and walked further into the room, her heels clacking on the stony tiles like horses' hooves. 'I'm glad I heard. At least I know where I stand now.'

He hung his head. 'I never meant to hurt you, Raquel.'

'Hurt me?' she said and stabbed at her chest with a long red fingernail. 'Oh, you haven't hurt me. I am angry though.'

He did not react. He knew that this was all a bluff, a performance. Of course she was hurt and she had every right to make him suffer. He deserved nothing less.

She circled him like a wolf, came to rest standing in front

of him and looked up at him with cold blue eyes. Her breath was stale and smelt of wine. 'I always suspected that you hadn't got over Sarah. There was only ever room in your heart for one woman and it was never me, was it, Ian? This marriage didn't stand a chance.'

'Wait a minute. That's not fair, Raquel. I did love you – at the start at least. I did try to make it work. Yes, I ... care for Sarah but it's not fair to blame me entirely. You're not interested in me either. All you want to do is party with your friends.'

She looked at the floor and shook her head. He softened. 'Raquel, I'm so sorry. I don't know what else to say.'

She lifted her head and gave him a terrifying, sort of triumphant, smile. 'You don't have to say anything. I'm actually glad. At least I don't have to feel guilty.'

'You've nothing to feel guilty about, Raquel. You haven't done anything wrong.'

She threw back her head then and laughed – a horrible, scary chuckle. Her amazingly bright teeth, the result of too much chemical whitening, glinted warningly. 'You have absolutely no idea, have you?'

He looked at her quizzically. 'What are you talking about?'

'You're so wrapped up in the fantasy that you and Sarah are going to get back together, so blinkered, that you can't see what's going on under your very nose.'

He shook his head, bewildered. She was taking this remarkably well. Better than he could have hoped, but he didn't like the hint of menace in her voice.

She sighed and looked at him with pity. 'I'll go and pack.'

He held out a hand and touched her arm but she pulled it away as if his touch was toxic. 'You don't have to leave, Raquel. I will.'

'No,' she said icily, 'I'm not staying here another minute.'

'But where will you go? Look, I'll go and … eh … stay in a hotel or something.'

She tutted dismissively, got out her mobile and started tapping the screen with the pad of her index finger.

'What're you doing?'

'I'm texting Jim to come and get me.'

'Jim?'

'Jim Proudfoot,' she said matter-of-factly. He was secretary at Ian's golf club where he used to take Raquel regularly for meals. He wasn't a close friend of Ian's, but they'd known each other from childhood. Ian had consoled him when his marriage had broken up last year.

'You and Jim?' he said stupidly, as the disbelief turned slowly into numb understanding.

'I haven't even tried to be discreet, Ian. At first I did it to try and make you jealous, to get you to just notice me. And then I realised that you didn't give a damn. You never once questioned where I was all those nights I came home late.' And with that she turned and strode determinedly out of the room.

He sat down abruptly on the chair and listened to her moving around upstairs, slamming drawers and wardrobe doors, stunned by the fact that she'd committed adultery. And yet he could not condemn her. Hadn't he done the same in thought, if not in deed, by yearning after Sarah? No, he could not blame her and he wished her well. Maybe Jim could make her happy in a way he could not.

Picking up the fallen chair and setting it to rights, he was surprised to find that his heart was not as heavy as it ought to be. In fact, it was not heavy at all. For even though his marriage was in tatters, he could not help but feel a great sense of relief.

Chapter 12

He was there, sitting on the bench by the river in front of The Big Fish, when Sarah arrived with her sandwich in one hand and a confusion of emotions in her heart. If he had not been here she would've been disappointed. But the fact that he was filled her with nervous apprehension. Evelyn had only been a slip of a girl when she'd risked everything she knew for an uncertain future. Was she brave enough to take a chance with Cahal, to risk being hurt a second time?

When she got close she saw that he had a phone pressed to his ear and she said, 'Sorry, am I disturbing you?'

He shook his head, removed the phone from his ear and smiled. 'Just listening to some voicemails the boys left me.' He pressed a button on the phone and the smile fell from his lips. 'Harry, the littlest, was crying.'

She sat down beside him on the bench. 'Oh, how awful. What was wrong with him?'

'I couldn't make out what he was saying. Something about a boy at school.' He pressed the phone to his chest and stared out across the river, the colour of sheet-metal under a blank grey sky. The sound of traffic and gulls calling filled the air. His throat moved. 'You know, I don't know what I'm doing here, Sarah. I hate being away from them. I can't even speak to Harry until late tonight by which time it'll be morning in Melbourne. I feel like I've let them down.' He paused and shook his head.

'I'm sure they understand that you had no choice.' She stared at the back of his hand where it lay on his lap, recognising the lump where a hurling stick had fractured it in the Ryan Cup finals at uni. She'd kissed his bandaged hand with such tenderness, feeling his pain as if she herself had been wounded.

He hung his head. 'I wanted to put as much distance as possible between myself and Adele and Brady.'

'Brady?'

He looked up. 'Adele's new husband. He's moved into our old house. It's one of the reasons I came here. I couldn't deal with it. Not because I still love Adele,' he added hastily. 'No, I'm pleased to see her happy. It's Brady.' He paused and stared hard out across the river before bringing his gaze back to Sarah. 'His favourite things in the world are beer and sport and he's more easy-going than me. I haven't told anyone this before, but … well … I'm worried that the boys'll like him more than me.'

'That will only happen if you let it, Cahal. You'll always be their Dad. And it's only six months.' Six short months and then he would be gone again. 'Maybe with a stepfather as well as a father, they get the best of both worlds.'

'What do you mean?'

'Just because Brady's different from you, it doesn't make him a bad influence. Maybe the boys will benefit from having two male role models in their lives.'

'I hadn't thought of it like that,' he said, frowning. He looked at her, a look of fierce determination on his face. 'I'll never leave them again like this. It was a mistake to come here.'

Her heart sank. She'd thought he still cared. Had she misread the signals?

'Except for meeting you again, of course,' he said, his voice soft.

She looked into his eyes. 'You mean that?'

His black pupils contracted. His hair, longer now than when he'd arrived, brushed the collar of his jacket. 'Yes.'

She swallowed. And could not look away. 'I know we said that we wouldn't talk about the past, Cahal. But there's something that I must ask you.'

'There's something I want to ask you too.'

She looked at him sideways and he said, 'You go first.'

'Okay.' She took a deep breath. Her heart pounded. Whatever he told her, she hoped she could forgive him for it. 'Why did you not write to me?'

He put a hand on his thigh, his elbow sticking out, and said crossly, 'What are you talking about? I wrote dozens of letters.'

She turned away from him then, sorry that she'd asked.

She felt so disappointed. An honest admission would've been so much more honourable than a blatant denial.

'Don't say that, Cahal,' she said quietly, looking at her hands. 'There were no letters.'

'Look at me.' Reluctantly she brought her gaze up to meet his. His eyes were grave and his chest rose and fell rapidly. 'I wrote to you, daily to start with, begging you to join me in Australia. But you never answered a single letter. That's what I wanted to ask you. Why you never wrote to me. I waited months and nothing came.'

She opened her mouth but no sound came out. What he said made no sense. She stared into his unblinking sea-green eyes and a creeping numbness spread through her body, like standing still in the freezing cold on a winter's day. She so wanted to believe him.

If what he said was true, he had not abandoned her. If she'd received those letters, they would've given her the courage to follow him. An alternative life played out before her in snapshots. She would've married him, she would've had his children and her life would've been so different, so happy, because he was all she had ever wanted. It was only after he'd emigrated that she'd realised that she would never be happy without him, but by then it was too late. She looked back at the wasted years and felt a terrible sense of injustice – and confusion. 'But I don't understand. How come I didn't receive the letters?'

A silence followed. Cahal screwed up his face in puzzlement. She said, 'Maybe you got the address wrong or put on the wrong postage or something?'

He shook his head firmly. 'I could see one or two going astray, maybe, but not every single letter. I wrote over twenty, Sarah. No, someone must have taken them.'

Immediately she was transported back to that long, miserable holiday. Dad was working day and night. Becky spent most of her time inside, unwilling to leave Sarah's side. Sarah lay in bed, physically sick with illnesses the doctor could not diagnose, and Aunt Vi was a constant presence, rarely going out, as if afraid to leave Sarah alone …

'Someone picked them up,' he said.

Aunt Vi! And though she said nothing, she slapped her hand over her mouth.

'And there's something else. I called your house and left a message with the man who answered the phone. He didn't say much, but I can only imagine it was your father.'

A chill ran down Sarah's spine. 'I never got any message.'

'But he told me that he would pass on the message that I had called – and give you my number in Australia.'

Sarah gasped. She didn't know what to think. She couldn't believe that her father had deliberately withheld this information.

'When you hadn't called back a week later,' he went on, 'I phoned again. But this time the phone was dead.'

Her mind raced. And then, like a light switched on in a dusty loft, illuminating all the things forgotten, she recalled a tiny detail. 'Dad had to change the number,' she said, becoming animated the more she remembered. 'We were getting nuisance calls. I remember thinking that was odd because our number was ex-directory – because of Dad being

in the RUC, you see. I stayed in my room most of that summer.'
She bowed her head, the misery of that time painful to recall.

Cahal blinked rapidly, colour rising to his tanned cheeks, and he said bluntly, 'Nuisance calls weren't the reason the number was changed. I was. Your dad changed the number because he didn't want you to speak to me.'

'No,' said Sarah with a firm shake of her head. 'He wouldn't do that without … he just wouldn't …' Her voice trailed away.

'And the letters?' he said.

She shook her head. She had never believed her aunt capable of such deception, but it seemed the only logical conclusion in the face of the facts. How could she do such a cruel thing? 'If only we'd had mobile phones and Twitter and Facebook back then. None of this would've happened.'

'If only.' He rubbed his chin and stared at her. 'What would you have done if you'd got my letters, Sarah?'

She pushed aside the nagging doubts that nibbled at her consciousness. 'If I'd received even one letter from you I believe it would've changed everything. I would've followed you to Australia.'

'It … makes me so bitter to hear that.'

She said, 'I sent you a letter shortly after you left. Did you ever get it?' She told him about slipping it through his parents' door. 'I assumed they forwarded it to you.'

He snorted derisively. 'They wouldn't have bothered going to the post office and buying a stamp. It would've gone straight in the bin.'

She swallowed, forcing down the lump lodged in her throat. 'I don't know what happened to your letters, Cahal, but I thought that you'd abandoned me,' she whispered. 'I thought that you didn't care.'

'That's what I thought too.' He paused, his eyes filling up, and said angrily, 'Our lives would've turned out so differently if we'd stayed together. And now we both have families and baggage and ...'

His voice trailed off and she finished the sentence for him. 'It's so complicated, isn't it? Before, in a way, it was so very simple.' Previously, it had been a straightforward choice between Cahal and her family. But now there were children and ex-spouses and thousands of miles to consider too.

There was a long silence. Against the grey, sunless sky, a lone gull swooped and dived. And the river, the tide about to turn, was still as glass. The unfairness of it all pressed in on her and she sniffed back tears. 'I thought of you every day for the last twenty years, Cahal.'

'Oh, Sarah.' His hand closed over hers. 'Is it too late for us? Or do you think we could start over?'

He was the only man she had ever wanted. But could she trust him? 'Maybe.'

His smile travelled all the way up to his eyes.

She so wanted to believe in him. She so wanted to believe that they had a future. What had Evelyn said? *The future has a funny way of taking care of itself.* She tried to cling to these wise words but they gave little comfort. For she could not honestly see how the obstacles that lay before her and Cahal could be overcome. And yet, she wasn't ready to give up hope altogether.

'But let's not rush things,' she said. 'Let's take it one step at a time.'

Sarah looked at the enormous bunch of flowers in her aunt's arms with dismay.

'Oh! They're absolutely gorgeous,' gushed Aunt Vi, her face partially obscured by lilac tulips, white germini and cream spray roses. 'How did you know it was my birthday, Tony?'

He winked at Becky, standing beside him in the small hall in her father's house. 'A little bird told me.'

Becky grabbed hold of his arm and grinned delightedly.

Tony handed Dad a bottle of wine and he said, 'Very nice.'

Sarah dusted her hands on her apron. 'Hi everyone. I'd better just see to the dinner,' she said, scuttling back into the kitchen.

Alone with her thoughts in the overheated room, she put on oven gloves, yanked the roast chicken out of the oven and set it on top of the cooker. Then she stabbed the thighs viciously with a metal skewer. Tony shouldn't be here. It was a family celebration. But Aunt Vi had insisted. Every moment in Tony's company was an agony for her, waiting for the awful moment she knew would one day come and ruin everything.

'How's it going?' said Becky coming into the room and filling a glass with water at the sink. 'Do you need a hand?'

'No thanks. I think it's all under control.'

There was a pause. 'Sarah?'

'Yes?' she said, ripping off a sheet of foil and placing it over the chicken before returning it to the oven.

'Is everything all right?'

'Of course.' Sarah smiled stiffly. 'Why wouldn't it be?'

Becky took a sip of water and frowned. 'Have I done something to annoy you?'

'Don't be silly. What makes you think that?'

'It's just … well, you do like Tony, don't you?'

Sarah swallowed. 'Yes, of course. It's just … well, things seem to be moving rather fast, that's all. You've only known him for a short while and here he is at Aunt Vi's birthday lunch.'

'Oh,' said a dismayed Becky. 'But Aunt Vi invited him.' She set down the glass of water and regarded Sarah coldly for some long moments. 'I expected more from you, Sarah. If Aunt Vi and Dad can welcome Tony into the family, why can't you? What's wrong with you?'

'There's nothing wrong with me. All I'm saying is –'

'Spare me the explanation,' said Becky and she walked out of the room slamming the door shut behind her.

Sarah ran her hand through her hair. Tony was coming between them and she didn't know what to do about it. She was on edge now in Becky's company in a way she had never been before, constantly worried that she would let slip her secret.

She tried to put Becky out of her mind and focused on Cahal and the conundrum of the missing letters instead. She wanted so much to believe he had sent them and made the phone call. It meant he had not abandoned her. But could he really be trusted after all that had been said and done? If he had sent the letters, what had happened to them? It was still inconceivable to her that her aunt and father who had done so much for her, had kept both letters and phone calls from her. The simplest thing was to ask them, of course, but she could not bring herself to do so. If they denied all knowledge, where did that leave her and Cahal? Was it better not to know, to take a risk in trusting Cahal, like Evelyn had done the night she eloped with Harry? Was it a risk she was willing to take?

Aunt Vi bustled into the kitchen with the flowers, laid them on the table and got out a vase. 'How's the chicken?'

'Nearly done.' Sarah took a tray of roast potatoes out of the oven. She glanced sideways at her aunt. Was this woman really capable of the deception Cahal would lay at her door?

Sarah took off the oven gloves and Aunt Vi peered at the potatoes doubtfully. 'Are you sure I can't do anything to help?'

'Absolutely not,' said Sarah, turning the potatoes with a pair of tongs. 'Just you relax and enjoy someone else cooking for you for a change.'

'Thanks, love. Aren't these just gorgeous?' swooned Aunt Vi, turning her attention back to the flowers.

'Mmm,' said Sarah, slipping her hands back into the oven gloves.

'So very thoughtful of him.'

Sarah shook the tray of roast potatoes so vigorously, fat splattered all over the place, narrowly missing the bare skin on her arms. 'Don't you think that he's a bit old for Becky though?'

'Oh, I don't think it matters too much,' said Aunt Vi, rummaging in a drawer for a pair of scissors. 'It's only twelve years, isn't it?'

Sarah closed the oven door with a bang. 'She told me he's been married before. Twice.'

'Well, a man in his forties is bound to have some baggage, isn't he?' said Aunt Vi, filling the vase up with water. She glanced at the door to the hall, went over and closed it. 'I'd be more worried if he hadn't.'

'But he's had four kids by two different women,' persisted Sarah, pulling off the oven gloves and throwing them on top of the counter.

Aunt Vi glanced sharply at Sarah, snipped the end of a germini, and placed the flower in the vase of water. 'I know he's not perfect, Sarah. But we have to take a pragmatic view of things.' She picked up a spray of cream roses and stripped it bare of leaves. 'He's the first man she's brought home that I actually like and he does seem very fond of Becky. And let's face it, she's not getting any younger. If she wants a husband and a family, well, this might be her last chance.'

Sarah swallowed. She felt like a juggernaut was racing towards her and she was powerless to stop it. The doorbell went. Sarah said, grabbing a spoon, 'That'll be Ian with the kids.' It was their weekend with him but he'd agreed to drop them over so they could celebrate their great-aunt's birthday with her.

Aunt Vi opened the door to the hall and called out, 'Sarah'll get the door. It's the kids.' Then she picked up the scissors and a tulip and said to Sarah, 'Go on then.'

'I can't. You go. I'm watching the dinner.' To prove her point, she stirred the sweetcorn with the spoon.

'Here, I can do that,' said Aunt Vi irritably and she held out her hand for the wooden spoon.

'No,' said Sarah, standing her ground. 'You go.'

Aunt Vi bumped her hip against Sarah's. 'Don't be ridiculous. They're your kids.'

'Mum?' came Molly's voice and the sound of feet in the hall.

'You can't leave the man standing there on the doorstep,' snapped Aunt Vi.

Sarah sighed, defeated. She wiped her hands down the front of the apron. 'Okay then.'

Aunt Vi grabbed the spoon out of Sarah's hand like a prize trophy and smiled triumphantly.

Ian, standing on the doorstep, looked a little dishevelled as he handed over Lewis' coat. He had bags under his eyes and what was left of his hair was sticking up all over the place. She was tempted to ask if he felt all right but stopped herself for fear of giving him further encouragement. 'Thanks for letting them come over for Vi's birthday dinner.'

'That's no problem, Sarah. Of course they couldn't miss it.'

'I'll drop them back before nine. Bye.' She started to close the door.

'Sarah?'

'Yes?'

He smiled. 'I haven't forgotten about the tap.'

'Er ... thanks.'

She narrowed the gap in the door even more.

'Sarah?'

'What?'

'Never mind. It'll keep.'

She closed the door, leaned against it and let out a long, loud sigh.

After dinner, with everyone sitting round the table in the cramped dining room, Aunt Vi asked, 'Didn't Ian want to come in?'

'I didn't ask him,' said Sarah sullenly and she looked around the table, avoiding eye contact with Tony. 'He was only dropping the kids off. He wasn't invited for lunch.'

'He's a good man,' said Dad, with a quick glance at Molly and Lewis' grave faces. 'You should be more civil to him, Sarah.'

Sarah opened her mouth to protest but shut it again. Being civil to Ian was what had gotten her into this mess. After giving her a lift home from Isabelle's party she couldn't get rid of him. She'd only agreed to let him come and fix the dripping tap in order to get him to leave. Since then she'd managed to avoid him, finding excuses to dash off when she dropped the kids or he appeared at Evelyn's bedside.

'Stop doing that,' hissed Molly at Lewis and then, addressing anyone who would listen, she said, 'He's kicking me under the table.'

'I am not,' said Lewis. 'You just keep putting your leg where I want to put mine.'

'Ahem,' said Becky. She touched Tony on the arm and grinned. 'We've got some news.' Sarah's heart jumped. There was a pause. Becky glanced sourly at Sarah, then delivered the hammer-blow. 'Tony's going to move in with me.'

So much for the relationship petering out, thought Sarah glumly. It appeared to be going from strength to strength. Something would have to be done.

'Oh,' said Aunt Vi and dabbed her mouth with her napkin.

'Ahem …' said Dad and started to cough.

'Now, before you say anything,' said Tony, addressing Aunt Vi and Dad. 'I know you don't approve but this way we'll be able to save up to buy somewhere together. And we're fed up being apart, aren't we, darling?' He placed a gentle kiss on Becky's nose and Sarah looked away. Her heart sank. Could things get any worse?

'But you really should be married,' said Aunt Vi. 'Or engaged at least.'

'Are you getting married, Auntie Becky?' said Molly, her face alight with anticipation.

Sarah swallowed, the idea filling her with horror.

'No, sweetheart,' said Becky.

'Oh,' said Molly. Her face fell and then she growled, 'Will you stop doing that, Lewis?'

Tony pushed his chair back. 'Tell you what, Lewis, why don't you and I go and play a bit of football? Did I tell you I played one season as centre half for Linfield?'

'Did you ever?' said Lewis, his eyes as big as plates, squeezing out of his chair and heading for the door. Molly went off to watch TV and, as soon as she was gone, Dad turned to Becky and said, 'Your aunt's right. You shouldn't be moving in together without a ring on your finger.'

But before Becky could say a thing, Aunt Vi rose to her defence. 'Your father's right, dear. But on the other hand, David, all the young ones live together nowadays.'

Sarah looked at her aunt in surprise and Dad said, 'You're very liberal all of a sudden.'

'We all have to move with the times, eventually,' said Aunt Vi, smiling at Becky. 'And Tony seems like such a nice man.'

'Yes, yes, he does,' said Dad thoughtfully, staring out at the garden where Tony and Lewis were kicking a ball about in the May sunshine.

'But what if things don't work out?' chipped in Sarah, clutching at straws.

Becky stared at her, stony-faced. 'I thought you'd be pleased for me, Sarah.'

Sarah cleared her throat and felt her face redden. 'I am pleased for you. I just don't want to see you get hurt. Or used.'

'Tony isn't using me,' said Becky icily. 'Any more than Cahal Mulvenna's using you.'

'What?' said Dad and Aunt Vi at the same time. Both their horrified gazes fell on Sarah.

'It's no big secret,' said Sarah, giving Becky the daggers. 'I met him for lunch a few times. As a friend.'

Aunt Vi put her hands to her face and whispered, 'No, Sarah.'

Dad flashed Aunt Vi a warning glance and said to Sarah, 'But I thought you were done with him? He's not a man to be trusted.'

Sarah rearranged the napkin on her lap. 'I'll be the judge of that.'

'You'd be a fool to give him a second chance, Sarah,' said Aunt Vi, fiddling with a dessert spoon. 'After what he did.'

'I agree,' said Becky folding her arms.

Sarah felt her face burn red. 'Well, that's my decision, isn't it?' She started collecting the dirty plates and forced a smile. 'Now, why don't we clear the table and have some birthday cake?'

Later, when she got to Ian's, dusk was falling and only his car was in the driveway. Sarah intended dropping the kids without getting out of the car but the front door opened and Ian came out, looking as unkempt as he had done earlier. His face broke into a grin when he saw the kids jump out of the car, leaving both passenger doors open. He kissed Molly on the head then lifted Lewis off the ground and turned him upside down before setting him back on his feet again. Lewis squealed with delight and cried, 'Again!'

Ian rubbed the small of his back, laughing, and embraced Lewis. 'Maybe later, son. You're getting too heavy for your old man.'

The children went indoors and Sarah got out of the car to shut the back doors.

'How was the party?' he said, coming up to the car.

'Fine,' she said, slamming a door shut. 'Listen, I'm going to be a bit late home from work on Wednesday. Is there any way you could pick the kids up from after school club this week? I'd be back by six.'

'Sure.'

'Okay, thanks.' She got back in the driver's seat, one foot on the tarmac.

'Sarah. Please come in for a minute.'

She froze and cursed under her breath. He'd come round the side of the car and was standing close, looking down at her.

'I haven't really got time tonight,' she said, looking straight ahead. 'I've an early start in the morning. And the kids really ought to be getting to bed.'

'I want to talk to you about something important.'

She glanced at the clock on the dash. The last thing she wanted to do was talk to Ian. But he had said it was important. It was probably about Evelyn. Or perhaps about the kids. Either way, she couldn't really say no. In turning down his suggestion of a monthly dinner date, she'd promised she would make herself available anytime to talk about the kids. And something about Ian's tone of his voice and his uncharacteristically scruffy appearance worried her. 'Okay.'

She knew something was wrong as soon as she stepped into the house. Unopened mail was stacked untidily on the half-moon hall table. And the carpet was stained with mud as if he'd let the kids walk in wearing their shoes. Raquel would have a fit when she came home and found grubby footprints on her pristine cream carpet.

He led the way through to the kitchen, and then sat down with his hands clasped together on the kitchen table, as if in prayer. Last night's dishes lay unwashed on the kitchen counter. The bin was overflowing. Something wasn't right. Concern for him began to grow. 'Where's Raquel?'

'Er, away ... but let's not talk about her.'

She slipped into a chair opposite Ian, fiddled with the car keys under the table, and waited.

'I was thinking of popping round this week to fix the tap. And I noticed last time I was round that the curtain pole above the kitchen window's coming off the wall. I'll fix that too. When would suit?'

She squirmed in the seat. 'Ian,' she said carefully, 'I don't want to sound ungrateful but I've been thinking about the tap and I really think it would be best if I got someone in to fix it.'

He laughed. 'You don't need to get someone in. You have me.'

'Still,' she said, meeting his sharp gaze.

The smile fell from his face. Her palms sweated. 'Well, if that's all you wanted to talk to me about, I'd really better be going.' She stood up.

'Don't go. Please,' he said.

He looked so miserable she sat down again and rested her hands on the table. 'What's wrong, Ian?'

He put his head in his hands. 'Raquel's left me.'

'What?'

He looked up and said flatly, 'She's moved out. Taken all her clothes and personal belongings. She says she'll be back for the furniture she paid for.' Sarah noticed a hole in the wall by the door and scuff marks on the otherwise spotless skirting board. Evidence of a fight?

'She can have it all, for all I care,' went on Ian, standing up and pacing up and down the room.

She put a hand on her stomach, tied up in knots. This was bad news on so many levels. 'Oh, Ian. I'm so sorry. What happened?'

But instead of answering her, he sat down abruptly and said, 'You and I should never have divorced, Sarah.' His eyes were watery, and there was a kind of jumpy energy about him that unnerved her. He ran a hand through his thin ginger hair. 'I don't know what I was thinking. We should've had more counselling. Or something.'

'We went to counselling for nine months, Ian, but it just wasn't to be.'

He smiled at her. 'The thing is, I still love you, Sarah. I want us to get back together.'

Sarah opened her mouth and stared at him in horror. Taking a deep breath, she tried to be kind. 'I care that you are happy, Ian. I couldn't be divorced from a better person. You're a wonderful father and a good son to Evelyn. I've always admired your integrity and your decency. But I don't love you.'

'Don't say that, Sarah. You loved me once.' He reached a hand across the table and she snatched hers away. He frowned. 'Surely you can learn to love me again? The way I love you.'

How could she tell him the truth? Ian's good qualities, and he had many, had never been enough to make her love him, not the way she had loved Cahal. Nothing before or since had ever come close to that. And she knew that nothing less could make her happy now.

'No, Ian.'

His face crumpled. 'Don't say that, Sarah. You have to give me … us … a chance.'

'I can't.'

'But these last few months we've been getting on so well. I thought –'

She stood up. 'If I've done or said anything to encourage you in thinking I wanted us to get back together, then I'm truly sorry.'

His face hardened and he stared at her, his blue eyes cold and accusing. 'It's because of Cahal Mulvenna, isn't it?'

Of course Vi must've told him that Cahal was back. The two of them were thick as thieves, always had been. 'How I feel about you has got nothing to do with him.'

His Adam's apple moved in his throat. 'I really care about you, Sarah. You know that, don't you?'

Reluctantly, she nodded.

'And I don't want to see you getting hurt. Or going against your family's wishes.' He paused and looked pointedly at her.

She bit her lip, counted to ten and squeezed the keys in her hand so hard one dug painfully into the palm. 'My family's affairs are nothing to do with you Ian. Not anymore.'

He sat back in the chair and regarded her for some time with a closed fist over his mouth, as if deciding something. At last he removed the fist and said, 'Do you know that Malachy Mulvenna, Cahal's father, has been in prison?'

She shrugged her shoulders dismissively. 'So what? Anyone can make a mistake, can't they? Everyone does things they regret. He was probably just young and foolish.'

Ian snorted, and shook his head in that knowing way of his that had always infuriated her. 'He was convicted of serious crimes, Sarah. Not petty ones. He served a long prison sentence.'

Sarah sat down again, trying not to show her surprise. Cahal had been vague about his father's criminal past but she was certain he'd told her the offences were minor, even though he didn't know what they were. Serious could mean any number of things. Drugs. Violent assault or burglary. Terrorist activities. Murder even. She shuddered involuntarily and said, 'Like what?'

Ian broke eye contact and looked to the left. 'I don't know the specifics.'

'And how do you know this?'

He stared at her, his eyes narrowed slightly, and she couldn't help but feel he was taking vindictive pleasure in telling her, 'I overheard my dad talking to yours once.'

'Well, maybe you … you misheard. Maybe he was talking about someone else.'

'I know what I heard.'

Sarah looked away. That might explain why Dad and Vi disliked Cahal so much. Dad had no time for anyone caught on the wrong side of the law and he had little faith in the redemptive power of the penal system. Once a criminal, always a criminal. A funny attitude for an ex-police detective, when you thought about it.

'It was years ago,' went on Ian, 'round about the time your dad found out about your fling with Cahal.'

She glared at him, hating the way he tried to belittle what she and Cahal had shared. 'Well, the father's sins aren't the son's. Cahal can't be blamed for what his father did.'

He sighed. 'You don't know what you're getting into, Sarah. You don't know the damage and the hurt you will cause your family if you persist in seeing this man.'

Sarah laughed. The situation was so ridiculous – her ex-husband telling her who she could and could not date. 'Well I've news for you, Ian. I'm a big girl and I think I'm old enough to make up my own mind.'

'You should make sure you're in possession of the full facts first.'

Anger rose inside Sarah. She'd let other people come between her and Cahal once before – she would not let it happen a second time. 'Look, the facts are these. Dad and Aunt Vi don't like Cahal because he's working class and he's a Catholic. If me seeing Cahal hurts them, it's because of their own snobbery and prejudice.'

'Please, Sarah,' he said, his voice catching in his throat. 'I'm asking you one last time. Please forget about Cahal Mulvenna and give us a chance.'

'No. Don't you understand, Ian? There is no *us*. You and me are over. Finished.'

A look of bewilderment crossed his face and then his features seemed to crumple in on themselves. She could not bear to look at him any longer. She stood up, took a step towards the door but was stopped in her tracks by a stifled sob. She turned. Ian's head was bent over the table, one hand over his face.

Filled with compassion, she went over, stood behind him and laid her hand softly on his broad shoulder. 'I'm sorry.' She stood like that for some long seconds until he composed himself.

'I think you'd better go, Sarah.'

'Do you want me to take the children?'

'No,' he sniffed. He shook off her hand and stood up. And looking at a space to the right of her he said, 'I'll be all right. Go, Sarah. Please. Just go, would you?'

Chapter 13

Sarah stood just inside the door of the pub blinking in the gloomy light. And then she saw him, sitting at a table for two, wearing a casual brown leather jacket over a grey T-shirt – the same understated style he'd always favoured. His jeans were blue and well-fitting, darker and smarter than the scruffy ones he used to wear as a student, and his tan had faded a little, making him look more like the old Cahal. They stared at each other, and though it could only have been for a few moments, it felt like forever to Sarah.

She went over and sat down opposite him.

'Thanks for coming,' he said.

Sandwiching her hands between her knees, she said, 'I guess this is our first date then?'

'It is. If you want it to be.' One corner of his mouth turned up in a half-smile and his blue-green eyes twinkled mischievously.

She stared into his eyes and grinned. 'Remember what I said. One step at a time.'

'Yes. And this is the first step, isn't it?'

'I guess so,' she said and, tearing her gaze away, added, 'So, are you all packed?'

'Yep. I'm on the red eye to London first thing. Then on to Melbourne.'

'It'll be odd knowing you're on the other side of the world. Getting up when I'm going to bed.'

'It's only for a fortnight. I'll be back soon.' He cleared his throat. 'What would you like to drink?'

'White wine please.'

He got up and went to the bar, the leather jacket, soft and buttery, skimming his slim hips. She wondered what had happened to his old jacket. She used to drape it over her shoulders sitting up in bed after sex, loving the way it smelt so strongly of him ... She ran her hands through her hair and pushed the image out of her mind.

He came back to the table with a glass of wine for her and a Guinness for himself.

'You might have stopped smoking but I see your tastes in beer haven't changed,' she observed, with a nod at the stout.

'Yours have,' he said sitting down. 'You used to hate wine. Your favourite drink was Babycham.'

She laughed. 'That's right. I don't know what possessed me. I couldn't drink it now. Too sweet and sickly.'

He picked up the glass and admired the thick, creamy head on the stout, 'Guess who I bumped into the other day in Belfast?'

220

'Hmm?' she said before taking a mouthful of wine.

He wiped froth from his upper lip. 'Anthony from uni.'

The shock nearly made her spit the mouthful of wine over him. She gulped it down, her throat feeling as if it had all but closed over. The drink settled halfway down her chest, burning a hole. 'Who?' she squeaked.

'You remember Anthony, don't you? I hung out with him a bit.'

She shook her head.

'You don't remember him? Blond curly hair, big nose.'

She shook her head dumbly, hoping that the dim lighting hid her reddening cheeks. What a stroke of bad luck for Cahal and Tony to bump into each other.

'That's odd. I could've sworn I introduced you.'

'You might have,' she said and shook her head. 'But I don't remember. It was a long time ago.'

He shrugged. 'That explains why you didn't mention that he was dating your sister, Becky.'

She tried to smile but it felt like stretching elastic, so she feigned surprise by placing a hand on her heart and opening her eyes wide. 'I didn't make the connection.'

'What a coincidence.'

With the moment of danger past, she smiled with relief.

Oblivious to her discomfort, he went on, 'He seems very keen on her. Told me they'd moved in together.'

Sarah tried to look indifferent. 'That's right.'

'He was some boy at uni,' Cahal chuckled in admiration. He supped some beer and wiped the creamy froth from his upper lip with the back of his hand. 'Quite the ladies' man.'

Sarah took a drink to hide her agony. 'What do you mean?'

'We used to joke that he could talk his way into any woman's bed. He's been married twice too.'

'I know.' Sarah gulped down another mouthful of wine and he said, 'Oh, I'm sorry, Sarah. That was insensitive of me. I got the impression he was really serious about Becky. You know what it's like when you really fall for someone? Well, that's how he seemed to me. Lovestruck. I'm sure she's the one to finally make him settle down for good.'

'Becky's really fallen for him.'

'I'm sorry,' he said again and reached out and touched her hand. Under his hot fingers, her skin tingled. 'I shouldn't have said that.'

She smiled thinly. 'It's okay. Really.' There was an awkward pause and she said, 'I've been thinking.'

He removed his hand. 'What about?'

'Something Ian said to me the other day about your dad.'

He leaned back in the chair and laced his hands across his flat stomach. His eyes narrowed. 'How come Ian got talking to you about my father?'

She twirled the glass of wine between her fingers. 'I'll tell you about that in a minute. But what I was thinking was … you know the way my dad and Aunt Vi were so set against you?'

'How could I forget?'

She inclined her head. 'Well, the thought occurred to me that it might have something to do with your father's prison record. Maybe him and my dad had a run in?'

Cahal folded his arms and shrugged. 'Maybe. But my dad

222

was in prison nearly half a century ago. You wouldn't imagine your father'd hold a grudge all this time.'

'You don't know him,' said Sarah. 'What exactly was your father convicted of?'

'Drunken assault, I think – he liked to drink back then; he was an angry man. Still is. And I think he got done for theft too. Nothing serious, just stupid.' He laughed, revealing strong white teeth and a pink mouth. 'He stole a bunch of TVs once. And another time he stole a delivery of tiles off a building site and was caught trying to flog them. What he didn't know was that they were a special one-off import from Holland. No one else in Northern Ireland was importing them at the time. Stupid bugger.'

Sarah smiled faintly. None of this sounded desperately serious. 'Nothing paramilitary, then?'

'God, no. The only cause my dad's interested in is his own.'

'You've never been arrested for anything, have you?'

He laughed at this. 'Not so much as a parking ticket. Maybe they don't like me because I'm a Catholic. Was a Catholic, I should say. I haven't been inside a chapel in twenty years.'

She shook her head. 'It's not that. Ian said something about hurting my family by seeing you.'

He said bitterly, 'Well, maybe it's just a case of good old-fashioned snobbery, me being from working-class stock and having a jailbird for a father.'

'I'm sorry,' said Sarah, looking at her hands. And yet she couldn't help but think that there was more to it than that …

Cahal took a long sip of stout. 'So, was Ian trying to talk

you out of seeing me too?'

She nodded. 'Yes. He wants us to get back together.'

His face paled. 'And do you ... is there a possibility ...'

'Oh, God, no,' she said quickly, keen to dispel any misunderstanding on this count. 'He just won't accept that I don't, and never will, love him.' She took a sip of wine and, emboldened by it, looked Cahal straight in the eye.

'But you must have once,' he said softly, his words cutting through her like a knife. 'You married him. You had his children.'

She closed her eyes in shame. She wanted to tell him the truth, but how could she when it reflected so badly on herself? And yet she had to make him understand. She opened her eyes and stared at a black-and-white print on the wall. 'I never loved him, not properly. I cared deeply for him and I believed that was enough. I thought that I could make a successful marriage out of respect and fondness. I'm talking only of my feelings, of course.' She braved a glance at him. He was nodding slowly, his eyes narrowed in concentration. 'Ian loved me. He still does. And to be honest, I don't know why.'

'I do,' he said and blushed.

She blushed too, momentarily lost for words, then gave him a sad smile. 'I don't deserve his love. I shouldn't have married him. My reasons for doing so were selfish. I wanted a family and I feared being alone. I couldn't return his love and I'm ashamed to admit that I made him miserable. And that was what destroyed the marriage in the end.'

He sighed gently and held out his hand across the table. Hesitantly, she reached over and he clasped her hand in both of his. Tenderly, he stroked the thin pale skin on her knuckles with a swarthy thumb. 'We all make mistakes, Sarah. I think you're being too hard on yourself.'

'Thanks for saying that.' She paused and stared at the back of his hand. The rhythmic movement of his thumb sent shivers down her spine. 'I'm going to miss you when you're in Australia, Cahal.'

'I know.'

She raised her eyes to his. His pupils had expanded into deep, dark pools. The roof of her mouth went dry.

He squeezed her hand, sending shivers down her legs. 'I'll be counting the hours till I come back to you, Sarah.' He leaned across the table till their faces were just inches apart. His warm, yeasty breath brushed her face. 'Every single one of them.'

Cahal pulled up outside the Edwardian timber house, partially hidden behind a cream stucco wall. It was autumn in Melbourne and the yellow fig leaves from the tree in the garden littered the pavement. Temperatures had plummeted in recent days and everyone complained of the cold, though back in Ireland where the weather he'd left behind was similar, the locals, declaring it summer, were running around half-dressed.

Compared to its bigger, moneyed neighbours, the house was modest but it was quaint too, pretty even, and Cahal was proud that he'd been able to provide his family with a home in one of Melbourne's most sought-after districts. But it wasn't his home now. It was Adele and Brady's. He tried not to resent it. He wished he could talk to Sarah. He pulled out his phone and looked at the time. She would be asleep now, waking soon to a new day.

He put the phone away, grabbed the brightly wrapped parcel and plastic carrier bag on the passenger seat and got out of the car.

'Dad! Dad!' called a child's voice, pulling at his heartstrings. Harry, tall and skinny in his school uniform, came barrelling towards Cahal and threw himself at him. Cahal embraced the child, only just managing to hold on to the parcel and the bag. Then he set them down on the pavement and ran his hands across the boy's bony nine-year-old shoulders and down his slender arms, feeling the shape and size of him as a blind man might.

'I missed you, son,' he said, tears welling up in his yes. He had not realised how much till now.

The boy sighed as if he'd been holding it in for a very long time. He threw his arms around Cahal's waist. 'I missed you too, Dad. I wish you would come home.'

The knife in his stomach turned. 'I will, son. Just as soon as this job's finished, I'll come home for good.'

Harry dragged Cahal by the hand into the large open plan kitchen and family room at the back of the house. As soon as he saw his father, seven-year-old Tom bounded over and jumped into Cahal's arms, clasping his hands around his father's neck and his legs round his waist. 'Daddy! Daddy!' he squealed, throwing his head back and giggling. Cahal held him tight and kissed his soft cheeks over and over until he wriggled to be free.

And when he released him, there was Jed, standing with

his hands in his pockets and sticky gel, a new development, on his dark hair. A gangly boy with too-big feet, and hands and arms beginning to muscle. A pang of regret pierced Cahal's heart. The door on Jed's childhood was slowly closing. Soon he would care more what his peers thought than his old man. And the siren call of women wouldn't be far behind.

'Happy Birthday, son,' he said, pulling Jed to him fiercely and kissing the top of his head. Jed's hands stayed in the pockets of his trousers but the boy leaned towards him, a subtle, yearning gesture that ripped at Cahal's heart. 'I missed you, Dad,' he said, his voice oscillating between the high pitch of his younger siblings and the deep tones of manhood.

'Hey you, want to stay for dinner?' It was Adele, standing barefoot by the cooker stirring something in a pot, her bare arms nut brown from the sun, her long dark hair loose in natural ringlets. She came over to him and they kissed each other on the cheek, friendly-like, if a little stiffly.

They'd met at an art exhibition fourteen years ago. He'd only gone because the company he worked for was a sponsor – and it was marginally better than sitting alone in his empty penthouse overlooking the Yarra River. He was no connoisseur of modern art, but her pictures, great canvases streaked with bold splashes of colour, had intrigued him. And so had she with her strong opinions, straight talking and exotic heritage – she was one-eighth aboriginal.

'Thanks Adele. I'd like that.'

Over on the sofa he handed out Irish rugby shirts, bags of Yellow Man and Tayto cheese and onion crisps, from Tangradee in County Down. Adele wandered over to watch and he said,

'I got something for you too, Adele.' He held out a large stiff envelope. A peace offering.

'Me?' she said, sounding surprised.

He nodded and she took the envelope. From now on, he thought to himself, he would make a real effort with her – and Brady. And he would stop resenting her. After they met at the art exhibition, it had all gone too fast. They'd dated, moved in together and she fell pregnant all within the space of six months. He'd done the right thing and, in doing so, condemned himself to a life with a woman he did not love wholly and fully.

She examined the little watercolour inside the envelope, a soft-hued scene of Carnlough Bay. 'A friend, Sarah, suggested it. It's by a local Ballyfergus artist.'

Adele smiled and said, 'Thanks. It's lovely.'

He sat with the boys while they tried on their rugby shirts and experimented with the crisps and toffee. Adele went over to the cooker and, after a while, he got up and followed her. 'I know it's been tough with my being away and you not getting a break from the kids.'

She shrugged, stuck a spoon in the pot and tasted the contents. 'Brady's pretty good with the boys. He helps out.'

Cahal swallowed the lump in his throat. 'Well, I don't take it for granted. I want you to know that.'

She nodded and said pleasantly, 'So, how's Ireland? Must've been nice to visit home.'

He paused to consider this. He had not thought of it as home. It was nice to see fields greener than anywhere on earth, to sup a good pint of Guinness and load up on an Ulster Fry.

228

And of course, there was Sarah. But home was where his boys were.

'The Sarah you mentioned, she's not *The* Sarah is she?' He'd told Adele all about Sarah when they'd first met. He later wished he hadn't. In the latter throes of their marriage, Adele had said it was like competing against a ghost.

He nodded. 'The very same.'

Adele's eyebrows rose a few centimetres on her forehead and she tapped the spoon on the side of the pot, then set it down. 'Are you back together?'

'Not exactly. We're sort of seeing each other. But ...'

'But what?'

'Oh, I don't know. She says she never received any of my letters.'

'That's odd. You wrote loads, didn't you?'

He nodded and Adele said slowly, 'And you don't believe her?'

'It's not that. I've just never quite forgiven her for putting her family before me. For not coming to Australia when I asked her. How do I know I can trust her?'

Adele frowned and folded her arms. 'We've been separated for how long?'

'Nearly five years.'

'And in that time, how many women have you dated?'

'Eh ... I've had a few blind dates. And more than a few one-night stands.'

'They don't count,' said Adele dismissively. 'But you do know the reason for that, don't you? Why you've not found a steady girlfriend?'

He shook his head stupidly. And she said, rather sadly, 'You've never gotten over her, Cahal. She was ... she is the love of your life, isn't she?'

He bit his lip and she smiled. 'Not many people get a second chance, Cahal. But it sounds as if you and Sarah have. Don't mess it up. We all make mistakes, and she was only a girl twenty years ago.'

He smiled his thanks, the lump in his throat making it impossible to speak.

'Is this for me, Dad?' Jed called out, holding up the present Cahal had brought with him.

Cahal swallowed. 'Yes, son. Happy Birthday. Go on, open it.' As he watched the boy turn it over in his hands, his eyes filled inexplicably with tears. His marriage may have been a failure but his sons were the greatest achievement of his life.

And then, to his dismay, the patio doors burst open and Brady came lumbering in, spoiling the moment.

'Hey, Cahal,' he said genially, filling the room with his sheer size and testosterone.

The doors crashed shut behind him. A former rugby league player turned high school sports teacher, he was blond and tanned and stood at six-foot-six. He must've weighed eighteen stone of hard-packed muscle. Tugging at the top button of his shirt with his huge hand – he never looked entirely comfortable in anything other than sports clothing – he tossed his briefcase on a chair like an envelope. He shook Cahal's hand vigorously, then looked at the parcel in Jed's hand. 'What's this, then?'

Adele went over to Brady, placed a proprietorial hand on

230

his chest and kissed him on the lips. 'Cahal's brought over Jed's birthday present. How was work?'

'Had to cancel the bloody after-school rugby fitness training again. Not enough turned up. Can't understand kids these days, Cahal,' said Brady with a heavy sigh, ripping off his tie.

Jed peeled the paper off the present and gasped.

'When I was their age all I wanted to do was play sport,' said Brady.

'It's an iPad!' cried Jed incredulously, holding up a sleek slab of grey metal and black glass, as thin as a magazine. He grinned, touched a button and the screen flicked into life. 'Oh, Dad, it's brilliant. I can't believe you got me an iPad.'

'It's the new one. Top of the range, son,' beamed Cahal.

Brady whistled. 'That'll have cost you big bucks.'

Cahal said, 'I thought you could use it for homework. You know, for browsing the web. As well as playing games, of course,' he added, not wanting to sound like a killjoy.

Brady sniffed, threw himself into an armchair and turned his attention to Cahal. 'Wanna sink some piss?'

Cahal bristled. He hated the crude way Brady spoke in front of his boys – his language belonged on the street, not in a family home. 'No thanks.'

Unperturbed, Brady shrugged his huge shoulders. 'Suit yourself. I'll drink with the flies then.'

'I'm driving,' said Cahal, a feeble apology for his terseness. He reminded himself that it was in everyone's interests, the boys' especially, if they all got on.

Brady smacked his lips together. 'Toss us a stubby, will ya, Adele? My throat's as dry as a nun's nasty.'

Jed sniggered and shared a secretive smile with Brady, sending a dart of jealousy straight through Cahal's heart.

'Brady!' said Adele in a tone that managed to be both remonstrative and indulgent at the same time. She retreated to the kitchen and Tom, who was hanging over Jed's shoulder staring at the iPad screen, looked up and said, 'What's a nun's nasty?'

'Nothing,' said Cahal coldly. Thankfully, Tom's attention was soon captured by the bright iPad screen once more.

'How are you getting on at school, Harry?' said Cahal, quickly changing subject.

'Okay.'

'Are you still in the top set for everything?'

Harry's shoulders sank and he shot a quick glance at his father. 'Everything but spelling. I'm in the second set now.'

Cahal frowned and Brady said, with a beaming smile, 'Did Harry tell you that he made the school swim team?'

Immediately Harry's body language changed. He sat up straight on the sofa with his hands sandwiched between his knees and smiled at Cahal.

'Harry, that's brilliant! Give me a high five.' They slapped palms and Cahal resisted the urge to return to the worrying subject of Harry's deteriorating spelling. 'Tell me all about it.'

Harry filled him in on the details – it turned out that he was swimming in a gala the very next day. 'I'll make sure I don't miss that,' said Cahal.

'When you come home, will you come and watch my basketball matches?' said Jed.

'Of course, son.' Cahal bent his head and picked the

discarded wrapping paper off the floor, rolling it into a ball as tight as his chest. His boys needed him so much. Their desire for his attention and approval was almost desperate.

Reality hit him square in the face. Even if things between him and Sarah worked out, how could they be together with families living on continents half a world apart? He looked at his children, his heart bursting with love for them, and knew he could never leave them. And how could he ask Sarah to come to Australia when it would mean taking her children away from everything they knew, and the father they adored? He tried to put himself in Ian's shoes – he tried to imagine how he would feel if Adele announced that she'd met some guy and wanted to take the boys to live thousands of miles away. He'd never allow it.

Adele came back with a small bottle of beer. She handed it to Brady, he tossed half of it down his neck and said, with a keen eye on the iPad in Jed's hands, 'You can watch all the rugby league games on that, Jed. You can watch sport all day.' He chuckled happily, like a big contented bear.

Tom came and sat on Cahal's knee, his tanned, bony knees sticking out from grey shorts. Cahal put a hand on his back and felt the heat of him through the thin cotton shirt. This wasn't how he'd wanted his life to turn out. It wasn't what he wanted for his children. And inside him, something broke.

'This feels very indulgent,' said Becky, staring at the opulent, faintly decadent surroundings of the champagne lounge in the Merchant Hotel, located in Belfast's Cathedral Quarter. Damask curtains framed the windows and light from the crystal chandelier bounced off the gilded mirrors onto the creamy-yellow walls. The carpet was black with a swirling gold pattern; the black velvet seats were low and wide.

Sarah sat opposite her sister in her best day dress. The square table between them was laid for afternoon tea with white china, a silver teapot, and napkins as stiff as the atmosphere between the two women.

'It's been a while since you and I spent time together. Properly. I've missed that,' said Sarah.

'Me too,' said Becky, with a small smile. 'I don't like it when things between you and me aren't right.'

'Me neither.'

Becky stared at the three-tiered tea stand between them on the table, groaning with dainty sandwiches, fat scones, and bright pink Parisian macaroons. In honour of the occasion, she'd donned a black mini skirt and a purple silk shirt that clashed marvellously with her red hair. 'You know, I don't think I've ever been anywhere quite so grand.'

'Well you deserve it!' Sarah, determined to lighten the mood and restore harmony between them, lifted a glass of champagne and smiled. 'Happy Birthday!' she said, and felt their mother's absence as sharply as a physical pain. She glanced at the ceiling, certain that she was watching over them like a kindly angel.

'Thank you!' Becky took a sip of the champagne, picked up one of the finger sandwiches and examined it. 'So how are you and Cahal getting on?'

'Slowly. I miss him.'

'He'll be back soon,' said Becky, taking a bite of the sandwich. 'Isn't it nice that he and Tony know each other? We'll have to organise a night out together.'

Sarah selected a white egg-and-cress sandwich from the display and set it on the dainty gold-rimmed plate in front of her. Changing the subject she said, 'I just don't know what to make of these letters. He says he sent them but I don't know if I can believe him. What happened to them?'

'Can't you just forget about them,' shrugged Becky, 'and start with a clean slate?'

'No, I can't. I have to know what happened to them. And I have to know if he made that phone call.' Sarah folded her hands on her lap. Becky lowered her eyes and mumbled, 'So what will you do?'

'I'll ask Dad and Aunt Vi when the moment's right. But I'm dreading it. What if they deny everything? Where does that leave me and Cahal?'

'I really don't know,' said Becky.

There was a long glum silence broken at last by Becky. She pointed at the untouched sandwich on Sarah's plate. 'Are you going to eat that, or admire it?'

Sarah laughed, picked up the sandwich and took a bite.

'I feel quite sorry for Ian,' said Becky, selecting a fruit scone and cutting it in half with a knife. 'He must've thought he was in with a chance and then along comes Cahal and blows all his hopes out of the water. Have you seen him since the night he told you Raquel had walked out?'

Sarah swallowed. 'Just to drop the kids off. But last night I saw Paula Dobbin in the supermarket and she heard, from her sister who works out at Carnfunock Golf Club, that Raquel's shacked up with Jim Proudfoot, the secretary there.'

'Oh my God!'

Sarah nodded grimly. 'Apparently they'd been having an affair for six months and, according to Paula, Ian didn't know a thing about it.'

'That's awful,' said Becky and she put a hand to her heart and said again, 'Poor Ian.'

'I know.' Sarah took a sip of champagne. 'Despite what Ian thinks, I never would've have got back with him. But I do feel sorry for him. He's having a crap time of it. His marriage is in tatters and his Mum's in a bad way.' Sarah set the cup down on the saucer and shook her head.

Becky frowned. 'How is she?'

'She's … she's dying, Becky.' Tears pricked her eyes. 'Her body's just slowly giving up. The doctors have done everything they can to make her comfortable but the children can't visit her anymore. It'd be too upsetting for them. And for her. She doesn't want them to see her like that.'

'Oh, Sarah. I'm sorry. Poor Evelyn.' Becky had known her as a kind family friend long before Sarah had married Ian.

'And poor Ian,' said Sarah. 'When she goes, he's going to be very much alone.'

Sarah finished off the sandwich, and they talked of happier subjects. 'Talking of birthdays, when's Tony's?'

'December. He'll be forty-three.'

Sarah dabbed the corners of her mouth with the napkin. 'There's quite an age difference between you then.'

Becky shrugged. 'So?'

'Well, it's just if you wanted to have a family, I mean, if you were thinking of having a baby in the next few years, he'd be quite an old dad.'

Becky looked in astonishment at her sister and laughed out loud. 'We're a long way from thinking about making babies, Sarah. Anyway, he's not old. And if I did have his child it wouldn't matter to me what age he was.'

Sarah smiled thinly and resolved to give it one last go with the most damning piece of evidence at her disposal. She leaned forward, rested her elbows on the table, and clasped her hands under her chin. 'I haven't wanted to say anything against him before, Becky, but Cahal told me he was a bit of a ladies' man at uni.'

Becky lifted her chin. Her eyelids flickered. 'What does that mean?'

'He's a womaniser. He hasn't exactly got a good track record when it comes to relationships, does he?'

Becky's eyes filled up and Sarah had to look away, feeling smaller than she'd ever felt in her entire life. She could have kept that nasty little piece of gossip to herself but she would do whatever she had to in order to protect Becky. Even if it meant hurting her.

Becky looked away and said thickly, 'That's a bit rich coming from a divorcee.'

'All I'm saying is tread carefully.'

Becky tossed her head and said defiantly, 'Tony's not going to hurt me. I trust him.'

Sarah smiled thinly. She was glad Becky had fallen in love. But why, oh why, did it have to be with Tony McLoughlin? 'I'm sorry I told you that.'

'Why did you then?' said Becky, touching the corner of her eye.

'I thought you should know, that's all. Look, let's not spoil our day together.'

'Let's not,' said Becky.

Sarah glanced at her watch. 'Why don't we finish off these goodies and then we'll hit the shops?'

'If you like,' said Becky without much enthusiasm. The day was tarnished and they both knew it.

Chapter 14

The warm spring had given way to a hot and sunny June. Aunt Vi had decided to throw an impromptu barbecue and everyone converged in the back garden on Sunday under a clear blue sky. Tomorrow, Cahal would return from Australia.

Sarah, in a printed cotton dress, was alone on the patio, the children and Becky were playing pig in the middle on the grass with a yellow tennis ball and Tony was over by the barbecue trading cooking tips with Dad.

Since she'd got to know Tony better, Sarah had come to the conclusion that he was a decent man. If she could just talk to him alone, if she could make him understand the terrible consequences of spilling the beans and make him promise to keep quiet, then maybe that was the best she could hope for. After some thought, she had decided that there was no reason to think he might tell Becky – or Cahal – but she had to be sure. Surely he would see that it was in everyone's interests to keep the past where it belonged?

Aunt Vi, in a long-sleeved shirt dress of white linen buttoned up to the neck, came outside carrying a wooden tray laden with condiments. She set the tray on the patio table and picked up a bottle of ketchup. 'So,' she said casually, though she was watching Sarah keenly out of the corner of her eye, 'are you still seeing Cahal Mulvenna?'

Sarah rolled a knife and fork up tightly in a white paper napkin. 'I see him from time to time, yes.'

There was a long, pregnant pause while Aunt Vi arranged ketchup on the table, along with onion relish, mustard and barbecue sauce. Then she held the empty tray across her chest and stood and stared at Sarah.

'What?' said Sarah, irritably.

'It's just … well.' Aunt Vi looked at the sensible walking sandals on her feet. 'You do know how your father and I feel about him?'

'I think I've got the message.'

'And you … you won't change your mind? About seeing him.'

Sarah sighed and looked out across the garden at Becky and the kids, red-faced and laughing. 'I really don't understand why you and Dad dislike him so much. I wish I'd followed my heart all those years ago instead of listening to you two.'

Without replying, Aunt Vi went inside to the kitchen and Sarah followed her. Gently, she closed the door on the shrieks of laughter outside and the two of them were alone. Aunt Vi glanced at Sarah, then lifted a packet of cheese out of the fridge.

Sweat pricked the back of Sarah's neck but her bare arms were cold all of a sudden and she had a bad taste in her mouth.

'Pass me a chopping board, will you?' said Aunt Vi, pulling a sharp knife out of the block by the cooker. Sarah turned around, retrieved a white plastic board from behind the bread bin and handed it to her aunt, who sat down at the table.

It was now or never.

Sarah took a step forward – and a deep breath. 'Cahal told me something very interesting.'

'Really,' said Aunt Vi. With a shaking hand, she cut an uneven slice of cheese off the orange block.

Sarah's mouth dried up with nerves. 'He said that when he went to Australia, he wrote many letters to me, none of which arrived.'

'Oh.' Aunt Vi placed the slice of cheese carefully on a small plate. 'Where did he send them?'

'Here, to this house.'

Her aunt paused momentarily with the knife hovering in the air over the cheese. Then she applied the knife to the cheese, her hand steady now, pressed down and another slice fell onto the board. 'And you believe him?'

'Yes.'

Aunt Vi snorted. 'Well, I think you're a fool. He'll tell you anything he wants you to hear. If he sent you all these letters, where did they go?'

'That's what I want to find out.'

'Well, I hope you're not suggesting that I had anything to do with it.'

Sarah cocked her head and stared hard into her aunt's clear, unblinking eyes.

Aunt Vi set the knife down on the table and shook her head, a look of incredulity on her face. She sighed loudly. 'Listen, Sarah. I can't believe that you're taking what this fella says at face value. Can't you see that he's ashamed of making promises he didn't keep and, now that his marriage's broken up, he thinks he can waltz back into your life and take up where he left off? With no regard, I might add, to where this situation is leading. Is he going to clear off back to Australia in a few months' time and leave you broken-hearted all over again?'

Sarah bit her lip and looked out the window. She could just glimpse Becky and the kids at the end of the long, thin garden, poking the compost heat with a stick. Smoke drifted across the grass. Hearing her aunt articulate her deepest fear made it even more real. Anxiety soared in her breast.

'This is how I see it, Sarah. If he has to tell a few porkies so he can have his fun while he's here, well clearly he's not above telling them.'

Sarah leaned on the table, her fingers splayed wide, the red polish on her nails like fresh blood. 'Someone's telling lies all right.'

Aunt Vi spoke quietly and calmly, without breaking eye contact for a second. 'You'd better be careful what you're saying, girl. Because you're very close to accusing me, or someone else in this house, of theft.'

Sarah stood up straight. 'That's right.'

Aunt Vi pushed her glasses up the bridge of her nose and this time her voice was far from calm and her hands on the table clenched into fists. 'I live by the Lord's word and I have never broken the law nor told anything other than white lies to protect the feelings of others.' The grey bun on the back of her head quivered. 'And if you think me capable of stealing letters, then quite frankly I'm disgusted with you.'

Sarah stared at her aunt, shocked, her heart pounding in her chest and her cheeks flaming with colour. She stepped away from the table and placed a hand on her throat. It wasn't the fact of her aunt's denial that came as a surprise – she could have rationalised the hiding of letters as an act of kindness to 'save' Sarah from the clutches of a terrible Mulvenna – it was the vehemence and utter conviction with which she defended herself that surprised Sarah. And left her feeling hurt and confused.

'There was a phone call too,' said Sarah. 'Cahal rang here and a man answered the phone. He said he would pass on the message that he had called and his number. Of course, whoever it was never did pass on the message to me and the rest is history.'

'And I suppose you're accusing your father?'

Sarah looked at the floor.

The back door opened. Dad came in, opened the fridge and peered inside. 'Seems I'm a little redundant. Tony's got the barbecue well in hand.'

'Sarah's got something to ask you, David,' said Aunt Vi, folding her arms.

He closed the fridge door. 'Oh, what's that?'

Sarah took a deep breath. 'Did you take any letters Cahal sent me from Australia?'

243

'There weren't any letters, love,' he said gently.

Sarah held on to the back of a chair. 'Can you answer the question please?'

He glanced at Aunt Vi, frowned and shook his head. 'No, I never took any letters.'

'And did you take a phone message for me from Cahal shortly after he went to Australia?'

He shook his head, glanced at Aunt Vi and sighed sadly. 'I always told you that fella was no good. I know you want to believe in him.' He placed a hand, solid and sure, on her shoulder. 'But don't you know a lie when you hear it?'

The door burst open and Lewis came running in all red-faced, his just-clean-on clothes covered in grass stains. 'Tony says he's ready for the cheese now, Aunt Vi.' Dad's hand slipped from Sarah's shoulder, though she felt the weight of it still, pressing down like a vice.

Aunt Vi smiled at Lewis. 'Just coming, darling.' She picked up the knife, expertly shaved off a few more slices of cheese and transferred them to the plate.

Molly appeared in the open doorway, wearing pale blue shorts and a multicoloured strappy top. 'Tony says can you bring plates out please?'

'Sure thing,' said Dad, handing the cheese to Lewis. 'There you go, son.' Then he lifted a stack of blue plastic plates off the counter and walked outside without so much as a glance in Sarah's direction.

Later, when everyone had eaten and the sun had moved round, casting a chilly shadow on the patio, Dad stood up and called to Molly and Lewis who were both lying on the grass in the sun, squinting at the sky. 'Who fancies an ice cream from the corner shop?'

Lewis jumped up immediately. 'Me!' he cried and ran over to his grandfather's side.

Molly hauled herself to her feet and brushed grass off her long, slim legs. She sauntered over to the patio and slipped her feet into a pair of turquoise flip-flops. 'Okay.'

'Becky,' said Aunt Vi, 'why don't you help me clear up?'

'Sure,' said Becky, standing up and stacking plates.

Sarah picked up a dirty glass but Aunt Vi said, coldly, 'It's okay, Becky and I can manage.' Becky frowned quizzically at Sarah and Tony said, rolling his sleeves up, 'I'll wash up.'

'No you will not,' said Aunt Vi, all sweetness and light again. 'You were slaving over that barbecue for ages. Anyway, more than two people in that kitchen and you can't turn around. Why don't you go and explore the garden properly? There's a pretty little wild area down there on the right full of primroses.' In order to make the garden look less like a tunnel, Dad had planted hedges and bushes at various points across the lawn, creating the illusion of width – and several secluded spots such as the wild flower garden.

'I'm no gardener but I'll happily take a look,' said Tony and he wandered off. Aunt Vi took the glasses inside and Becky hissed at Sarah, 'What did you say to upset her?'

'I'll tell you later.'

Sarah was none the wiser about the letters but watching Tony disappear behind a laurel fence, she decided she might salvage something from today.

In the kitchen she grabbed the white plastic container – a

245

two-litre milk carton with the lid cut off – filled with apple peelings, two egg shells and some wet teabags. 'I'll just put this on the compost heap.'

'But I emptied it only this morning,' protested Aunt Vi.

'It needs doing again. It'll go all smelly in this heat,' said Sarah and went outside, before her aunt could pass further comment.

She found Tony crouched in front of a white cabbage butterfly that had settled on a flower. He stood up when he felt her presence and the butterfly flew off over Mrs Riley's fence, zig-zagging like a drunk.

'Sarah,' said Tony and he shoved his hands in the pockets of his chinos and looked at the toes of his scuffed suede loafers.

Sarah looked nervously towards the house, over the hedge. She could see only the upper windows of the house, which meant that they could not be seen from either the patio or the kitchen. But she only had a few minutes. Dad and the kids would be back soon. And Becky or Aunt Vi could appear at any moment.

'We need to talk,' she said briskly. 'I'm sorry to be so abrupt, Tony, but we don't have much time.' She glanced at the house. 'I'm really worried that Becky will find out about … you know. I got a terrible shock when you walked into that party.'

'You're telling me. Becky told me she had a sister called Sarah but how was I to make the connection? I never knew you were from Ballyfergus. You shouldn't have pretended not to know me when we met at that party.'

'I know. I saw straight away that it was the wrong thing to do. Why didn't you say something?'

'Well, excuse me for trying to save you embarrassment. Perhaps I should've blurted the whole story out.'

She took a step towards him and placed a hand on his chest. 'Oh no, you mustn't ever do that, Tony. We can't undo what's done.' They both looked at her hand at the same time and she snatched it away. 'But you must never tell Becky. She would be so hurt.'

He looked away and pulled a grim face, fair curly hair falling in front of his eyes. 'I love her, you know.'

'I know you do. And she loves you, Tony. You do understand that she can never find out, don't you?'

He stared at her for a few long moments, then nodded slowly. 'Yes.'

'Swear that you will never tell anyone. And we'll never talk about this again.'

'Okay. I swear.'

She let out a long loud sigh and placed a hand on his arm. 'Thank you. Thank you. You don't know what it means to hear you say that.'

'I think I do.' He smiled. 'You're a great sister, Sarah.'

Sarah's face coloured once more. He thought her motive a selfless one but it wasn't. She glanced at the container in her hand. 'I'd better go before someone comes looking for me,' she said and slouched off.

Cahal answered the door of his temporary home in Grace Avenue, wearing jeans and a red checked lumberjack shirt. Sarah smiled, her stomach full of butterflies. 'How was Australia?'

'Oh, Sarah, I missed you.' He hugged her there, on the doorstep, and she closed her eyes. A small tear trickled out the corner of her right eye. Why did she feel as if she had to choose between him and her family? Why couldn't she have both?

'How were the boys?' she said, pulling away and discreetly flicking the tear away.

'Great. But it was hard leaving them.' His brow furrowed. 'I tried really hard with Brady but ...' He let out a long sigh. 'Let's put it this way, I don't think we'll ever see eye to eye. We're just too different.'

He closed the door and led her into a lounge with red flock wallpaper on the walls and a swirly green carpet. She said, 'Did Adele like the picture?'

'She loved it. Really. Anyway, how have you been?'

She smiled weakly, sat down beside him on the green velvet sofa and stared into his eyes. His countenance was so open, his eyes so clear and unblinking. Was it really possible that he had lied to her? 'I asked my aunt about the letters. She said she never took them.'

'I see. Well, she's hardly going to admit to it, is she?' he said, without breaking eye contact.

Sarah was first to look away. 'I asked my dad too. And he said he never took them either.'

'And the phone call?'

'He denied that too.'

Cahal bit his bottom lip and waited. She sniffed and wiped her nose with the back of her hand. 'I believe they're telling the truth.'

There was a long silence. 'And I'm not?' he said.

'I didn't say that,' she said quickly. 'It's possible something else happened to the letters, isn't it?'

'Like what? And who else could've taken the phone call?'

'I don't know,' she said glumly, and looked at the palms of her hands.

'Are you forgetting just how much your father hated me back then, Sarah? And probably still does. Even decent, moral men can be corrupted by hate.'

Her stomach was a ball of nerves, like tangled Christmas tree lights. 'I don't believe my father is one of those men. I don't believe he would lie to me.'

'I feel as if you're choosing them over me. Again.'

'That's not true!' she cried and her bottom lip quivered. 'I'm here now, seeing you, aren't I, against their wishes? Do you have any idea how hard that is for me?' She took a deep breath and said sadly, 'I don't have the answers, Cahal. All I know is that they're telling the truth. Please don't be angry with me.'

'I'm not angry with you, darling. I'm angry with them. For breaking us up in the first place.'

'But they didn't, Cahal, did they?' A single tear slid down her right cheek. 'I did that all by myself.'

'Don't cry, Sarah,' he whispered, wiping the tear away with his forefinger. He pulled her to him and held her tight. 'You were only a girl. It was expecting too much asking you to stand up to them.'

'But it was my fault, Cahal,' she said into his chest. 'It was my fault I lost you.'

It was June 1992. Sarah sat on the bus headed for Ballyfergus with her head full of the promises she'd made to Cahal – and her heart full of fear. She'd persuaded him that breaking the news of the engagement to her family before the exams was a bad idea. The ensuing uproar would be too much of a distraction.

'I'll tell them as soon as the exams are over. I promise,' she'd said, clinging to him in the darkness of the night. In her heart she knew she could put it off no longer. She knew he was hurt and his rising resentment was pushing them apart, a dark cloud over their happiness.

And now the exams were finished and she had no more excuses. Only the dread that grew with every mile the bus travelled, bringing her closer to Ballyfergus. She stared out the window and tried to calm her frazzled nerves. It had rained on and off all day but now the clouds had broken up and late afternoon sun bathed the lush green fields and the white-washed cottages, lending everything a golden hue.

Cahal had offered to come with her but, in anticipation of her father's reaction, and her aunt's, she turned him down. This was something she must do alone. Cahal made telling them sound so simple but she knew it would change her relationship with them forever.

She'd tried to tell them before, but this time it was different. The Claddagh ring she'd worn constantly on her ring finger for the past six weeks filled her with courage and reminded her that she was an adult now, free to make her own choices in life. So why, by the time the bus pulled into town on Friday teatime, did she feel so nervous she thought she might vomit?

Aunt Vi had gone to a lot of trouble. 'I've made your favourite, Sarah,' she said, wiping her hands on her apron.

'Homemade chicken and leek pie.'

They all sat round the small square table, Dad and Aunt Vi facing each other, Sarah facing Becky. Sarah feigned relish as she forced down the food, each mouthful tasting like mud, her right temple pulsing with pain. She asked Becky about her week at school and enquired after Mrs Riley and smiled tolerantly when Aunt Vi complained about a new recruit to the choir who couldn't sing. No one listening would've known that her heart beat so fast her ears were ringing with it. Or that her stomach felt like it had been turned inside out. When they were all finished eating and the plates had been scraped clean, Sarah knew this was the moment. She opened her mouth to speak but the muscles in her jaw refused to co-operate.

'Can I go and watch *Brookside*?' said Becky.

Sarah grabbed a glass and took a long drink.

Aunt Vi, sitting on Sarah's left, tutted. 'You know we don't like you watching that rubbish, Becky. It's not suitable for a girl your age.'

'Maybe we can find something suitable for everyone to watch,' suggested Dad. He put his hands on the table and started to ease himself out of the chair.

'I've made apple crumble for afters,' said Aunt Vi.

'Oh, thanks Aunt Vi! Can we have it in front of the TV?' said Becky hopefully.

'You know we eat at the table, love, not in front of the TV,' said Aunt Vi, not unkindly.

Sarah dug her nails into her palms and almost shouted, 'Actually, I've something to tell you all.'

'Oh?' said Dad and he eased himself back into the chair.

Aunt Vi pushed her plate away.

Sarah glanced at Becky for support but, bored already, she was idly kicking the table leg with the toe of her plimsoll. She was only a kid.

Sarah tried to recall the preamble she had so carefully prepared on the bus journey home. But staring into her father's calm blue eyes, her mind went blank. Time passed and she felt Aunt Vi tense. She always anticipated bad news, and this time she would not be disappointed. 'What is it, love?'

Sarah turned to look at her aunt's grey eyes, magnified behind the wire-framed glasses perched on her nose. Then she looked back at her father and remembered what Cahal had said to her boarding the bus. 'Remember how much I love you, Sarah. And no matter what anyone thinks or says, we are meant to be together. Don't ever forget that.'

Her heartbeat slowed and she felt a growing warmth in her stomach. 'I'm engaged to Cahal Mulvenna.'

Becky's eyes opened wide and she clapped her hands and cried out, 'Oh, Sarah's going to get married. And I'm going to be a bridesmaid!'

Sarah smiled thinly. But the silence that followed this outburst was the most deafening she had ever heard. Aunt Vi clasped her hands together on the table and bent her head. Her knuckles went white. Dad stared at his sister, then touched his right eyebrow with his index finger, the muscles on his face all working at once. Becky, sensing the awful atmosphere, stared at the table and bit her bottom lip.

The warmth in Sarah's stomach turned to ice. She tried to recall Cahal's image and feel his touch, knowing that it would give her strength. But she could not bring to mind his face and all she felt was fear.

Dad spoke first. 'Becky, go and watch the TV.'

She slid off the chair. 'Don't I have to help clear up the dishes first?'

'Not tonight,' he snapped, without looking at her. She gave Sarah a woeful glance and slipped quietly from the room. Sarah's heart sank as the door closed behind her little sister. With her only ally gone, she felt like a lamb to the slaughter.

'How long have you been engaged?' said Dad, his head quivering as if he had a touch of Parkinsons.

She lifted her chin. 'Six weeks.'

'Where's the ring, then?' said Dad scornfully, with a sharp glance at Sarah's left hand.

'In the pocket of my jacket.' She'd slipped it off before the bus reached Ballyfergus. That had been a mistake. It made her look like a coward and undermined her credibility.

Aunt Vi blew air out of her nose, lifted her head and gave Sarah a filthy look. 'I can't believe you've done this. And without even telling us, David. What kind of man would enter into an engagement without asking for your father's permission first?'

Sarah steeled herself. 'Why do you think he didn't ask? We knew you'd never agree to it.'

Aunt Vi went on, addressing Dad, 'He hasn't even got the decency to come here and face us himself.'

'He wanted to come but I told him not to. Do you think I'd ask him to sit here and listen to you two denigrate him and his family, just because they're working-class Catholics?'

'Sarah, please,' said Aunt Vi, softening. 'You're too young to understand.' She glanced at Dad. He lowered his eyes and Aunt Vi said, 'If you marry him, it will be a disaster for you and your family.'

'No it won't. I love him and he loves me. And it'll only be disaster for you and Dad if you refuse to accept him.'

'Sarah,' said Aunt Vi sadly, 'we can never accept him into our family.'

Sarah fought back the tears. 'Yes, you can. Just give him a chance. I promise you, if you get to know him, you'll like him. No one could help but like him. Cahal's parents have met me. Why can't you meet him?'

Aunt Vi's face went red and Sarah said, 'Dad?'

'Ian Aitken doesn't like him,' he said, sitting upright in his chair, his rigid physical posture akin to his moral one.

'What's this got to do with Ian?'

Dad inclined his head a little. 'He's a trusted family friend, Sarah. He's simply trying to look out for you. And I consider his judgement very sound.'

'He's trying to break me and Cahal up,' said Sarah angrily. 'Not because he's concerned about me, but because he wants us to get back together.'

'You could do a lot worse,' said Aunt Vi.

'Oh, for heaven's sake,' snapped Sarah. 'Why are we talking about Ian?' Taking a moment to compose herself, she ran a hand through her hair. The anger made her both brave and surprisingly calm, in spite of the way her left leg jiggled under the table and a muscle in her cheek twitched uncontrollably. 'You've both made your feelings perfectly clear. I'm sorry that you can't be happy for me. But we're going to get married this summer and there's nothing you can do to stop us.'

She stood up. Her legs felt like jelly and, though the room was only a few paces wide, the kitchen door seemed like a long way away. She started to move towards it, praying she would make it to her room without collapsing. She was shaken but she'd stood her ground. Cahal would be proud of her. The sooner she and Cahal were married the better. 'Sarah,' said her father's voice, freezing her to the spot.

She turned and stared at him. She should've known he would not let it go at that. 'Come and sit down.' His voice was quiet and, unnervingly, utterly devoid of emotion.

She obeyed, as her heart sank into the boots she'd travelled home in and still not taken off.

Once she was seated at the table again, he stared straight ahead. 'I'm not going to discuss this with you, Sarah.'

'There's nothing to discuss. I've made my mind up.'

He dismissed her comment with a blink of his eyelids and carried on as if she had not spoken. He still treated her like a child and, infuriatingly she still acted like one sometimes. 'As long as I'm paying for your education and you're living under this roof, you'll do as I say. You are to break off this engagement and promise never to see Cahal Mulvenna again.'

She opened her mouth in astonishment. How could he do that to his own daughter? He couldn't possibly be serious. 'You can't do that.'

'Don't think for a minute that I don't mean it. If you don't do as I ask, I'll throw you and all your possessions out of this house and we'll see how long you last on your own.'

She felt empty inside as if her guts had been hollowed out. Her own father would do this to her? She stared at his square jaw and rigid back and realised that he meant every word. But she would not let him blackmail her. She thought of the long hours Cahal spent working in The Anchor bar, the awful digs he lived in, how he had to be so careful with money. But if he could do it, so could she. Her cheeks burned with indignation. 'I'll get a job to supplement my grant. Lots of people do it. I don't need your money.'

He stared at her coldly. 'Do this, and I will make sure you never see your sister again.'

Appalled by this, she hesitated, glanced at her aunt's unreadable face and said, 'You can't stop me seeing her.'

'So long as she's a minor, I can stop her doing anything I want.'

Sarah gasped. Becky, whom she loved as much as Cahal, was just twelve years old. How could she bear not seeing her for years to come? She stared at the door through which Becky had just exited, but it wasn't Becky she saw in her mind's eye. It was her mother in that hospital ward and the words of her promise rang inside her head. Much as she loved her father, he had never been a hands-on Dad and he left the raising of his children to Aunt Vi. She did her best, but she was too strict and old-fashioned and she got more and more paranoid with each passing year. Without Sarah to moderate her aunt's controlling tendencies, Becky's life would be hell.

Hot tears sprang to her eyes and curses sprang to her bloodless lips. 'You evil bastard,' she cried. Aunt Vi put her hands to her mouth and Sarah stood up knocking her chair over in the process.

'Don't you dare use that –' began Aunt Vi but Dad shook his head, and that was enough to silence her.

She stared at her father's immovable face, her legs almost buckling beneath her, and waited. But he just sat there implacable as a cow chewing the cud and said nothing more. Sarah's gut felt like it was spilled. Her dreams fell about her in tatters, all her brave words and heroic plans crushed to smithereens under the boot of his ultimate authority. Her situation was impossible.

Three weeks later she stood on the Nun's Walk, a dramatic cliff path on the southern edge of Portstewart Bay. Cahal put his arms around her shoulders and pulled her close, but his embrace gave her no comfort, no respite from the torment that was tearing her apart. She shivered involuntarily though she wore a jacket and the June evening was warm and pleasant.

Far below the safety railing the sea crashed against the rocks throwing up furls of white froth and a light breeze blew in from the west. Behind them the white walls of the Dominican convent rose straight into the sky, as forbidding as any fortress.

'I love you, Sarah,' he said into her hair, as the setting sun, orange as a glowing ember, touched the edge of the horizon.

'I love you too,' she said but her voice sounded disconnected, unreal, and her heart was numb.

He released her and took a step back. 'Don't do this, Sarah. Don't hold back on me.'

He was wearing his waiter's uniform of black trousers and white shirt, his leather jacket on top. Now that his exams were over, he'd started a second job waiting tables in the Strand

Hotel and worked fifteen hours a day. He said he could go without sleep, so long as he had her.

'We've been over this a hundred times,' he said, his tone somewhere between irritation and despair. 'You can't let him blackmail you. Even if he means it now – and I'm betting it's just a bluff – he'll mellow once we're married and he realises there's nothing he can do about it.'

'You don't know my father.' She had never seen him back down, or change his mind even in the face of evidence that he was wrong.

He sighed. 'It's nearly the end of June. Your lease on the flat runs out next week.'

'I know,' she said quietly, thinking of Becky's pale, round face at the window as she'd walked away from the house the morning after the row, bag slung over her shoulder.

'Look.' He grabbed her hand. 'Let's just do it and then nobody and nothing in the world can ever keep us apart. You can move in with me straight away. I know my lodging's not up to much but we'll find something better.'

Her whole body shook. Slowly, she slipped her hand from his grasp and stared down at the rocks below. The sheer drop was terrifying – and inviting. For the past weeks she'd barely slept, and every waking minute her thoughts went round and round in circles, ending up exactly where she had started. Her father was immovable. If she stood on the other side of the railings and let go, all this would be over …

'What do you say, Sarah?'

'I can't. Not yet. I have to sort this out first.'

'But how?' exclaimed Cahal. 'He won't speak to you – or

me.'

'What?' Her head snapped up.

He looked a little sheepish. 'Last weekend when I said my Ma was ill and I had to go and see her, well, she wasn't ill. I went to see your father.'

'And?'

'He told me that if he ever saw me on his doorstep again, he'd call the police. Then he slammed the door in my face.'

Sarah clawed at her cheek with bitten fingernails. She was proud of him for braving her father, but she could've told him it would be utterly pointless. Once David Walker had made up his mind, he was like a runaway train going downhill. 'Why didn't you tell me?'

He shrugged. 'Didn't seem like much point. I didn't want to upset you.'

But to Sarah it was a defining moment. Her father would never budge, not while he was in this mindset, not while he felt like his back was up against a wall. But maybe there was another way.

'I have to do what my father says. I have to finish with you.'

'What?' he cried and his eyes blazed with fury.

'For now. Let's have the summer apart and I can use the time to persuade him to change his mind.' Her father was pig-headed and stubborn, but so was she. There must be some way to get through to him. Maybe she could work on Aunt Vi first. She'd never married, but surely she must've loved? If she could win her over to her cause, maybe they could both change Dad's mind. But even as she internalised these thoughts, the task seemed unreachable, like scoring a hundred per cent in an exam – possible in theory only.

His nostrils flared and his chest rose and fell like a bellow. 'No Sarah, you finish with me now and it's over.'

He turned abruptly and stormed off in the direction of Portstewart and she called out, 'Please, Cahal, just give me more time. I'm sure I can win him round ...'

He stopped.

'Somehow ...' she added, pathetically.

He turned to face her and took a few steps. His fists were clenched into tight, white balls. 'You're nineteen years old, Sarah. Do you have the courage to face up to your father, once and for all?'

She looked at the ground. She had faced up. And she had lost. He didn't understand. She was the linchpin of her little family, holding it all together. What he was asking was impossible. She could not leave Becky. For she could never be happy knowing that she had.

'I thought not.' There were dark rings under his eyes. Black stubble shadowed cheeks that had grown thin. 'I thought you loved me,' he said in a broken voice.

Her eyes stung but no tears came. There were none left. 'I do love you.'

His eyes burned. 'Then marry me.'

She stared into his eyes – and she blinked first. 'I just need more time, Cahal.'

The fire went out of his eyes, and his face hardened. He looked at her with a mixture of disgust and rage. Then he turned and started to walk away.

Her heart beat so hard it hurt. 'Please, Cahal. Give me more time,' she screamed. But he put his hands to his ears and simply carried on walking.

She watched his back, shoulders squared with resentment, disappear round a bend in the path. And on the horizon, the sun, now burning red like hell itself, slipped below the horizon and the light was gone.

Chapter 15

'It wasn't your fault,' said Cahal's voice, bringing her back to the old-fashioned furnishings of Grace Avenue.

'You thought it was,' she said, sadly.

He took her hands in his and stared at them for some moments before looking into her eyes, the muscles in his right cheek pulsing. 'Well, I was wrong, Sarah.'

A tear pooled in the corner of her eye and spilled down her cheek.

He let go of a hand momentarily and wiped the tear away. 'I hate to see you cry.'

But the tears came unchecked now, a relief after all these years. 'I should've told my father to go to hell.'

He let out a long sigh. 'What if your father had carried out his threat? What if he'd barred you from seeing Becky for all those years? I don't blame you for choosing her. But it was a choice you should never have been forced to make – by me or by him.'

'I was scared. Of him and of losing Becky.'

'I know.' He pressed her hand to his lips. He smelt of beer and citrusy aftershave she did not recognise, and underneath that, the unmistakable earthy scent of him. He stared deep into her eyes. 'It's true. I did blame you for breaking us up. But I see now how unfair that was of me.'

'And I blamed you for being so stubborn.'

'I *was* stubborn. Maybe if I had stayed around, things would've worked out differently.'

Salt and pepper curls brushed the collar of his shirt. Her hands felt small and safe in his. 'I wish we had our time over again. I'd do things differently.'

'So would I.'

The dark stubble on his light brown skin made his face look thinner, his blue-green eyes more vivid. 'But we can't, can we?' she said.

'It's true we can't go back and change what happened.' His lips parted to reveal the little sideways tooth she had always loved. 'The past is what it is, Sarah. But it doesn't have to govern our future.'

She broke eye contact. She wanted him more than she'd ever wanted anything but all she could think about was Tony. How long could she trust him to keep his mouth shut? And then there was Cahal's family on one side of the world and hers on the other. Last time it had been her father who stood between them. This time it was vast oceans and continents.

'What?' he said.

'I know it's defeatist of me but maybe it's too late for our happily ever after.'

He squeezed her hand tight. 'I've been thinking that too. But you know what, Sarah? It's never too late. In fact I think you and I are looking at the start of a fairy tale, not the end.'

Her heart leapt but just as quickly fell again. 'But we've carved out lives on different sides of the world. How –'

'Sshhh,' he said and touched her lips with the tip of his finger, sending a little shiver down her spine. 'Don't let's talk about that now. Do you still love me?'

His grip on her hand was tight and hot. She could feel the pulse of the blood in his veins. Her heartbeat quickened. 'Yes, with all my heart.'

His grip loosened a little and he grinned, a smile so wide and so open, it filled her up with happiness. 'And I still love you. Don't think of the past or worry about the future. It's our destiny to be together, Sarah. And this time we will be. Somehow.'

He leaned in and kissed her, and it was like fireworks going off inside her head, eclipsing all the doubts. She oughtn't to get involved with him. It was too complicated. Too messy. But she couldn't help herself.

He led her along the dark corridor by the hand. In the bedroom he kissed her again. His touch was like a spark, lighting up her insides. Tentatively, she slid her hands under his shirt where it was warm and hot. He kissed her harder, cradling the back of her head in his hands, pressing his fingers into her skull. Becoming bolder, she worked her fingers across his shoulder blades and her hands, travelling downwards, found the small of his back and then his firm buttocks. She moved against him, oblivious to everything but his solid body pressing so exquisitely against hers.

When they parted at last he kissed her nose and she said, slightly breathless, 'Well, that much hasn't changed.'

He threw his head back and laughed. In the soft orange glow of the setting sun, he looked like the old Cahal, when they thought the world was theirs.

'You're still the best kisser,' he said.

'Kissed a lot of women, have you?' she teased and he chuckled.

'A few. But none that ever came close to you.'

She slipped her hand inside her coat pocket and pulled out the Claddagh ring. 'I brought this to give back to you.'

'My grandmother's ring!' he exclaimed, his face lighting up with surprise and pleasure. 'You still have it? I thought you might have thrown it out when we lost touch – or when you married Ian.'

'I would never have thrown it out.' She placed it gently in the centre of his palm and though she knew it was the right thing to do – the ring was not hers after all – she felt bereft.

He picked it up between finger and thumb and examined it. 'You've looked after it.'

'I kept it in a box in the bottom of the wardrobe. I never told anyone about it. Only Molly's seen it and that was by accident.' She paused, remembering all the dreams and hopes the little ring had once encompassed. Swallowing the regret, she smiled. 'You should have it back. I've had it too long.'

'No, I'd like you to keep it. I want you to wear it. I mean, if that's what you want too.'

A jolt went down her spine. All her senses tingled and she stared stupidly at him, unable to speak.

'Do you remember the promise that came with that ring?' he said.

How could she ever forget? *One day it will seal our marriage, Sarah.* 'I remember.'

'I still feel the same way about us. Nothing's changed for me.' Gently, he clasped her right hand in his and held the ring up between them.

She looked into his eyes, dark and gleaming and her heart unfolded like the blooms of morning glory that grew by her back door.

He slipped it onto the ring finger of her right hand, the point of the heart facing in. She imagined the veins and arteries channelling the love towards her heart, filling her up with so much joy, her body ached. It felt so right to have the ring on her finger once more. Her life had come full circle, back to Cahal, the place she never should have left.

'Hey, where've you been?' said Sarah, when Becky came into No. 11, the pub they always went to on Quality Street. 'I've been trying to get you since Sunday but you didn't reply to any of my calls or texts.'

'I've been busy.' Becky looked at her watch and threw her bag on a chair. 'I haven't got much time. What did you want to see me about?'

'Well, let's get a drink first,' said Sarah, a little put out by Becky's brusqueness.

When she came back from the bar with two glasses of wine,

Becky was still sitting in her coat. 'Bad day at work?'

'I had to stay late and sort out the mess the new guy made of the monthly reports.'

'I think you're wasted in that office.'

'So do I. Thanks for the wine,' she said, lifted the glass and took a long drink. She set the glass down and rubbed her hands. Sarah regarded her thoughtfully. 'Are you all right?'

'I'm fine. Why wouldn't I be?'

'I dunno. You just seem a little ... grumpy. Have you and Tony fallen out?'

'No.' Becky's eyes flashed warningly. 'Me and Tony are absolutely fine.'

'Okay.' Sarah took a sip of wine.

'So, what was so important that you couldn't wait to tell me?'

Sarah inched forward on the seat, anxious to share recent events. 'At the barbecue on Sunday I asked Aunt Vi and Dad about the letters and the phone call. They both denied knowing anything about them. In fact, Aunt Vi was really offended. You know what she's like. The thing is, I believe she was telling the truth. And Dad.' She sighed and ran a hand through her hair. 'So where does that leave me and Cahal?'

Becky stared at her long and hard. 'Frankly, Sarah, I couldn't care less.'

'What?' said Sarah in astonishment.

There was a long, unbearable silence. 'I saw you, Sarah. In the garden at Dad's. With Tony.'

Sarah froze and then her heart went ka-thump, ka-thump so loudly Becky must've heard it. 'Oh that,' she said casually, unable to maintain eye contact. 'We were just … talking. What about it?'

The muscles across Sarah's chest tightened until it hurt. Becky, her eyes full of tears, shook her head. 'I saw you … I saw you put your hand on his chest and on his arm. I know what's going on, Sarah. I'm not stupid. I've put two and two together.'

'You have?' Sarah swallowed and hung her head. Oh God, her lies and deceit had been discovered. How could she ever forgive herself for hurting her little sister? She looked up sheepishly, her hands shaking in her lap and said, 'What did Tony say?'

'Oh, Tony's far too decent to drop you in it. He said you were just talking. But I could tell he was trying to protect me from the truth.'

Sarah frowned, a little confused. If Tony hadn't told Becky, then how did she know?

'I should've known from the start,' blurted out Becky. 'From the minute you met Tony you acted weird. You were all formal and polite, not exactly unfriendly but reserved in a way I've never seen you before when meeting new people. At first I thought that you just didn't like him. And then the other day at the Merchant Hotel, when you tried to talk me out of seeing him, I started to suspect the truth. But I didn't want to believe it. I couldn't believe that you would do such a despicable thing.'

Sarah stared at Becky, dumbfounded. What was she talking about?

'But it all adds up, doesn't it? When I saw you run out into the garden, I went upstairs and watched from the landing window. You went straight to him, not the compost heap.'

'What adds up?'

'Oh, don't give me that, Sarah. You're jealous that I've finally found someone I love and who loves me. You're trying to break us up because you're jealous. Just because you and Cahal can't make it work.'

Sarah stared at her in astonishment. 'No. No. You're wrong. That's not it at all. Me and Cahal … we've sorted things out. Look. He gave me this ring to wear.' She thrust out her hand. 'I spent last night with him.'

But Becky did not look at the ring. 'You were trying to get Tony to dump me, weren't you?'

'No, of course not!'

'Then tell me why you went looking for him in the garden? And what did you say to him?'

Sarah broke eye contact yet again. How could she convince Becky without telling her everything? Becky might hate her now, but she'd hate her more, and Tony too, if she found out the truth. 'All I care about is your happiness, Becky. You must believe me.'

Becky glared at her. 'What did you say to him?'

Sarah opened her mouth and closed it again. She struggled desperately to come up with a plausible explanation but her mind went blank. 'I can't tell you that.'

Becky stood up and grabbed her bag. 'I would never have believed you capable of jealousy, Sarah. I thought I *knew* you. I thought if there was one person in the world I could trust it was my own sister. But it turns out I was wrong.'

*

Cahal turned up for work feeling like he'd the hangover from hell, though he'd not had a drop to drink the day before. His mouth was dry and he'd bags under his eyes.

'It's the air con in the plane,' said Jody sagely, perching her trim bottom on his desk. 'They re-circulate the air, spreading everyone's bugs about. You've probably caught something.'

'Thanks, Jody.'

She laughed and picked up a pen. 'So, how are things between you and Mrs Aitken? You two are always sneaking off to have cosy lunches together. The whole building's talking about you.'

Remembering what they'd done in his bungalow the night before, he rubbed his chin in an attempt to hide his smile. 'I'm sure they're not. I'm sure they've better things to talk about.'

'You'd be surprised.' Her smile faded. 'Well, I don't blame you.'

'Huh?'

'I'd have an affair to spice up life a bit,' she said, casting a disparaging glance at a bald man with middle-aged spread walking past. 'But you're the only decent man in the place and you're taken.'

'You don't mean that, Jody.'

'Sure I do. We're a long way from home. Why not have a bit of summer fun, when you can?'

Something in her tone jarred and he said, 'Sarah's not a bit of summer fun, as you put it.'

Jody laughed again. 'Course she is.' She paused, set the pen down on his desk and fixed him straight in the eye. 'She's got two kids and an ex-husband here. And you've got three kids and an ex in Melbourne. If you're telling me that this is more than a short-term fling, then tell me exactly how you plan to make that work?'

He blinked, then said coldly, 'I've work to do, Jody. I'm sure you have too.'

She gave him a smile that looked like a lot of effort, then sauntered off. And the rest of his day was spoilt.

Work was a nightmare and there was no opportunity to slip away at lunchtime and meet Sarah for the rest of that week. It wasn't until the weekend that they saw each other again. They went for an early supper at No. 11 and then decided to walk out to Ballygally along the Coast Road. He held her hand all the way, marvelling that she was his again. But while she chatted away he could not help but notice that she was preoccupied, distant. He couldn't seem to connect with her the way they had done the other night. Just beyond the Black Arch they stopped to stare at the lapping waves crashing into the Devil's Churn – a cave where, legend had it, a drunken piper went in to explore and never returned.

'Tell me about your trip to Australia,' she said. 'Were the boys pleased to see you?'

He tucked a lock of hair behind her ear. 'Very much so. It was awful leaving them, though.' Tom had clung to him and sobbed till Cahal thought his heart would break and, when he locked eyes with Jed, leaning against the wall with a studied nonchalance, he saw a look of resentment in his eyes that he had never seen there before. Harry had been stoic and brave but, when he gave him a hug, his little body was shaking all over. 'It nearly broke my heart. And it made me realise that I can't do this to them again.'

Her hand went limp in his. She stared at him, the vast blue sea framing her face, the wind blowing in her hair.

'I miss them too much,' he said. 'And I can see how much my absence hurts them.'

Sarah nodded grimly and, slipping her hand from his grasp, shoved it in the pocket of her pink fleece.

'Brady's not a bad sort of bloke,' he went on, 'and he'd never be unkind to them, but all he thinks about is beer and sport. He's not a bad influence but, well, the boys need their father. I don't want them to grow up strangers to me.'

Sarah bit her lip and there was a long silence. 'What are you saying, Cahal?'

He swallowed and forced himself to go on even though each word felt like a betrayal. 'I'm saying that I won't leave my boys, Sarah.' She flinched and he had to look away. 'They need me. As much as I need them. I …' He looked at the ground. 'I couldn't live with myself if I did.'

'More than you need me?' she said and when he looked up, her face was pale and stricken.

He grasped her by the shoulders and squeezed. Her bones felt small and fragile. 'No, not like I need you. I need you like I need air in my lungs and blood in my veins. But I need them too, Sarah, in a different way. And they so desperately need me. I could never be happy, knowing that my actions have made them miserable.'

Sarah gave him a sad smile. 'I understand how you feel, Cahal, and I respect you for it.' She stepped closer and stroked his face with her hand, as gently as if he were a wounded bird. 'If you felt any differently, I wouldn't love you the way I do. And though I love and adore you with all my being, I would never leave my children for you either.'

'Oh, Sarah. If only we'd made it the first time round. If only we hadn't let other people tear us apart.'

He pressed his forehead against hers and they stood together like that for a long time, as cars roared past and the sun sank behind the Antrim hills. It was nearly the end of June. He was more than halfway through the contract. In three short months he would have to return to Australia. 'Do you think ... would Ian ever agree to the kids moving to Australia? I mean if you would consider it, that is?'

She gave a little sob. 'I would, if it was the only way we could be together.' She took a deep breath and shook her head. 'But I can't see Ian agreeing to it. He adores those kids and for all his faults, he's a good father.' She paused and said, without much hope in her voice, 'There's no way Adele and Brady would consider moving here is there?'

He shook his head. 'Adele only visited once and she hated it. And Brady's a dyed-in-the-wool Aussie. He's never even been out of the country on holiday.'

'I see.'

'Will you ask Ian?'

She lifted her head and stared at him with sad eyes. 'I'll ask him, Cahal. But what kind of a man would let his ex-wife take his kids to the other side of the world? And what kind of a woman would take them away from the only father they've ever known?'

He had no answers. He just held her tight and looked out at the deep blue sea, his eyes stinging with unshed tears. Ian Aitken hated him. And he could not help but ponder, with wonder and dismay, how it had come to pass that his greatest enemy held the key to his happiness.

Cahal grasped a handful of weeds with his gardening glove, loosened the roots with a trowel and yanked them out of the flower bed. He tossed them on the growing pile behind him on the lawn and wiped his brow with his forearm. It was a futile task, of course. He would not be here in a few months' time, when the front garden would again become overrun, but the simple physicality of the chore appealed. It was what he needed to soothe his troubled mind. If only he could root out his problems and cast them aside just as easily.

He stood up and surveyed the patch he'd just cleared and a sense of misery overcame him. He never should've come to Northern Ireland, not without thinking through the consequences of what might happen. He knew Sarah was divorced. He should have realised she would have kids. If he'd only stopped for a moment to consider the difficulties they'd face, he might never have pursued her. For now she was hurting, and he was the cause of it.

Weeks had passed since their walk to Ballygally and they were no further forward. Sarah had yet to put the question to Ian, but he knew in his heart what Ian's reply would be. They both did. That was why Sarah had not broached the subject with Ian, and it was why he had not pressed her. While that shred of hope remained, they could pretend, clinging to each other in desperate throes of love-making, that they had a future, that somehow it would all come good. But time was running out. The change management programme was running horribly to schedule and the team were scheduled to return to Australia in mid-September.

The thought of having to wait until all the kids were independent before he and Sarah could be together broke his heart. He could not imagine living another decade, or longer, without his darling Sarah by his side. They'd already missed out on the best twenty years of their lives. With a flash of bitter rage he threw the trowel across the garden. It clattered against the garden fence and disappeared amongst a thriving patch of nettles.

A car screeched to a sudden halt on the road and Cahal turned to look, shading his eyes in the evening sun. The driver's door burst open and a tall, well-built man leapt out, leaving the car door open and the keys dangling in the ignition. The man marched down the gravel drive and across the lawn towards Cahal, anger and determination etched into his familiar features. It was Ian, his hands clenched at his sides. He came to a halt and glared at Cahal. Cahal glared back, refusing to be intimidated.

'I want to talk to you,' said Ian, the anger in his voice barely controlled.

The muscles in Cahal's body tensed and he squared up to Ian, planting his feet a shoulder-width apart on the dry grass. 'Fire away.' Ian glanced at the house and Cahal said, with a nod at the ground, 'Here's as good a place as any. Say what you came to say.'

'You put her up to this, didn't you?'

'What?'

'She just asked me if I would let her take Molly and Lewis to Australia. For good. So that you and she can play happy families.' The skin just above his collar went red and spread upwards until his freckled face was crimson and his pale eyes bulged with rage under almost transparent eyebrows. 'Well, I've news for you and I don't care who hears it,' he roared.

Across the street, a man watering his hanging baskets put down his watering can and leaned on his garden fence.

'I will never ...' Ian bared his teeth and struggled to contain his rage before going on. 'Those children are my life. No one is taking my children away from me. Do you hear? No one.'

'I'm sorry,' said Cahal, shame engulfing him. He could not blame Ian for his reaction. If anything, he had reacted with admirable restraint in not decking Cahal on sight. 'We had to know.'

Ian's shoulders sagged a little and he exhaled long and loudly. And when he spoke his voice was calmer and quiet. 'Well, now you do.' He turned and started to walk away and, then, thinking better of it, came back. 'Jesus Christ, did you think I'd say yes?' His eyes filled with tears, whether of rage or sorrow, Cahal could not be certain. 'Did you think I'd let you have my children? They're all I have left in this world.'

Cahal swallowed the lump in his throat. He had never before felt so ashamed.

Ian sniffed, wiped his nose on the back of his hand and said with a tone of utter contempt, 'Why don't you just get on a plane and go back where you came from? No one wants you here.'

He looked up quickly. 'If Sarah tells me she doesn't want me, I'll go.'

'Sarah?' Ian gave a hollow laugh. 'Can't you see that all you've done is cause her misery and heartache? She left my place in tears.'

Cahal's heart leapt. He must go to her.

Ian went on, 'We were on the verge of getting back together before you came on the scene. And now you've ruined everything.'

Cahal stared at him in astonishment. 'She was never going to get back with you, Ian. She doesn't love you. She loves me.'

'Don't tell me what Sarah feels. You don't know anything about us.' Ian stabbed at the middle of his chest with his forefinger. 'I'm the one she married, Cahal.' His voice rose to a crescendo, like a minister delivering an impassioned address. 'I'm the one who gave her children. No power on this earth can break the bonds between us.'

Cahal stared open-mouthed. Ian had clearly deluded himself into believing this fantasy and yet, in spite of his aggressive manner, Cahal felt a wave of incredible sympathy for him. 'She divorced you, Ian,' he said calmly. 'You had your chance and you blew it. You cannot make her happy because she does not love you.'

'And you think you can?' said Ian, sizing him up and down with a look of disgust on his face. 'You might have set yourself up as a fancy consultant but you don't fool me. I know who you really are, Cahal Mulvenna.' He shoved his face in Cahal's. Sweat beaded his brow and his breath was stale. 'You're nothing but a low life with a benefit sponger for a father who crawled out of the Drumalis estate. Oh, don't look at me like that. Sure he's been dragging that leg round behind him for decades but there's nothing wrong with it when there's a bet to be placed or a drink to be had, is there?'

Cahal stared at him coldly, refusing to rise to the bait. He may not feel much in the way of love for his father, but he still felt loyalty.

'I'd be careful what you say about my family, Ian.'

'I'll say what I like because it's true. He's not just a sponger, he's a liar and the worst sort of criminal.'

Cahal shrugged, determined not to let Ian see that he had got to him. 'He stole a bunch of TVs and got in a few fights. So what? He served his time. He paid the price.'

Ian nodded his head slowly. His eyes narrowed and what came out next was injected with pure venom. 'You think the time he served was justice for what he did? You think he deserved to go free after just five years to carry on his life where he left off, when other people's lives were ruined? Well, I'll tell you what would've been justice. He should've hanged for what he did.'

Cahal felt like all the blood had pooled in his feet. He could not move, he could only stare in horror at Ian's vengeful face with white spit on the centre of his bottom lip and burning hatred in his eyes.

'What are you talking about?' he eventually managed to blurt out. But, by then Ian was halfway across the lawn. Across the street, the man picked up his watering can and scurried inside.

Chapter 16

Ian sat in the car outside the nursing home in the golden sunshine of a fine late July evening, and took long, deep breaths until the blue veins on his wrists stopped throbbing and his heartbeat slowed. He checked his appearance in the mirror, straightened his tie and wiped the sweat off his brow with a folded paper hanky. He must not let Evelyn see him upset. He would not trouble her with his worries.

A month had passed since Sarah had asked him if he'd give permission for her to take the children to Australia and, even though it had not come as a surprise, he was still furious about it. He knew from Vi that Cahal had an ex-wife and three kids in Australia, but there was no talk of uprooting *his* kids and taking them away from their mother. Of course Cahal wanted it all his way.

Sarah had looked thoroughly ashamed of herself when he'd told her he would never give up his kids. And now he worried that Cahal was planning some other way to get what he wanted, maybe through the legal system. Everyone knew it was stacked against fathers. Hadn't he read only the other day about a similar court case where the judge ruled in the mother's favour and permitted her to take her child to the US against the father's express wishes?

He took a deep breath and resolved to put them out of his mind. He must concentrate on Evelyn. The doctor had said it could be a matter of weeks now. He tried to tell himself, as she herself had done, that she'd had a good and happy life and her death would be no more than the next step in the natural order of things. But he could not accept it. He lived each day on edge, dreading it every time the phone rang and lying sleepless in his bed at night, rigid with fear.

Evelyn was just as he'd left her the day before, lying with her head propped up just slightly, her eyes closed and her lips slightly parted. Jolanta, who was sitting by the bed when he came in, got up.

'Any change?' said Ian fearfully.

'No. She just the same.' She placed a hand on Ian's shoulder and a little of the fear subsided. 'She seem a little unsettled to me. She keep asking for you.' She touched him lightly on the arm then left, closing the door behind her.

'Hi Mum. It's me,' he said, taking the seat Jolanta had just vacated. He watched her for a few moments then placed a kiss on her papery brow.

Evelyn's eyes flickered and opened. She turned her head towards him and the muscles in her cheeks worked but didn't quite manage to produce a smile. 'What time is it?'

'Eight thirty at night, Mum.'

She frowned. 'Have I slept all day?' Her brow smoothed again and the thought was gone. 'When did you last come and visit me?'

'This afternoon.'

A long pause. 'Oh. Don't you have to go to work?'

He smiled, his insides all twisted up like knotted rope. 'Not today, Mum.' His employers had been incredibly understanding. He'd barely been in the office the last fortnight, working mostly from home and spending as much time as possible by his mother's bedside.

'Your face is thin. Are you eating properly?'

'As well as I ever did,' he said truthfully. Raquel had rarely cooked and the kindness of near-strangers kept him going these days. 'The women from the church are determined I shan't starve. I found a shepherd's pie on my doorstep this morning. Nearly tripped over the darned thing! And yesterday it was Irish stew. Emily Ferguson made that.'

Evelyn sighed, a substitute he thought for the smile that would no longer form on her face. 'People are so very kind.'

'Yes, yes they are,' he said, dropping the pretence of humour. He glanced at the table against the wall, crammed with flowers and cards from well-wishers. 'And I appreciate it.'

'I'm glad Raquel left,' said Evelyn.

He looked at the floor. He was glad too but it seemed terribly disloyal and shallow to say it, so he kept quiet.

'You love Sarah.'

He looked at her unreadable face. Her eyes had closed again. Was he that transparent? 'What makes you say that?' he said, playing for time because he wasn't quite sure how to respond to this. He wanted his mother to die peacefully, untroubled by worries about him.

Her eyes flickered open. 'I see the way your eyes never leave her when she's in the room, Ian. You look at her like she's the sun. You always have done.'

'Let's not talk about Sarah and me.'

'I want to.'

'Oh.'

'You do love her, don't you?'

It was pointless to deny it. She would know he was lying. 'I've loved her from the first day we met.'

'I'm sorry. I wish I could wave a magic wand and cure you of it, of her. But I can't.'

He laughed lightly. 'I don't wish to be cured of Sarah, Mum. I'm going to win her back.'

She sighed. 'You do know she's seeing someone, Ian. An old sweetheart.'

Ian frowned. Sarah must've told Evelyn because he certainly hadn't. 'I know. But it won't last,' he said confidently. 'It can't. She's still my wife.'

'Ah.' A long pause. 'She might be in your eyes, Ian, but not in hers. Nor in the eyes of the law. She divorced you. And she loves this man Cahal.'

Her words struck him like darts. 'Did she tell you that?' What was Sarah doing talking to Evelyn about another man?

'She didn't need to tell me. The facts speak for themselves. In seeing him, she's going against the deeply held wishes of her family. Yet, she's happier than I've ever seen her and she wears his ring on her finger.'

Ian swallowed. He'd seen the ring too, a symbol of owner-ship, and he hated it. 'She'll tire of him and I'll find a way to win her back.' He shuffled forward in his seat and lowered his voice. 'When I was growing up you always told me that nothing was impossible. That if I really, really wanted something, there was always a way.'

Her chest moved rapidly up and down, her breathing was shallow and laboured. 'Not in affairs of the heart, Ian,' she said quietly and the hope that he had kept alive in spite of the events of recent weeks, began to falter. 'Sarah cares for you, but she doesn't love you. And even if she and Cahal cannot be together, she will never love you the way she loves him.'

The truth of this statement struck him like a slap in the face. Sarah had told him herself, of course, but he'd refused to accept it. But hearing it from his mother, whose wisdom and counsel he had always valued, was devastating.

He put his hands over his face and his resolve crumpled. He wept, for his dying mother and for himself. Soon he would be all alone in the world. And the two women he had loved the most would be lost to him.

He sobbed for a few long minutes and then wiped his eyes with the back of his hands, ashamed of himself for bringing his sorrow to his mother's bedside.

'All I ever wanted was to make her happy,' he said. 'Why won't she let me? Oh, what am I to do, Mum?'

She reached out a hand and he took it gently in his own. Her skin was dry, bones showing beneath pale, transparent skin. 'You must take joy in the good things in your life, Ian. Find things to be grateful for, like your darling Molly and dear, sweet Lewis.'

He grasped her hand a little tighter. It seemed so frail, so insubstantial. Was this the same competent hand that he remembered from his childhood? The firm hand that had kept him safe crossing roads, whipped cream till it peaked in soft crests, and rubbed his wet hair with a rough towel when he came out of the bath? 'I will, Mum.'

'And if you love Sarah the way I believe you do ...' She paused to rest and he leaned closer. When she spoke again, her voice was barely audible. 'Take joy in her happiness, even if it comes at the price of your own.'

Cahal walked up the steps to Ballyfergus library on a wet Saturday morning and snuck inside like a thief, the collar of his jacket turned up, his hands thrust deep in his pockets.

Even since Ian had paid him that visit he'd been unable to put what he had said about his father out of his mind. At first he dismissed it as spiteful gossip, but the more he thought about it, the more he thought it had a ring of truth about it. Could it hold the key to why Sarah's family hated him so much?

He only found out that his father had been in prison at all, when Uncle Vincent let it slip one New Year's Eve when he was nine. When he asked questions, thinking this might be something to boast about at school, he was told in no uncertain terms to shut up. So how did Ian know, for example, that his father had served five years? And who were the people Ian had alluded to, whose lives had been ruined? Were they victims of his father's crimes? Had he accidentally hurt someone in a blundering burglary or robbery? Or was it more serious than that? Ian had said he should've been hanged. Had his father killed someone? A chill went down his spine even though the day was warm and muggy. No, that couldn't be it. He would've served a lot more than five years if he had.

Inside, the matronly librarian with a head of wild salt-and-pepper curly hair smiled radiantly when he approached the counter.

'I rang earlier about looking at old papers,' he said and she stood up.

'That was me you spoke to. Follow me please.' She led him to a bank of computers in a quiet corner of the library, trailing the way in a floor-length floral skirt and open-toed walking sandals. 'We have *The Ballyfergus Times* going back more than a hundred years. Have a seat and let me show you how to access it.'

He sat down and, leaning over him in a cloud of jasmine, she cradled the mouse with her right hand, necklaces jangling between her breasts. 'All you do is click on the year you want, like this,' she said, clicking on 1970. 'Then the month and then the date and *voilà*, up it comes!'

'That's great, thank you,' he said with relief, as she stood up and folded her arms. She watched him tentatively move the cursor round the screen. 'What year do you want?'

He did a quick mental calculation. 'I want to start with 1952.' His father turned eighteen that year. And if he had been convicted of a serious crime, surely it would've been reported in the local papers?

'Those papers were originally stored on microfiche, which was subsequently converted to computer. So they won't be the best quality.'

'I'm sure they'll be just fine,' he said dismissing her with a polite nod of the head, anxious to get cracking.

He waited till she disappeared then clicked on the first edition of the year. He put a hand over his mouth and stared at the front page. Someone had died in a car crash on the icy roads. There were plans to expand the port terminal creating fifty new jobs. On the next page, letters to the editor complained about bus services, pub closing time and the dilapidated state of the town parks. He skipped to the court pages, full of reports of drunken brawls, petty thefts and an assault on a policeman. But no mention of Malachy Mulvenna.

He searched all through that year and the next, by which time hours had passed, his head was sore, and he was hungry and thirsty. He leaned back in the chair and letting out a long sigh, dragged his hands down his face.

It was a hopeless task. What was he looking for? A crime that may or may not have taken place decades ago. It was like looking for a needle in a haystack. And did he really believe the word of Ian Aitken, a man who hated his guts?

He glanced across the library, quiet save for a few well-behaved youngsters with their mums and old-age pensioners sitting in red bucket chairs, reading the paper. The table from where he had once spied on a teenage Sarah was now gone, replaced by racks of children's books.

He stared at the bookshelves, seeing once again the back of her blonde head, the slope of her shoulders, the curve of her neck. What would happen to him and Sarah now? Ian's refusal to let Sarah take the children to Australia felt like the final nail in the coffin of their hopes. As the summer waned, there was a kind of desperation between them. It was as if they were going through the motions of building a relationship that they both knew was doomed. Because once September came, he would have to go back to Australia and she would have to stay here. He did not think he could bear to lose her a second time. Anger at Ian, at her family, at God Himself, rose up in his chest. He had never asked for much – only Sarah. Why couldn't he have her?

'Researching a bit of family history?' said a voice behind him and he snapped his head round. It was the librarian, standing with a pile of books in her arms, smiling.

'Huh?'

'That's why most people want to look at old papers.'

'Well, I wonder how they get on.' He folded his arms across his chest and said crossly, 'Because this morning's been a complete bloody waste of time.'

She bristled. 'There's no need for language like that,' she said coldly. 'I came to tell you that we're shutting for lunch in five minutes.'

'Oh, thanks. Sorry,' he said sheepishly, collected his jacket, and went out onto the street.

He found a takeaway place at the top of Main Street and ate a greasy kebab, sitting in the car while he pondered what to do next. He couldn't do anything about the terrible predicament he and Sarah found themselves in, but he could do something about Ian's accusations against his father. He could find out if they were true. Of course he knew what he must do, he just didn't want to do it. He put the key in the ignition, shoved the car into first gear and drove off.

He was surprised to find his elder brother, Sean, sitting on his parents' sofa, smoking roll-ups, looking as thin and badly dressed as any of the down and outs on the corner of Victoria Parade and Smith Street back home. He'd visited him in Carnlough a couple of times, where he lived alone, eking out a living as a farmhand, supplemented by a bit of poaching and lobster fishing on the side. Though he loved his brother, or perhaps because of it, the visits to his squalid room above the chippy had been depressing affairs. The vast age difference between them ensured they had nothing in common, except a shared hatred of their father.

The two men shook hands. Sean said, 'What about ye?'

Malachy, sitting in the same chair, and wearing the same clothes as last time with a folded paper on his lap, said, 'Look what the cat's dragged in.'

Cahal tensed and Bridget came scurrying into the room, brushed Malachy's knee lightly with the feather duster she'd had in her hand when she opened the door, and laughed. 'Ah, now don't be teasing him, Malachy.' She smiled rigidly at Cahal, willing him to go along with this pantomime. But this time he didn't feel in the mood for playing her silly games.

'Oh it's all right, Mum. I'm used to him behaving like an arse.'

Bridget gasped and Malachy glowered.

Cahal sat down on the sofa beside his brother, crossed his legs and stared coolly at his father. 'You've never said a civil word to me my entire life. No point in breaking the habit of a lifetime.'

'Tea?' said Bridget in a voice so high it might have broken glass.

'Yer all right, Ma,' said Sean, lifting the mug off the arm of the sofa and bringing it to his lips.

'No thanks,' said Cahal.

'So what brings you here, son?' said Bridget perching on the arm of the sofa, the duster in constant motion, held by hands that could not be still. 'Did you bring those photos of the kids from when you were over?'

'Sorry, Mum, I forgot. I'll bring them next time.'

'You'll be going home soon,' she said quietly, looking at her hands.

A wave of panic made him tense. Time was running out and he hated to be reminded of it.

'I hear you've been sniffing round that Walker woman,' said his father. He took a puff on the cigarette between his yellow-brown finger and thumb. 'I thought you'd have more sense.'

Beside him, his mother's hands stilled. And something in the atmosphere shifted.

Cahal leaned forward, his hands resting on his knees, and he said, 'What were you in prison for?'

Malachy's eyes darted to the left, then at Bridget and finally came back to rest on Cahal. 'This and that. Sure, I was a head case when I was young.' He tapped ash into the glass ashtray on the arm of the sofa and took a last, long haul on the cigarette. 'I did a bit of time for theft and breach of the peace. Not that it's any of your business.'

'Breach of the peace?'

'That's right. Man picks a fight with me in a pub, he's not going to get away with it.' He pressed the spent cigarette into the ashtray, twisting and squeezing till it was a pulp.

'Theft and breach of the peace. And you expect me to believe that they gave you five years for that?'

'Who told you he got five years?' said Bridget sharply.

'Doesn't matter,' he said, and sensing he was onto something, he pressed on, keeping his eyes on his father. 'You don't get five years for petty crimes like that.' He inched even further forward on the sofa, his heart pounding. 'What did you really do?'

'I fecking told you,' said Malachy and he threw the newspaper on his lap across the room. 'Are you fecking deaf?'

Malachy was lying, he knew it.

'Do you know, Sean?' said Cahal without taking his eyes off his father.

'Nah. Why are you asking?'

'Because,' said Cahal, staring at his father's red and furious face, 'I think he did something he doesn't want us to know about.'

Bridget jumped to her feet all of a sudden and screamed, 'How dare you come into this house and start accusing your father of ... of lying.'

Everyone stared at her in stunned silence. She waved the duster in the air. 'Didn't he tell you it was for theft and fightin'? You've no right coming in here, throwing lies around and digging things up from the past.' And then just as suddenly all the fire went out of her and she sat down.

'Do you hear your mother?' Malachy roared. 'Get out of here, Cahal. And don't be bringing your filthy mouth back here again.'

Down on the street Cahal found his car untouched. The rain had stopped and the sun, peeking between grey, bubbling clouds, sent up hot steam from the black tarmac. A group of teenagers loitered at the end of the street, their winter hoodies exchanged for singlets and tattoos on red, sunburnt arms and necks. He raised a hand and one of them returned the gesture.

'Cahal!' said Sean's gravelly voice. The door to the building slammed shut and Sean came down the steps.

Cahal opened the car door and put his arms on the roof of the car. 'What did you think of that then? There's something he's not telling us, isn't there? And I'm going to find out what it is.'

Sean glanced up at the windows of the flat, then grabbed Cahal by the forearm. His grip was firm and his eyes pooled with tears.

Alarmed, Cahal said, 'What is it?'

'You did the right thing getting out of Ballyfergus, Cahal, boy. I'm proud of you, my wee brother.' He smiled. 'You're the only one of us that did good, Cahal.' His grip tightened. The back of Cahal's throat felt like it was closing over. 'Go back to Australia,' went on Sean, 'and live the life the rest of us dream about. Live it for me. Forget about them.' He looked again at the top-floor flat. 'There's nothing for you here.'

Cahal stared into his brother's face but he saw not a haggard, broken man but a thirteen-year-old boy with blond hair and an angry, pure heart. A boy who had stood up to his father to protect Grainne, when she'd accidentally smashed the TV screen with a wooden sword, only to take the beating himself. A boy who'd started smoking at ten and drinking at twelve, all his promise withered by the age of eighteen.

Tears flowed freely down Cahal's face but he did not wipe them away. He pulled a wad of notes from his jacket pocket and pressed them into Sean's hand. 'See that Ma gets what she needs,' he said, his voice small and reedy. 'And you too.' Sean let go of his arm and stared at the money.

'I'm sorry, Sean,' said Cahal, his voice choked with years of regret and guilt. Then he got in the car and drove off.

Chapter 17

Sarah opened her front door on a balmy Saturday night and Cahal immediately scooped her up in his arms and kissed her like she'd been gone a month instead of a week. She clung to him, her face pressed into his warm neck, his scent filling her nostrils and fuelling her desire. Inside her head she battled the fickle demons that whispered *you are going to lose him again.*

'I missed you, gorgeous!' said Cahal, when he eventually pulled away. Plastic bags rustled at his feet and he wore a short-sleeved blue shirt and tan jeans.

She brushed a curl off his forehead, his healthy tan partially restored over the summer by the Irish sun. She disliked her pale skin but Cahal loved it. He called her his alabaster queen. When they lay together, limbs entwined, they looked like lovers of different race. 'I missed you too. Dreadfully,' she sighed. 'I wish you could've come with us.'

She'd taken a farm cottage in Donegal for the week for herself and the children, and Dad and Aunt Vi had come too. It had been booked long before Cahal came on the scene. She had hoped that the holiday would be a chance for her to reconcile with her aunt. Unfortunately, it had turned out exactly the opposite.

'What's that ring on your finger?' Aunt Vi said when they were alone in the kitchen doing the dishes together on the first night.

Sarah lifted her hands out of the basin and wiped the suds off the ring. It glinted, wet and shiny in the evening sun coming through the window. 'A Claddagh ring. Cahal gave it to me.' She smiled. 'Pretty, isn't it? It's an Irish marriage ring.'

At once, the plate she was holding slid out of Aunt Vi's hands and smashed to pieces on the stone floor.

'Oh,' cried Sarah and she jumped away from the sink, her hands dripping suds onto the floor. 'Are you all right, Aunt Vi?'

Aunt Vi held on to the counter and stared at Sarah, seemingly oblivious to the shards of china at her feet. Her face was pale as a ghost. 'You … you married him?'

'No,' she said irritably. 'It's only a wedding ring when it's on your left hand.'

Aunt Vi held on to the counter with both hands and bent her head. 'Oh, thank God.'

Sarah's stomach tightened into a hard, cold knot.

Aunt Vi lifted her head and stared at Sarah, her voice little more than a whisper. 'Promise me you'll stop seeing him. I beg you, Sarah. Please.'

*

Cahal picked up the bags at his feet and Sarah led him into the kitchen. 'I got enough Chinese takeaway for the kids too. They like lemon chicken, don't they?'

'Oh, that was thoughtful of you.' Sarah picked cutlery out of a drawer and tried to inject some enthusiasm into her voice. 'They're over at Becky's just now. But maybe they can have some for their supper.' Even though they were barely on speaking terms, Becky still acted as though nothing was wrong around the kids. The situation between them was awful but how could Sarah resolve it without telling the truth? Even though she had Cahal, she'd never felt so alone. Or so sad.

Glancing out the window, she noticed the evening sun had already fallen behind the garden shed. It was nearly the end of August, September loomed ever nearer and with it a mounting sense of dread. Maybe she shouldn't have introduced Cahal to the kids after all. They liked him but when he went away they would be left confused and she would have to carry on. But how could she, without him?

'These don't feel so hot,' said Cahal, setting the containers on the granite worksurface.

'Let's pop them in the oven for a bit. It's a little too early to eat anyhow.' She switched the oven on and got plates out while Cahal opened a bottle of wine. She was busy filling a jug with water at the sink when Cahal came up and wrapped his arms around her from behind. 'Leave that a minute.' She turned off the tap, set the jug down and swivelled round. He nuzzled her neck. 'Tell me all about the holiday? Did you have a nice time?'

'Yeah, it was fine. The kids loved it. The farmer let them

collect eggs every day and took them for rides on his pony.'

'I bet Lewis loved that. And what about you?' he said pulling back a little to look at her face. 'Did you enjoy it?'

With her hands behind her back she held on to the kitchen counter and looked at the floor. 'It was okay.'

'Did Becky come in the end?'

'Yeah, she came for one night.' And though Becky had avoided her as much as possible, she was still glad to see her. 'A week in a cottage with just Dad and Aunt Vi is a long time,' she joked, making light of what had, in fact, been a difficult week.

'Well, that'll be because I wasn't there,' he teased and she looked into his eyes and tried to smile.

His smile faded and he hooked a lock of stray hair behind her ear. 'What is it, love?'

She looked away. 'I ... I couldn't relax properly. I was worried Evelyn would pass away while we were on holiday. We were in constant contact with Ian, which kind of spoiled it a bit for me.'

'But she didn't.'

'No, not yet. But it's going to be any day now.' She put her hands to her face and though she tried to hold the tears back, they came anyway.

He squeezed her upper arms. 'I'm sorry. I know you're very fond of her.'

She sniffed. 'I'm not crying just for Evelyn. I'm crying for us too. What are we going to do, Cahal?'

'Oh, Sarah,' he said and held her tight while all the sorrow seeped out of her. 'I don't know, darling.'

She pulled away and looked up into his sad, dark eyes. 'But you're going back to Melbourne in three weeks and I can't see where we go from there.'

His chest rose and fell. 'There's always hope, Sarah.'

She folded her arms. 'You keep saying that, but what's going to change, Cahal? We'll both still be parents with all the commitment that entails.'

'Look,' he said, holding her by the elbows, though her arms were still stubbornly crossed, 'why don't you bring the kids out to Melbourne at Christmas? I promise you, they'll love it.'

She sighed. 'What for? To show us what we can't have?'

His hands dropped to his sides. 'Please, Sarah. Don't make this any harder than it already is.'

'I'm sorry.' She put her arms around his neck and leaned against him. He wrapped his arms around her waist and they stood like that for a long time just holding each other.

She loved him so much she would give up her house and her job and all that was familiar. But even being prepared to give up all this was not enough. Because she would never leave her children. And she would never ask Cahal to leave his. It would destroy him and, in the end, it would destroy them.

The back door clicked open. Sarah fixed a neutral expression on her face, expecting it to be one of the kids. But when she looked across the room, it wasn't Molly or Lewis, it was Aunt Vi.

'Your Dad's waiting outside –' began Aunt Vi but, as soon as she saw them, the cheerful words died on her lips.

Cahal and Sarah sprang apart. Aunt Vi stood stock still in the doorway, a metal loaf tin, partially wrapped up in a tea towel, in her right hand. The evening breeze carried the smell of warm gingerbread, fresh from the oven, across the room.

'Hello, Vi,' said Sarah, trying not to show she was unnerved by her aunt's unexpected presence. She glanced nervously at Cahal. Unlike Sarah, he appeared completely calm, and even gave her a small reassuring smile. Taking courage from this, she said, rather stating the obvious, 'You haven't met Cahal, have you?'

Aunt Vi stepped inside and shut the door. 'I thought your father asked you to stop seeing him only this week.'

Sarah glanced at Cahal. His brow furrowed.

'And you told him you would,' went on her aunt.

At this Cahal flinched, then turned his shocked and wounded gaze on Sarah.

'That's not true,' she blurted out. 'I said I would think about what he said. That was all.' To reinforce the truth of this, she went over to Cahal and put her arm around his waist.

This action seemed to incense Aunt Vi who shrieked, 'Are you going to defy your father?'

Sarah hesitated, momentarily surprised by this outburst from her normally mild-mannered aunt. 'For heaven's sake. Stop talking to me as if I'm a child.'

Cahal put his arm around Sarah's shoulder and pressed his fingers into the top of her arm. At this, Aunt Vi's eyes narrowed meanly, and her upper lip curled. 'Your father didn't raise you in a good Christian home to consort with low-class people like this, Sarah. You're breaking his heart. Can't you see that?'

298

Sarah slapped her forehead with the palm of her hand. 'I'm sick of you and Dad loading all this emotional blackmail on me. I'm not breaking Dad's heart. He's breaking his own heart with his pig-headed narrow-mindedness and prejudice.' She spat the words across the room. 'I'm not responsible for how he chooses to react to Cahal.'

Aunt Vi's lips pursed momentarily and then she turned her attention to Cahal whom, up until now, she had not looked at, nor acknowledged, in any way. She glared at him and hissed, 'They're all evil criminals, the Mulvennas. Men of violence. And this one will turn out to be just the same.'

Sarah put a hand to her throat, horrified both by her aunt's outrageous words and the hateful manner of their delivery. Beside her, Cahal tensed.

'If you've something to say about me,' he said, maintaining admirable calm in the face of her aunt's spite, 'say it to me. Don't talk about me as if I'm not here.'

'Aunt Vi, please,' said Sarah disentangling herself from Cahal and taking a few steps towards her aunt. 'What has Cahal done to make you hate him so much?'

Vi's eyes bulged behind her glasses and the tendons on her neck stood out like wires. 'You mark my words,' she said pointing an accusative finger at him, the loaf tin still balanced in her right hand. 'You're just like your father. From the way you look to the way you talk. And inside you're the same too.'

Cahal gave Sarah a perplexed glance then addressed Aunt Vi. 'Does this all come down to my father? Is that why you hate me so much? This is madness,' he said with a shake of his head and an exasperated glance at Sarah. 'Look, I know he's no angel,' he went on reasonably, 'but I don't see how what he did has got anything to do with me. Anyway, he paid for the things he did wrong.'

Aunt Vi's nostrils flared and she pulled herself up to her full height. 'No he didn't. That sentence never even came close to being enough for what he did,' she said in a voice so low it scared Sarah. And then her voice rose. 'I hope God can forgive him for the ... the violence he committed, for I can't. I hope he burns in hell for all eternity!'

'Aunt Vi!' cried Sarah. What had transformed her placid aunt into this ranting madwoman? 'Stop!'

Cahal raised his hand against the onslaught of her aunt's vicious words. Both women fell silent. How he kept his temper, Sarah didn't know. Every fibre in her body was on fire, blood pumping so fast inside her head, she thought it might burst.

'Okay,' said Cahal and, though his voice was calm, the muscles in his right cheek twitched and his eyes were hard and cold. 'He has a bit of a temper on him – I'm not denying that – but only when provoked.'

'Only when provoked!' screamed Aunt Vi, as the last semblance of self-control fell away. There was a terrible pause. She raised her right hand, the loaf tin balanced precariously on her palm. 'Your father is evil. Satan incarnate.'

And then the tin was in the air, moving so fast that neither Sarah nor Cahal had time to react. It sailed past Sarah, there was a dull thud, and when she spun round, Cahal was bent over, leaning against the sink, with his hand pressed to his left temple. The tin skidded to a halt by the skirting board. The gingerbread, split in two, lay on the tiled floor at Cahal's feet.

'Cahal!' she cried and dashed to his side. She put a hand on his shoulder. 'Are you badly hurt? Let me see?'

'It's … nothing,' said Cahal, straightening up, but when he removed his hand, blood seeped from a gash just below the hairline. Fear filled her head and anger filled her heart.

'You stupid woman. You could've really hurt him!' She kicked the gingerbread out of the way and grabbed a tea towel off a hook. 'Here, use this.'

He pressed the towel to his head. 'I'm okay, really.' He removed the towel and frowned at the blood on the cloth. 'It's not serious. Bloody hurts though,' he grimaced.

'Oh, darling,' said Sarah, examining the wound. It was an inch long, but not deep. Satisfied that he was not seriously hurt, she turned to face her aunt. 'What the hell is wrong with you?'

Aunt Vi's face was livid, her expression unrepentant. 'I won't let you destroy her life. Not the way he destroyed mine!'

Cold dread stilled the fire in Sarah's breast. She paused, took a deep breath and said, 'What did you say?'

But her aunt didn't seem to hear. She glared at Cahal for a few, short seconds. Then, without any warning, she took three nimble steps over to the island unit, and grabbed a boning knife, long and slim, from the knife block.

Sarah screamed. Cahal grabbed her shoulders and pulled her back. Aunt Vi raised the knife in the air, every muscle in her puce face contorted. Cahal pushed Sarah behind him and growled, 'Don't you touch her.'

'For God's sake, Aunt Vi. Put it down!' sobbed Sarah,

clawing at Cahal's back.

'That's enough!' said a voice from the doorway.

Everyone froze. It was Dad. Before anyone had time to think or move, he walked over to Vi, took the knife out of her hand and said, 'That's enough, Vi.'

The fight went out of her instantly and the madwoman was suddenly gone, replaced by a harmless, confused-looking old woman. Dad put his arm around her shoulders and she began to cry, holding on to the back of a chair. 'There, there, now,' he said, gently.

Sarah came out from behind Cahal's back and stared in numb astonishment at the scene before her. Her aunt rarely cried and never like this. Her whole body heaved with sobs and the sound that came out was a pitiful sort of wailing. In the face of her obvious distress, Sarah couldn't help but feel sorry for her, but she was furious too.

'Dad, did you see what she did? She came in here and just went completely bonkers and threatened us with a knife.'

Aunt Vi's sobs slowly ebbed. Dad removed his arm from her shoulders. 'It wasn't you she was threatening. It was him.' He gave Cahal a grim, resigned sort of look. 'And she has every right to hate him.'

Cahal said, 'Right, I've had enough of this. You either tell me what the hell this is about, or I'm going to the police.'

'I don't think you want to do that, son.' Dad pulled out a chair and Aunt Vi sank gently into it. She put her elbows on the table and her face in her hands.

Dad said, addressing Cahal, 'You've probably gathered by now that this is to do with your father.'

Sarah took Cahal's hand and squeezed, a horrible sense of foreboding taking hold.

'You'd better sit down. Both of you.'

Cahal gave Sarah a questioning look and in response she shook her head, utterly baffled. They sat at the kitchen table, a pile of unopened mail and letters from school piled up on one end, place settings for two between Sarah and Aunt Vi. Dad sat down beside his sister, placed his hands on the table and stared at them. Everyone waited and eventually he said to Sarah, 'Well, I suppose you were bound to find out one way or another. I'm surprised you never told her, Cahal.' He glared at him. 'You've some nerve coming near my family.'

Cahal shook his head in bewilderment and said grimly, the tea towel still pressed to his head, 'I have no idea what you're talking about.'

Dad said, 'Maybe we should have told you, Sarah.'

Sarah hid her shaking hands under the table and leaned forward. 'Told me what?'

Another silence. Dad took a deep breath. His eyes were heavy and sad and his breathing was slightly laboured as if this was all suddenly too much for him. 'What happened to your aunt,' he said flatly.

'No, David,' said Aunt Vi and everyone looked at her. Her face was white and composed, all trace of rage gone. 'I don't want to be here when you tell them.' Without looking at anyone, she got up out of the chair slowly as if every bone in her body ached. She touched Dad on the shoulder. 'I'll wait in the lounge.'

When she was gone, Sarah stared at her father, her eyes

303

wide with fear, her left leg twitching uncontrollably. Beside her, Cahal was still as a rock, his hands clenched into fists on his lap.

'It all started when Vi met Malachy Mulvenna at a dance in Ballymena in May 1957.'

Sarah let out a little gasp of surprise and Cahal sat up straighter in his chair, his jaw clenched tightly shut. Aunt Vi *knew* Cahal's father?

Dad stared at the back of his hands and spoke as if reading out the lines and furrows on his skin. 'She was a nurse, just newly qualified, working at the Cottage Hospital and he'd come over from Ballyfergus on some labouring job. I don't know why she agreed to meet him again after that dance.' He shook his head. 'But she did. She was on her own, a naïve and vulnerable young woman.' He sighed so sadly and deeply, a sound so full of regret, it pulled Sarah's heartstrings taut. 'Anyway, after the first date she found out that he was married and she told him she didn't want to see him again. And then she met this lovely lad, Robert Sinclair – a merchant navy man, and four months later they were engaged. And I wish to God that had been the end of it.' He paused, looked up at the ceiling and blinked, his eyes filled with tears.

Sarah, trembling with fear, put a hand to her mouth and waited.

Dad brought his gaze to bear on Sarah. 'They were going to get married in October the following year and Vi decided to continue working till then. The Cottage Hospital in Ballymena was built on the edge of the millpond in the People's Park. They've got CCTV and security gates and lighting now but back then, they'd none of that.' He paused and shifted his cold gaze to Cahal. 'On her way home from a late shift that autumn, a man accosted her in the grounds of the hospital and attacked her.'

Cahal made a horrible gurgling sound in the back of his throat. Sarah cried out, 'No.' She did not need to hear the rest, she knew what was coming, but Dad pressed on, in a horribly disconnected, monotone voice. 'A porter putting out bins heard her screams. He was too late for Vi – she was raped and badly beaten – but he caught the man. He was tried and convicted. He served –'

'Five years,' said Cahal, and a deathly silence filled the room.

Dad nodded slowly, his penetrating gaze never leaving Cahal's face for a second. 'You know who that man was, don't you, son?' he said quietly.

Cahal hung his head.

Sarah closed her eyes and silent tears ran down her cheeks. Inside her head flashes of memory – words and faces, whispered secrets, fear. Slowly, piece by piece, everything made perfect sense. It explained why her aunt had been so protective of her and Becky growing up, why she worried when they were out with friends and went frantic if they were as much as five minutes late. And most importantly of all it explained why Aunt Vi and Dad hated Cahal. Why they could never countenance him joining the family. Why they never would.

The legs of Cahal's chair scraped the floor. Sarah opened her eyes and he stood up. His face was pure white, his expression one of horrified shock. Oh God, how must he feel knowing that his father was a rapist, knowing that he was the reason they had been apart all these years and not her family. For Sarah, in all honesty, could not blame Aunt Vi or Dad for what they'd done.

'Cahal,' she said and touched his arm, her heart aching for him.

He turned his head slowly towards her, his face so miserable it broke her heart. He looked from Sarah to her father and back again.

'I have to … I have to think,' he said and, ducking his head, he hurried towards the back door.

Sarah jumped up. 'Please, Cahal. Wait. Please don't go.'

He paused with the door wide open, his foot on the threshold. 'I'm sorry, Sarah. I need to be alone.'

Chapter 18

Sarah sat across from her father at the kitchen table and for a long time neither of them spoke. Only the soft whirr of the fan oven and the distant sound of a lawnmower broke the silence.

Dad spoke first. 'I've nothing against Cahal personally.'

Sarah nodded and finally managed to speak, her throat so tight it came out a whisper. 'I know that, Dad. I see that now.'

'I couldn't care less if he's a Catholic or a Jew or a Muslim, working class or royalty but this ...' His voice tailed away and he bent his head so that she could clearly see the bald patch on the top of his head. 'This, I cannot bear. Malachy Mulvenna ruined your aunt's life, Sarah.' He paused for a moment to compose himself, then lifted his head. 'Very few women went through with rape cases in the fifties, Sarah. You have to understand how very brave she was. Rape victims didn't have anonymity in those days but she was determined to have justice. She had to stand up in court and describe every little detail of what happened. She'd fought, you know, until every one of her nails was broken and she was covered in bruises. He knocked out one of her teeth. You should've seen her face.'

Sarah let out a little sob and a wave of compassion made her regret every horrible thing she'd ever said to her aunt.

'The court case was terrible,' Dad went on, 'I don't know how she did it, standing up there, day after day, while that lawyer tried to make her out to be a liar and a slut. It didn't work. Mulvenna was found guilty and he got five years because of the level of violence. But in his summing up the judge said it would've been more but for the fact that Vi had willingly dated Mulvenna. He made it sound as though she'd led Mulvenna on.' He ground his teeth together.

'Oh, Dad, that's awful.'

'Well, the sentence broke her. She changed after that. She was never the same girl again.'

'What happened to Robert Sinclair?'

Dad's eyebrows went up and the corners of his mouth went down. 'He said he didn't care about the rape, but she couldn't handle it. She broke off the engagement and she never looked at another man again. She moved to Coleraine shortly afterwards. She couldn't bear that people knew. I wish now that I had dissuaded her from going to court. But I'd not long joined the force. I didn't know how these things worked … I didn't know how she would be treated. And she was adamant that he shouldn't get away with it.'

'I'm so sorry, Dad.' Poor Aunt Vi. Malachy Mulvenna hadn't just raped her. He'd taken away her prospects of marriage and children. She'd devoted herself to her career, to helping people, and later, she'd devoted herself to her brother and his broken family.

He looked at her sternly. 'Your aunt made a very great sacrifice in coming back to Ballyfergus to care for you and Becky after your mother died. She not only gave up her career, but she came back to Ballyfergus even though Malachy Mulvenna still lived here. I told her she didn't have to, I didn't expect her to. But she could see I wasn't coping.'

Vivid memories sprang to mind. Sarah remembered the weeks after her mother's death: baked beans on burnt toast, night after night; un-ironed laundry piled up in great heaps around the house. Sarah had tried to fill her mother's shoes, but she was slow – and she had school and homework, and Becky to soothe to sleep every night in the double bed they shared. Dad went to work as usual but at home he was bewildered and utterly incapable of addressing the growing crisis.

And then Aunt Vi came and, though Sarah had resented her, she was relieved too. Soon the house was shipshape and routine reigned once more; clean, folded clothes appeared on the end of her bed, meals appeared regularly and they never ran out of milk or bread or breakfast cereal. 'I resented her coming. I was horrible and difficult.'

'You'd just lost your Mum, Sarah. You were only a child. And you didn't understand. How could you?'

Sarah bowed her head in shame, her father's words doing little to assuage her guilt. 'I understand now why she stole the letters Cahal wrote me from Australia. She was only trying to protect herself – and me.' She could not blame her aunt and the unfairness of it all – what had happened to Vi, what had happened to her and Cahal because of it – made her eyes prick with tears.

Dad's face clouded. 'Yes, she told me about that. She was very upset that you'd accused her of theft. She didn't take any letters, you know.'

The blood drained from Sarah's face. 'You took them!'

He smiled sceptically and said calmly, 'I never took any letters, Sarah.' He paused and his blue eyes narrowed. 'I think you place too much faith in Cahal Mulvenna. How come you believe him over us?'

'I … don't. I do believe him. But I believe you too.' She ran a hand through her hair. 'I know that doesn't make any sense.'

There was a pause and Sarah said, 'What about the phone call?'

'I took the call.'

'But you said –'

'I know what I said. But it was me.'

Sarah froze, stunned by the news and utterly dismayed both by the fact that Dad had failed to relay the message and had lied about it. She tried to take in this new reality but her head hurt and her brain would not function. 'I need a drink of water.' She got a glass and filled it and stood at the sink to drink. Her father came and stood beside her.

She shook her head, looking out onto the garden. The late evening sun cast long shadows across the grass. That summer so long ago was a hazy memory. She closed her eyes and drank half the glass of water wishing it would wash her clean. He cleared his throat. 'Granny was getting double glazing put in that summer. She came and stayed with us for four days.'

Sarah looked at him. 'What's this got to do with Granny?'

'I told her about the call,' went on Dad. 'She made me promise not to tell you and the next day she reported nuisance phone calls to BT and had the number changed. Mulvenna had destroyed her daughter's life. She hated him as much as I do.'

Sarah chest rose and fell rapidly, like a small animal breathing. If only she'd known about the call, it would've been enough. She slammed the glass down on the counter and water sloshed over the edge and onto the floor. Angry at everyone and everything and God Himself, she blurted out, 'You ruined my life. All of you!'

Dad gave her a hard stare. 'We did what we thought was right. I acted as I did to protect Vi. And to protect you from getting involved with that dreadful family. If you're looking for someone to blame, then blame Mulvenna.'

Sarah let out a sob and put her hand to her mouth. Dad touched her arm but she brushed him away.

'I'm sorry that you've been hurt by this, Sarah. But can't you see that I had no choice? I could not allow Cahal to break up our family.'

'You could have told me.' And then what would she have done?

Dad shook his head. 'Vi never wanted you girls to know. She didn't want you to be afraid, the way she'd become.' He smiled. 'She's always been so proud of you two.' He paused. 'But I don't make any apologies for what I did in breaking you and Cahal Mulvenna up, Sarah. But if I had my time again, I'd do things differently.

'I wish I'd persuaded Vi to keep her mouth shut and not go to court. I should've have waited for Malachy Mulvenna one night on his way home from the pub and put a bullet through his head.'

'You don't mean that,' gasped Sarah.

'Yes I do. Don't you see how it would have solved more than one problem, Sarah? This Cahal of yours, for one, would never have been born.'

Cahal found his father in Ballyfergus Social Club. A band strummed out desultory hits from the sixties but the dance floor was only half full, for the big attraction of this club was not the dancing, but the discounted drink.

Malachy slumped on a barstool, a pint of dark brown bitter on the bar in front of him. His walking stick rested against his right leg. Ignoring the chatter and interaction between the men around him, he lifted the glass to his lips and took a long sup of beer. His hand shook as he set the glass on the bar. He looked old and harmless.

But he had not been harmless as a young man. He had been a brute and a bully as a father and, looking back, Cahal believed him perfectly capable of worse. A hard, cold lump formed in Cahal's stomach. He did not doubt David Walker's story. He could check the facts himself, but he had no need to. The truth in David Walker's eyes, and the old, tired anger in his voice, was confirmation enough for Cahal.

His own flesh and blood had raped a young woman. It was

the most heinous of crimes. A crime committed by weirdos and woman haters, not your own father. But Malachy was both these things. He had no true friends, and he treated his wife worse than a doormat.

Cahal fought against the nausea in his stomach and anger replaced it. Anger for the suffering of Vi Walker at the hands of this brute – and for his own and that of his siblings. Malachy had smashed Vi's life into smithereens and, in doing so, he'd shattered Cahal's chances of happiness with Sarah. She would not want him now.

All these years he'd nursed hatred in his heart for David and Vi Walker but they could not be held responsible for their actions. He understood now why they had gone to such lengths to keep him and Sarah apart. And all along, the architect of his heartbreak had been his own flesh and blood.

His mother, sitting with a group of old women nearby, a tumbler of amber liquid in front of her on the table, caught sight of him. She smiled hesitantly, rose uncertainly out of the chair and fired a nervous glance in Malachy's direction. She wore the same clothes she wore indoors – polyester trousers and a woolly cardigan. He'd always assumed she was unhappy with her life, but now he wondered if it suited her well enough. She was as fond of a drink as her husband.

Cahal flashed her a warning glance and the smile faded from her lips. She sat down abruptly and Cahal crossed the room on shaking legs towards his father. His face burned and sweat beaded his brow. People looked and whispered – strangers were uncommon here, prodigal sons even more so – but he paid them no heed.

Pushing his way through the crowd, someone tugged on his sleeve. He looked round and found Grainne standing there with an empty glass in her hand. She was drunk – or worse. Her eyes were half-closed and bleary and she swayed in time to the music.

'Fanks for sorting out Beaky for me, Cahal. You're a good brother, so you are.' She raised a yellow index finger, dirt under her nail. 'And I swear to you, I won't touch that stuff again. Fries your brain it does.'

'Not now, Grainne.'

He turned to go but she grabbed his arm and dug her nails in. 'Lend us a tenner, will ye?'

She looked so pathetic he was filled with compassion and repulsion in equal measure. His hand moved towards his back pocket where he kept his wallet. But the money would only go on more drink or drugs. 'No.'

She pulled at his arm. 'Ach, come on, Cahal. You've loads of dosh. You won't miss one wee tenner.'

'I'm sorry.'

Her eyes narrowed. 'Buy your big sis a drink, then? For old times' sake?'

He stared at her and something inside him snapped. He shook off her grip roughly. 'Is that all I am to you, Grainne? A cash machine?'

Her eyebrows came together in confusion and she swore. 'You're a mean bastard, Cahal.'

'Yeah, right,' he said and pushed on into the crowd, her curses ringing in his ears. He reached his father and, leaning close to his balding head, he said, 'I want to talk to you.'

His father jumped, startled from his reverie. 'Huh! What are you doing here?'

Cahal met his father's bleary gaze with a cold, hard stare. He leaned even closer until he could smell his hair cream and cigarette smoke, and whispered in his ear. 'I know what you did to Vi Walker.'

Malachy grabbed the handle of his walking stick and thumped the floor. 'Who have you been talking to? You don't know anything. Whatever you heard is lies. I'm innocent.'

Cahal, who had expected no less of him, let out a cold, false laugh. 'So the police and the jury and the judge were all wrong, were they?'

Malachy, his face red with fury, hauled himself off the barstool, gave Cahal a shove and pushed through the crowd. Cahal caught up with him on the edge of the dance floor, a few feet short of the crush at the bar. He grabbed Malachy's arm and raised his voice. 'Answer me. Were they wrong?'

Malachy shook off Cahal's grip with surprising strength. 'I don't have to listen to this, especially not from a jumped-up snob like you. You weren't there. You don't know anything about it.'

'Cahal,' said Bridget appearing by his side. She touched Cahal's arm. 'People are looking.'

'I don't care who looks or who hears,' he said, raising his voice and Malachy headed for the exit while Bridget held on to Cahal's arm, dragging him back. 'Leave it, Cahal. Just let him go.'

'No.' He prised his mother's hands off his arm and pursued Malachy towards the foyer, Bridget following right behind him.

Outside in the foyer, the door closed on the noise of the band and the three of them were alone. Malachy turned to face him, leaning unsteadily on the end of the stick with both hands. Bridget stood between husband and son, nervously scratching at her neck. 'What are you two arguing about now? Can't you just get on?' Her breath smelt of malt whiskey.

'You stay out of this,' said Malachy without taking his gaze off Cahal.

'Da was just about to explain to me how an innocent man gets convicted of rape.'

His mother let out a soft cry and something about that quiet, knowing sound cut him to the core. She *knew*.

Malachy licked his lips. 'I'll tell you how. That bitch stood up in court and told a whole pack of lies about me. And who do you think they were going to believe – me or the sister of David Walker?'

'I'll take the word of Vi Walker before yours any day.'

Malachy's head quivered. 'That's always been your problem. You've never had any loyalty to your family. You couldn't get away fast enough, could you? And now you're Mr Big Shot.' He paused to look Cahal up and down in disgust. 'You think you can come back here, looking down on the rest of us like we're shit on the sole of your shoe.'

Cahal blinked. His father's words though crude, had truth in them. 'I don't owe you anything, Malachy Mulvenna. And the only thing in my life that I've ever really wanted, I can't have because of you.'

Malachy raised the stick in the air and shouted, 'What're you blethering on about, man?'

'Sarah Walker. Her family can't stand the sight of me because of who I am. And now she knows the truth as well.'

Malachy laughed and stabbed the floor with the stick. 'Poor wee heartbroken Cahal. You always were a whinger. Well, that's not my problem. You tell her that her aunt is a lying cow. She led me on, so she did. And what she got, well, she had it coming.'

Cahal recoiled in horror, his father's words so hateful that he felt physically repulsed. He took a step backwards. 'I never want to see you again.'

'Think I care?' Malachy spat out. He added a curse, turned and hobbled back into the function hall.

There was a long silence. Cahal pressed the heels of his hands to his throbbing temples and leaned against the wall. His father's blood ran in his veins. He felt contaminated, spoiled, the black stain of his father's sin passed down to him like a genetic disease. He closed his eyes and placed his hand on his heart. But hadn't he escaped once? Hadn't he reinvented himself? He would not let his father's actions determine who he was. He was Cahal Mulvenna – flawed in many ways – but he tried to live a decent life and do the right thing. He would continue to do that; he would not let his soiled bloodline determine his future.

He opened his eyes to find his mother staring at him, not in horror, but in trepidation. The cold, hard lump in his stomach intensified. Her gaze fell to the ground. 'You knew he was guilty all along, didn't you?'

She fidgeted with the collar of her blouse. And then, without raising her eyes, she nodded.

He had always seen her as a victim.

'And Sean and Grainne?'

'No.'

'How could you have stayed with him?'

She pulled her cardigan tighter round her frame. 'We'd only been married for a year and he was off working most of the time. He couldn't get work in Ballyfergus. When the ... when Vi Walker claimed he raped her, I was pregnant with Sean. I believed him at first. It wasn't till it went to court that I started to have ... doubts.'

'Why didn't you leave then?'

'It was too late. I had a baby to look after and I had nowhere to go. You don't understand how it was then, Cahal. I couldn't leave.'

'Gran would've taken you in. Or your sister.'

She shook her head. 'My Ma told me it was my duty to stand by him. And my sister's husband didn't want to have anything to do with us. And Malachy always denied it ... and if I hadn't stayed, you wouldn't have been born!' she said angrily.

He snorted. 'And that's supposed to make me feel better?'

She pressed her lips together in anger and then blurted out, her grey head shaking and spit on her lips, 'Don't judge me for it, Cahal. Unless you've walked in my shoes you have no right to judge me.'

The anger drained away. Inside he felt hollow. 'I don't judge you, Ma,' he said quietly. 'I feel sorry for you. I'm sad that you settled for this.' He touched her wrinkled cheek with his hand but he could not bring himself to kiss it. 'Goodbye, Ma.'

He thought of Sarah and the dreams and hopes he had carried in his heart since that night he saw her in the Europa

Hotel. How terribly mistaken he had been. The cards were stacked against them from day one, they just hadn't known it until now.

'What will you do now?' said his mother's voice.

He looked her in the eye. 'Go back to Australia. What else can I do?'

Aunt Vi sat on the sofa in Sarah's lounge cradling a mug of hot, sweet tea and staring straight ahead, her back erect, her lips sealed in a straight line. Sarah, watching from the doorway, put a hand on her stomach, nauseated by what she'd learnt in the last hour. Sounds floated up the hall from the kitchen – Becky's voice; the ping of the microwave; the kids arguing over who was having lemon chicken or crispy beef.

She padded quietly into the lounge on bare feet and shut the door behind her, blocking out the racket. Vi did not stir.

Sarah's chest tightened, and the space between her shoulder blades burned. She felt weighed down by a sense of guilt that, not only had her aunt endured a horrific, life-changing ordeal, but Cahal's presence here today had forced her to relive it all over again. In the space of a few short moments, Sarah's whole world had shifted and it would never be the same again.

She sat down beside her aunt and said, 'I'm sorry about what happened to you, Aunt Vi,' the clumsy sentence failing to convey the depth of her compassion and grief.

Aunt Vi set the mug down on a coaster and touched the back of her grey bun as if checking it was still in place. Then she looked Sarah in the eye, her gaze behind her glasses as calm and collected as ever, though she now looked incredibly tired. 'You don't have to be sorry, love. You had no part in this. You didn't do anything wrong.'

'But I did. I … I wasn't nice to you when you came to live with us after Mum died.'

Aunt Vi smiled sadly. 'We were all hurting then, Sarah. We were all just trying to do the best we could. It was only natural for you to resent me. It must've seemed as if I was trying to take your mother's place.'

Sarah looked away and blushed. 'I thought Mum wanted me to be the mother, not you. She asked me to look after Becky.'

'I know she did, love. But she was very ill, I'm not sure she knew rightly what she was asking of you. It was a very heavy burden to place on the shoulders of someone so young.'

Sarah put her face in her hands. 'Oh Aunt Vi, I feel it still.'

'I know you do, love. But it's time to let that sense of responsibility go.' Aunt Vi patted her on the knee and Sarah looked up into her kind, wise eyes. 'Do you think you can?'

Sarah nodded. 'I'll try.'

Aunt Vi smiled. 'You mustn't beat yourself up about being difficult. All teenagers rebel and you had more to cope with than most. And I made a lot of mistakes. I was too strict.'

Tears spilled out of Sarah's eyes. 'But I understand why now. After what you'd been through, you were afraid for us.'

Aunt Vi nodded slowly. 'Yes, I was. I didn't used to be such a worrier, you know. But Malachy Mulvenna changed that. He made me afraid of my own shadow.'

'There are people who can help with that, Aunt Vi,' said Sarah earnestly, wiping the tears away. 'I could find a good counsellor for you.'

Vi pushed her glasses up by the bridge. 'I think the time for that's long past, Sarah. I'm an old woman now. My life, such as it was, well … it's lived, isn't it?'

Sarah blinked back tears. 'And I accused you of stealing Cahal's letters. I know you didn't take them. I'm sorry.'

'Thank you for saying that, Sarah. I appreciate it,' she said graciously and then added, her eyebrows raised questioningly, 'You still believe him about those letters then?'

Sarah, her doubts increased by tonight's revelations, looked away and said nothing. Aunt Vi forced a smile. 'I should be the one apologising to you. I'm sorry I lost it in there. It was just that … when I saw him, Sarah.' She paused and shook her head, a grim expression on her face. 'It was like looking at Malachy Mulvenna all over again. I couldn't bear it. Something inside me just snapped.'

Sarah gave her aunt a brief, awkward hug. She stiffened in Sarah's arms and she released her. They had never been tactile with each other. 'I don't blame you. I don't know how you coped all these years.'

Aunt Vi sniffed and stared grimly at the ring on Sarah's finger. 'By putting others before myself. Family and duty first, Sarah.'

Sarah stared at the ring on her finger. She had put family and duty first once before too and it had brought her nothing but misery.

'I want you to stop seeing him,' said Aunt Vi, and when Sarah did not answer, she added, 'He can never be part of this family. You do see that, don't you?'

Sarah's heart stilled. She looked at her aunt and in her cold, hard eyes she saw a life wasted, hope quashed, dreams shattered. And she saw her future too – a lonely life of duty and service, dedicated to her children and the care of her ageing aunt and father. A life without Cahal. It would be unbearable. 'I'm sorry, Aunt Vi. I can't do that.' And with that Sarah walked out of the room.

Chapter 19

Later, when the kids were in bed, and Dad and Aunt Vi had gone home, Becky and Sarah sat opposite each other in the lounge on armchairs, talking in low voices in the fading light. Plates of half-eaten food covered the coffee table and a stiff gin and tonic sat on the table by Sarah's right hand.

The extraordinary events of the evening had resulted in a sort of truce between them, though the atmosphere was strained.

'I'm going to try him again.' Sarah hit the redial button on the mobile she'd had in her hand constantly for the last hour. The phone tripped straight to Cahal's voicemail – a female computerised voice. She threw the phone down in frustration. 'He's not answering. Or replying to any of my texts.'

'He must've switched his mobile off.'

'He's not picking up at home either.'

'Maybe he's gone for a long walk. Maybe he just needs to

be on his own for a bit.'

'I suppose so,' she said despondently, peering anxiously at the small screen on the phone. But what if he wasn't okay?

Becky took a long drink of gin and tonic, then shook her head in disbelief. 'What a night. Poor Aunt Vi. I can't imagine what she suffered.'

'And not just the rape, which must've been awful,' said Sarah, getting up and switching on the lights. 'But everything that happened afterwards. The court case and missing out on marriage and children. And all because of that evil man.' She sat down, lifted up the glass by her side and stared miserably into her drink. 'I just wish they'd told us a long time ago.'

'It's not the sort of thing you want to tell young, impressionable girls, is it? It would have scared us witless. And the chances of you meeting and falling in love with Malachy Mulvenna's son must've seemed like one in a million to them.'

'I suppose so. But still, it might have saved everyone all this heartache.' She pressed the glass against the place between her breasts, a knot of pain caught there like indigestion. Tears seeped out of the corners of her eyes. 'But then I would've missed out on the only real love I've ever known. And for all the pain this has caused, I wouldn't have missed that for the world.'

As if sensing her distress, Bisto, who'd been lying on the rug, jumped onto her lap and rubbed his face against her arm. She stroked his hard little skull and he curled up in a ball on her lap. Smiling bravely, she wiped away the tears, and tried to hold back more. Crying didn't change anything. It only made her feel worse. 'I feel terrible for accusing Aunt Vi of stealing those letters. But I still can hardly believe that Dad lied about the phone call.'

'What?'

'It was him.' Sarah told **Becky about** the confession Dad had made and Becky said carefully, 'Well you can't really blame Granny and Dad, can you? Not in light of what we now know.'

'No, I can't blame them.' She set the glass down and raked both hands through her hair. 'Cahal hasn't done anything wrong. It's not right for him to suffer.' And, though she tried to hold it back, a little sob escaped.

'About the letters,' said Becky and something in the tone of her voice demanded Sarah's full attention.

'What about them?'

Becky's hands shook so much she had to set her glass down. And there was a long pause before she spoke again. 'I took them.'

Sarah leaned back in the chair and put her hands over her mouth, too shocked to speak. Why had it never occurred to her that Becky might have taken them? Because she loved and trusted her sister more than anyone. And she expected the same loyalty back. Finding her voice at last, Sarah said, 'But you knew how much the truth meant to me. You stood by and let me doubt Cahal.'

Becky lowered her eyes. 'I know. And I'm sorry.'

Sarah's brain whirred into action sorting facts, putting two and two together. 'Did you know about the rape?'

Becky shook her head. 'No. That wasn't why I did it.'

'Then why did you take them?' said Sarah angrily. 'And why didn't you tell me? Since Cahal told me about them, I've talked of nothing else for months. I confided in you. And you sat and let me point the finger at Aunt Vi and even Dad.' Her throat constricted with hurt, making further speech impossible for the moment.

'Please Sarah, just listen will you?'

Sarah took a deep breath and tried to calm herself. She stroked Bisto again – long, hard strokes down the length of his spine.

Becky wet her lips. 'I took them because I thought that you were going to follow Cahal to Australia. I was afraid you'd leave me, Sarah. Dad was so angry and Aunt Vi so upset, the atmosphere in the house was unbearable. The three most important people in my world were at each other's throats.' She paused and some of Sarah's anger leached away.

'And when that first letter fell onto the doormat,' Becky went on, looking into the empty fireplace, 'I was standing right there. I picked it up, saw the Australian stamp, and slipped it into the pocket of my dressing gown. I don't know why I did it. I don't know why I didn't just give it to you straight away. But later that night I took it out –'

Sarah gasped. 'You read it?'

Becky shook her head. 'No. Nor any of the others that came after it. I … looked at it and I thought that if I hid it, then you'd forget about Cahal and everything would go back to the way it was and everybody would be happy again …' Her voice tailed off and Sarah stared at her sister, stunned.

'I never thought you could betray me like that.'

Becky hung her head. 'I'm sorry, Sarah. I thought I was doing the right thing. I thought that if Dad and Aunt Vi didn't like Cahal they must've had good reason. And it turns out they did. But that doesn't excuse what I did.'

'Oh, Becky,' whispered Sarah. 'What have you done?' She paused. 'Where are the letters now?'

Becky lowered her eyes. 'I burnt them the day after you and Ian got married.'

Sarah gasped. So she would never read Cahal's love letters. His words were gone, along with the lost years. She felt she had been robbed of so much.

'I thought that you were happy,' said Becky earnestly, inching forwards till she was on the edge of her seat. 'I thought that you'd forgotten all about Cahal. How was I to know that you still loved him? Or that he would come back one day?'

Sarah blinked back tears and stared at the ceiling. Then she brought her gaze to bear on Becky. 'Do you know what, Becky? I'm sick of all these secrets and lies. They've brought nothing but misery.'

'So am I,' said Becky, miserably. 'I swear to you, Sarah, if I had known how much my actions would hurt you, I never would've taken those letters.'

'I know that. And I forgive you.' Sarah stared at Becky, her heart pounding in her chest. Here was her chance to come clean about Tony, to trade one secret for another. Did she have the courage? And could she live with the consequences? 'I only hope that you can forgive me too.'

Becky stared at her coolly and folded her arms. 'So, you're finally going to tell me what you said to Tony at the barbecue, are you?'

Sarah took a deep breath and closed her eyes. When she

opened them, she looked not at Becky but at Bisto's little brown and white body. 'I knew Tony at uni.'

'But I thought you said you'd never met him before,' said Becky, puzzled.

'I know.'

'So why would you say that?'

Sarah glanced into Becky's perplexed face, then looked away, unable to bear her scrutiny. 'Because I had something to hide. And so had Tony.' There was a long pause. 'Cahal introduced me to him shortly after we met. I saw him occasionally, at parties and in the uni bar, but we never talked – just nodded in passing, that was all.'

Becky unfolded her arms slowly and Sarah took a deep breath to try and calm her jangling nerves. 'Well, that autumn after Cahal went to Australia, I went back to uni. One night I got drunk at a party – I did that a lot that term – and Tony was there. We talked about Cahal and I was so hurt and angry, I would've done anything to injure him. I thought that ...' Her voice started to break up but she pressed on, her face burning, determined to reveal the truth. For if she didn't do it now, she never would.

'... I thought that if I slept with one of his friends, word would get back to him.'

Becky cried out, her eyes open wide in horror.

Sarah fixed her eyes on the clock on the mantel and dug her fingers into Bisto's fur. 'I thought I would show him that if he didn't care for me, then I didn't care for him either. And so we ... we did it.'

A long silence followed. Sarah looked at Becky. She was

still as a statue and just as white. 'And did you … have you …'

Sarah shook her head vehemently. 'No, it was just that once. And it was nothing more than a drunken –'

'I don't want to know!' cried Becky, slapping her hands over her ears.

'You have to understand that it meant nothing to either of us,' said Sarah, her stomach muscles tensing. Bisto leapt off her lap and trotted out of the room, tail erect. 'He never told Cahal so my stupid plan didn't even work and now I'm glad it didn't for Cahal might never have come back. I avoided Tony for the rest of the year, and after that he went off to Queen's and I never saw him again, until he turned up at Isabelle's seventieth.'

'You slept with Tony,' said Becky, removing her hands from her ears. 'And you were always banging on to me about what a slut I was for sleeping around!'

'I never said that, Becky.'

Becky jumped to her feet and shouted, 'You're no better than me! At least I slept with men because I liked them, because I thought we might just have a future together. Not to get back at someone, not as a twisted act of revenge.'

'Keep your voice down or you'll wake the children.' Sarah's cheeks burned with shame. 'That's one of the reasons I didn't tell you,' she said quietly. 'You've always looked up to me. I couldn't bear you thinking ill of me. And I didn't want to ruin your relationship with Tony before it had a chance to get off the ground.'

Becky stared at her for some long moments, her tongue

bulging in her left cheek. 'Why did you have to spoil this for me, Sarah? Tony's the only man I've ever loved.'

'I didn't do it deliberately! How was I to know that you would meet him all these years later and fall in love?'

Becky said, more to herself than Sarah, 'I don't understand why Tony didn't tell me.'

'I asked him not to. That's what we were talking about in the garden.'

'And how many other secret rendezvous did you and Tony have?' demanded Becky, her eyes ablaze.

'None. That day in the garden, I got him to swear that he'd never tell you.'

Becky stared at her open-mouthed, then said, 'So you weren't jealous?'

'No. I was pleased you'd found happiness. I just wished it had been with someone other than Tony.'

Becky folded her arms. 'But you did try to break us up.'

'At first, yes. You see, if you broke up, the problem would vanish. But later, when I saw how great you were together and realised that wasn't going to happen, all I cared about was making sure that you never found out. I thought it would destroy your relationship with me – and with Tony.' She put her head in her hands. 'It's all my fault. At Isabelle's party, I leapt in before he could speak and pretended I didn't know him – and then he just went along with it to save me embarrassment.'

There was a long silence and Becky sat down suddenly on the chair and ran her hand through her hair. 'You should've told me.'

'I know. But please don't let this affect your relationship with Tony. I've watched him these past months, Becky. He's devoted to you and you're perfect together. It's not as if you don't have histories. He's got two marriages behind him for heaven's sake and God knows how many ex-girlfriends.'

'Thanks for reminding me.'

'Look,' said Sarah, feeling as if her life depended on persuading Becky. 'You never placed much emotional importance on sexual relationships before you met Tony. Do you think Tony cares who you slept with before him?'

'No.'

'And what would you think of him, if he did? If he gave you a hard time about it?'

Becky shrugged.

'You'd think he was creepy, wouldn't you?'

'I suppose so.'

'So, why should you give a toss who he slept with? Especially when it was twenty years ago.'

Becky rubbed her eyes and sighed. 'I'm not angry with Tony. I'm angry with you.'

'But you do see why I didn't tell you, Becky, don't you?'

'You were doing your usual.'

'What do you mean?'

'Protecting me. Making decisions on my behalf. You should've told me and let me decide whether I wanted to keep seeing Tony.'

This had not occurred to Sarah. 'Oh, I hadn't thought ... you're right. I'm sorry.'

Becky sighed and her voice softened. 'I know you did it for

331

all the right reasons. But you have to stop doing this.'

'What?'

'Making decisions on my behalf, behaving as if I'm some sort of ward that needs your protection. You've been doing it ever since Mum died.'

Sarah looked at her lap. 'You're right. I'm sorry. Do you forgive me?' She looked up and held her breath.

'Of course I do. Come here you big idiot.'

The two women met on the rug and hugged each other and Sarah, her heart soaring said, 'Oh, Becky, I've missed you. It's been awful not having you to talk to.'

'I know, me too. I'm just so glad you told me the truth. And I thought you were jealous of me and Tony!'

They pulled apart and Sarah smiled. 'I'd never be jealous of you.'

'What are you going to do about Cahal?'

'I don't know.' Sarah's smile faltered but inside a steely determination rose up from somewhere. 'All I know is that I love him and I won't let this destroy us. I have to find him.'

'Well go and look. I can stay the night and get the kids to school in the morning.'

'Are you sure?'

'I'm sure. And if you don't come back tonight, I'll phone in sick for you tomorrow.'

Sarah's heart pounded and the hairs stood up on the back of her neck. 'Thanks, sweetheart. Tell the kids I had to leave for work really early.'

She hesitated for a moment then ran out into the hall.

Becky followed her and sat down on the stairs. Sarah took one look in the mirror and groaned. Her hair was a mess from running her hands through it, and her face was streaked with tears. She licked the tips of her fingers and rubbed at her cheeks. 'Oh, what the hell does it matter what I look like?'

'You look fine,' said Becky, standing up and holding on to the newel post.

Sarah grabbed keys off the hall table and opened the door. The night was still and warm. Neighbours two doors down were barbecuing, smoke and the sound of laughter permeating the air. She stepped onto the doorstep and took a deep breath of the smoggy air. 'Wish me luck.'

'Sarah?'

'What?'

'You should go to Australia.'

She paused, came back inside and partially closed the door. They had talked about the possibility before but Becky had never before given her assent. 'You wouldn't mind?'

'Not if it made you happy. And I believe that without Cahal, you won't be. I'd miss you terribly of course, but I don't need you to look after me anymore. I have my own life.'

Sarah realised with sudden clarity that this was true. Since she'd started dating Tony, Becky's life had taken a more settled path and, though the sisters remained close, their relationship had changed. It was as if Becky had, finally, grown up.

Sarah felt the burden that she had carried since the day her mother died, lift. And a tear slipped out the corner of her eye.

'Oh, come here, you big cry-baby,' said Becky and she gave

Sarah a fierce hug.

'I'm sorry,' said Sarah. 'It's just that I'm really, really happy for you.' She thought for a few moments. 'But it wouldn't be fair to leave you with Dad and Aunt Vi to look after. I mean they're both great now but –'

'Sure, the two of them have constitutions like oxen,' laughed Becky.

Sarah forced a smile. 'But it's only a matter of time before they start to fail, isn't it?'

'I know. But I don't mind, Sarah, really.'

'You're saying that now. You might not feel the same when the time comes.'

'Honestly, Sarah, it's all right. I have thought about it. You can't stay here waiting for one of them to fall ill.'

'Well, it's really sweet of you to say that, Becky, and I appreciate it. But talk of me going to Australia is all pie in the sky. Ian would never agree to me taking the kids away.'

'He might not be able to stop you. Not if you go to court.'

Sarah was momentarily speechless. The idea had never occurred to her and she was shocked that Becky had suggested it. It seemed such a crude and brutal tool to accomplish what ought to be achieved through compromise and agreement.

An image came to mind. Ian in the hospital cradling newborn Molly the morning after the night she had been born. Sarah remembered drifting in and out of consciousness, exhausted by lack of sleep and loss of blood. But she recalled quite clearly, how he'd stood by the window in the grey morning light with this tiny, swaddled scrap of life in his arms – and cried silent tears of joy.

'Oh, Becky,' she said, her eyes brimming with tears. 'I might not love Ian, but I could never do that to him.'

Every house on Grace Avenue was shrouded in darkness, cars nestled in the narrow driveways, curtains drawn. Down in the town centre the church bell chimed midnight, the sound carried far and wide on the still night air.

The battery on her mobile was almost dead and Sarah's bottom ached from sitting on the cold concrete doorstep outside Cahal's house. His car was gone. She'd searched every pub she could think of and driven out to Ballygally and back, in case he'd taken a midnight walk to clear his head. She'd even braved the Drumalis estate to visit his parents' flat, but no one answered the door. And now she circled the bungalow, her arms wrapped around her body, while her mind began to suspect the worst. Where could he be? The noise of a car pulling up on the street sent Sarah racing to the front of the house. She saw at once that it was Cahal's car and ran down the drive to meet him, her heart pounding.

'Oh, darling, are you all right?' she cried, running into his arms. He had no jacket on, only the blue shirt and trousers he'd been wearing earlier. 'I've been so worried.'

His embrace was lacklustre and he did not reply at once. She pulled back. In the yellow light of the streetlamp, his eyes were black and wet and he smelt of beer. 'I'm all right,' he said, his voice heavy as lead, his face all shadows.

She grabbed his limp hand and said, 'Where have you been? I looked all over town. In every place I could think of. I've been texting and phoning all night too.'

'I'm sorry. I switched the phone off.'

'That's okay,' she sighed and her heartbeat slowed. 'I'm just so relieved you're all right.'

He smiled faintly then and said, 'You came looking for me?'

'Of course I did.'

He hung his head. 'You still love me then?'

She squeezed his hand tight. 'Oh, Cahal, how could I ever stop?'

She let go of his hand and slipped her arm round his waist. He draped his arm over her shoulder and together they walked to the house. Inside, he threw his keys on the coffee table and slumped on the sofa. He leaned back with his knees splayed apart and closed his eyes.

'Shall I make us some coffee?' she said.

'Please.'

When they both had mugs in their hands, Sarah curled up on the velvet armchair.

'What a night,' he said and shook his head sadly. He had dark rings under his eyes and his face was shadowed with black stubble. 'What happened after I left?'

Sarah looked into the milky coffee. 'Quite a lot. I had a chat with Aunt Vi and I found out from Dad that it was him that answered your phone call.'

'No surprise there.'

'But Aunt Vi never took your letters. Nor did Dad. It was Becky.'

'I thought you two were like this.' He lifted up his hand, middle and forefinger entwined together.

'We were. In a way, that's why she took them. She was afraid

I'd go off to Australia and leave her. She was only eleven, Cahal. She thought if she took them, I'd forget about you and everything would go back to the way it was.'

'And I suppose it did,' he said, one eyebrow raised cynically, his mouth unsmiling. 'So she got what she wanted.'

'Except that my heart was broken, Cahal. And I was never the same girl again.'

'Oh, sweetheart.' He knelt on the floor in front of her. His long black eyelashes brushed his cheek, and he said shyly, 'Have you had a chance to read any of the letters?'

Sarah's eyes filled with tears. 'I'm sorry, darling. She destroyed them a long time ago.'

'Oh.' He sat back on his heels and thought for a few moments. 'Maybe it's just as well.'

'What do you mean?' cried Sarah, who was still reeling from the injustice. 'Now I can never read them for myself. I'll never know what was in them.'

He sighed and smiled, and tucked a lock of hair behind her ear. 'Those letters were love letters, bursting with passion and feeling. I loved you so much I thought I would die without you. But they were also bitter and full of hateful recriminations against your family. They were meant for the eyes of a nineteen-year-old girl, Sarah, not a beautiful, confident woman. I'm afraid if you read them now you'd think them immature, childish even. So don't fret. The things that matter, we hold here and here.' He placed the flat of his hand over his heart, then touched his head. 'Not on pieces of paper. Okay?'

'Okay,' she smiled. Perhaps he was right. The letters were part of the past – it was time to let it go and look to the future.

He took his place on the sofa again. Rubbing his hands together he hung his head and looked up at her, his eyes narrow and small. 'I can understand now why everyone in your family hates me so much. I hate who I am.'

'Oh, Cahal.' His words tore at her heart. She uncurled her legs, went and sat beside him and placed a hand on his arm. 'Don't say that.'

'How would you feel if you found out you were the child of a rapist?'

Sarah tried to put herself in his shoes, to feel what he was feeling but it was beyond her comprehension. She felt so desperately sorry for him. 'I can't imagine what you must feel like.'

He rubbed his face with his hands. 'I feel like I've been contaminated by something evil. It's as if part of him lives inside me. Here.' He thumped his chest with a balled fist. 'I knew he was capable of violence of course. He used to knock us about – and my mother.'

Sarah tried not to wince. Cahal had never spoken explicitly about his father's violence though reading between the lines, and having met the man, she was not surprised. He had an aura of suppressed rage about him.

'But a sex crime against a defenceless young woman? It's … it's revolting. And do you know what he said to me when I confronted him? He said she asked for it.'

'Oh my God. How awful.' The statement hung in the air, vile and repugnant. Sarah had never hated anyone more in that moment than she hated Malachy Mulvenna. 'You saw

338

him tonight then?'

'Yes. When they weren't at home I went straight to Ballyfergus Social Club. They're never out of the place. Cheapest drink in County Antrim.' He gave a small cynical laugh. 'My mother was there too.'

Up till now he had avoided looking Sarah in the eye, as if he could not bear to look at her. But now he stared at her intensely, his eyes full of tears and his face all crumpled up. 'She knew all along, Sarah. She knew about it and she stayed with him.' He curled his lips up in disgust and looked away. 'You know, I've always seen her as a victim,' he said angrily, 'I've always stood up against him to protect her. But now I see that she's no better than him. Well, that's it. I'm finished with the two of them. I never want to see either of them again. I don't even want to be in the same country as them.'

Tears blurred Sarah's vision. Blinking them away, she took his hand in hers and unfurled his fingers. 'Cahal, darling, look at me.' She held his hand, her fingers interlocked with his, and when he did at last look at her, she said, 'You are only your father's son in the biological sense. You can't change the fact that he fathered you, but you can rise above it. Haven't you already? You have a pure soul, you are a good person and no one who's met you can possibly think otherwise.'

'Your family do.'

'No, they don't, Cahal. They just can't bear the thought of being connected in any way to your father.'

'I won't blame you if you feel the same.'

'Nothing could make me feel differently about you, Cahal. You are the love of my life. You always will be.'

'And you are mine, my darling Sarah. You are the only thing I need in this world to be happy.'

She felt like she was floating. Her worries momentarily evaporated and all that mattered was this moment with his hand in hers and his dark eyes drawing her closer, filling her up with desire. His face leaned towards hers and he kissed her on the lips, soft and tenderly. She closed her eyes and the old fire ignited, just as it had always done.

When they pulled apart, he smiled. 'That's what I love about you, Sarah. I know you always tell me the truth.'

Her mouth went dry. If she let that pass unremarked, her chance may never come again. She closed her eyes fleetingly and prayed for strength.

'What is it, Sarah?'

Tonight had been all about the truth and she still had one secret to tell. But would Cahal forgive her as easily as Becky had done? She cleared her throat, opened her eyes and untangled her hand from his grasp.

'There's something I have to tell you.'

A guarded look crossed his face and he waited.

She swallowed. 'Something happened a long time ago that I should've told you about.'

'Not more secrets?' he joked, but when she did not smile but only stared grimly at him, the humour faded from his face.

'When you went to Australia …' Her voice caught in her throat. 'I … I … don't know how to tell you this.'

She stared at the swirling pattern on the carpet. In the silence of the night, the house creaked. She must shake free of this secret or it would, like a weed, eventually strangle the trust between them.

'I did something that I'm deeply ashamed of. But you have to understand that I did it because I was angry and I thought you no longer cared for me, and I wanted so desperately to hurt you.' She looked up. His brow was furrowed in concentration. 'You see, I'd waited all summer for you to write and when I went back to uni in the autumn ...' Her voice trailed away.

He stared at her. The Adam's apple in his throat moved.

'I ... I slept with Tony McLoughlin.'

There was a long, awful moment of silence. A sequence of emotions rippled across Cahal's face – disbelief, hurt and finally, anger. He jumped off the sofa, his eyes bulging. 'Jesus, Sarah. Tony McLoughlin. That bastard?'

'Don't blame him, Cahal. You were long gone and I suppose I more-or-less threw myself at him.'

'But why?'

'I told you why. I was angry. I hated you, or rather I thought I hated you.' She paused and pleaded, 'But aren't love and hate flip sides of the same coin, Cahal?'

'You hated me so much, you loved another man,' he said in a scathing voice, his bitter gaze unbearable.

Blood pounded through her veins, filling her ears with noise and her head with a sharp, intense pain. She wiped her damp palms on the thighs of her jeans. 'It wasn't love, Cahal. There was no emotion involved. It could've been anyone. I was so drunk I barely remember it.' She blushed with humiliation. 'I avoided him after that. And when he went off to Queen's at the end of that year, I hoped never to see him again.'

He flopped down on the sofa, folded his arms and stared straight ahead.

'You've every right to be angry with me, Cahal. It was a very stupid thing to do but it was a long time ago. And I'm very sorry.'

He turned his head slowly and stared at her for a long time and then he said, 'You were drunk?'

'Very.'

'And you believed that I had dumped you.'

'Yes.' He paused, his eyebrows almost meeting in the middle, and she said, 'Tony didn't do anything wrong. As far as he was concerned I was no longer your girlfriend.'

All of a sudden the anger seemed to go out of him.

'It hurts, Sarah. To know that you were in bed with him when I was thousands of miles away with a broken heart.' He shook his head.

'I'm so sorry. I wish I could turn the clock back.'

He sighed heavily. 'Don't we all?' He stared into her eyes, his pupils huge and black. 'To me you've not changed at all. You are still the girl I fell in love with.'

Her body shook like a leaf and she barely managed to contain the tears that threatened to spill out. 'Oh, Cahal, please say you forgive me.'

'Come here.' He pulled her to him roughly and hugged her tight. 'Of course I forgive you.' She pressed her face into his hot, hard chest, and silent tears streamed down her face.

'Does Becky know?' he said.

Sarah sniffed. 'Yes.'

'And?'

'We talked. She's okay about it.'

He kissed the top of her head and held her tighter still. 'I don't blame you for anything, Sarah. I blame my father for all of this. You ever heard of the butterfly effect?'

She looked up into his face. 'If a butterfly flaps its wings in one part of the world, it can cause a hurricane in another.'

'Exactly,' he said, wiping her tears away with his thumb. 'The effects of what my father did all those years ago have rippled down the years, and left us where we are today.'

She placed a hand on his chest and felt the beat of his heart, steady and strong. 'Thank God we found each other again.'

His expression darkened. 'But if we'd never been forced apart in the first place, we wouldn't have married other people, had kids with them and we wouldn't now be where we are, with my family on the other side of the world and yours here.'

She tried to close her ears. She did not want to hear. Talking about it did not change anything, though she wished with all her heart that it would. She put her hand on the back of his head and pulled his face down. She kissed him long and hard on the lips, as more silent tears crept out the corners of her eyes.

He pulled away and she sat up straight. 'I'll wait for you, Sarah. You do know that. I'll wait until we can be together and I don't care how long that takes.'

'Please, Cahal, don't,' she said, choking up. She placed a finger over his lips. 'I can't bear to think it, let alone talk about it.'

'We have to face up to reality, my darling, even though it breaks my heart.'

'Well, I don't want to, not now, not ever,' she blurted out childishly, tears streaming down her face. She threw himself into his arms. 'I can't bear it.'

Chapter 20

The nursing home was quiet and still, all the residents tucked up in bed for the night. In Evelyn's room the blind was drawn and a single lamp burned on the bedside table casting a golden glow on the shrunken, motionless figure in the bed. Evelyn lay as if asleep, her mouth open, her head tilted back, her face grey as dust. Her breath was audible in the silence, raspy and laboured, every inhalation a gargantuan effort, every exhalation a relief to Ian who sat on a chair by her bed.

The get-well cards and the flowers were all gone from the room, the hope that she might recover from this last bout of pneumonia quietly surrendered weeks ago. There was no hope now, only the reality of the minutes ticking by, each one of which might take her. But she was a fighter. Every time she breathed in, he held his breath expecting it to be her last. But then the air would come out again and she lived a moment longer.

The door opened and Sarah slipped quietly into the room with a fearful glance at Evelyn. She went over and held Evelyn's hand for a long time, then released it and sat down on a chair on the other side of the bed. 'I just checked with Dad,' she whispered, setting her bag on the floor. 'The kids are fine. They can stay there as long as …' Her gaze travelled to Evelyn's ashen face. '… as it takes.'

He rubbed his eyes, dry and itchy from watching. Sarah said softly, 'You haven't eaten all day. Jolanta's on duty tonight. She'll make you a sandwich or something. Shall I go and ask?'

He shook his head. 'Dr Glover said he thought it would be tonight. I can't see her going on like this much longer, can you?'

He glanced at Sarah and her bottom lip wobbled and he could see from the way her jaw worked that it took every ounce of control to stop herself from breaking down in tears. 'No, Ian, I can't.'

He nodded and bit the inside of his cheek. Everything that needed to be done was done. The arrangements with the funeral directors were all made. It felt as if time itself had stopped, suspended like Evelyn, between life and death.

'Oh, Jesus,' he said and put his hands over his face. It was unbearable. Every rasping breath raked across his brain like chalk on a blackboard. Why wouldn't God take her? 'Why does she have to suffer so?'

'I don't think she feels any pain,' said Sarah firmly. 'Not with the morphine.'

Panic filled his chest, sending his heart racing, sweating his palms. 'I'm afraid, Sarah.'

346

'Don't be. She needs you to be strong now.'

He felt so useless. He could not help his mother now. Evelyn breathed in and Ian closed his eyes and waited. One second. Two seconds. Three seconds. No sound, just silence pressing down like a dead weight. He opened his eyes, leapt out of the seat and leaned over his mother's body, his heart pounding, his body bathed in sweat.

And then it came, the crackle of breath leaving her body once more.

Sarah, who had jumped to her feet at the same time as Ian, stared at him across the bed, her hand on her heart, her eyes wide. 'Dr Glover said that the last thing to go is the hearing, Ian.'

'Okay.' Blood pumped round his veins too fast, making it hard to think clearly, to think at all. He felt a change in the room. Tension crackled like electricity. His chest felt like it was being flattened by an enormous weight, making it hard to breathe in the stuffy room. He took his mother's limp hand in his. It felt like ice. 'Her hand is so cold, Sarah.'

'Shall I leave you?' said Sarah, moving towards the door.

Without taking his eyes off Evelyn, he said, 'No. Stay. Please.'

He leaned close and whispered in his mother's ear. 'It's Ian here. I love you, Mum. I love you so much. You are the best mum in the world and I'm going to miss you very much.'

Sarah stifled a sob and Evelyn breathed in once more, but shallower than before. And then the agonising wait before the breath left her body once more, gurgling like water down a plughole.

She breathed in. Ian held his breath and steeled himself

for the horrible rattling sound of her breath coming out. But this time, the long seconds ticked by. Her chest stilled and she breathed no more.

He breathed out slowly and the tension in the room dissipated, replaced by a calm sort of peace. The worst had finally happened. It was over. He stood for a long time, composed and grave, with her cold hand in his. When he was absolutely certain she was gone, he arranged her hand gently on the bedspread and looked at Sarah. 'What am I going to do without her?'

'I'm sorry, Ian.' Tears streaked her face but she was calm. She came round to his side of the bed and held out her arms. He stepped into her embrace and her arms closed round him, like a soft and gentle blanket. He hugged her back, pressing his face into her fine, sweet-smelling hair. And then the sobs came, jerking his whole body, a release of the tension that had built up like a pressure cooker these past months. He cried for a long time and she simply held him, wordlessly, the two of them united at last, not in love but in grief.

Later, after the doctor had been and they were waiting for the funeral director, they sat in the empty day room, with a cold grey dawn cracking the edge of the world. Ian held a mug of untouched tea in his hand. 'It's strange,' he said to Sarah, 'I knew the moment she died. Not because she stopped breathing ... it was more than that. She, her spirit I suppose I mean, was there one moment and the next it was gone. And the body lying on the bed ... it wasn't her.'

Sarah looked into her mug of tea. Her face was grey as the dawn, her lips pale. 'I was there when Mum died and I felt it too. I remember I turned to Dad – and this sounds weird but it's true – I was kind of elated. I said, *She's not here, Dad. She's gone.* I was glad because, after all the suffering, I knew her soul was free.'

Ian nodded. 'I know what you mean. And I know Mum's gone to a better place.'

Sarah smiled, though her eyes were wet with tears. 'Yes, Ian, I'm quite certain of that.' She looked at her watch. 'Dad'll be up by now. I'd better ring and let him and Aunt Vi know.' She rummaged in her bag and pulled out a mobile, the little gold ring Cahal Mulvenna had given her glinting on her finger. 'I'll make the call outside.'

He thought back to the last proper conversation he'd had with Evelyn when he finally realised that Sarah was lost to him forever. 'Sarah?'

She'd almost reached the door. She stopped and turned round. 'Yes?'

'Are you still seeing Cahal?'

She hesitated. He had never asked her about him, not since he'd come back from Australia. 'Yes,' she said cautiously. 'Why?'

'I just wondered. Doesn't he go back to Australia soon?'

She looked at the floor. 'Yes.'

'And what are your … your plans after that?'

She shrugged and said tonelessly, 'We'll stay in touch. See each other during the holidays, I suppose. Wait till the kids grow up.'

'And then?'

'Then we'll be together.' Her eyes flashed. 'The way we should have been from the very start.'

Ian flinched, steeled himself and said, 'And he'll wait for you?'

'He says he will. I'll definitely wait for him.' She smiled through the tears streaming down her face. 'But who knows what the future holds? You see, Cahal and I found out something that changes everything.'

'I know. Your Dad told me. But I knew about the rape long before that.'

Sarah stared at him in astonishment. 'How come?'

He scratched the back of his neck. 'I overheard your dad and my dad speaking about it when you started dating Cahal Mulvenna at uni.'

Sarah put a hand to her heart. 'You knew all these years and you never told me?'

He lifted his shoulders. He had felt guilty knowing when Sarah hadn't, but he also admired and respected Vi for her stoicism. 'It wasn't my secret to tell, Sarah. If your aunt had wanted you to know, she would've told you, wouldn't she?'

Sarah bowed her head. 'Yes, I suppose so.'

'You mustn't blame her – or your Dad – for not telling you. Or for holding it against Cahal Mulvenna.'

'I don't blame them. And neither does Cahal, though it's turned his whole world upside down. Even if he was willing to leave his kids for me – and I'd never ask him to do that – he can never settle here. Not after this. Aunt Vi can't bear the sight of him. He reminds her too much of his father.' She sniffed and wiped her nose on the back of her hand. 'So you see, it's really rather hopeless.'

*

Two weeks later, Sarah pulled up in front of Ian's house and her anxiety for him went up another notch. The grass was six inches high and the borders were knee-deep in weeds. He had always been a house-proud man but, since Evelyn's death two weeks ago, he'd completely lost interest in everything domestic.

Her heart ached with grief, not only for Evelyn, but for a future that had slipped through her grasp like sand. For tonight, in the early evening, Cahal would fly to London and, from there, on to Australia. She would not be there to see him off.

She bent over the steering wheel and a long, low wail of anguish escaped her. Fighting for breath with lungs that no longer had the will to work, she waited for her chest to implode with the unbearable pain. But it did not. Slowly, amazingly, the intense ache ebbed away, to be replaced with a dull, dead feeling between her breasts.

A single bronze leaf, crisp and dry, fell onto the windscreen of the car. It clung to the window wiper for a few moments, then blew away. Against the fence dividing Ian's house from the neighbours, the roses were all blown, heads bent as if in shame, their pink and yellow petals scattered across the unkempt garden. All around her death was on the march.

She took a deep breath, dug her nails into the palm of her hand and told herself to buck up. Even though her heart felt like it might crack in two, she had to be strong. It might be many long, lonely years before she and Cahal could be together, but she must take comfort from knowing that he lived and he was hers. Theirs would not be a life lived together after all, but lived apart. The Claddagh ring glowed amber in the afternoon sunshine, a reminder not so much of a promise made but one thwarted.

Maybe happiness had never been her destiny. Her future, it seemed, would bear more resemblance to her aunt's than she had ever dreamed possible. Her life would be one of duty, after all, a life where the happiness of others – her beloved children and Ian – would come before her own. And she must find a way to live that life with gratitude and serenity, taking joy where she could find it.

Pulling herself together, she got out of the car and retrieved a plastic bag from the boot. She let herself in the side gate and hooked the bag on the handle of the back door. She was just in the process of popping a note through the front door, when it opened, making her jump back in surprise.

'Hello,' said Ian, dressed in loose-fitting jeans and a grubby polo shirt.

'Ian! Aren't you working today?' she said, feeling a little guilty for having timed her visit with the express intention of avoiding him. As for herself, she'd arranged to work from home today because she couldn't bear being in the office knowing that Cahal was somewhere in the building clearing out his desk.

'I didn't feel like going in.' His face was unshaven, his eyes bloodshot and swollen. If she didn't know him better, she would've thought he'd been drinking. But then what must she look like? She'd hardly slept for weeks and spent most of today in tears.

'I left Molly's PE things on the back door,' she said. 'She forgot to pack them. She won't be allowed to do the fun run at school tomorrow without them.' It was because of the children she hauled herself out of bed every morning and carried on as if her world was not coming to an end.

'Thanks.'

'Molly has art after school and Lewis is going to Matt's for a play. You've to pick them both up at five.'

'Yeah, I haven't forgotten. Have they been okay?'

'Molly was crying again last night but she's okay now. We had a long talk about Evelyn. I don't think it's affected Lewis as much.' She regarded him thoughtfully, wondering if he was up to looking after the children. 'I'm worried about you, Ian,' she said gently. 'Maybe you should try to get back to work. A bit of routine might help.'

He shrugged and shoved his hands in his jeans pockets. 'Maybe in a day or two. I've been … I've had a lot to think about.'

'Of course. Look, if you're not up to it, I'm sure Dad and Aunt Vi would take the kids.'

'No, I want to see them. It helps,' he said simply.

There was an awkward silence and he said, 'Won't you come in?'

'I can't. I'm working from home and I really need to get on.'

'Please. I have something for you.'

She glanced at the car, and then back at Ian's wretched face. All she wanted to do was go home and curl up on the sofa and drink herself into oblivion. But she wasn't the only one suffering.

The coffee table was hidden under old papers, half-drunk mugs of tea and smoky bacon crisp packets – Ian's favourite snacks. The white marble mantelpiece and the gilt side table were littered with condolence cards. Sarah perched on the white sofa and placed her hands on her knees while Ian went off to make them both tea. She'd only been inside the house on a few occasions and she'd never felt comfortable. It was too perfect and too white. Now that Raquel was gone the décor felt too frivolous for a single man.

Ian came in carrying a mug in each hand. He kicked the door closed with his foot and handed her a mug. 'She didn't even send a sympathy card.'

Sarah stared at him uncomprehending and he said, 'Raquel.'

She hadn't come to the funeral either. 'I'm sorry,' she said, thinking that her dislike of Raquel had been well-founded after all. No matter what had gone on between her and Ian, she should've been there.

He sat down opposite her on a matching armchair and set his mug on a glass side table. 'Cahal's due to go back to Australia soon, isn't he?'

She eyed him warily. Oh God. Surely he wasn't thinking that with Cahal off the scene, there was hope of a reconciliation between them? She looked into the mug. Her hands were shaking, sending little ripples across the surface of the tea.

Last night she'd lain awake in Cahal's bed, his arm wrapped tightly round her waist, listening to the sound of his breathing and the creaks of the house. All night her emotions lurched from rage to despair and, when she finally fell into a doze around 6 in the morning, she awoke an hour later, consumed by sadness and the awful knowledge that no matter how she raged against the injustice of their circumstances, she and Cahal were powerless to change it.

In the morning, she sat across the kitchen table, and watched him butter toast, resentful of everyone who had played a part in this sorry tale – his father, Dad, Aunt Vi, Becky. Her eyes were dry and sore from lack of sleep. 'How can you leave me and go back to Melbourne?'

He paused with the knife in his hand. 'Oh, sweetheart, how can I not?' He set the knife down, leaned across the table and squeezed her hand so tight it hurt. 'We've been through this a hundred times. And I wish to God I could change things, but I can't.'

'Stay.'

He bowed his head and when he looked up his eyes were wet with tears. 'I can't, darling. The boys are expecting me. I can't let them down.'

She'd folded her arms stubbornly and sulked. 'So the boys are more important than me?'

He raised his eyebrows and his expression hardened a little. 'That's not fair, Sarah. And you know it. They're as important to me as your children are to you.'

She looked away and scowled. Frustration made her unreasonable and bad-tempered. And though she did not want to spoil their last moments together, she could not stop herself.

'I won't let you fall out with me,' he said, tilting her chin up with his forefinger.

She yanked her head away and glared at him. 'I don't understand how you can just accept it. Where's your fight?'

'Tell me what to do then, Sarah!' he shouted, bringing his

355

closed fist down on the table between them. 'Tell me how to change the past and by God, I'll do it!'

Her entire body shook. 'I just don't think you love me as much as I love you,' she blurted out.

'I do, Sarah.' His eyes bulged and the tendons on his neck stood out. 'But if I can't make you believe it, what chance do we have?'

'Sarah?' said Ian's voice, bringing her back to the present. She coughed and took a sip of tea to steady her nerves. She'd thought her relationship with Cahal strong enough to survive the separation but now she wasn't so sure. If this morning was anything to go by, it didn't bode well for the future. They'd kissed and made up, sort of, but the argument had left a sour, unfinished note between them. 'He flies home tonight. London first, then on to Melbourne tomorrow.'

'I see.' He rubbed his chin.

There was a long silence. Ian said, 'Tell me something, Sarah. Would you go to Australia if you could?'

'In a heartbeat.' She smiled sadly and added hastily, 'But I would never do that to you, Ian. I would never take the kids away from you.'

'You would leave your job and Becky and your Dad and Vi?'

She nodded. 'Yes.'

He stared at her for a long time with his hand over his mouth and then at last he stood up and said, 'Evelyn left you something in her will.'

'Oh.'

'She left some things for the kids, some jewellery, and

investments too,' he went on, rummaging in a lacquered jewellery box she recognised as Evelyn's, his big, broad back silhouetted in the light from the window. 'But I'll tell you all about that later.'

He closed the lid and came and knelt in front of Sarah. 'I'll never forget what you did for my mother, Sarah. Not just at the end but over the years, even after we'd split up. I'll never forget your kindness to her. She loved you.'

Sarah, all choked up, nodded.

'Here, take this.' He held her hand in his and pressed something into her palm. It was a gold chain with an emerald pendant on it. 'This meant a lot to her. Dad gave it to her on –'

'Their first wedding anniversary,' said Sarah, setting the mug down and fingering the pendant. How kind of Evelyn to give her in death something that had meant so much to her in life. 'She told me. She wore it in that picture of her and Harry all dressed up in their finery.'

Quickly, Ian wiped away tears. 'That's right. She wanted you to have it.'

'Thank you. It's lovely. And I shall treasure it always.' She closed her fingers on it and fought back the tears. 'I should go now. Thank you for this. And if you ever need a friend to talk to, you know where I am.' She stood up and took an uncertain step towards the door, her heart as heavy as lead, her legs like wood.

'Wait. There's something else I have to tell you.'

She turned and waited.

He rubbed his face with his hands. 'Mum said something

357

to me before she died. It was the last completely coherent conversation I had with her, in fact. And it was about you.'

'Oh,' Sarah's interest quickened and she sank onto the arm of the nearby chair.

'She knew that I loved you.' He paused and gave her a small, quick smile before looking away and addressing his hands. 'Love you. I didn't have to tell her. She just knew.'

Sarah pressed her lips together and closed her eyes. Why did he persist in talking like this when she'd made her feelings perfectly clear? It was torture for both of them. She opened her eyes. 'Ian ...' she said, a gentle admonishment, and left the sentence unfinished.

He went on, 'She said: "Take joy in her happiness, even if it comes at the price of your own". I know what she meant of course. That I should be glad for you and Cahal even though you being with him means that I will never be happy.'

'Oh, don't say that, Ian,' she said softly. 'There's someone out there for you. You just haven't found her yet.'

'Maybe, maybe not.' He looked at the palms of his hands. 'But I've thought about what Mum said over the past fortnight. I've thought of little else in fact. And I've come to a decision.'

Sarah's heartbeat quickened. What could he possibly mean?

He cleared his throat. 'There's nothing for me here in Ballyfergus anymore, not with Mum gone.' He paused and swallowed. 'And if I'm the only reason you can't go to Melbourne, well what would you say if that impediment was removed?'

'How?' she said fearfully. Was he offering his assent for her to take the children to Melbourne? Even if he did, the children would never be happy without their father. They would blame her for taking them away from him. And in her heart, though she loved Cahal with all her being, she would not take them away from the father they adored. And then another, awful thought occurred to her. Surely he wasn't talking about taking his own life? Her heart pounding, she put her hands to her face.

He fixed her with his steady blue gaze. 'What would you say to me emigrating to Australia too?'

'To Melbourne?' The blood drained from her face. 'You can't possibly be serious, Ian.'

He held out his big hands, palms upwards, and looked about the room. 'What is there for me here, Sarah? Raquel's gone, Mum's gone, I hate this house and I'm bored in my job. It would be a fresh start for me. For all of us.'

'All of us?' she said, a horrible sinking feeling in her stomach.

'Not together, obviously.' He gave a nervous little laugh. 'I'd get a place somewhere within driving distance of you so that I could see the kids easily. I wouldn't be riding on your coat tails, Sarah. I'd make my own life out there.'

She stared at him in puzzlement, barely able to take in what he was saying. 'You've spoken to the kids?'

'No, not yet. But I think they'll be fine so long as you and I are both there for them. They'll miss Becky and their grandad and Vi, but they can come out for holidays, can't they?'

All of a sudden happiness exploded in her heart, pushing aside the pain, like a flood bursting a dam. Her head felt light and fluffy inside like cotton wool, her thoughts jumbled and confused, joy and guilt and terror all competing for a place in her heart. She stood up abruptly, then sat down again, and covered her face with her hands. Tears came easily but this time they were tears of relief.

And then, just as quickly, her euphoria died away. She wiped her cheeks and stared at Ian. 'It's sweet of you to make the offer, but you've only just lost your mother. You aren't thinking straight.'

One side of his mouth turned up in a cynical smile. 'You always did try to tell me what to think, Sarah. But you're wrong. I've never before had such clarity of thought. I love you, Sarah, and I know that I can't make you happy. But Cahal can. Why should we both be miserable?'

She went over and sat on the coffee table in front of him with her hands between her knees. 'You'd do this for me?'

'For no one else.'

'But you hate Cahal.'

He shook his head. 'No, you're wrong. I only ever hated him because you loved him.'

Her heart filled up with guilty gratitude. 'Oh, Ian. You have no idea what this means to me.'

'I think I do.'

'I can never repay you.'

He nodded and, though his eyes were full of tears, he smiled. She jumped up and planted a kiss on the top of his balding head. 'You are a good, kind man, Ian Aitken. The very best. And someone will love you for it one day.'

'Yes, well. Hadn't you better go and tell Cahal?' he said,

without looking up.

'Yes, I must, right away.' Her heart skipped a beat. 'We argued this morning. I said some stupid things.' She glanced at her watch. 'Oh my God, his flight leaves in three and a half hours!'

She ran to the door, paused and looked back at Ian. His head was still bowed, as if he did not wish her to see his face. 'I'll never forget this, Ian,' she said, then slipped quietly from the room.

Once in the car, she grabbed the mobile she'd left lying on the passenger seat. She called Cahal but there was no answer. Throwing the phone to one side, she fired up the engine and drove off, tyres screeching on the tarmac.

The house at Grace Avenue was locked up. She ran around the building, stopping to peer in every window. The bed was stripped and all his things were gone. She dashed back to the front of the house, pulled the phone out of her pocket and tried a different number.

'Jessica,' she said breathlessly, running back to the car, 'has Cahal left for the airport?'

'I saw him get into a taxi just now. Why? What's up?'

'I'll explain later.'

She hung up. They were flying out of Belfast International. The airport was just outside Templepatrick and roughly equidistant from Belfast city centre and Ballyfergus. If she put her foot down, she might just make it in time … On the main road, she put her foot down. Sweat pooled in the middle of her back as she struggled to resist the urge to overtake where it was not safe. The road was choked with elderly drivers going too slow. A stream of lorries, just off the ferry, chugged and wheezed up the slow incline out of the town. Occasional tractors trundled onto the road without a care in the world. And all the time she had one eye on the clock.

At last, after an agonising journey that felt as if it had lasted for hours, though it was only forty minutes, she pulled into the airport car park. Ditching the car in the first space she could find, she sprinted across to the check-in lounge, hair flying out wildly behind her, blood rushing in her ears.

Inside, she paused to catch her breath and looked around. She searched desperately for Cahal's face amongst the crowds of business people, families, and a hen party checking in for Larnaca, all dressed in pink T-shirts and wearing sparkly silver cowboy hats. But he was not in any of the queues. She peered at the exit that led into departures and caught a glimpse of a man, the same height and build of Cahal, just disappearing round the corner. She bolted across the hall, rounded the corner and almost bumped into a female official at a desk.

'Boarding pass, please,' said the woman.

'I ... don't ... I just need to speak to that man.' She pointed at his rapidly disappearing back.

'I'm sorry, madam, but you need a boarding pass to enter this area.'

'Cahal,' she cried out. 'I'm here.' He ignored her and she took a couple of steps past the official's desk and screamed again, this time so loudly everyone in the building must've heard. 'Cahal. Over here!' The man turned his head, but it was not Cahal, just another businessman in a suit. Her heart sank.

'Madam, you are not allowed beyond this point without a boarding pass,' said the official and before she knew what was happening two strong arms had grabbed hers behind her back.

'Let's just calm down, darling,' said a voice in her ear and she cringed with embarrassment.

'Sorry. I thought he was someone else.'

The arms released her and she turned to find herself face to face with a security guard who, though big and burly with a florid face, had kind eyes. She looked down at her grubby sweatpants and trainers — he must think her some sort of chav. 'I thought he was my boyfriend,' she said lamely.

He squinted at her and said, 'Are you flying today?'

She shook her head.

'Then I'll have to ask you to leave the building. Come on, darling, this way.' And though he took her by the arm, his grasp was gentle.

He escorted her through the check-in lounge. Everyone turned to look at the source of the commotion and Sarah wished the ground would swallow her up. And then she heard a female voice call out her name.

'Sarah?'

She glanced up to find Jody towering over her on legs like stilts, her big teeth exposed in a grin. Inside, she groaned and then brightened. Where Cahal went Jody usually wasn't far behind. She craned to see past her but there was no sign of Cahal.

Jody walked over, touched her perfect jaw with the tips of her perfectly manicured fingers, and said, 'What are you doing here?'

The security man stopped dead. Jody had that kind of voice. Commanding.

'I … eh … I was looking for Cahal,' she said.

'Oh, he's right here,' she said and stepped to the side. He appeared from nowhere, staring at her in bewilderment and looking incredibly handsome in a navy suit and blue shirt, briefcase in one hand, coat in the other. Promptly she burst into tears.

'So this is the boyfriend, love?' said the security guard.

She nodded and he let go of her arm. And then suddenly she felt Cahal's arms around her. She pressed her face into his neck, her salty tears running down the collar of his shirt. He smelt of spice and soap and his hands on her back were firm and strong. He held on to her for a long time and, when she'd composed herself, they pulled apart. Cahal's briefcase and coat lay at his feet and his face was stricken. 'What's wrong, Sarah? Has something happened?'

The security guard said, 'Guess I'd better leave you to it. But no more of yer carry on, do you hear me? Next time, you'll get arrested.'

'Okay,' she said sheepishly and, when the guard walked off, she smiled at Cahal. 'I couldn't let you go without saying a proper goodbye, could I?'

He touched her hair. 'I'm sorry we quarrelled this morning.'

'Me too. Oh, but never mind that now.' She placed a hand on his chest. 'Cahal, I have the most wonderful news.'

'Jody! Cahal!' someone called from the front of the queue. 'Time to check in.'

Cahal grabbed her hands. 'What news, Sarah?'

'You'll never believe it. Ian's going to move to Melbourne.'

'Who's Ian?' said Jody.

He thrust his head forward, his eyes wide and startled. 'You mean emigrate?'

Sarah nodded her head, unable to keep the big, foolish grin off her face. 'Yes. He says that there's nothing for him here now that Evelyn's gone. And he knows the only reason I won't take the kids to Australia is because of him.'

A slow, incredulous smile started at his mouth and spread upwards until the corners of his eyes were all crinkled up and his lips stretched in a wide grin. He had never looked so gorgeous. 'Does this mean that you'll move to Melbourne?'

Giddiness fizzed up inside her like the bubbles in a washing-up bowl. 'Yes!' she squealed, clapping her hands to her face and jumping up and down on the spot. 'Yes!'

'Oh sweetheart, that's the best news I've ever heard.' He hugged her tightly and when they parted said, 'But why would he do that?'

'He says he can't make me happy but he knows you can.'

Cahal brushed a strand of hair off her forehead and smiled sadly. 'Poor Ian. He must love you very much, Sarah. Possibly as much as I do. You always said he was a good guy, well, I don't know many men who would do this.'

'Cahal,' said Jody, coldly. 'Check-in's closing. We're going to miss our flight.'

'You go, Jody,' he said, without taking his eyes off Sarah. 'I'm staying.'

Jody stomped off with a flick of her blonde hair, her pert bottom wiggling in a tight skirt, the wheels of her trolley bag clicking on the tiled floor.

'Somebody's not happy,' said Sarah and giggled.

Cahal glanced at Jody and rolled his eyes.

She said, 'But what about your boys?'

'One more day won't make any difference, will it?' he said, nuzzling her neck. 'You and I have a lot to talk about. We've got a future to plan.'

Chapter 21

'You've just missed them, mate,' said Brady as soon as he opened the door to Cahal in baggy surfing shorts and flip-flops. 'Adele's taken them down to the mall. Tom's just gone and grown out of all his shoes. Again!' He laughed heartily and put a hand on his belly.

'Actually, Brady, it was you I wanted to see, not the boys.'

'Oh, right. You'd better come in then.' He ambled down the hall into the kitchen cum family room, the hub of this home, and Cahal followed.

Brady opened the fridge and said, 'Wanna beer?'

'No thanks.'

Brady closed the fridge door, folded his beefy arms and said, 'What can I do for you?'

Cahal shoved his hands in the front pockets of his jeans. It had not been easy to come here today. He'd arrived home a month ago and he'd only just strummed up the courage to make this long-overdue visit to Brady. He cleared his throat. 'I hardly know where to begin, Brady.'

Brady cocked his head and looked at him curiously. 'The beginning's usually as good a place as any,' he said genially, leaned against the counter and waited.

Cahal smiled at this dose of homespun wisdom which he would normally have scoffed at but which, today, seemed wise and apt. 'When Adele got together with you, I wasn't in a good place. I resented you moving into my house.' He paused to look round the room. 'With my kids.'

Brady acknowledged this with a twitch of his big head. 'Couldn't have been easy.'

'And the more the boys came to like you, the more jealous I became.'

Brady looked perplexed. 'Jealous of what?'

'Your relationship with them and the fact that you live with them and I don't.' He looked at his shoes. 'Sometimes I think that they like you more than me.'

Brady snorted. 'You're their Dad. They love you.'

'I know. But I think … what I'm trying to say is … I'm trying to apologise, Brady. For being a drongo. I know I haven't always made things easy for you and Adele.'

Brady acknowledged this by puffing his cheeks up with air then blowing it out.

Cahal went on, 'I just want to say that I'm glad Adele married you. You've made her happier than I ever did, I think. I want to thank you for that and for everything you do for my boys. I appreciate it.'

Brady blinked and poked the inside corner of his right eye

with the tip of a big, stubby finger. 'They're good kids.'

Cahal looked at his feet. 'We bring different things to the party, Brady, and I see now how much the boys benefit from having you as a stepdad.'

Brady sniffed and looked out the window. 'You're making me embarrassed now.'

'I don't mean to. We kinda got off on the wrong foot – you and me – and I was wondering if … if you'd be willing to give it, give us, another go. I don't suppose we'll ever be best buddies, but, you know, it'd be good if we got on.'

Brady looked at him for a few short moments. 'Sure, mate. I'd like that. And so would the boys and Adele.' He came over and slapped Cahal on the back so hard he stumbled forward.

Recovering, Cahal grinned. 'How about that beer then?'

Brady grinned back. 'Thought you'd never ask.' He opened the fridge, lifted out two bottles of beer with one hand and expertly twisted the lids off with the other. He nodded at the big-screen TV on the other side of the room. 'The footy's just coming on. Geelong's playing St Kilda in the semi-final. Why don't you stay and watch it?'

Sarah picked the photograph up off the shelf and smiled. It had been taken on Chelsea Beach, Melbourne at Christmas. Molly and Lewis, standing between her and Cahal, were holding up huge ice creams as were Adele, Brady, her three kids and Brady's grown-up daughter, Michelle. Everyone had big grins on their faces. An unconventional family, but a family none the less. It had been a happy, exciting visit, seeing the sights and looking at houses. She'd liked Adele and Brady from the off, both down-to-earth and genuinely pleased, it seemed to her, to see Cahal happy. And now, three months later, here she was, packing her life into cardboard boxes.

'Do you think I should take this one on the plane, Mum?' said Molly, coming into the room, wearing pink skinny jeans and holding up two fleeces, one white, one red. 'Or this one?'

Sarah swathed the photograph in bubble wrap and tucked it inside the sturdy cardboard box along with the others. 'It's a long flight and things'll get grubby. The red one won't show the dirt so much.'

Lewis wandered in with a Nerf gun in his hand, took aim and fired a soft foam bullet at Molly's bum. His hair was gelled into a ginger Mohican.

'Stop that, Lewis,' shouted Molly, chucking the fleeces on the floor. 'Mum, look what I have to put up with! And you've been at my hair gel again, haven't you, you little creep?' She made a lunge for Lewis but he sidestepped out of the way.

'Lewis, don't do that to your sister,' she said, suppressing a laugh and scooping the fleeces off the floor. 'Molly, do try to be more tolerant.'

Lewis charged around the room, making noises like a siren. Molly let out a big, heartfelt sigh, placed her hands on her hips and rolled her eyes. 'But he's so annoying, Mum. I don't go into his room and use his hair gel.'

'That's because I haven't got any,' said Lewis, sticking out his tongue.

'Enough!' cried Sarah. 'Come here, you two.' Reluctantly both children approached, Lewis with a mischievous look on his face, Molly a thunderous one. She encircled both children with her arms and pulled them close. 'Come on, hug it out.' They embraced each other and she kissed the tops of their heads inhaling the scent of them. Their babyhoods were long gone but the smell of them was still as recognisable to her as their faces. 'I'm not letting go until you do it properly.'

The arms around her tightened and Molly pulled away first. 'All right, Mum. Enough,' she said, trying to suppress a smile.

'That's better isn't it?' said Sarah. 'Sure you love each other really, don't you?'

Lewis giggled and Molly said, trying but not quite succeeding in sounding cross, 'I suppose so.'

'But not as much as I love you,' said Sarah. 'You two are the light of my life.' Both children's chins lifted and they smiled contentedly. 'Are you excited about going to live in Melbourne?' she said.

'Yes!' they both cried in unison.

'We'll have a lot to do when we get there.'

'I'm going to swim in the pool all day!' said Molly. They'd found a house to rent in upmarket Toorak. It was costing them an arm and a leg but it wouldn't be forever. Once Cahal found a buyer for his apartment, and she sold her house, they would buy a place together.

'I'm going to have a Nerf gun fight with Tom.' The children had met Cahal's three boys at Christmas and, so far, so good. Lewis had taken to them straight away, deciding Tom was his best mate and hero-worshipping cool Jed. Molly had been more circumspect but that was only to be expected in a girl her age.

'Hmm,' said Sarah. 'School starts in two weeks. I was thinking more along the lines of school uniforms and registering us all with a doctor and a dentist.' She frowned, thinking of something else to add to her already too-long 'to do' list. 'Oh, and we'll have to find out about the buses to school.'

Molly and Lewis exchanged glances and Sarah said, 'But we'll take time to do some fun stuff too. It'll be a wee while before I start work.'

Cahal staggered into the room under the weight of the box in his arms, his shirt sleeves rolled up, sweat beading his brow. 'That's the last of the boxes from Molly's room. Hey, what you got in this, Molly?'

'Books.'

He set it down, rubbed the small of his back and gave Sarah a peck on the lips. 'Right, I'm going to start on the garage.'

She ran her hand through her hair. 'There's loads of old toys and bikes out there. I think most of it'll have to go out.'

Cahal turned to the kids, hands on slim, jean-clad hips. 'Kids, you wanna tell me what to keep and what to throw out?'

'I want to keep my dolls,' said Molly.

'I want my stunt scooter,' said Lewis and raced Molly out the door. Cahal chuckled, scooped Sarah up in his arms and lifted her right off her feet in a bear hug. He twirled her round until her head was spinning and she begged for him to put her down. 'Dad or Aunt Vi might come in,' she giggled. 'Or Becky.' They were all working in different parts of the house. Tomorrow the removal company would come and, in the evening, they would fly to London on the first leg of the most exciting journey of her life.

He set her on her feet, and traced the curve of her T-shirt down and across her chest with his finger and his eyes. Then he cupped her face in his hands and looked deep into her eyes. 'I love you, Sarah.'

'And I love you too.' She slipped her hands into the back pockets of his jeans and looked up into his face. 'You know Cahal, I've never been so happy in my entire life. I'm sad to leave my family but I know that we're going to be so happy together.'

He took her hands in his and they both looked down at the small gold ring that now resided on the ring finger of her left hand. When they married in a few months' time, it would turn the other way, the point of the heart facing inwards. And then her happiness would be complete.

'My grandmother would've loved you, Sarah. She was a good person, just like you.'

'Just like you,' she said and smiled and he rubbed the contours of the little ring with his thumb.

Molly's voice carried in from the hall. 'Are you coming or what, Cahal? We've been waiting ages.'

Cahal grinned and lightly smacked her bottom. 'I'd better go.' Sarah watched him walk out of the room, and a little bit of her went with him. It was as if they were not two separate people but joined by an invisible connection. Her life was so full and rich now, and she saw the world through a different lens. Everything was bright and clear, as if someone had switched on the lights, or cleaned a grubby window she had been looking out of all these years. And she wondered how she had survived without him.

Later, when Cahal had gone to the dump and the children were playing with old toys newly discovered in the garage, Aunt Vi called, 'Tea-break!' Sarah went straight into the kitchen to find all the cupboards open and the shelves bare. Five mugs and a plate of homemade, buttered gingerbread sat on the table. Dad, his glasses slipped down the tip of his nose and a pink sponge in his hand, peered inside the empty cutlery drawer.

Aunt Vi poured tea into a mug on the table. 'Where's Cahal?' she said as soon as Sarah came in.

Sarah told her and she said, 'Oh, I would've waited if I'd known.'

'Sure, he can have a cuppa later,' said Sarah, filled with admiration for her aunt, who not only had accepted the plan to move to Australia with resignation, but had been civil to Cahal ever since. She had even apologised to him for her outburst that day in this kitchen. The same day that Sarah had finally learned the meaning of duty and self-sacrifice.

'Do you never clean out your kitchen drawers?' said Dad, flicking crumbs out onto the floor. 'You should see the muck in here.'

Sarah suppressed a smile. 'Don't be wasting your time on that, Dad,' she said, taking her usual seat at the table. 'It's not going to make any difference to the selling price.'

He sighed and frowned. 'I suppose not,' he said, chucking the sponge in the sink. He came over, pinched the fabric of his trousers just above the knee and hoisted them up an inch, before sitting down at the table with a soft sigh. He placed one liver-spotted hand on his knee, the other on the table.

'Well, love,' he said, looking at Sarah with bleary eyes. 'Tomorrow you start a whole new life. I hope it makes you happy.' He paused and glanced at Aunt Vi who was topping up the teapot by the sink, her head turned so that Sarah could not see her face. 'Me and your aunt, well, we'll miss you and the children.'

A hard lump formed in Sarah's throat. For she knew her happiness came at the expense of her father and her aunt. She would be forever grateful to them for their stoicism.

Aunt Vi set the teapot on the top of the cooker with a dull clang and sat down at the table opposite Dad. 'I remember the day you and Ian got the keys for this place,' she said and Dad nodded and smiled wistfully.

'I'm sorry that things didn't work out with Ian,' went on Aunt Vi, looking at her hands. 'I had such high hopes for you both. And I'm sorry that you've had to wait all these years to be with your one true love.'

Sarah put a hand out over her aunt's and gently squeezed, painfully aware that Vi had lost the only love of her life. 'You don't have to apologise, Aunt Vi. If I had been you, I would have done exactly the same thing.'

Aunt Vi looked up and smiled. 'Thank you for saying that, Sarah. It means a lot.'

'And it means a lot to me that you've been so good about all this. Especially with me taking the children away.'

Everyone fell silent for a few long moments and Dad said, his voice all choked up, 'We only ever wanted you to be happy, Sarah.'

Sarah's throat burned and tears bound her eyelashes in

clumps. 'I know that, Dad.'

'It's what your mother would've wanted too.'

Sarah let go of Aunt Vi's hand and grasped her father's instead as he went on, 'We just want you to know that ... we ...'

His voice tailed off and Aunt Vi finished the sentence, blinking rapidly behind thick glasses. 'We want you to know that what you're doing is the right thing.' She looked at her brother. 'The only thing. For all of us. If you stayed here ... well, you know how your Dad and I feel about the Mulvennas.'

'Yes,' said Dad, who'd regained his composure. 'It's for the best, love.'

They all straightened up at the sound of Becky coming up the hall. Sarah let go of her Dad's hand and deftly flicked the tears from her eyelashes.

'What's for the best?' said Becky, coming in and flopping down on the seat opposite Sarah.

'That Cahal makes an honest woman of her!' said Aunt Vi cheerfully and drank some tea.

'Course he will.' Becky took a slice of gingerbread and crammed half of it into her mouth. 'God, I'm starving,' she said, chewing her food. 'Can't seem to get enough to eat these days.'

'Watch yourself, girl. You'll get fat,' said Aunt Vi. Becky rolled her eyes, shoved another bit of gingerbread into her mouth, and Sarah smiled inwardly.

'So when do you plan to marry?' said Dad.

'We have to get married within nine months of my arriving in Australia,' said Sarah, playing with a teaspoon. 'So we were thinking Christmas. It'll be a very quiet registry office wedding, but I was hoping you'd all come out for it.' She added hastily, 'None of Cahal's family will be coming.'

Dad looked at Aunt Vi and said, 'Well, I don't see why not. What do you think, Vi?'

'A visit around Christmas time might be nice.'

Sarah's spirits lifted. She had worried they would say no.

Becky said, 'And you don't mind not having a fancy wedding?'

Sarah smiled broadly. 'I'd happily marry him in a sewage works wearing my gardening clothes, Becky.'

Later, when she was alone in the still and quiet house, Sarah stood in the lounge, her life stacked around her in cardboard boxes. Dust motes circled in a beam of late afternoon sun that shone on the dark patch of carpet where the rug had lain for the past eight years. Outside in the garden, the snowdrops were bent and withered and the white fluffy catkins on the pussy willow were almost finished. In a month's time the cherry tree would be heavy with lush pink blooms and the yellow daffodils and red tulips would jostle for space in the borders.

And she and the children would be on the other side of the world, where the seasons were upside down and everything was new. Sarah tiptoed quietly out of the house that no longer felt like it belonged to her, and locked the door.

Later, at Dad's, the table in the cramped dining room was laid with Mum and Dad's wedding cutlery and crystal glasses that spent most of their life on display in the corner unit. Aunt Vi was putting the finishing touches to the table – salt and pepper, and expanding metal table mats.

'You've gone to a lot of trouble, Aunt Vi,' said Sarah. 'It's only a carry-out.'

Aunt Vi looked up and said brightly, though her eyes were sad, 'It's the last meal we'll have together as a family for a very long time.'

'The last supper,' observed Sarah, her voice catching in her throat.

Aunt Vi came and stood beside her and together they surveyed the table. 'You could say that.' She gave Sarah a brief, self-conscious squeeze across the shoulders, then let go. 'So let's make it a good one.'

The back door bursting open in the kitchen made them both go and look. The children came running through from the hall, nearly knocking over Dad. 'Hey, take it easy!' he called out genially.

Cahal came through the door first, jacketless and laden down with white carrier bags, the muscles in his forearms standing out like ropes. The smell of Indian food filled the small room. He grinned at Sarah and winked. 'Where do you want these?'

'Let me take them,' said Aunt Vi, bustling into action. She took one bag out of his hand and he jerked a thumb over his shoulder and said to Sarah, 'I picked up two renegades on the way over. And Ian's car's just pulled up out front.'

Tony came through the door next with Becky right behind him. He said something over his shoulder and she giggled, then slapped a hand over her mouth. Tony held up a bottle of red wine in one hand and a bottle of white, wet with condensation, in the other. 'I hope you don't mind, David, but I brought these.'

Dad chuckled. 'Not at all, Tony, just don't make me drink any of the stuff! I think you'll find a corkscrew in that drawer there.'

Tony went over, rummaged in a drawer, pulled out an ancient corkscrew and set to on the wine.

Ian appeared at the back door then, wearing a smart navy jacket and tan chinos. He stood uncertainly on the doorstep, holding a big box of Thornton's chocolates in both hands. Sarah went over to the door and smiled. 'Come on in, Ian. Getting a bit chilly out there now, isn't it?'

'Yeah.' He stepped into the by now packed room, and smiled, 'It's like church on Christmas morning in here!'

Everyone laughed, Lewis cried out, 'Dad!' Then he pushed past his grandfather and threw his arms round Ian's waist. Ian ruffled the top of his head and said to Molly, 'And how's my girl today?'

'Starving!'

'Well, let's get everybody round the table before this food gets cold!' said Aunt Vi.

'Oh, these are for you, Vi,' said Ian, handing her the chocolates. 'Thanks for having me over.'

'Oh, they're lovely, son. Thank you. But, sure, it's only a wee supper. You shouldn't have bothered,' said Aunt Vi, but she beamed with pleasure all the same. 'And don't thank me, thank Sarah. It was her idea.'

He smiled his thanks at Sarah.

'Thanks for coming, Ian. I'm really pleased you did,' she

said in a voice loud enough for only him to hear, hoping that he understood how much she appreciated the gesture. It couldn't be easy for him sitting round the same table as her and Cahal. She doubted that there were many men in this world as selfless as Ian.

Aunt Vi clapped her hands. 'Come on now, everyone. Let's go next door and sit down.'

Once everyone was seated elbow to elbow around the table, had food on their plates and drinks in their glasses, Dad said to Ian, who sat between the children, 'So how are you getting on with the visa application?'

'Good.' He paused to chew and added, 'The immigration consultants that Cahal recommended have done a great job. I'm lucky because of the job I do – they're desperate for sales and marketing managers out there.'

Aunt Vi, who was sitting on the opposite side of the table beside Dad, speared a piece of lamb. 'And how's the job hunt going?'

Ian crossed his knife and fork on his plate and set his elbows on the table. 'Well, I have some good news on that front too.'

Everyone paused and looked up from their plates.

'Do you remember I flew out for that interview with Fulcrest?'

'The insurance company?' said Cahal, sitting between Sarah and Lewis.

Ian nodded. 'Well, they offered me the job and I accepted.'

'That's great news, mate,' said Cahal raising his glass. 'Cheers!'

Everyone followed suit and Lewis said, 'Does that mean

you'll be coming with us tomorrow?'

'No, darling,' said Ian, picking up his knife and fork again. 'It'll be a month or two before everything's sorted out. Don't look so sad, son. You'll be so busy you'll hardly notice I'm not there. And I'll speak to you and Molly on the phone almost every day.'

The conversation revolved around this news for a few minutes and then Molly, who'd been quiet up till now, said, 'How's Bisto?'

Becky, on Sarah's right, smiled. 'Oh he's very, very happy, sweetheart. He's used to my place already. I got a cat flap in my front door yesterday so now he can come and go whenever he pleases. So you don't need to worry about him. Him, me and Tony are very happy together.'

She helped herself to more rice while Molly, smiling happily, loaded her plate with chicken korma.

Sarah said, 'You'll be starting your archaeology course in September, won't you, Becky?'

Becky glanced quickly at Tony, sandwiched between her and Dad, and Lewis said, 'What's arch-e-logically?'

Molly sniggered then gave him a withering look. 'Digging up things from the past, isn't that right, Aunt Becky?'

'That's right, pet.' Becky ripped a bit off the communal naan bread and set it on her plate, before wiping her hands on her napkin. 'Why do you ask about my course?'

'Oh, I was just thinking.' She turned to Cahal. 'Dad and Vi are going to come out at Christmas for the wedding.' Cahal's mouth was full of food and he could only nod in reply. She squeezed his knee under the table, then turned to Becky. 'You'll not have to worry about taking time off work. And you'll get a nice long holiday at Christmas. We'd love you to come too, Tony, of course.'

'I always meant to visit Australia,' he said.

Becky leaned over, whispered something in Tony's ear, and he nodded.

'Ahem,' said Becky and everyone stared. She and Tony grinned foolishly at each other and held hands on top of the table. Becky looked round and took a deep breath. 'Actually I'm not sure we'll be able to come out at Christmas.'

'Oh,' said Sarah and the room fell silent. Sarah could've kicked herself. With Becky not working and Tony supporting her, of course they wouldn't have the money for an expensive holiday. She shouldn't have suggested it.

But Becky didn't look in the least embarrassed. Her eyes sparkled and her smile was wide and full. Tony stared at her as if she was the only woman in the world. He gave Becky an encouraging nod and she said, 'Because we've got some very exciting news to tell you.'

Everyone waited. Sarah noticed that the glass in front of Becky contained not wine, but water.

'We're going to have a baby.'

Sarah's eyes travelled down to Becky's plump belly and for a moment it was inconceivable. Her little sis a mum? And then for the first time in her life she saw Becky as others must see her – a capable, intelligent, grown woman. A woman on the road to motherhood.

'Oh, my,' said Vi, putting a hand over her mouth. 'A baby!'

Molly said excitedly, 'That means we'll have a cousin, Lewis!'

Sarah threw her arms round Becky and found her voice. 'Oh, Becky, that's the most wonderful news. I'm going to be an aunt!'

Cahal stood up, leaned across the table and shook hands with Tony. Ian and Dad followed suit and Dad patted Becky's shoulder.

Lewis, watching all of this with a look of puzzlement on his face, said, 'What's the big deal? It's only a baby?'

When the laughter had died down, Ian said, 'What about your uni course, Becky?'

'All sorted. They've said I can defer for a year, no problem.'

Dad dabbed his mouth with a folded napkin and set it on the table. 'Well that's wonderful news, all right. Another wee bairn in the family. My goodness.' He paused to let this sink in and then a frown passed across his face like a cloud. 'But you don't want it to be born out of wedlock.'

'What's wedlock?' said Lewis.

'Never you mind,' said Aunt Vi, with a sharp glance at his plate. 'Finish your dinner.'

Becky laughed. 'Oh Dad, you're so old-fashioned.'

'We have talked about marriage,' said Tony, apparently taking Dad's concerns more seriously than Becky. 'Haven't we, Becky? But we're not in any rush.'

Becky wrinkled her nose. 'Maybe after the baby's born.'

'When's it due?' said Aunt Vi, her face all red and shining.

'End of August. We're not ruling out a trip to Australia,' said Becky, looking at Tony. 'But the baby'll only be three and a half months old come Christmas.'

'Oh, you can't be too careful with wee ones,' said Aunt Vi,

her hand shooting up to her neck. 'You don't want to be taking risks. The air pressure could damage their wee ears. And you can catch some horrible infections on these planes.'

Sarah smiled good-naturedly, while her heart soared with happiness. Becky's timing could not be more perfect. The baby would distract Aunt Vi and Dad from the loss of Molly and Lewis. 'Well, let's just wait and see how things go. And if you can't come out, Becky, I'll try and swing a trip back with the kids in January, before they start back at school. What do you think, Cahal?'

'Great idea.'

'I'd better get the knitting needles out!' said Aunt Vi. She fanned her face with her napkin. 'Well, what an eventful year this is proving to be!'

Later, when darkness had fallen and the kids had gone home with Ian, Sarah lay in Cahal's arms in the lumpy bed in Becky's spare room. The streetlamp outside cast a golden glow through the thin curtains and Sarah thought that she would not sleep a wink. Her head was full of Becky's happy news and excitement about the future. But her joy was tinged with sadness at leaving Ballyfergus and those she loved.

Cahal, lying on his back, stroked her bare arm absentmindedly. As if he could read her mind, he said, 'I feel as if you're giving up your family for me.'

She swallowed. 'It's not so bad. We can talk on the phone every day and visit.' She paused and added, 'But it is a very big thing to move the children to the other side of the world and for Ian to come too. I hope things work out for him.'

'I'm certain they will.'

'I'm doing it because I love you so much, Cahal.' She paused, and traced a line down his chest. 'And I feel as if you've given up your family for me.'

'How's that?'

'Well, you're not inviting them out to the wedding, are you?'

'They wouldn't come anyway, Sarah.' He kissed the top of her head. 'They only visited once in all the time I lived in Melbourne and, to be honest, I don't want them there. I'll still send Mum money but I have a new family now. It's you, my boys and Molly and Lewis.'

'That's sweet.'

'I mean it. You and the kids are all that matter to me. Don't ever forget that.'

She reached for his hand and locked their fingers together. 'I won't.'

They lay in silence for a long time. Sarah's head on Cahal's chest rose and fell gently in time with his long, deep breaths. She imagined Evelyn looking down in approval.

'I've waited twenty years for you, Sarah. And do you know what?'

She pulled herself up onto her elbow, her fair hair falling round her face. 'What?'

'You've been worth the wait.'

'And so have you, my darling man.'

ERIN KAYE'S THOUGHTS ON WRITING *ALWAYS YOU*

Erin Kaye talks about the themes within *Always You*

What inspired you to write about star - crossed lovers?
It's a universal theme and because I experienced opposition and prejudice when I got together with my now husband. It takes quite a lot of guts and a very deep love to risk losing everything for the one you love. I wanted to explore the idea of two lovers being given a second chance and how they overcome all the obstacles placed in their path.

Is there such a thing as a 'happy divorce'?
Every divorce is sad, especially where children are involved. But that said, some ex-couples manage to make a better job of it than others, rising above grievances and recriminations for the sake of their children. I've a great deal of admiration for people who manage to put the welfare of their children before their personal feelings.

Was it fair of Sarah's mother to ask Sarah to look after Becky once she was gone?
Maybe a little unfair, but understandable. Perhaps she didn't mean Sarah to take it so literally.

Why does Sarah find it so hard to stop being so protective of Becky?
I think being a pseudo mother to Becky gives Sarah a sense of identity. She's been doing it so long, it's part of who she is. Also, it's because of Becky that she wouldn't go to Australia, so she finds it hard to let go. Only when she sees Becky as an

adult is she finally able to relinquish the responsibility.

What do you think of Sarah's father in forcing her to break up with Cahal?
This story is all about impossible choices. He did what he thought he had to in order to protect his sister and his family.

What effect does Evelyn's death have on Ian?
When we meet him, Ian is self-centred and determined to get back with Sarah, with little regard for poor Raquel. His mother's death transforms him from a selfish man to a selfless one. Evelyn's death isn't a transformational experience for Sarah, but what Evelyn tells Sarah about how she ran off and married Harry is. Evelyn's story gives Sarah the courage to follow her heart and trust Cahal, even though she believes he wronged her.

Sarah and Cahal pick up where they left off. Is that realistic?
I don't think people change very much over time. The essential character remains the same. When a person falls out of love, it's because the scales have fallen from their eyes, not because the object of their love has changed dramatically.

Do you think Sarah is wrong to take her children away from their extended family?
It's sad that she has no choice, but it's not wrong. Very little in life is black and white and this is one of those situations where there is no right or wrong answer. She put the wishes

of her aunt and father first when she was nineteen. This time she puts herself and Cahal first.

The book ends on a bittersweet note – Cahal estranged from his family and Sarah leaving hers behind in Ireland. Why?
It was the only way the book could end. When people have that much baggage there is no perfect ending.